The
GREEN
SHORE

NATALIE BAKOPOULOS

Simon & Schuster
New York   London   Toronto   Sydney   New Delhi

Simon & Schuster
1230 Avenue of the Americas
New York, NY 10020

For epigraph permissions see page 350.

First Simon & Schuster hardcover edition June 2012

SIMON & SCHUSTER and colophon are registered trademarks
of Simon & Schuster, Inc.

For information about special discounts for bulk purchases,
please contact Simon & Schuster Special Sales at
1-866-506-1949 or business@simonandschuster.com.

The Simon & Schuster Speakers Bureau can bring authors
to your live event. For more information or to book an event,
contact the Simon & Schuster Speakers Bureau at
1-866-248-3049 or visit our website at www.simonspeakers.com.

Designed by Jill Putorti

Manufactured in the United States of America

10 9 8 7 6 5 4 3 2 1

Library of Congress Cataloging-in-Publication Data
Bakopoulos, Natalie.
    The green shore / Natalie Bakopoulos.
        p. cm.
1. Greece—History—1967–1974—Fiction. 2. Domestic fiction.
I. Title.
    PS3602.A5933G74 2012
    813'.6—dc23   2011032325

ISBN 978-1-4516-3392-4
ISBN 978-1-4516-3395-5 (ebook)

For Eleni, in loving memory

Will the gift and good fortune be granted to us
that one night we can go to die
there on the green shore of our native land?

—KOSTAS KARYOTAKIS, "SLEEP"

The
GREEN
SHORE

Prologue

That April, just weeks before national elections, three men in dark suits met in the center of Athens. In a small house on Aspasia Street they spoke briefly, shook hands, and left in separate cars. At the Greek military headquarters—a massive cement structure surrounded by tall walls topped with barbed wire and studs of glass—senior military commanders held forth around a table.

Earlier that day at the Hilton Hotel, the king and queen had dined and a political party meeting convened—all signs of routine democratic activity. Now a middle-aged sentry stood on a balcony. Through binoculars he looked out at the lit-up city, waiting. There was the Acropolis, there was Lykavittos Hill, there were the lights that lined the avenues. Athens still looked like Athens.

As the evening turned to night, men in plain clothes assembled inconspicuously, through the narrow, tree-lined streets of Kolonaki, from the residential section of Papagos. From Pangrati, from Kypseli, from Ambelokipi, military men kissed their wives and left them sleeping in their beds. Behind the old soccer stadium at the heart of the city, restless soldiers smoked cigarettes and a few played cards. Some, filled with nervous apprehension, told off-color jokes.

In Psychiko, men with bayonet-tipped rifles gave orders, rousing a couple from sleep and shoving them into a car. "Hurry up," they shouted. The woman was without her eyeglasses and both wore pajamas. Nearby, another man climbed to his roof while his sons took cover beneath their beds.

Three in the morning and the military headquarters were alight, as if manned by careless children whose parents have left them alone. In an empty room, a record player left on by a second lieutenant from Kyparissia blared to no one. One soldier from Kalamata pored over a map of the city; another two argued over the proper frequency of a radio signal. Obsessed with valor, one young officer cocked his rifle, released it, and cocked it again. In a pane of glass he caught his reflection and was startled by what he saw.

Outside the illuminated windows, most of the city slept.

Part One

April to November 1967

The night that is only night I no longer know
—ODYSSEUS ELYTIS, "I NO LONGER KNOW THE NIGHT"

1

Just after midnight, Vangelis—trusted neighborhood cab driver, friend of her uncle, and painter on the side—delivered Sophie and a few other girls to a party in Psychiko, a winding, lush neighborhood filled with stately homes and embassies. Sophie's recent love interest, Nick, was throwing the party because he had the house to himself. His parents, both left-leaning lawyers, had gone to Thessaloniki to promote the rights of a local political campaign, and in those few days they had transformed that elegantly run-down house with its curvy French furniture and old, expensive rugs into a student headquarters: making posters and distributing leaflets, writing letters to newspaper editors, and mostly discussing their visions for their country and what it could become.

After Sophie's friends crawled out of the backseat, bare legged with scarves in their hair, and disappeared behind the wrought iron gate, Sophie leaned forward between the seats to pay Vangelis. As always he refused her.

"I work until sunrise," he said. "Shall I collect you then?" His deadpan delivery was intentional. Some nights, when she was out pasting up flyers, she knew he idled nearby. Other nights she had been creeping up to her gate just as he was driving in from his shift. He'd nod to her, tip his hat, and bring in the milk bottle from his front porch.

Sophie slumped back in the seat and returned her drachmas to her purse. "I'll pay you next time," she said.

"Is that a yes?" Vangelis asked. His gaze shifted to the side mirror, as if someone was behind him. Then he turned to her, waiting for her reply.

"If it's on your way," Sophie said. They both knew, though, she didn't need to answer his question. As dependable as the rising sun, Vangelis would be at the curb, holding his cigarette between his pinkie and ring finger, like a *bouzouki* player. She thanked him and kissed him on his rough, unshaven cheek.

Behind them the music from the back garden drifted to the street, along with a medley of enthusiastic voices. The air was heavy with honeysuckle, so sweet Sophie could taste it in the back of her throat, like wine. Others arrived on foot and motorbikes, and a handsome guy in a leather jacket opened the wrought iron gate and she and others passed through the blossoming grounds. Three young men with thick sideburns and turtleneck sweaters stood on the Doric-style entrance porch, smoking. Only after she moved past them, down the lantern-lit walkway to the back of the house, did she hear Vangelis drive away.

The party was at maximum blare, with students everywhere, women in miniskirts flirting with men in tight jeans and slim shirts. She could hear the excitement in the loud music and the clink of ice in glasses, the profusion of words and ideas and the overlaying thing nobody spoke of but everyone felt. Sex. The yard vibrated with the combined heat of politics and passion. The elections were slated for the next month, at the end of May. Would the king allow the elections? A woman with a large purple flower in the middle of her dress insisted that he would not. She sipped her drink through a straw; two young men nodded eagerly in front of her. On the house's large back porch, bodies she didn't recognize moved closely together, and Sophie brushed through a crowd of chirping girls, barely managing to survive yet another squad of men, and was nearly dragged to dance by a short insistent law student with wild, curly hair.

Nick. Where was Nick? Their situation was not exactly clandestine, but it wasn't particularly open either. He was two years her senior, having finished his undergraduate work in chemistry, and was now planning to study medicine abroad. But even had he still been a student, their paths wouldn't have crossed much because she was studying French. Sophie didn't know exactly how he spent his days because mostly she met him in the middle of the night. She had noticed him at several student-based political meetings, and they had officially met marching in the center of Athens, day after day, supporting former prime minister George Papandreou. Their physical connection had been so strong that it had embarrassed her, the way they kept brushing up against one another, like aloof but aware cats. The first time he drove her home and kissed her outside the arched gate to the yard, she wanted to drag him up to the roof or into her bed. Instead she went inside alone and didn't fall asleep for a long time. Two nights later, she snuck out of her house and met him in a park, and there began a pattern of moonlit coupling.

Mostly they met up in groups and then they'd sneak away together later, after she was allegedly safe at home. But a *relationship*? She wasn't sure if it was, or if she even wanted it. The sex was entangled with the urge of their commitment, which seemed to spill into bed, and sometimes when they made love she saw him speaking and sometimes when she saw him speaking she couldn't help but think of his arched body.

In the parlor, a group gathered around a young man dancing *zembekiko;* one student strummed a guitar and another played a *bouzouki,* and people drank wine and *raki* out of goblets and tumblers that seemed reserved for special occasions. A few gathered around a baby grand, but no one played it. "Nick's looking for you," a blond boy called to her, and she felt a pleasurable shiver to be identified so closely with the host and relaxed into the party, trusting he would find her.

Sophie wandered through the large manicured garden. Rows of lanterns threw eerie, lovely glows across people's faces. She approached the small bar set up in the corner, where Nick's cousin Loukas, home for Easter, was pouring himself a cheap-looking yellow whiskey over shards of ice.

"What can I get you?" he asked.

She eyed the variety of bottles on the table. "Whatever you're having," she said.

He went for the whiskey but instead reconsidered and poured her a glass of red wine. "I brought it from France," he said, and smiled at her. They'd been briefly introduced three nights before, when he'd arrived. She finally saw a chance to ask him about France but before she could a spritely woman took his arm, stood on her tiptoes, and whispered something in his ear, her light-brown hair shiny and straight and so long that it almost reached the hem of her impossibly short paisley dress. Loukas laughed, squeezed Sophie's shoulder, and told her to enjoy the party. Then, he set off rather deliberately across the crowded garden, arm in arm with the girl.

Sophie wanted to call after him: *Wait! Don't walk away!* She felt good in his presence, Nick's older *cousin,* she reminded herself. She had heard much about Loukas, but had he heard about her? Did men share their most intimate details that way? When Nick talked about Loukas it was more an outpouring of random facts, often divulged as trivial bits but always with a fraternal sort of pride. Sophie knew Loukas had completed his undergraduate studies in the States, at Cornell, and graduate school in Paris, and now he worked for an architectural firm in Lyons. He and Nick smoked the same brand of loose tobacco; Loukas had been the one to teach him how to roll a cigarette.

But Sophie held back and instead went inside. In the center of the dining room was a large teak table. The chairs had been pushed against the wall and a group of students assembled a newsletter, spreading the leaflets across the tabletop and poring over them like generals planning a war. Glasses, coffee cups, and ashtrays overflowing with cigarette butts and pistachio shells dotted the sides. Any degree of formality the room usually held had been temporarily suspended.

She joined a group and immediately began to talk. While she was giving her opinion on the placement of an editorial she had written on the upcoming elections, Nick appeared and slid his arm around her waist, looking over their work.

"Hi," he said. He kissed her on the lips, full, suggestive. Sophie realized this was the first time they had admitted any affiliation in public. "Looks good," he said.

For the next few hours they drank and danced and she enjoyed the glow of the evening. No matter where Nick was, Sophie was aware of him: beneath a huge, ancient fig tree; underneath the trellis covered with grapevines; or dancing with others in the crowd. While Nick mingled, flirting with girls who beamed at him, he always found her again. Sophie felt an odd charge from this jealousy and liked this approach and retreat, a dance in itself. Before her friends could tell her they were going to a club in Kypseli, she caught Nick's eye and he motioned for her to follow him. They slipped through the tidy maze of vines and apricot trees, back around the house to the side spiral staircase.

Nick's bedroom was remarkably spartan compared to her cluttered one: a bureau, desk, and mahogany bed covered in faded linens. A dark red robe hung from the bedpost, and the large desk in the corner was neatly stacked with books. Though it was late, the party had hardly quieted, and a group of slightly older guests, perhaps Loukas's friends, gathered around a small bonfire in the far back garden. When Nick opened the shutters, the flicker of the flames delineated his face. Just the two of them now, and Sophie stepped out of her shoes and pulled her dress over her head. Nick watched her from near the window, and then he moved toward her. In the dark the two of them fell together, in secret, once again. Hushed, attentive, close and ready.

Suddenly came the sounds of men shouting, nothing more than the noises of persistent revelers, they assumed, the whoop and fuzz of a late-night second wind. Until they heard a sharp scream, not celebratory but distressed, at which Nick lifted his head. The fire of a gunshot brought him out like an animal into traffic, and within seconds he was on the dark terrace, pulling on his shirt and pants almost simultaneously while looking over the edge. Sophie dressed and hurried after him.

First came a surprising silence, like the beats between a concerto's slow movement and its louder, faster finale. The bark of voices and slap of footfalls and panicked start of motorbike engines. Chaos.

Nick urged her to duck and motioned for her to follow him into his parents' bedroom, which faced the street. They kept the lights off and peered out the windows.

Soldiers with rifles surged through the front garden, around the side of the house. Sophie and Nick watched, speechless, as more soldiers entered. Nick headed toward the stairs, ready to run down. But Sophie grabbed his hand and stopped him.

"The newspapers, the flyers," he said. "All those things on the table."

"Too late," Sophie said. They could hear noises coming not only from below but from down the street as well. "The roof. We'll be able to see what's going on from there." She pulled him to the back terrace. Unlike her home in Halandri, no staircase provided easy roof access, so Nick grabbed a chair and stood on it to help her up. Then he climbed up himself. Together, they crawled across the flat roof to the front of the house, where they lay, side by side, looking down into the yard. They watched astounded as friends were handcuffed and thrown into trucks, the menacing growl of their engines filling the night, while others tried to scale the wall. Sophie moved to get up and Nick stopped her. "Just stay low," he said, his arm arched over her like a fence. "Oh, God," he whispered. "My parents'—"

"Your parents' what?" Sophie asked. The sound of her own voice frightened her.

"My parents' everything."

Maybe they had come for Nick's parents but the whole mess of bearded and denim-clad and miniskirt-wearing student radicals they found instead was a veritable windfall. And his was not the only family targeted: in a house down the street, many lights were on, thrown open in a careless rage. More men in black berets stood in the burn of the headlights. A large truck and a few jeeps crammed with more soldiers filled the street. A man and woman, in pajamas and handcuffs, were being forced into a large black car. The motorcade moved down the road, stopping farther down. Vigilantly, methodically, yet as casual as the postman going door to door. Shouting, shouting, there was so much shouting. In the distance, a dog barked, croupy and erratic, and after another short and swift gunshot, it stopped.

Sophie spotted Vangelis's cab one street over and had the sudden urge to flee. "I have to get home. I have to go."

"You're crazy," Nick said. "You can't go anywhere."

"Come with me," Sophie said. "We should get out of here." She knew Nick wouldn't let her go alone.

"I can't leave. Please just wait. Let me think for a minute."

But Sophie didn't know how long Vangelis could wait, and who knew if there were soldiers still in the house? Think, think, damn it, who had time to think? She threw herself onto Nick as if he were ablaze, a flat, forceful hug. Before he could grab her she scrambled to the back of the roof, lowered herself to the terrace, and slipped down the metal spiral staircase that led to the ravaged empty garden. The bonfire smoldered.

This was not the first time she had had to sneak out of Nick's house, though the other times had been because of a sudden, unexpected arrival of parents, not soldiers. Her best bet seemed to be to climb over the cement wall and into the neighbor's yard; she didn't know who might still be lurking in the front or inside. From there she could get to the street where Vangelis waited. More voices shouted in the distance.

She gathered her courage and ran for the back wall. Scaling the blocks, she scraped her knee. She dropped over the other side, landed awkwardly, and scampered through the neighbors' yard and out their front gate. It squeaked and clattered shut, and Sophie cringed, but she was away.

Sophie headed toward the corner where she had seen Vangelis but stopped abruptly when down the street from the cab she saw a military jeep and a barricade. The cab's lights were off, but the jeep's were on, and in the glare Sophie could not make out what was happening. She couldn't tell if Vangelis was there but where else would he have gone? She crouched behind a hedge of jasmine just as a military truck rumbled onto the street.

Then, one soldier opened the jeep's door and motioned to the people inside. They emerged, and Sophie thought she spotted Vangelis in the crowd, but she wasn't sure. One by one the prisoners, partygoers only moments before, were transferred to the truck and driven away. Two remaining soldiers got back into the front seat and dimmed the lights. But a beam of moonlight still shed light on their faces, and Sophie thought they looked younger and more confused than any of those who had been taken away. One leaned his head down on the steering wheel, and in the passenger seat the other rubbed his eyes.

A wash of guilt rose inside her so suddenly her body ached. She imagined Vangelis's wife asleep, waiting for him to return with the dawn. She wanted now to return to Nick's but just the thought of walking back into that yard scared her. Forward, forward. Traipsing through the street like a mangy dog was obviously not a good idea either. Those soldiers had a reason for raiding Nick's house in the first place. Or had the party been an unplanned detour, an opportunity?

She hoped Nick had stayed on the roof and she was cursing herself for not doing the same. The two soldiers still idled not far away from her, though they seemed half as alert as she. Still. What if they saw her? She shifted her weight and then crouched lower behind the bushes. To walk to her house in Halandri from here was not impossible, though it would take her a very long time. Or she could try to hail a taxi. She had nothing with her: her purse sat on Nick's desk. She wondered if anyone had found it, riffled through it, added her name to some sort of list.

The driver started the jeep and the men pulled away as quickly as they'd come. The only evidence of their presence was the paltry barricade. She could walk right around it and back to Nick's. Yet Sophie knew she needed, for once, to think before she acted.

What if they were waiting for her at Nick's? What if they'd come back and found him on the roof? She crawled out from the bushes to Vangelis's cab. Maybe he was hiding somewhere too. Maybe she hadn't seen him in the crowd. The window was halfway down, and she tried the door. It was open, so she crawled into the backseat and lay down, covering her cold, bare legs with Vangelis's cardigan sweater. When he returned, she would be waiting for him. She couldn't allow herself to imagine another outcome.

2

Across the city, in a chic neighborhood in the foothills of Lykavittos, Sophie's uncle Mihalis was drunk. Crumpled in his pocket was a letter from his estranged wife, Irini.

In the corner of a terrace, Mihalis poured himself a drink. A group of remaining guests sat around the patio table; a couple who had just met talked quietly in another corner. Evan, the host, sat among them while his wife, Simone, cleared abandoned glasses. Inside, a group of women washed dishes and put food away. Mihalis watched through the kitchen window as a gregarious, balding professor in Evan's department—irritatingly, Mihalis thought—tried to coax the women to dance.

Evan wandered over to Mihalis. "You're brooding," Evan said. "I can see that." He began to pour himself another drink but the bottle he chose was empty. "One moment," he said. He disappeared inside and came back with a few beers and some *tsipouro*, which he arranged on the bar, and a bag of hazelnuts, half of which he poured into a bowl and set on the table.

"Don't encourage the locusts to stay," Mihalis remarked. "Let them go home to drink their own liquor and fuck their wives."

"You've been like this all night," Evan said.

"Irini has written me. She wants to come back to Athens."

Evan poured his drink.

For the past three years, Irini had held a position at the university in Thessaloniki. The job offer had come at a good time: she and Mihalis had been fighting incessantly. To friends they maintained the move was strictly professional—but to themselves they could not ignore the truth. They had been living disconnected lives for months. Holidays came and went, and though they'd plan to reunite for those, Irini would at the last minute decide to visit friends in Paris or join her sister in Santorini, and would Mihalis like to come? But Mihalis hated leaving Athens, and she knew this. Sometimes, she'd plan a visit back and then say she had fallen ill, a claim whose veracity Mihalis never doubted. After all, he had thought for a long time that he made her sick. Other times, she'd simply have too much work, and Mihalis never offered to visit *her* instead, though he had no work at all. Soon they ignored the topic of holiday visits entirely. They were better together when the pressure of being together lifted. Or maybe they were just better apart.

Before Irini had left, she and Evan, a literature professor and critic, had taught in the same department in Athens. They knew each other very well. Mihalis had expected Evan to be surprised by the news of her return, or delighted, or to let on that he had already known. Something. But Evan seemed blasé, noncommittal even.

"I tell you my wife is coming back and you have nothing to say?"

Evan sighed. "It's a little strange you even call her your wife, don't you think?"

"She still *is* my wife," Mihalis said.

Evan parted his lips to speak but was interrupted by a couple who were leaving. He stood to wish them good night and to accept their compliments for the evening. Evan seemed to know everybody in Athens, and while he accompanied these guests to the door more guests arrived.

It occurred to Mihalis then that Irini might already be back in Athens. Evan had gone out a few nights before, and when Mihalis had asked him whom he had seen, he had been evasive and quickly changed the subject. Maybe in a crowded, dark bar she had touched Evan lightly on the arm and said, "Don't tell him I'm here yet." He and Evan had a lifetime of complexity and conflict and familiarity between them—Evan's own wife, Simone, was a fiery Brit who Mihalis knew firsthand could be itinerant—and he wouldn't put it past his friend to withhold this information just to have one up on him.

Mihalis went quickly from sulking to seething. He stood up, snatched the new bottle of *tsipouro,* and stormed out past the guests, bumping shoulders and upsetting drinks. He left out the front door and walked up the block.

Away from the party the night felt quiet, but he felt edgy and apprehensive. Mihalis had lived in Athens long enough to intuit its mood, its opinions, its underbelly. The air, it was in the air. Something imminent. He was overcome with the urge to walk.

Rising above Athens was Lykavittos Hill, crowned by a small, whitewashed chapel that Mihalis could see, at turns, glowing during his climb. His sober self might have taken the funicular railway to the top. To not slip while sober was a feat of balance; to not fall while drunk would be a feat of the divine. And because he was not a believer, Mihalis took those broken steps slumped on his hands and knees, like some nocturnal beast.

Almost to the top, next to an overpriced café that was closed for the night, Mihalis sat down on a bench beneath the calm, unfinished moon. He felt a little dizzy. From behind him he heard breathing, murmuring, and turned to see two teenagers in the shadows. The boy had the girl pressed against the wall, her skirt riding up to expose a long, lean thigh.

"Hey," the boy said. "What are you looking at?"

"Oh, go fuck yourself silly in the bushes," Mihalis said. He rested his elbows on his knees and hung his head, catching his breath.

The girl came around in front of Mihalis. "Are you okay?" she asked. Her face, reflected in the lights that lined the flights of steps, was delicately beautiful. And as he stared at her, her expression changed. "You're the poet," she said, excited to recognize him. "Aren't you? I've seen you around Omonia. Do you need help?"

"No," he said. What sort of help would she offer him? Had she been just a little older Mihalis would have made an inappropriate comment, but he resisted.

The boy joined her. He shifted on his feet and blew air from his mouth, clearly impatient. "Come on," he said. "He's fine. Just drunk." He took her hand and began to pull her away.

The girl resisted. "Are you sure?" she asked Mihalis.

Mihalis waved them on. "Go," he said. And the girl allowed herself to be led back toward the shadows of the café. The boy, emboldened, called back, "Write us a poem, why don't you!"

Now Mihalis wished he'd spoken more to the girl, just to spite the little prick. But they were gone, so he continued up the last several steps to the top.

To stand at the narrow promontory beside Saint George Chapel was to gain a tremendous view of the city's vast constellation of lights. From there, Athens looked as though it had been built in a bowl. And in the farthest distance he could see the red bow lights of ships on the blackened sea.

Mihalis was grateful to be alone. Now he felt his exhaustion. He sat down and rested the bottle of *tsipouro* between his feet, wishing he had instead taken some water. His mouth was dry. The sense of foreboding had returned. Mihalis removed the crumpled letter from his pocket and folded and unfolded it a few times. He used his lighter to read the words. Then he lit a cigarette and gazed out at the city.

Over the past few days he had countless times tried to write a reply, only to stop. How to begin such a thing? With too much to say, Mihalis simply said nothing, and the longer he went on saying nothing, the more saying anything at all seemed an insurmountable task. He had often thought, over the three years of their separation, to send Irini copies of his most recent poems, an indirect way of communicating, but he never did. When he'd imagine them through her eyes, they were suddenly not good enough.

Some nights, when their marriage had become difficult and Mihalis had slept on the couch, he'd awake to find Irini sitting on the floor next to him, her head near his face. She'd press her cheek next to his, or her nose to his forehead, and close her eyes. Other nights, she led him back to bed with her, not necessarily for sex—though there were nights when this ultimately led to sex—but to sleep with their bodies entwined, as they should, as was expected of husband and wife. But inevitably the next morning, the light filtered in and with it the harsh reality of their marriage. In the day, they were accustomed to their misery, and the sweetness of night couldn't defeat it. In the day, they behaved as they expected of each other.

Mihalis took up too much emotional space, Irini had said, and left no room for her. He found a small piece of comfort in the fact that she seemed happy these days, at least when this observation didn't enrage him with jealousy. Her voice, during their phone calls—the frequency of which decreased by the season—seemed content and at ease, and it was almost as if he were talking to a woman he didn't know or one he had just met. He tried not to think about what she was doing for companionship or any other things that threatened his sanity. He knew he should probably let her go but no man wants to think of his wife with another. Eventually, he knew, she'd want to marry again. Wouldn't she? Was this what her letter was about?

Mihalis stood, walked to the edge of the wall, and climbed atop it, looking down at the dark café. He wondered if the teens were still somewhere below. Then he unzipped his pants and relieved himself over the edge. "Underneath an incomplete moon," Mihalis said in his best oratory voice, "the poet pisses on young love."

When he was finished he walked over to the row of telescopes set up for tourists. But instead of the usual movement of nighttime traffic processing down the main streets, he saw stern, neat lines of military trucks and tanks. He pulled his head back for a moment, then looked again. He was torn between staring through the telescope, looking out with his naked eyes, and returning to the city itself. It felt very surreal.

Then the alarm and the panic set in. He swore, he spit, he peered once again through the telescope and saw more tanks positioned in the central square of the city. Trucks were lined up nearby, probably full of soldiers or citizens roused from sleep. He looked to the north near Halandri and thought of his sister, his nieces and nephew. What in the world had happened? Up there, alone, he felt removed and powerless. *Fuck,* he thought. *Not again.* Would they ever have any peace? He stumbled back to the steps of Saint George's and grabbed the bottle of *tsipouro*. He meant to hurl it out into the night, but instead when he chucked it it smashed against the low stone wall. The sheer force of this awkward fling set him off balance, and he fell, sprawling onto the uneven, jagged ground.

There Mihalis lay. His lungs felt as if they were shrinking, his chest tight; the dread pressed down on his shoulders, pinning him to the ground. He tried to get up again but felt light-headed, so he stayed still on the path and stared at the sky, hoping the moon could soothe him while the rest of the country derailed. But the bleating background soundtrack of sirens finally forced him to get off the ground. He moaned, lifted his head, and pushed his body up with his hands. Then he began to make his way down the brittle steps.

Past the café he encountered the two teenagers again, giggling and running through the darkness like scurrying mice, oblivious to the momentous shift taking place in the city below them.

"Listen to me," Mihalis called after them. "Get yourselves home. Don't walk the main streets. There's been some sort of takeover."

But the two disappeared again, behind a trellis lined with jasmine and lantana. For a moment he wondered if he had imagined them. But no—he was in control of his faculties again, like the drunk who sobers up upon glimpsing the reflection of his own slack-jawed face.

He knew what he was witnessing, and it terrified him. There had been talk of a coup for weeks; who exactly had succeeded in pulling it off was unclear.

He wouldn't go back to his sister's, where he was currently staying, more or less. Halandri was much too far so he headed back to Evan and Simone's. It was a long way to the bottom, but he had no choice but to slouch his way back toward Athens.

By the time he reached their house at the base of the hill, he was sore and exhausted. Early light spilled through the citrus trees, and a cool, sharp-toothed wind blew over the garden. Evan was awake and sitting on the back veranda, a transistor radio in front of him and a heavy wool sweater wrapped around his shoulders.

When he saw Mihalis, he jumped up. "What happened to you?" he asked. "You look like a wild man." Military music blared from the radio. "What are you doing wandering around during this?"

Mihalis collapsed into a chair and took a sip from Evan's glass of water. Then he helped himself to Evan's cigarette burning in the ashtray.

"There's been a coup," Evan said. His brown eyes, the chiseled Byzantine features that women could not resist, were strained, as if he had been in and out of sleep himself.

"Yes," Mihalis said. "I see that." He brushed off his suit, which was covered in dust. His pants had ripped open and his knee was a bloody, dirty mess. Somewhere on the climb down, he had taken off and lost his tie.

"So where the hell have you been?" Evan asked.

Mihalis wiped his raw and grimy hands on his thighs and winced from the sting. "What are you, my wife?" he snapped.

Evan glanced toward the house, and a strange look came over his face. The military music stopped and a forceful voice declared that anyone out on the streets would be shot down without warning. Evan gestured to the radio and lit himself another cigarette. "Arrests all through the night. You should stay here awhile." His voice was strangely monotone. He seemed to be in shock.

Mihalis closed his eyes. His mind gave him an image from the civil war, years and years before: young Evan sitting across from him in a tiny, dirty, sickly lit cell, sleeping upright against the damp wall while his head lolled down on his chest, like a child who had fallen asleep in a stroller. *No,* he thought. Not prison again, not the constant fear of being chased again. When he opened his eyes Evan was watching him but didn't say anything.

Mihalis stood up. "I'm going inside to clean up, make some coffee," he said. It was one thing he knew: through all sorts of imprisonments and wars, the body continued to need what it needed. And now his body felt as though it were falling apart. He thought of the young couple, making love in the bushes while a coup raged below. "Keep the radio on, in case there's any news."

Inside, he was careful to be quiet. Simone, pregnant, was surely sleeping. He stepped into the first-floor bathroom and flipped on the dim light. He looked at himself in the mirror, searching for signs of decay. He could already hear it in a poem: *The morning after the coup, the poet undergoes a narcissistic fit.* He tightened his right bicep and felt it with his left hand. Still young. He was strong, he was slim, and he supposed he was handsome enough. He felt hungover and wanted to lie down. *The morning after the coup, the poet realizes his age.* Chronologically forty-four, but much older by any other measure. He took a shower, not bothering to wait for the water heater.

As he passed the den with only a towel around his waist, he noticed a small figure curled up, asleep. It was not Simone's golden head but a raven-haired one. Sensing movement, the figure rose up to face him.

The corridor was dim, and the shutters of the den were closed, but still he was flooded by so much sensation: her perfume, a strong gardenia; her high cheekbones, almost sharp; her black straight hair and her heart-shaped lips. She was thinner, but her skin was still bright and youthful. She touched his hair, messed and wet from the shower, and took his torn-up hands in hers and examined his face.

The morning after the coup, the poet reunites with his wife.

3

In the northern Athenian suburb of Halandri, at the end of a block lined with citrus trees and bitter laurel, sixteen-year-old Anna woke to the early wobbly light and morning sounds that usually lulled her insomniac self to sleep: the clink of spoons against coffee cups; the scattered shifts of frequencies and squawk of stations as her mother adjusted the radio, which she was having particular trouble with that morning. These familiar sounds reminded her of being a child and listening to her father do the same. Sometimes, in that in-between time of sleep and consciousness, she thought she could still hear him, swearing when he couldn't get a strong broadcast signal. On these mornings she would wake with an even deeper sense of his absence, which sometimes lingered into the afternoon.

That morning, she heard Taki trudge into the bathroom and then flap down the stairs. His dry voice already rambled at this early hour but she wasn't sure about what. The radio grew louder. Instead of the usual morning program, Anna heard military music. A strange choice for any time, let alone breakfast.

She rubbed her eyes, rose from bed, and set her bare feet on the cold tile floor. The morning was cool but soon it would break into April's midday warmth, and Anna was reminded that Easter, then summer, were just around the corner. Her neighbors were having breakfast on their veranda, wearing sweaters. The small radio in front of them played the same music that sounded downstairs. She waved at them and they nodded back at her, looking a little grave.

She found her mother and Taki at the table, sitting completely still and staring at the radio as if it were a television. Anna had walked into not her kitchen but a painting of it.

"What's going on?" Anna asked. Neither answered her.

Both Taki and her mother looked stunned. "It's the goddamn communists," Taki said. "It's why I'm leaving this place. The country's a disaster."

"You don't know that," her mother said quickly. "It's unclear." Something in her voice, an uncertainty and kind of resignation, scared Anna, and she didn't ask questions. With the stir of the upcoming elections, the recent street demonstrations, and an overall restless populace, Anna had been on edge for weeks, and she had come to know the nighttime workings of the house as if she were the director of a play and the stage a cross section of the dwelling's two levels, like the dollhouses she had played with as a child.

Anna usually heard Sophie run the water full blast while she brushed her teeth, and Taki wake to take an unbelievably loud piss without lifting the toilet seat. She knew Sophie often climbed from her terrace down to the garden, barefoot so her landing would not sound, and disappeared, slipping into a pair of shoes she kept behind the shed. And shortly before daybreak, just when Anna's eyelids were finally growing heavy, her sister would return. Around this time, her uncle Mihalis either woke to get a drink of water or was just himself returning home. He stood by the back door to let their new cat Orpheas in from its midnight wanderings, and Anna heard his gentle calls: *psst pssst pssst*. She liked the image of their uncle expecting the cat and instead discovering Sophie emerging from behind the shed, bleary eyed and barefoot and undeniably sheepish.

But Anna had finally slept and missed the usual nighttime routine, and the bizarre, frightening news coming from the radio alarmed her. She went upstairs but instead of finding her older sister in a tangle of sheets, her eyes covered with a lavender mask, Anna faced an empty bed with neatly made corners. No, it wasn't because Anna had finally slept—she hadn't heard Sophie because Sophie had not come home at all.

Anna swept past her mother and brother in the kitchen without mentioning Sophie; they were as usual arguing about something. She went outdoors and called to the cat, who didn't come. Around the side of the house, she descended the cement stairs that led to the basement room where her uncle stayed. She knocked on the door and without pause pushed it open.

He wasn't there either. His bed was also made and the stack of clean T-shirts and underwear Anna's mother had put there the day before, ironed and folded, was not disturbed. On his dresser was the usual pile of notes and notebooks, worry beads and small jars of medicine. Sometimes Anna wouldn't see him for days. She had no idea where he spent most of his time. He had a secret life all his own; he just happened to live in their house.

Back in the house, her mother was trying to use the phone. "It's dead," she said. She returned it to its cradle, letting her hand linger.

"Sophie isn't here," Anna blurted.

"What do you mean she isn't here? Where is she?"

"She was at Nick's party last night," Taki told her.

Anna's mother looked at them both. "Who's Nick?" Her voice was sharp, startling. "Where does he live?"

"I can't stand the guy," Taki replied, as if this precluded him from knowing anything else. But when pressed by their mother he revealed that he knew Nick lived in Psychiko, the suburb next to Halandri, though neither he nor Anna knew his last name or address.

Anna walked over to the window and opened the shutters. More of the neighborhood was awake now and some brave neighbors stood out on their terraces, waiting for an explanation. Someone knocked on the door, and her mother went to answer it.

Anna listened to Vangelis's wife talking to her mother downstairs. Though Vangelis's shift had finished two hours earlier he still was not home, and Anna heard her say that many people, mostly leftists, politicians, and students, had been arrested, including another neighbor whose children were terrified and now wouldn't answer the door. There had been tanks in Syntagma Square, and though Halandri normally felt far removed from the center of Athens, suddenly now it did not. From an adjacent balcony one man argued it was a collaboration with the Soviets; another that it was an American conspiracy; another was sure it was conservatives; another said definitely the king. It was his voice on the radio, was it not?

Anna heard her mother respond, "Well, I can't just sit here and wait." Then came the jangle of keys. "Do not leave the house," her mother called to them.

"They're telling everyone to stay inside," Taki said. "You're just going to drive up and down the streets, looking for Sophie?"

For a moment their mother paused. "Yes," she said finally, and she left. Anna and Taki watched her drive away. With his typical insolence Taki pulled a sweater over his head and said he was going to see his friend Spyro, who lived two blocks down. The heavy front gate to the yard banged shut. Anna did not like to be alone in the house in general and that morning was no exception. Had she not still been in her pajamas she would have chased after him. Her only option was to wade through that familiar anxiety, telling herself that, like all other things, it would pass. She wanted to go for a walk but was too frightened, so she wrapped her wool blanket over her shoulders and went up to the roof. As eerily quiet as it was that morning, from there she felt the kinship of the neighborhood. She could even see Spyro's house. She sat down at the wrought iron table that Taki had dragged there. Sophie, in an attempt at elegance, had covered it with a worn, red-and-black embroidered cloth.

Come on, she thought. Where was everybody? She stared out across their garden, the grapevines, her mother's favorite *mousmoula* tree, already bearing its orange-brown fruit, always the first of the season. Any bit of movement in the neighborhood relieved her; one neighbor folded laundry on her porch and from another house she could hear the rise and fall of quiet conversation. Radios tuned to the only station accessible, a sort of draconian stereophonics.

Two toddlers played in the garden across the street, babbling and shrieking with delight. Anna envied their unawareness. They didn't know their country was in shambles. They didn't know of her recurring nightmares from having years ago watched men arrest her father for helping to organize dock workers or for being seen with a certain newspaper. Always charges of communism that led to lost jobs, a few months in jail. Taki told Anna he was going to the States because he didn't want to pay for what he saw as his family's mistakes. Only a few days ago he had repeated this to their mother, and she had slammed her bedroom door behind her and not come out for hours. It was the word *mistakes,* she knew, that had set her mother off.

She stretched her legs. Her slippered foot banged into something, and she yelped. She bent over and peered under the tablecloth. There was Taki's radio transmitter. Strange. He was always very watchful of it and when he was finished, he carefully brought it back to his room, where he kept it in a box underneath his bed. He didn't like anyone else to touch it. Though he only used it for entertainment purposes, nothing political or subversive, he guarded it as if it were the key piece of a revolution.

One year earlier, when Taki had returned from the army with a short haircut, an expertise in poker, and some old military radio parts, he built the transmitter. After he and Anna had attended their English lessons, they perused the flea market in Monastiraki, where he bought what to Anna seemed like a box of junk. But soon he had the transmitter working. To test it, they called Spyro, instructed him to tune his radio to the correct frequency—1590 AM—and started talking. Spyro was on their roof before Taki was done with his ranting and chatter. And within minutes they had dragged Taki's turntable up there as well, powered by a long extension cord hanging down to his bedroom. For the rest of the hour they played music—from Manos Hatzidakis to the Beatles. Soon Taki was broadcasting regularly: Friday nights at eight P.M. Word of mouth was a strong force in Halandri and within two weeks many had begun to regularly listen. Though he kept his identity ambiguous, many knew it was him, and Anna knew he liked it when a pretty girl at a party murmured a song request in his ear or winked at him in the square. Anna liked it too, the pride that came from hearing her brother's voice.

Anna moved from one corner of the roof to the other, surveying the streets like a hesitant guard. *Any moment now,* she thought. She imagined Sophie climbing from the back of someone's motorbike, the glossy curtain of hair covering her face; she imagined her waving up to the roof, as if nothing were wrong. Over and over, Anna counted to ten then said to herself, *Okay, now.* She'd look in four directions, thinking for sure she'd see Sophie ambling down the street in that lackadaisical way of hers. Her older sister had always behaved as if the world knew it was obliged to wait for her, whereas Anna always felt herself chasing behind.

The morning sun was strong but there was still a slight chill to the air. From their roof, you could see all the way to Lykavit-tos, awash in the early morning light. One month before, on Clean Monday, the start of Lent, Anna and Mihalis had perched on the roof and watched the colorful display of kites. On Filopappos Hill south of the Acropolis, in unbuilt stretches of the city, and all over the countryside, people flew kites to commemorate the lifting of sins. When they had been children, Taki and Sophie had each flown their own in the large empty lot across the street. As a girl, Anna had been afraid the kite would lift her up and carry her away. Instead, she kept her hand on Taki's, as her brother suggested. He always told her she was helping.

Anna still preferred to watch the bright shapes flutter and soar. It was strangely moving, that vast skyline bursting with such color. At a house a few doors down, she saw a torn kite strewn on a terrace, flap-ping in the breeze. She stood up and walked to the edge of the roof again. No sign of her mother, no sign of Sophie. Anna descended the winding staircase and halfway down jumped onto the balcony outside her room. She thought she heard a car door slam, and because few people had cars in their neighborhood she expected her mother's key in the heavy front door, the sound of her footfalls on the stairs. But the house and the street stayed quiet.

Anna crawled into bed, where she felt slightly more protected. She knew that whatever had happened during the night was more than serious. Yet she found herself intractably separated from it all: politicians, armies, student groups, kings. Who was running things? What side was anybody on? What did it matter? She felt groggy. She didn't want to think about Sophie, God knows where; or Taki and his anti-everything attitude; or her uncle Mihalis, probably already arrested, one of the usual suspects who had been rounded up before and who always expected he'd be rounded up again. She wanted to think about nothing.

There was nothing to do but wait.

4

In April, fecund and green, Athens erupts with life. The trees rustle in the wind, and hyacinths and lupine bloom in the parks. In the summer, the land is sun baked and dry, resigned to a barren calm, but in the spring, it writhes and it kicks. There was a particular smell of the city at this time of year that Eleni had always associated with spring, a heady mixture of earth and spice and wet foliage, with a hint of gasoline. But now she'd forever associate it with something else.

That morning, Eleni drove aimlessly through the winding streets of Psychiko. It was not easy. At every corner, she encountered police: there one day to protect, the next to inspect. They stopped cars, checked identification cards of passengers and drivers, and sometimes searched the trunks. Each time she was stopped she affected a bored look when she rolled her window down, as though all this fuss were of no concern to her. Yet her pulse raced. A question, a wrong look, or an impudent response could make her sound guilty. With her political history, and that of Christos, her departed husband, it wasn't as if she were above suspicion. Each time she was stopped she was simply told to go home, and each time she said that's where she was going.

What was most surprising to her was this: the police seemed just as uneasy as any of the passersby. Some had the startled looks of six-year-old boys woken from sleep; others looked like they were being pestered by gnats.

The neighborhood was winding and dense, with its grand houses set back from the road, their lush entry gardens hidden behind walls. Large trees loomed over the streets. The avenues seemed deserted but in her chest Eleni could feel the distant thunder of trucks. The barrel of a tank peeked out from a narrow street, and she diverted quickly onto an even quieter road, worrying the hum of her engine was too conspicuous. Surely there were people in all these houses, having breakfast, drinking coffee, listening in shock to the radio, but you wouldn't know it from the outside. It seemed the entire neighborhood had evacuated.

Realizing the road was a dead end, she quickly turned around in front of a magnificent yellow house. *This one?* she wondered, looking a moment at its large, empty porch before driving away. Eleni continued to drive up and down the streets that had not been blocked off. Now she almost wished she had bought Sophie the Vespa she had been asking for; at least she'd have something substantial to spot. Because what, really, could she be looking for? An abandoned hair band? A purse? A shoe on the sidewalk? Sophie rarely rode a bicycle and she didn't have a car. Beyond knowing he was in this neighborhood, Eleni had no idea where this boyfriend lived; she now couldn't even remember his name.

She tried to temper her anger. Sophie could be in trouble, and Eleni felt a horrible tightness throughout her body, in her temples, her stomach, her chest. She imagined her daughter's face approaching these officers, accusing and confrontational, afraid of nothing. Eleni fought the urge to go to Dimitri, the man she had been seeing for the past year. He lived not far away, in Filothei, but as adults with separate pasts, they kept the workings of their households separate too. She did not want to involve him but more specifically was embarrassed to tell him she had no idea where her daughter was.

Finally, Eleni turned toward home. Her daughter was okay, she thought, trying to reassure herself, only unable to call because the lines were down. She had simply not used her judgment; Eleni had certainly not been the perfect twenty-one-year-old. This was just bad luck, getting caught at a friend's house. And, speaking of poor judgment, here she was actually endangering herself by ignoring the warnings on the radio.

At the next intersection was a greengrocer. Eleni was about to continue when she noticed the grocer in his store, standing near the front windows. He stared at her, as if he didn't know whether he should hide or wave. She stopped the car and got out. The sign read CLOSED, but when she went to the door he opened it for her. She could hear him playing the Greek military radio, she hoped more out of astonishment than allegiance.

"You're open?" she asked.

"No," he said. She could feel him watching her, wondering what she was doing driving around at a time like this.

"May I buy a few things?" If she couldn't find her daughter, she could at least make sure the rest of the family had plenty to eat. Who knew what would happen next?

He motioned for her to get what she needed. In the cramped store she gathered more than they could probably eat before it went bad; as much as she hated to waste food, it was worse to not have it at all. She felt a horrible sense of déjà vu, back to the Nazi occupation, during which many, including her grandparents, had starved. She added rice, macaroni, and two bags of lentils, and was suddenly grateful for all the tomatoes, green beans, and olives she had canned and stored in the cellar.

As she cautiously moved through the narrow aisles, the grocer didn't take his eyes off her. "You shouldn't be out," he said. "It's not safe."

"I'm headed straight home," she said. "I'm a doctor," she added. "Night shift."

For some reason this, or the fact that her stocking up indicated her preparation for a disaster, made him warm to her a little. "Have you heard anything?" he asked.

"No more than you," she said, motioning to the radio.

"They took my brother last night," the grocer said quietly. "My nieces are staying with us upstairs now. One of them won't leave the closet." His shoulders slumped a bit, as if admitting this made it a little less frightening. "As soon as I find out where they've taken him I'm going to show up there and raise hell. I just don't want to scare the girls."

Eleni watched his lips move but didn't hear anything else. She had been so preoccupied with her missing daughter that somehow she had dismissed the idea of Mihalis being arrested. A nihilistic poet was sure to be high on the list, though her brother seemed, to her, such a free spirit she couldn't imagine his being considered any sort of threat. Then again, he was no longer the ten-year-old boy she sometimes imagined him to be.

"You've been very kind," Eleni said. She paid him.

He handed back her change. "It's nothing," he said.

But they both knew it wasn't. She loaded the bags into the backseat and drove down a few more winding streets of the neighborhood until she reached the same police checkpoint again, though this time the officers were not so indifferent. When she showed them her identification, one of them recognized her. She remembered the mole on his cheek and the reek of his cologne.

"You just passed here," he said. "Now where are you going?" Two other officers stepped closer to the car. A third stood on the other side of the road, smug, smoothing his mustache like some comic-strip villain.

"The hospital sent most of us home," she said. "Because of the—" She wanted to say *curfew,* or *coup,* but stopped. Perhaps it was insulting to the soldiers, who had, in a sense, caused this. Or maybe they liked having such power. Then she added that she had stopped for groceries; her nerves made it hard for her to stop rambling.

The police officer looked her up and down, and Eleni tugged her skirt over her knees. To verify her story, she pointed to the snake and staff on her front window—the mark of a physician—but the man's eyes were still on her legs.

"Step out of the car," he said. Slowly, she did. He made her stand on the curb. Then he crawled into the backseat, where he pawed through the bags of food, spilling much of it onto the floorboards. Behind her, only one other car waited, idling. Normally at this hour the side streets would be teeming with cars: people headed to work and negotiating the neighborhoods to avoid the traffic on the main roads. But as she waited for the man to decide whether her second pass or those groceries were enough to detain her—she wondered if stores had been forbidden to open; would they ask her to turn the grocer in?—she noticed the silence. No cars, no horns, no buzzing of motorcycles or people double-parking. Just the sound of the officer grunting as he heaved himself back out of the vehicle. He slammed the door and shook his head to the other officers. "Last time," he warned her. "Go home."

"Thank you," she said, ashamed at her deference. She got back in the car and he waved her forward. Then, by way of dismissing her, he banged on the trunk as if slapping her ass.

*   *   *

When Eleni arrived at the house, she had convinced herself that So-phie and Mihalis, Anna and Taki, would all be having breakfast and listening to the radio together at the kitchen table. In fact, she had imagined it down to ridiculous detail: Sophie in her father's pale, old pajamas that she insisted on wearing; Mihalis in his blue robe and slippers; Taki eating toast with honey; Anna looking happy just to have everybody nearby.

But when she got home, she only found Taki and his friend Spyro sitting on the front porch, staring into the street. The radio blared from inside. Spyro's tousled light-brown hair, heavy-lidded eyes, and uncharacteristically worried expression brought to mind her holding both little boys' hands as she had walked them to primary school. The news that morning had reduced these two young men to diminutives.

"Well?" Eleni asked.

They shook their heads. "Phone lines are still down," Taki said.

"I saw Sophie last night, at the party," Spyro said hesitantly.

This gave Eleni some comfort. Still, hours had passed, not to mention a shift of power, and the comfort was fleeting. She walked outside to unload the car, and the boys followed to help.

Taki took one bag in each arm. "What—for the bomb shelter?"

Eleni glared at him, placed a bag atop her hip, and shut the car door with more force than she intended.

"Shut up, Taki," said Spyro. He took the bag from Eleni.

"What?" said Taki. "It's probably just some idiots playing some stupid joke."

"In NATO tanks?" Eleni stopped on the front porch and looked at him, incredulous.

Inside, she plopped the groceries on the kitchen table, not both-ering to put them away, and walked upstairs. She knew her older daughter hadn't returned, but she felt compelled to check her room anyway. She sat down atop the neatly made bed. Sophie's dresser, in contrast, was cluttered with poetry books and makeup, dozens of hair ties and headbands, a few bottles of French perfume—gifts from Irini. Her closet was messy and overflowing, and one dresser drawer was not quite closed, a pair of black stockings hanging out. For a moment she thought of calling to Anna, who was embedded somewhere in her mess of blankets. But if she was sleeping, a rarity for her youngest, why wake her? For what?

Her children had not even been born yet that April twenty-six years before, when the Nazis had plowed in with their tanks and cars and motorbikes and raised their flag over the Acropolis. Few could forget the way it hung there, a red and black and haughty splotch over the bright blue sky. Now whoever this was had taken over Athens in the same way, their tanks barreling through the streets, a fresh horror of humanity. There had been rumors of a king's coup or a communist takeover—tensions between left and right only mounted, never went away—and though it was the king's voice purportedly on the radio, Eleni thought the suddenness, the shock of it all, suggested another agenda entirely.

She wondered how Christos would have reacted to this new incursion. His absence, particularly strong that morning, was the reason she had no idea where Sophie was half the time. Once a parent becomes missing, she had come to understand, whether by death or disappearance or the rare and often undiscussed divorce, the entire system of domestic checks and balances becomes void. The one who is left either becomes strict and tyrannical with the children or allows the children to exist on their own. Autocracy or anarchy. Eleni chose the latter, or, more precisely, the latter chose her. Even though her children were small at the time of Christos's death, after the initial pain, the grieving, the loss, something else settled in, a new system of quasi-collectivism that even Anna, the youngest, was aware of. They lived in that house as individuals with the same rights, like students in a dormitory. The People's Republic of Iliopoulos.

She remembered well this loss of control, how one day it seemed the power dynamic had shifted, and she felt strange telling her children to go to bed, to clean their rooms, to wash their faces. That, too, was when the odd hours began; it was not unusual to come downstairs at three A.M. and find two of her children playing quietly on the floor—Taki with his train, Sophie with a doll, or Sophie with the train, Taki with the doll; even the specificities assigned to gender were overturned.

But summers, when the children were no longer in school, this domestic coup was at its strongest. Even their diurnal rhythms were up for question. They slept during the day—not the usual late-afternoon nap, but through the mornings, through the afternoons, arising sometimes not until the evening sun dropped. Many times, she'd hear her children traipse down from the roof at sunrise, when she was getting up for her shift at the hospital. Other times, she'd wake to find their bedrooms empty and all three of them asleep on the roof, lined up with blankets and pillows like campers far from home.

Now they came and went without so much as a question, and evidently at all hours of the night. Order had unquestionably gone the way of their father. And now order in the entire country of Greece was being imposed by some new, self-appointed "father," their supposed savior whose name was being bellowed out.

When she came back downstairs, Taki and Spyro, to her surprise, were putting away the groceries. Taki looked up at her. "I'm just saying, this might blow over in a day or two," he said.

Eleni could see fear behind his nonchalance. Yet how wonderful it would be if her son were right. Not knowing what else to do, she made herself another coffee and sat on the porch.

5

Reuniting with one's estranged wife is never without trouble, though one way to do so with minimal altercation is during a military coup. And when you've known each other since you were teenagers, Mihalis thought, decades could pass with minimal communication and countless damages, and you still could find some sort of comfort in each other. Add political instability and fear of arrest to the equation, and there they were: Mihalis and Irini sitting across the kitchen table from one another as if it were any Friday afternoon.

Except that it wasn't any Friday afternoon. Together Evan and Simone, Mihalis and Irini listened to the dreadful things the radio was blaring that morning, the military marching music interspersed with a harsh voice that hailed the coup as a triumph against immorality, communism, and atheism.

People were told to stay home, stay quiet. Many streets were closed to traffic, and phone lines remained cut. Yet friends in the neighborhood dropped in anyway to share any sort of news. One friend of Evan's had been on his way to the airport when his taxi was stopped and told to turn around. They learned a friend of Simone's had been arrested, as well as a neighbor's uncle who was a member of parliament. A voice on the radio announced the numbers of the articles of the constitution that had been revoked. Anything defending the right to free speech was annulled. They no longer had any sort of protection from arrest. These things were announced as casually as a weather forecast.

"Insanity," Evan kept mumbling, standing up to pace.

Late that afternoon, after the visitors craving news had stopped arriving, after it seemed they had learned all they would learn that day, they encouraged one another to rest.

Mihalis lay in the small upstairs den, the lights off. The couch pulled out into a bed, though Mihalis didn't bother. Sleeping on a couch held a certain lure of familiarity. Simone, holding a clean set of sheets, was a bit quick to offer Irini a bed at the other end of the house. Irini followed her, looking back at Mihalis, saying, "We'll talk more about this later?" Whether she meant the state of the country or the state of the marriage was unclear. Irini had always wanted to discuss *everything,* until she hadn't wanted to talk about anything at all. In fact, Mihalis was sure his inability to *talk* finally made her desist, detach, and eventually depart. "A poet who won't articulate," Irini often said. "Brilliant."

Now Irini was staying in Kifissia, in the old villa she had inherited from her aunt. A perfect country escape, tucked away at the end of a dirt road, the place was modest but charming, and thinking of it made him nostalgic. He and Irini had often visited her aunt there; some nights after dinner, the two of them, still young lovers, climbed to the roof to stare at the night sky, and from there the stillness and beauty made them feel they were in another world. Right now, to be in another world sounded ideal.

Despite his exhaustion, he moved in and out of a restless sleep. Sometimes he'd wake up and think, *What if they come to arrest me here? What if they come now? In five minutes?* He had vivid, unsettling dreams. In the early evening, he heard Evan and Simone murmuring in the kitchen below. Though heavy shutters covered most of the house's windows, in the kitchen they were always wide open. In the twilight, Evan and Simone were on display to the street. Mihalis thought of those stories from the night before, the soldiers breaking down doors with axes. Here they could simply step right in. He wondered if Irini also lay awake and he took some reassurance from the fact that Simone was a foreigner, and foreigners were usually spared.

He washed his face, used Evan's toothbrush, and joined Evan and Simone in the kitchen, where Evan was wondering if the arrests would lead to executions. Though he was exaggerating, the basic idea of civil rights had become a past luxury. Strangely, no matter how disconcerting, they longed for these bits of information. The more knowledge they had, the less anxious they felt.

But anxious all the same. Though they did not know it exactly, they could construe the truth, which was this: Ten thousand people had been arrested in a matter of hours, including not only the current prime minister but the former, seventy-nine years old and ill; his son, who was set to begin campaigning for the election; a leader of the left in parliament, as well as many other members of the legislature. Young and old men and women. Students. Garden-variety intellectuals. Factory workers, publishers, cab drivers, whores. Actresses exiting the stage, journalists typing their bylines, and an assortment of leftists who'd paid their dues after the civil war and would now fill the old jails again. Mihalis wondered if they would be among them. He looked at Evan, drinking his coffee and staring at the kitchen table. Irini appeared in the doorway and adjusted her glasses. They were all thinking the same thing.

Simone filled the *briki* to make Irini some coffee. "I don't remember how you like it," Simone said.

Mihalis did remember and thought the comment, innocent on the surface, was meant to be a passive-aggressive insult, the sort Simone coaxed into an enviable art. *You've just been gone so long.* Is not a woman who stays with her less-than-ideal husband always a bit guarded around a woman who leaves? Simone had always been bothered by Evan's friendship with Irini, and Mihalis was certain this was why, one late night when Irini and Evan had been away at a translation conference in Paris, Simone had come to Mihalis. But that had been years ago.

Irini told her heavy-sweet—*vary glyko*—and Simone added the sugar and stirred. The two women watched the coffee boil and foam, their shoulders touching in some strange, newfound solidarity that Mihalis irrationally but intensely felt was directed against him. When it was ready, Simone poured Irini a cup and one for herself.

Irini brought the demitasse to her lips and held it there. "Maybe we should leave," she said. Not until Evan responded for them to please stay put for now did they all realize Irini meant something else.

"As protest or precaution?" Mihalis asked.

Irini shrugged, as if motivation was beside the point. She lowered her chin and narrowed her eyes. Oh, how he knew that look! For a moment he wanted to pull her toward him.

"We could go to Paris. We both have friends there," Irini said.

His affection lifted. What Irini said was true, though it annoyed Mihalis the way she said it: we *both* have friends there. Implying she had her *own* set of friends there, friends he didn't even know.

"Athens is home. If anything, we should stay and fight."

"From jail?" Irini quipped.

Mihalis shrugged. "That hasn't happened yet."

Evan agreed that leaving until things blew over was not a bad idea. "But actually doing so might be difficult," he added. "Who knows what's happening at the ports, the borders?"

"What do you mean? We know the airport has already been shut down," Simone said.

Mihalis sipped his coffee and looked straight at Irini. "I don't believe in running away from things. It's cowardly."

Irini sighed, set down her cup, and stretched her hands above her head. Then she settled back into her chair, crossing her arms over her chest. "It's not cowardly. It's proactive."

Both Evan and Simone held their tongues. Mihalis could feel that this conversation was now between himself and his wife. He stared at Irini. He noticed faint lines at her forehead, her first signs of aging.

"We should stay," Mihalis said.

"You're not scared they're looking for you?" she asked.

Mihalis glanced around the room. Once more he thought of Evan across from him, the two of them in that tiny, dirty cell. He set his coffee cup back on its saucer.

6

For Sophie, morning arrived all at once, a grotesque assault of light that startled her awake. She didn't want to move, fearful that what had actually awoken her was a gunshot or worse.

Keeping her head low, Sophie cranked down the window for some air. She lay on her back and tried to straighten her legs. Her hips ached from sleeping in the cab's backseat. She'd spent half the night trying to get comfortable, her body tense from every sound outside the car. Dozens of times she'd nearly left, only to convince herself to stay, to wait for Vangelis. But now, with morning, it was clear she'd made the wrong choice. Still, at least she hadn't been discovered.

On the floor she found a pack of Vangelis's cigarettes and a matchbook inscribed with the name of a gritty bar in Exarheia she knew both Vangelis and her uncle frequented. Her mouth tasted awful; she needed something to drink. Instead, out of nerves, she sat up and lit a cigarette, blowing her smoke out the window like so many SOS rings. Then, realizing she didn't trust who might be out there to save her, she put the cigarette out.

Her mother. Her mother must be panicked. If her absence had

gone unnoticed through the night, it was surely clear by now. And her mother had one weapon left in her arsenal: shame. Still, Sophie would take the humiliation her mother's cold glances incited if she could just be safe in her own bed.

She squinted out through the dusty windshield. For a Friday morning the neighborhood was bereft of movement, as if everyone had been sucked into the core of their homes. No one walked to the market or the train station, no gardeners trimmed rosebushes or watered plants. No hum of morning traffic, no buzz of motorbikes, no hiss and halt of buses drifted from the avenue. Somewhere nearby a baby cried an incessant, inconsolable wail, and it pierced the stillness like a bad dream. One lone car passed her, headlights still shining, and Sophie ducked, feeling a punch of panic.

While the cab had seemed an unlikely comfort in the middle of the night, now with the glare of the sun, the dirt on her dress, the bloody scab on her knee, and one sharp pain in her neck, she felt like a wild animal who'd been lured into a trap. She peeked out once more to survey her surroundings and climbed out of the cab. A few steps away she smoothed out her dress and hair and began to walk back to Nick's.

The neighborhood was winding and dense and not easy to navigate. In the light Sophie almost didn't recognize it and was glad she was only around the corner from the house. Sophie did not drive, and sometimes as a passenger she'd be sure they'd turn the corner and be at Nick's; instead, there would be the park, dark and dense with pine, or the gates of a foreign embassy. Now, so disheveled, unkempt, the only person on the streets, she felt frighteningly displaced and conspicuous.

Though the gate had been unlocked for the party, an easy access point for the soldiers, now it was locked. Sophie reached for the hidden spare key and let herself in. A black bicycle with a front basket was propped up against the house on the large porch. The door was not closed all the way, and Sophie pushed it open and quietly called for Nick. She heard hesitant footsteps but instead of finding him or his cousin she faced Mrs. Popi, the maid. Leaflets from the student newspaper were scattered over the floor. The overflowing ashtrays, the half-drunk bottles of beer and diluted glasses of whiskey and *tsipouro* would any other day have looked like a morning-after scene. Sophie would not have been surprised to see clothing items strewn over the light fixtures or someone tumble forth from a closet. But now, the way Popi stood amid the mess, perplexed, picking pistachio shells from the rug, the sight was not riotous but simply ominous. All the windows were open, and the breeze coming through felt equally portentous. From the kitchen Sophie could hear the radio.

"What happened? Where is *to paidi*?" she asked. To Mrs. Popi, who had raised Nick, he would always be a child. *The* child, as she referred to him now.

"He's not here?" Sophie asked.

Popi shook her head. "The house was empty when I got here."

Sophie said, "I need to call my mother."

"It's no use," she said. "The phones are dead." Popi pointed in the direction of the front porch. "And the buses aren't running either. I had to ride my bicycle." She motioned for Sophie to follow her to the kitchen, where they saw a small window that had been broken.

While Sophie told her what had happened there at the house, she felt the fear rising up inside her all over again. And she watched that same fear well up in Popi's face as she pieced together the past few hours in her mind.

"I had thought it was a bus strike," Popi said.

Because she wasn't sure what else to do, Sophie helped Popi gather the pages of their newspaper that had been strewn around the room. But even this small act exhausted her. Her nerves rattled and her limbs felt like someone else's. She slumped onto the couch and put her head between her knees. The alcohol and lack of sleep and water and food made her light-headed, and coupled with the fear, she thought she might faint. Popi sat next to her and smoothed her hair, which fell over her bare legs.

"You should stay here awhile. It's not safe," Popi said. "Why don't you take a bath."

Sophie didn't object. She was grateful not to be alone and was overcome by the urge to be taken care of.

Upstairs she peered into Nick's bedroom. Popi had already made the bed, surely aware that it hadn't been *slept* in. Sophie's pocketbook was still on Nick's dresser, where she had left it, along with her cardigan and her earrings. She lay back down on the bed and closed her eyes a moment. Downstairs Popi continued cleaning the mess, as if she was used to Nick and his parties and this was another morning she'd arrived while his parents were gone. The way she was in alliance with him made Sophie think of Vangelis, and she hoped he had somehow made it back to Halandri.

In the bathroom she looked at herself in the mirror. Mascara had collected underneath her eyes; there was dirt on her face and arms. Her hair was unkempt, and her beige shift was soiled with dirt and blood from her skinned knee. No wonder Popi had suggested a bath: she looked like a street urchin. She scrubbed her face and used her finger to brush her teeth. Then, she filled the tub with hot, sudsy water.

When Popi pushed open the door Sophie sank down into the suds, shy. Popi handed her a cup of tea. Sophie felt small and scared yet appreciated the company. The woman sat down at the edge of the tub. "I don't know how to reach them," she said, referring, Sophie assumed, to Nick's parents. She didn't expect advice from Sophie but needed to voice this concern aloud. It didn't feel so strange to be taken care of by someone other than her mother; stranger would have been having her mother act that way. From the time Sophie was very young she craved the attention of her mother, but once the other two siblings came around she prickled at any sort of hovering, as if her parents had betrayed her by having more children. As a result her mother learned to treat her with a bit of detached indifference that was probably the opposite of what she had wanted, but it was the way it was. Her mothering instincts went mostly to Taki, with a little bit left over for Anna.

"If you need anything else . . . ," Popi said, standing to leave. Then she smiled wanly and Sophie nodded.

After what felt like a long time, Sophie got out of the tub and wrapped herself in the robe Popi had set out for her. She left the bathroom and went back to Nick's room. But when she pushed open the door, she found him standing there in the same clothes he'd been wearing the night before.

"What the hell happened to you?" Nick asked.

For a moment she wasn't sure how to take this. He was angry, but seeing her safe softened him a bit, and this moved Sophie. He asked her if she was okay. He told her which of their friends had been arrested but didn't mention where he had gone. Plenty had also managed to escape, he told her. He had been up all night, it seemed, though with no signs of sleepiness.

"We're going to fight this," he said. "Whatever it is."

"I need to get home," Sophie said.

Nick nodded but wasn't quite listening. "Something that comes about so abruptly can just as abruptly be toppled." She wanted to believe him but his reasoning seemed faulty. He touched her shoulder and kissed her cheek. "Here are some clean clothes," he said, and left the room.

Sophie brushed her hair. Her own clothes looked so filthy, crumpled on the floor. She examined what Nick had given her: a white oxford shirt, jeans, even a pair of white cotton underpants (his mother's?), which embarrassed Sophie, but she was happy to have clean things to wear. They smelled like Nick, the same laundry soap. The jeans were soft and old and loose on her, so she threaded her long scarf through the belt loops to keep them up. She braided her damp hair and went downstairs.

In the kitchen Popi washed dishes while Nick and Loukas sat at the dining room table. On a tray in front of them was toasted bread with butter and honey, and Sophie devoured three pieces. She could have eaten the entire loaf. Popi gave her a glass of juice. Some things went along as usual, she supposed. Loukas gave her a once-over, and she blushed at his attention.

"You could have given her your mother's clothes, you know," Loukas said to his cousin. Then Nick jumped at a knock at the back door, and from the table Sophie watched him talk to a broad-shouldered rakish guy she recognized from the party. He left quickly on foot and Nick came back to the table.

"Some people are meeting," Nick said.

Sophie must have looked alarmed because Loukas shrugged and said the longer people were passive the worse it would get. "The earlier the better," he said. His tone wasn't so much condescending as it was acquiescing, as if they were all in this together. Nick took her hand and pulled her over to him, putting his hands on her hips. "We can take you home, if you want." In front of his cousin, Nick was weirdly nonchalant, sensible, a stark contrast to the panicked boy on the roof. And suddenly a little proprietary? Why hadn't he specifically asked her to come along? At this point, so exhausted, she didn't know what she wanted.

On the road checkpoints were everywhere as they had expected, and the police were rerouting traffic it seemed just for the sake of making things difficult. They were stopped first by an officer who looked younger than they were. But Sophie, with her loose boyish clothing, her face scrubbed clean, and her hair pulled back, perhaps looked no more than fifteen, because he only asked Loukas and Nick for identification and, after barely even glancing at the documents, waved them by. Every few minutes, Loukas checked his rearview mirror and met Sophie's eyes, and she grew hot under his intense gaze. They were stopped twice more by the police, quickly showed their ID cards, and were waved off again, as if their being on the streets at all was simply a nuisance. "Just go home," the officer told Loukas.

"That's where we're headed," he said. Sophie thought about the warnings on the radio, to not be out after eight o'clock. Shot dead, they had said, but Sophie had a hard time believing the threat. Regardless, the police were making it clear it was best they weren't out at all. It was a gloomy, late Friday morning. "Feels like a Sunday," she mumbled. There was a despondent quality to Sundays that she hated. Her father had died on a Sunday, but Sophie swore this outlook originated much before that, when she was very young.

Time had virtually stopped. The atmosphere of the city felt how Sophie imagined the bombarded cities of France during World War II did, though nothing had been bombed, at least not yet. As they drove north on Kifissia Avenue toward Halandri, Sophie noticed two older men in suits being harassed by several officers half the men's age. She was angry and embarrassed by the scene but also grateful that they had slipped by virtually unnoticed. She wondered from which houses people had been taken and how many had been arrested. Earlier, she had placated herself by thinking that Nick's neighbors were part of a select few. But the desolate feel of the streets, the police and military officers and their checkpoints, the cut lines of communication—she had to acknowledge an alternate reality. Athens was under siege.

It was an act of defiance simply to be out, a fact they were all aware of. Nick smoked and flicked the ash out the window while Loukas drove. Loukas's presence had soothed her and as they crept down the street toward her house, she grew edgy at the idea of separation. Why had she felt so desperate to get home? The thought of being in the house with her family, though at first comforting, made her feel as though she was choking. From the time of her father's death this confined, cramped feeling had thrust her to the roof, the only place that gave her relief, the potential of open air and freedom and the fantasy of being able to soar into the open sky. Suddenly to stay with the two cousins seemed the only option. All the rules had been dismantled and reassembled in different ways, and at that moment she could have convinced herself that two plus two equaled five.

Sophie pointed to her house, and Loukas stopped in front of it. "Be careful," he said. Nick turned around and took her hand. His overprotectiveness irked her.

"Let me come with you," Sophie said. "To the meeting. How am I supposed to just sit inside, staring at my family?"

Out of the corner of her eye she saw Loukas's face brighten. He had been very quiet during the drive, and Sophie wondered if he was kicking himself for not staying in France, the way seemingly benign, ordinary decisions often led to extraordinary results. Everything was still changing. Sophie felt it and wanted to be there. More importantly, she thought, looking again at her house, she couldn't be here.

Nick nodded toward the house. "Is that your sister?"

Through the gate Sophie could see Anna on the porch, watching them like a cat. She could go inside, see her mother, put on some different clothes. But something told her if she got out of the car, she wouldn't get back in. Anna rushed to the gate, and Sophie rolled the window down.

Anna stared at the balled-up dress in Sophie's lap, her odd clothes. She glanced in at the boys shyly but then turned back to

Sophie. "Where have you been? She's going nuts. No one knows where Mihalis is, and Vangelis never came home—"

Sophie interrupted her little sister. "Quiet. I know," she whispered. "Tell her I'm fine. I'll be back before dark." She looked at Nick and Loukas in the front seat.

"Of course," Nick said.

At the sight of her house, the lush garden, the comfortable front porch and trellised grapevines, Sophie hesitated. She looked up to the second floor, her mother's bedroom, the balcony. Maybe she did just want to put on her pajamas and close her eyes. But then what? Here she had a chance to be a part of something.

As they drove away Sophie felt yet another rush of adrenaline. She had almost forgotten about Vangelis until her little sister brought him up again; she noticed the space where he usually parked was empty. His cab was probably still waiting around the corner from Nick's and Vangelis was god knew where. She knew the right thing to do would be to stop, to get out of the car and talk to Vangelis's wife, to tell her she had seen him and show her mother she was okay.

When they reached the corner of the main road, Sophie craned her head back.

7

Eleni hadn't heard the car with Sophie pull up. She'd simply become aware of the sound of the motor running out front, the way she'd sometimes suddenly notice the humming of bees in her garden. By the time she went to the front window the car was already pulling away and Eleni ran into the yard.

"I don't believe this," Eleni yelled. "The day of a coup and the child drives off? Has she lost her mind?"

Had the circumstances been different and Sophie simply stayed out

all night, it would have come as no surprise to Eleni. All her life Sophie
had been trying to get out of the house. She emerged from the womb
with her hands out first. Christos had once joked that Sophie cut the
cord, bathed herself, put on her shoes, and walked out of the hospital room, fully formed and bossing the nurses around. Anna, on the
other hand, two weeks late, had been a grueling thirty hours of labor to
boot—rare for a third child—and Eleni sometimes wondered if Anna
still wished to be inside the womb, warm and safe and enclosed in darkness. Eleni had miscarried a child after Taki, before Anna, and though
Eleni was far too pragmatic to ever admit this to anyone, she sometimes
wondered if Anna was that miscarried child who came back, defeated.

She hurried out to the porch. In the garden, Anna stood by the
gate. She was strangely reminded of the time Anna had, when visiting
their friends in a small village, witnessed the killing of a lamb. Her
daughter's wrists were raw and red; she had even made herself bleed.
Eleni took her hands to stop her from scratching, something she had
been doing since Christos had died. A nervous habit.

"Don't you know what's happening, Anna? You let her drive off?"
Eleni walked outside the gate and stood in the road. Anna was too
scared to say anything, though her silence made it seem as though
nothing out of the ordinary had happened. Eleni saw nothing in the
road of course and walked past Anna and into the house. She'd distract
herself by cooking something. As if it were an evening like any other.

The evening Christos died had also been an evening like any
other: the neighborhood arose and continued its business. Some went
back to work; others walked, read the paper, prepared dinner. Another evening of clattering dishes and the tinny clink of silver, of
walks to tavernas for some fish, some greens, a glass decanter of wine
on the table. This ordinariness, in Eleni's mind, was as startling as her
husband's death had been itself.

Eleni remembered the way her green tumbler of water had per-
spired—it had been hot, and she had been baking an herb pie, wishing instead she had decided on salad and smoked fish or anything that
wouldn't involve the oven. On the front porch, Taki and Anna had fought
over a toy—or was it a comic book?—like territorial, hungry dogs.

Sophie, only eleven then, but already aligning herself with her parents and not her younger brother and sister, read at the kitchen table, holding her book open with one hand and chopping tomatoes with another. With each hard whack of the knife on the cutting board, Eleni looked up, but Sophie's eyes never left the page. When Eleni did finally catch her daughter's eye, Sophie didn't acknowledge her dodgy cutting technique, and before Eleni could tell her anything, Sophie rolled her eyes to refer to her squabbling siblings and returned to her book and her slicing.

Eleni still tried to remember what it was her eldest daughter had been reading that day, as if it would hold some clue, some answer, but she could only remember the worn edges of a dark red hardback. No, even the color was questionable; at times she thought it was gray or blue. Maybe even a cheap paperback with a torn cover. Or a comic book, which Christos always hated. In fact, in this image, she envisioned the refrigerator in the background behind Sophie, shiny and new, but this was impossible; Christos died in 1957, and they had used an icebox until 1961. She wondered how many of her other memories were fabricated, inauthentic. Even so, what about memory *was* authentic?

Then, that evening, had come a strange, painful yelp. At first, Eleni had thought Sophie had chopped off a finger, what with the haphazard way she was slicing. But looking at Sophie's small, blank face, the way she held the knife midchop, her book flapping closed, she realized it had come from Christos. A fall, too, a horrible thump, the crash of a stack of books to the floor. Sophie ran from her seat, still holding the wet knife.

Within hours Christos had been pronounced dead. There he had been, sipping brandy in his den, reading the paper, when an aneurysm had ruptured in his brain. The news had spread quickly but quietly through the neighborhood. It was common for information to drift between the houses, roof to roof, balcony to balcony, over the courtyards and verdant gardens, the same way it had when the Germans had left the city in 1944 and all of Athens had flooded the streets.

A good seven years passed before Eleni began to abandon the requisite black of widowhood, to allow herself freedom from grief. No one—well, perhaps some in her ancestral village, but surely none of her friends and colleagues in Athens—would have expected her to remain draped in black forever. But over the past decade, she had become so used to herself in dark tones that to see herself in red or light blue seemed garish, like so many tourists who emerged from the ports on the islands, ready to buy souvenirs. Wearing color to her seemed akin to the mating strategies of certain animals: swollen backsides, bright plumage, a confident strut. She certainly did not want to announce to the world, "Okay, *now.*" Then again, she would not be like the widows of her mother's generation, who wore black for the rest of their lives and who, inevitably, moved into one of the households of their grown children and did all the cooking and cleaning and much of the child rearing. She was young still and did not know many widows who were her contemporaries, and perhaps they too would follow in their mothers' footsteps. But she did not fit the stereotypical portrayal of the young widow either, also forlorn and black clad, with an alleged insatiable sex drive that fueled the town gossip, and the object of the affections of a hapless young man who drove himself crazy trying to satisfy her.

Though was she to turn off all swells of desire? Not to mention of loneliness? So when Dimitri, head of surgery at the hospital, began paying attention to her beyond just polite work banter, she didn't know how to react. Soon they had coffee, and after that dinner, and then it seemed they were simply together.

He was an incredibly conscientious man. He rarely arrived at her house without something sweet, or a bottle of wine, or tomatoes from his large garden in Filothei. When she worked late at night he'd either pick her up or call to make sure she was home, safe. At first Eleni thought it was a little much—she had been on her own for some time—but she quickly began to appreciate those kind, chivalrous gestures, still common in her generation, but because he was ten years her senior there was something that felt decidedly old-fashioned about him.

So it shouldn't have surprised her to hear the doorbell that late afternoon and to find Dimitri on her porch. "How are you?" he asked, coming into the foyer and placing his hat and jacket on the coat rack.

She told him about Sophie.

"Something like this was bound to happen sooner or later," Dimitri said.

Eleni was about to ask him what he meant until she realized he was speaking of the coup.

"I'm sure it will pass over, once things stabilize," he said.

He spoke of it as if it were just a little civil unrest. Eleni didn't respond. Instead, they went inside, Dimitri poured them each a glass of wine, and they sat on the front porch. At first Eleni was hesitant; she didn't want to be in view.

"Who are you afraid will come looking for you?" Dimitri asked. "No need to overreact."

Eleni acquiesced. She and Dimitri rarely talked about politics. Not that she was uncomfortable expressing a dissenting opinion; it was that Dimitri saved these discussions for other men, away from her. Sometimes, Eleni would read the paper over Dimitri's shoulder and comment on a piece of news. "Hmm," was all he'd say in response. And that was that. Conversation canceled.

She supposed all this was fine. They talked about books, and films and theater productions they had seen, avoiding the more blatant political themes; they spoke of their children. They talked about work, this patient, that patient, this nurse, and so forth. Often they sat quietly, not saying anything at all. Eleni supposed this was how couples behaved after many years, but she and Christos had been together twelve when he died and had not yet reached that point. There had always been something to say and she never came to dread him the way other friends came to dread their spouses. She wondered if they ever would have moved beyond that state. Maybe it was only youth, raw and idealistic and bellicose. For whatever reason, she and Christos had often found themselves in trouble for their fervent idealism—lost jobs, arrests, allegations of communism and the like—and maybe in her fifth decade, temperance was not a bad quality. Less than one year and she behaved with Dimitri as if they'd been together thirty. Was this duplicity or deference?

Later, Eleni took some vegetables and rice out of the oven, and the two of them ate with the radio on dimly in the background. She was soothed by his presence and was glad he had come over. Anna and Taki appeared, ate quietly, and left the table. By that time of day they had learned it was carried out not by the left, nor the king, but by colonels in the army, in the name of defending the country against the barbarism of communism. When their conversation turned back to

Sophie, Dimitri's expression looked vaguely condescending. "I'm not saying anything," Dimitri said. "I have three boys, remember." But his three boys were older, and serious, conservative young men. One was a major in the army, stationed in northern Greece, and she wondered if he had known about the previous night's events far before they had occurred. Dimitri certainly didn't seem too shaken, though it was not like him to exhibit emotion.

His presence did temper her nerves a bit, but it was not enough at ten minutes to eight to squelch the desire Eleni had to throw a wet dish towel at Sophie when she appeared in the kitchen. Anna and Taki both came down to the kitchen immediately thereafter.

"Up to your room, right now," Eleni said. "Now. I don't even want to look at your face." Sophie looked at all of them, began to try to explain herself, and then huffed and turned away. But no sooner did Sophie's long braid disappear into the foyer and up the stairs than Eleni let the dishes drop and clatter in the sink and chase after her.

She followed Sophie into her room and slammed the heavy door. Sophie collapsed onto the bed, and the bundle with dress and purse she let fall from her hands.

"What in the world do you think you're doing?" Eleni asked.

"It wasn't exactly easy to get home last night," Sophie said, her voice muffled by her pillow. She lifted her head and looked around: her drawers were all still wide open from Eleni's earlier ransacking. "There were arrests all up and down Nick's street. The phone lines were cut."

"And today, all day? Where? With this Nick?"

Sophie parted her lips but then flopped her head down on the pillow. She rolled over to face the wall. "I came home to say I was okay. Then I had to do something."

"What?" Eleni asked. "Don't you realize what sort of danger *doing something* could put you in?" Eleni looked at her daughter's thin, long frame, clad in boys' clothing. How could it be she wanted to shake her and hold her all at once?

"If there's no danger," Sophie said, "then probably nothing that important needs doing."

Eleni heard the echo of Christos there, that glimpse of him in

Sophie's dark, deep-set eyes, and she recognized a young idealism that she herself had once felt, and maybe this was why she did not stay in that room, arguing with her daughter until her voice became hoarse or she slapped her across the face. Instead, she stood up, closed the shutters, and left the room.

Back downstairs, Anna was in the kitchen finishing the dishes. Taki sat at the table, his physics text open in front of him. He had turned the radio louder now and from it the same tired military marches blared.

"Please, Taki," Eleni snapped. "Turn that damn thing off." He did, and she heard both Anna and Taki slog up the stairs to their rooms.

In the living room, she sat next to Dimitri, who was leafing through a book with the look of a man who didn't want to get involved. She covered her face with her hands, and he put his hand on her back. Eleni leaned into him, hoping contact might help make sense of what had happened.

8

The Monday after the coup, when the phones were on and the buses were running, Mihalis declared at breakfast that he was going back to Halandri.

Evan asked him if he thought that was wise.

"I can't stay here forever," Mihalis said. "And do you think these idiots are organized enough to be going door to door?"

"If these idiots are anything, they're organized," said Simone.

"Regardless, they wouldn't be looking for you here," Evan said.

"Why not?" asked Mihalis. "If there's a list, you're as likely to be on it as I am. There's probably an ivory tower at the prison for the bourgeois intellectuals." He finished his breakfast and wiped his hands on his pants.

"You're ridiculous," Irini said. "You should come with me to Kifissia. Better yet, we should just go to France."

"Or London. You could stay with my family," Simone said again. They'd been having the same conversation for days.

"I'm serious. Maybe we should try to get out of here," Irini said. "Both of us. All of us. And go from there."

"It's dangerous," Mihalis said. "To try to leave." He didn't know if that was really true, but Irini's continual suggestions about leaving were beginning to irritate him.

"Really?" Irini asked. "More dangerous than here?"

When the Second World War ended, Mihalis joked that another battle had begun, which was true, but he meant not the civil war but marriage. Things between himself and Irini had always been electric, glowing one minute and short-circuiting the next. Within the same fifteen-minute period they'd be shouting at one another and making love. Mihalis and Irini had barely consummated their marriage before he disappeared into the mountains with Evan to fight, this time against not Germans but other Greeks in a conflict that still lingered, with wounds that were reopened with this recent turn of events.

As much as Mihalis complained about Greece—he would die complaining, Irini had often said—he couldn't imagine living anywhere else. He knew Irini knew this, and he wondered if she suggested such things simply to provoke him. Someday maybe she would use his obstinacy as a reason to divorce him. No, he would not leave the country, but he would leave Evan's house. He went upstairs to get his coat. Irini did not follow him as he had hoped she would. When he put on his suit coat, he checked the pocket. Her letter was still there, and in the other pocket was his crumpled tie.

When he came back downstairs, no one was talking. Evan stood but the women remained seated. Evan hugged and kissed him, and then Mihalis bent over to kiss Simone. When he said good-bye to Irini she, out of character, hugged him tightly. "Be careful," she said.

Mihalis took the walk down to the main avenue slowly. Kolonaki's tree-lined streets were in furious bloom, and the yeasty, warm smell of bread drifted from all the bakeries. Owners swept the stoops of their shops and wiped down the tables in their cafés. Two teenage boys unloaded a delivery truck outside a grocery, and near a newsstand, two old men had coffee. Men in suits bought newspapers. Mihalis stopped at a kiosk to get one for himself but then reconsidered: if the radio blaring its same announcement days earlier was any indication, surely the newspapers were heavily censored. Some foreign papers still graced the newsstands, but Mihalis was reluctant to buy one, as if it would somehow implicate him.

He continued to Vassilissis Sofias Avenue, where he'd catch the bus to Halandri. He could hear the incessant jabbing of a jackhammer and the hiss and spew of garbage trucks. On the corner near the National Gardens, two young military police stood looking overly serious. Mihalis passed them without much recognition. When he walked through Exarheia or Omonia people recognized him just the way the young teenagers on Lykavittos had. It didn't matter how large Athens was; the area around Omonia was his village. People waved, they called out, sometimes they even bought him a coffee. Bookstore owners asked him if he'd read the newest volume of poetry or the latest translated novel. But here, now, he was grateful for his anonymity.

In Omonia or otherwise, he was rarely in Athens this early. The masses of people emptying from the buses, continuing their business as though nothing had happened, working and running errands before they slowed down again for Easter, troubled him. As he was waiting to get on the bus, two women disembarked with shopping bags full of cleaning products hanging from their hands. They pushed past him, glaring.

Save for some odd jobs here and there, Mihalis had never been employed. He had gone to work once with his friend Mina, who over the years had had various jobs—sometimes she worked in a factory in Piraeus, sometimes she picked fruit, and she had even been the children's nanny when they were very young, which is how Mihalis had befriended her. At that time she had been cleaning houses and needed help, so Mihalis had agreed to go with her for two weeks, cleaning grand homes and both spacious and cramped apartments, ironing underwear and expensive French linens and scrubbing shit from the toilets. After that, during dinner one night in Halandri, he seethed about the poor conditions Mina worked in, the low pay, the rude and thoughtless employers, how sometimes she needed two or three of these jobs to support her children. During this rant, Taki had scoffed, a bitter, angry huff, and Mihalis, although he would not let his nephew see it, had carried with him a cloud of embarrassment for days. Taki knew his parents supported Mihalis, and in some way this gave Taki, even as a boy, the power to humiliate.

Somewhere deep down this did embarrass him: as a poet, he couldn't align himself with the workers, whether they were high-class professionals, factory laborers, or olive farmers. A poet's life was different; surely there were starving artists in Greece and abroad—he knew many—but he had rarely if ever been one of them. His ability to write his poems did depend on a certain privilege, he knew, the security of his sister's family and their support, and, of course, Irini's. But didn't it also depend upon vision and voice? And didn't this in itself carry a certain worth, a gravitas? He had a cousin who once told him that he, too, would have chosen to be a writer if he had the time. Mihalis had shrugged and said, "It's not a choice." And his cousin, an accountant, had simply laughed. "Come to think of it I also wish I had your naïveté," he'd remarked.

Over the past few days at Evan's, friends and neighbors dropped by with news of meetings and opposition. A network of resistance was forming, but Mihalis couldn't help but wonder what strong voices already were silenced in jail. And he was wondering what his role would turn out to be.

On the bus, his feelings of remove were heightened. The poet was an observer and as such he could never truly be a participant. He was both nestled firmly in the center of society and lurking on its fringes. Mihalis stared out the bus window. Nothing seemed different except for the faces, all of them slightly rattled, the morning after a nightmare.

When he disembarked from the bus, Mihalis paused. Halandri had always felt as if it were another world from Athens, his village away from the city, and in many ways it was. That morning, the square was quiet. A grandmother dressed in black wandered with two small girls holding dolls. Several cats dozed in the sun. Mihalis noticed that a few shops were closed, but otherwise, the neighborhood continued its dealings. Two priests talked outside the church, and another young mother pushed a stroller.

As Mihalis turned the corner to his sister's, he noticed Vangelis alone on his back porch, which surprised him. His cab wasn't parked in its usual spot. Mihalis called out a hello, and Vangelis motioned for him to come to the side gate, which he opened. He looked horrible, as if he hadn't slept in days. His skin was craggy and he hadn't shaved. His lips were so dry that they were cracked and bleeding. A tall glass of orange juice sat in front of him, and a package of tobacco.

"I haven't been back to the house yet," Mihalis said. "Since." He hoped Vangelis could fill him in. If you want to know the workings of a city, ask its taxi drivers.

"My wife was there this morning," Vangelis said. He motioned at the kitchen window, as if she were standing in it, but the shutters were closed. "They all seem okay."

"What have you heard?" Mihalis asked.

Vangelis didn't say anything at first. He glanced around, as if others were in the yard with them. He sat up in the chair and winced, rubbed his back. "I just got home last night myself," he said.

Mihalis stared at him but didn't say anything.

Vangelis continued. "I was taken in for questioning."

Mihalis looked around the yard. Weeds sprang up from beneath the cement blocks, and Vangelis's old dog, Goya, slept in the sun. An abandoned canvas was propped in the corner, on an easel, as if he had thought to paint but then changed his mind. Upright against the small shed underneath a trellis of grapevines were several other paintings—finished or unfinished, Mihalis couldn't tell—and a small pail of brushes sat next to them. He remembered when they had been young, in the island prison where they had first met, and Vangelis etched images into the earth while Mihalis scratched out words to accompany them. He remembered when Vangelis and his new wife had bought the house next to his sister and Christos and what joy and safety he felt to have everybody so close. "We've known each other a long time," Mihalis said.

Vangelis looked at him. "We're old."

"In twenty years we'll scoff that we thought this was old," Mihalis said. From inside, he could hear the sounds of the television. "What did they do to you?" he finally asked.

Vangelis sighed and stood up. He held his lower back and shuffled inside, as if it hurt to lift his feet off the ground. "What they always do," he said.

Mihalis followed him into the house. Unlike Evan's, which had been drenched with the morning light, Vangelis's living room felt dark, closed up. A small stand in the corner held a few icons, where a candle burned. His wife stood in the living room, folding clothes. Mihalis greeted her with a kiss and followed Vangelis into the small kitchen. "Do you want something to drink?" Vangelis asked. "Coffee?"

Mihalis nodded. "You should see the center of Athens. Business as usual. As long as everyone has their morning cookies, their newspapers, they're happy."

Vangelis turned the water on to boil and opened the tin canister of coffee.

"And you were arrested why?" Mihalis asked.

Vangelis looked at him sharply. "Wrong place, wrong time," he said. "That's all."

Had Vangelis not looked so demoralized, so beaten; had his eyes not seemed so sunken and his skin so ashy; had Mihalis not noticed the bruises on his arms, like someone had been holding him down, he would have prodded him for more details. But he didn't. He knew them, anyway.

Vangelis's wife came into the kitchen then. "Let me take care of the coffee," she said. "You rest."

"I think I need to lie down," Vangelis said. "I'm sorry."

"Don't worry," Mihalis said. He put his hand on his friend's shoulder. "We can talk later."

When Mihalis began to walk toward the side door, through which they had just entered moments before, he was surprised to see that Vangelis's wife had already locked it. She followed him to the door. "I'll let you out," she said.

*   *   *

His sister's house was quiet. Eleni usually worked at the hospital Monday mornings. The kids were probably home, already on Easter break. But after he let himself in the yard's iron gate he didn't go up the steps and into the house to say hello. Instead, he walked through the garden and down the cement steps that led to his basement room.

Mihalis plopped down on the small narrow bed. His sister had changed the sheets, anticipating his arrival. He closed his eyes. Vangelis had already been broken by these bastards. Only a few stupid army colonels and the entire country was afraid. But Mihalis was angry.

On the nightstand next to his bed was an old coffee mug stuffed with pens. In the drawer were various notepads. He drew one out and held it on his chest. He wanted to write but at the same time felt too distracted, and he let the notepad fall to the bed. He took out a red marker and on the wall, just above his pillow, wrote in small blocky letters one word, both statement and reminder: RESIST. He said it a few times, angrily.

Then, too restless to sit in that cool, dark basement, he went upstairs to see who was around.

9

Over the next few days, that false state of the ordinary persisted: buses and trains were running, the military songs stopped blaring over the radio, and a few tanks dozed outside parliament as seemingly benign as they had been when they barreled through the Independence Day parade one month before. But the populace was on edge, waiting for the next calamity, the next arrest. Because it seemed here that no one was safe: members of the left and right had been arrested, and the center, too. That week, Athens slept in fear of hearing banging on the door, of being dragged away.

One week after the coup, the colonels had temporarily lifted the ban on large gatherings—"large" being more than five people—and encouraged everyone to attend Easter services, their way of showing that there was no need to worry and their transition into power was seamless and benevolent. Sophie, as a result, was all the more adamant about doing no such thing. "They may have checkpoints set up around Saint Constantine's," she said to Anna. Since the coup, she and her mother had barely spoken. "It may be all a hoax to get people into one place. They're no better than the Nazis. They're the same people who collaborated with the Nazis."

Sophie's comments made Anna nervous. Her older sister always seemed privy to some large, looming secret. But Anna hadn't left the house all week, and she hoped their attendance would bring something numbly soothing, a hint at a return to normalcy. Or, at least, the familiar. Though they were decidedly not churchgoers, Easter services were another matter, an almost secular event.

On the walk to the square with her mother and Taki, although she was happy not to be in a car, Anna held her breath at every corner, expecting some sort of confrontation. There was none, though the streets did feel a little more chaotic. She kept watch for military police, those colonels' uniforms, and wondered why Sophie had been so insistent. When they neared the church, she did not feel the normal bursting of her chest that the bells usually roused; instead, her heart beat so quickly at times she thought she was having a heart attack. She shivered beneath her thin coat; it seemed colder than usual for Easter.

Outside the church, where people gathered, a young man walked past Anna wearing a military uniform. The way the crowd was aware of him! They moved aside or looked away or glared at his back. There were plenty of young men in the army; all Greek men had to enlist for two years of service. Just because this man wore a uniform it did not make him a fascist coup mastermind. But in the last week, the military uniform had been transformed regardless, and it was impossible not to associate the uniform with the dictators. Soldiers were certainly out, patrolling, but his inclusion in the middle of the crowd was particularly unsettling. Perhaps a more smug officer would have gloated at the power and attention, but Anna could see a flush rise up into his ears. She wondered why he was alone. Was his family embarrassed? Or maybe he'd had them arrested. Maybe they were here, in the crowd somewhere, but he had to arrive late, after questioning a roomful of men.

Anna stared at the back of the soldier's head. His brown hair had been cut very short, and he had a cowlick in the back. If his hair were long, it would have stuck up there in an unruly tuft, no matter what he did to smooth it down. It probably turned reddish brown in the sun. Every so often, he turned to his right slightly, and then to his left, to catch a glimpse of who might be around him.

Anna tried to better see his face. She pretended to be staring off into the distance, past him, and she was able to look for a good few seconds. His skin was a pale, pale olive, like Sophie's. His jaw was strong but not too square, and he had dark circles below his eyes.

Candles were distributed through the crowd—when she had been younger, there had been fireworks, outlawed now; too many injuries to both those setting them off and unsuspecting bodies was the claim. When the soldier turned to offer his candle to light hers, Anna blushed. He was directly in front of her now, talking to no one, and Anna imagined leaning forward too quickly and singeing the stray hairs on his neck. She wondered if he could feel the heat.

Anna noticed her mother looking uncomfortable, glancing over her shoulder, one deep wrinkle between her eyebrows. Was it the soldier making her that way? She had seemed hesitant about going out for services at all.

"I don't want to bother going in," her mother said. "Do you?"

They often didn't stay for the Easter services, but that year, it seemed important. "I'm going to stay," Anna said.

"Let's go," Eleni said.

Without Sophie around, their mother had only Anna to disagree with. Anna was about to protest, but her mother pushed through the crowd as if there were a fire. She turned around and gave them a look that suggested they should accompany her. Anna and Taki obliged, their burning, flickering candles highlighting their perplexed expressions. On the walk home, she and Taki kept their candles lit, and around them, others did the same.

"What is it?" Anna asked her mother.

Her mother looked at her as if she didn't know what she was talking about. "Enough," she said. "Just enough."

On the walk home, Anna saw neighbors and families whom she hadn't seen in weeks, it seemed. There were people behind her, in front of her, walking through the streets of Halandri, walking through all of Athens, and in Thessaloniki and in Patras and all the villages too. Something about this mass movement, the idea that the entire country was doing the same thing, soothed her. If only for a moment.

10

Saturday night, with the rest of the family at the Resurrection service, Sophie and Nick waited on the roof for Mihalis to arrive. From there, a great horizon encompassed them: Ymittos, Penteli, Parnitha, the rocky hills that rose above Psychiko. There was Mount Lykavittos in the distance, blinking white and violet in the night sky.

"For a while, he stayed here," Sophie said, explaining her uncle's vagabond ways. "This past week, I think he's been moving around a bit. Avoiding one place for too long." She told Nick about Irini, the way she had just returned to Athens.

Nick lay back, placing his arms behind his head. He was wearing a gray suit and white shirt, though still untucked, the last few buttons undone, like he had dressed on the way over. His shirt lifted a bit, exposing his taut stomach, and Sophie leaned over and touched it absentmindedly. Despite the cool air his skin was warm. Then, she lay back, too. For a moment they both looked up at the starlit sky. Though their bodies were barely touching, Sophie could feel the rise and fall of his breath.

"Are they separated?" Nick asked after a moment. Sophie liked the way he was so intrigued by her uncle. Upon hearing that she was Mihalis's niece, Nick had called his poems "underappreciated and revolutionary." She had no basis to judge him as a poet; his work she liked because it was his. But she knew he occupied a certain space in Athenian life—this, in light of that week's events, made her nervous and proud. Still, to her, he was simply her uncle, her mother's little brother.

Sophie told him yes, they had been separated physically, but she had no idea where their relationship stood. Even when they were both in Athens, allegedly living in the same place, Mihalis often turned up in their basement for days at a time. He had been a constant fixture in Sophie's life, but she didn't know much about his personal world. But this much she did know. As they spoke, Mihalis was attending a resistance meeting at his friend's print shop—one to which he did not suggest they come along, to her disappointment—but would pick them up at midnight. He knew she wanted to be involved but she knew he was also trying to protect her. All he told her was to dress for Easter, to look presentable and pious and inconspicuous. If for some reason they were stopped and questioned, they'd simply say they were going to church, whichever one they were near. Together, they'd appear a family: a father and his two children.

"And your cousin?" she asked. Had the party been only one week ago?

"He went back to France," Nick said. "Decided not to stay for Easter."

Sophie tried to hide the surprising wave of disappointment that arrived with this news. For some reason she had imagined Loukas staying, leading a resistance movement maybe, being nearby. That he had an entire life in France that perhaps he was happy to return to made her irrationally jealous. Why did it matter? "I think that's him," she said. The basement door pulled open, grating against the cement, and Mihalis talked to the cat.

When he came up to the roof, Nick and Sophie were lifting themselves up, brushing off their good clothes.

"Well," he said. "Cozy." He lifted his hands: *Let's go, kids. What are you waiting for?* He held a paper bag of things retrieved from the basement: glasses, hats, even fake mustaches. Nick peered into the bag and chortled, but when Mihalis shot him a look, he went poker-faced.

"This isn't a joke," Mihalis said. "Can I trust you two?"

Sophie and Nick both told him that he could.

Down the stairs they went and into the house, where Sophie helped Mihalis secure his wild curls into a tight knot and hide them beneath a hat. He stood at the bathroom sink, and Sophie watched him shave his beard. He eyed her in the mirror, glanced at her conservative blouse and skirt. Then he motioned to her hair, which was loose around her shoulders. "Tie it back," he said. When he was done shaving, he handed Nick a pair of horn-rimmed glasses and a newsboy cap.

They both obeyed him. Nick put on the glasses and Sophie brushed her hair into a chignon, the way her mother wore it. She almost didn't recognize herself.

"Where are we headed?" Nick asked as they were walking out.

"Let's tack the flyers outside of Saint Constantine's," Sophie said. "People will see them when they're leaving the church."

"Never shit where you sleep," Mihalis replied. "Besides, we're not just putting these up arbitrarily. We've got a plan. You think it's just the three of us, randomly putting up flyers?"

Sophie shrugged. He was gently teasing, but she could detect an underlying frustration, even disgust, in his voice. Mihalis saw her suggestion as irreverent, and there was little that struck him so. She didn't want him to think they were just silly schoolkids, charged up by the idea of breaking rules. She was grateful he was including them in this underground world.

He handed Sophie and Nick each a stack of flyers. Sophie put hers in her large handbag and Nick shoved his beneath his suit coat. "We're responsible for the area around Plaka."

"So who else is a part of this network?" Nick asked as they headed out onto the sidewalk.

"The people who are," Mihalis replied.

Sophie imagined her uncle's many friends moving carefully through the city around them—Evan, Simone, perhaps even her aunt Irini. Though not Vangelis, she knew. Vangelis was back at home tonight, his shutters drawn and the house eerily quiet. Though he had told Sophie he was okay, his sunken eyes and slight limp betrayed his words.

They walked to the bus station in silence. Sophie, who rarely saw Mihalis without facial hair and his trademark dark glasses, kept glancing over at him. "Yes, Sophie," he'd say each time he'd catch her eye. "It's really me."

He turned to face them, walking backward. "It's going to be busy there," Mihalis said quietly. "And probably a lot of soldiers, police, checkpoints. We're just to take care of the flyers. Try to act nonchalant." He ran his hands over his newly shaven face, as if he were trying to pull off his skin.

On the bus, Nick and Sophie took a seat in front, together, and Mihalis sat a few seats behind. When Sophie turned to catch his eye, he looked away. She knew he was just trying to keep a low profile, but it stung, that second of rejection. All she wanted was for her uncle to be proud of her, to see her as a young revolutionary like he had once been. But about this he didn't seem particularly excited; it seemed he was operating more out of obligation than passion or principle.

"Don't do anything stupid this time," Nick said, referring, she knew, to the night of the coup, when she had raced from the roof.

"You neither," Sophie said.

Once they got off the bus, they posted flyers on telephone poles, mailboxes, and the closed windows of kiosks. They dropped them on the benches that lined the National Gardens, being careful not to linger below streetlights. She and Nick, on a dark street, plastered the front windows of some shops, regretting this later because they didn't want the owners to be held responsible. All this was difficult; there were many people around, and to affix each sheet of brightly colored paper onto something took stealth. Then again, because there were so many people around, small actions like these perhaps were less noticeable.

Around one dark corner, Nick, handsome with his suit and smooth, shaved face, grabbed her by the shoulders and kissed her. And each time she pasted up a flyer, it felt as though she were on fire, exploding from the inside out.

Plaka, the old district of Athens at the base of the Acropolis, was always bustling, and that night was no exception. Tourists and natives alike filled the narrow cobblestone streets. But there was a forced feeling to it all, like a smile feigned to not offend an overbearing host, like eating food placed before you regardless of hunger or appetite. Sophie had always loved Plaka—its lively nightclubs and *tavernas,* the *bouzouki,* the sellers peddling their wares, the visitors from all over— and she liked being there after a very isolated and hesitant week. She loved the way the Acropolis ascended over the city, its ancient, rocky guard, the way the Parthenon stood majestic and alight like a shining, golden crown. She loved the depth and pull of history everywhere, the endless excavations and archaeological sites where the very old became very new again.

Sophie knew Mihalis, more than anyone, felt this weight of the past. For many like her uncle who had been involved in the resistance, fighting the Germans during World War II, great pride came from combating a malevolent force. While Mihalis himself was always left-leaning, in theory, he didn't ever like to affiliate with a party. Mihalis told Sophie, "Sometimes you have to choose one side or the other, even though the intricacies and the truths are far more complicated than that." As Sophie had understood it, he, along with her father, had joined the left-wing resistance army to fight the Axis powers as well as to prevent the return of a British-imposed monarchy. And slowly this confrontation with the Germans became an internal confrontation with the royalists—left versus right, Greek against Greek. Even those who didn't completely identify with the far left but were against the German occupation were grouped in by default. "Is there no worse ideological fallacy than 'If you're not for, you're against'?" Mihalis had once asked her. Perhaps his past actions, things he did not talk about but Sophie knew involved the atrocities of war, had now made him more careful, more reserved. Perhaps this is why his approach was so serious and methodical. "Organization," he had told them on the walk to the bus stop, "is the key to all resistance. It's deliberation, not happenstance, that brings the people out in droves. I never understood that when I was your age."

Sophie remembered something their beloved former minister had said, that if there were ever a takeover in Greece, the church bells would ring and all of Athens would rouse and pour into the streets in defiance. The Greeks were no strangers to protest; only weeks before the coup, workers and students and all sorts of others had marched through the streets in the fervent name of democracy. Were they really doing all they could? Were they all just waiting to be mobilized, organized, slapped into action?

Because now? Yes, now the church bells rang; yes, people filled the streets. But that was all. It was as if Plaka, and all of Athens, had become a movie set and they the actors. And though they created a believable Easter scene, they really only counted the hours before they could dismantle the set, return indoors, and draw the shutters closed.

Outside the Mitropoli cathedral near Plaka, a large, tentative crowd gathered. Then, when the more devout went inside for the remainder of the service and the rest went home, Sophie, Mihalis, and Nick surreptitiously scattered tiny, colored pieces of paper printed with the words LONG LIVE DEMOCRACY, and, Sophie's favorite for its slightly surreal take, THIS IS BIRD SHIT.

After she'd kissed Nick good night and she and Mihalis had returned home, Sophie couldn't sit still. She was bursting, exuberant. And so while her uncle poured himself a drink she took advantage of her family's absence and rummaged through Taki's closet until she found his radio transmitter.

"Let's not call it a night yet," she told Mihalis, and asked him to come up to the roof.

He obliged, drink and book in hand. He removed his cap, and his curls sprang out every which way. With his floppy hair and smooth cheeks Sophie could imagine him as a boy.

After Sophie set up the transmitter and the microphone, she and Mihalis took turns reading poems over the air: Ritsos, Sikelianos, Seferis. Then Mihalis followed with a few of his own. When they heard the rest of the family come home, Sophie turned off the transmitter, unplugged the microphone, and wound the cord around it. She covered it with her sweater and hoped no one would notice until she could get it back into Taki's closet. When she went to sleep that night, though she was relieved the evening was over, deep in her gut she felt the pull of something else. Something new.

11

Easter Sunday, Dimitri arrived at precisely four o'clock, holding a bouquet of white and yellow flowers and a bottle of wine. Eleni kissed him on each cheek. Then she took the flowers and headed back into the kitchen to find a vase.

As she let the tap run, she realized she should have taken his coat or asked if he wanted a drink. But he knew where the coats hung and Eleni was already reaching for the whiskey when she had this thought. Such familiarity was a comfort, wasn't it?

Eleni came back into the living room, holding a drink for Dimitri, who stood with Taki in the corner, looking through Taki's records. Eleni was surprised by the way Taki had taken to Dimitri, not at all what she had expected. She could never even imagine what it would have felt like to have one of her parents dating, and she didn't expect her children to completely accept it. Sometimes she couldn't accept it herself: often she had sat at cafés with Dimitri and looked around nervously, thinking, *What am I doing here?* Sometimes, she felt as if she were having an affair. Still, she was lonesome, and her children would inevitably be gone soon, or at least have lives completely separate from hers, and shouldn't she have another shot at happiness? Or intimacy? Or, at the very least, companionship?

Dimitri thanked her for his drink. He sat down in a tall wingback chair and seemed completely at ease. He asked Anna and Taki about their studies, and Eleni was relieved to hear them all talking. Outside the window, she saw Mihalis tending to the roasting lamb. Sophie stood nearby, wearing a lavender shift with eyeshadow to match. She held a cigarette and a glass of wine, and the two of them were laughing. There was something about the way Sophie and Mihalis looked when together that suggested to everyone else to stay away. And when had Sophie started smoking?

Eleni sat down next to Irini on the couch.

Irini sighed. "So much for our elections," she said. Eleni could tell

Irini wanted to talk about it. The two of them had always discussed politics together, often quietly, on the periphery of a conversation. Even during Irini and Mihalis's estrangement they had still written to each other, a fact that Eleni did not hide from her brother but did not broadcast either. But Eleni wasn't in the mood just then, and she tried to steer the conversation to something with more levity, to fill Irini in on the social gossip she might have missed. But all she could think of was who so far had been arrested. Vangelis, and a union organizer from down the block, and a physician with whom Eleni worked at the hospital, on the way out from his shift, no less. Close to home on all counts. And she was sure she'd soon hear of more.

Yet in the adjacent small dining room, the Easter bread, not yet cut, looked like something from a cookbook: the decorative twists of dough adorned the top like a golden, toasty crown.

Irini motioned to it. "I've never been able to make one so perfect," she said.

Eleni knew the irony was not lost on her sister in-law, such pretense while their world was pandemonium. She hesitated to slice the bread, and so it still sat there, untouched, atop the red tablecloth. A white bowl filled with dyed-red eggs sat beside it.

They were happy to continue with the charade, however. With the first toast of wine, the passing around and breaking of the bread (Taki was the one to slice it), the *magiritsa* soup, the conversation was light and the bright buzz of the room surprised Eleni—perhaps everyone had already exhausted themselves discussing the current political disaster. She herself was grateful to escape it, if even for a few hours. In her cozy, light-drenched home, away from battle-clad soldiers and tanks and military checkpoints, Eleni could almost pretend nothing out of the ordinary had happened.

"Shall we crack the eggs?" Eleni asked. As was tradition, they would each take a hard-boiled, bright red egg and hit it together with the adjacent person's, first the pointed end and then the round. The last one with an intact egg was destined to have good fortune for the rest of the year.

Anna bent over the silver bowl, considering each egg closely as if one were destined for her. She chose and passed the bowl around the table. When everyone was holding an egg, Anna turned to her left and challenged Irini (this was how their family did it; the person who won the year before started the ritual, picking her first opponent). The two of them struck their eggs together, as if they were jousting. Irini's broke.

"I'm sorry!" Anna blurted.

Irini laughed. "You're not supposed to apologize for winning," she said.

Taki, then, won the match between himself and Mihalis, about which he'd gloat the rest of the evening. Sophie held her shoulders back, tossed her hair, and like a deranged, confrontational soldier met Dimitri's eyes. When he gingerly held his own egg up, she smashed her egg to his, not minding that the hard strike she had given his egg had shattered hers, too. It was as if her egg staying unbroken wasn't even the goal, only destroying his. Eleni couldn't tell if it was his politics or his mere presence that so antagonized Sophie. Probably both.

Anna's egg, after an exaggerated showdown on Taki's part, broke, and Eleni could detect a bit of sheepishness here from Taki instead of the aggressive victory she would have expected. But when her son took his egg to Eleni's, he seemed purely at ease when his light tap cracked his mother's egg in one small place.

Eleni could feel the anomalous lightness in the room peeling away with the red coating of the eggs. She knew the conversation and the mood would turn quickly—it had only been one week since the coup. Mihalis and Sophie talked nearby, their heads already bent close together like conspirators. Eleni stood up to clear the dishes, and Irini followed her to help.

After the dishes had been washed and the coffee and sweets served, Mihalis turned to Dimitri and asked him what he thought about the current political situation. But Dimitri, gentleman that he was, tried to answer in a nonpartisan, unbiased way—a true rarity, as far as Eleni was concerned.

"If it wasn't one side, it would have been the other," Dimitri said. Perhaps in a less politically charged group, this response would have worked.

"What's that supposed to mean?" Mihalis asked.

"It's not supposed to mean anything," Dimitri said. "Things have been unstable for a while. It was just a matter of who pulled it off first—the left, the king, the right. Whatever."

"Exactly," Taki chimed in.

"So you don't find this at all to be a problem?" Sophie asked. "The suspension of civil liberties, the reinstatement of Nazi laws? The arrests?"

"I'm not sympathetic to the regime," Dimitri said, putting his hands up, as if surrendering to them both. And it might have ended there, and perhaps if Eleni had come up with a joke or offer of food she could have stopped the conversation. But her brother wasn't about to let it go.

"The right is full of fanatical idiots," Mihalis said.

Dimitri scowled. He put both hands on the table, ready to push himself to his feet. "And the left isn't fanatical? They act as though they're the only ones with any intelligence. As if they've exclusive rights to art and music and literature. They seem to think they're the only ones with brains."

"Well, this regime isn't going to support you there," Mihalis said. "Not exactly the most introspective bunch."

Sophie rolled her eyes. "The right is too reactionary to appreciate art," she said. She pointed to the living room. "Half the books in there have been banned."

Irini turned toward Dimitri. "What about at the hospital?" she asked. "Have there been any torture victims?"

Dimitri looked startled. "No," he said. "There haven't."

"Well, we've heard accounts," Irini said firmly, and everyone turned to her. Irini had never been particularly vocal, but perhaps her three-year absence from her husband had reshaped her. Eleni didn't want to think about how she herself had been reshaped. She knew it was in the opposite direction. She had hushed through the years and become more interested in peace and quiet than anything else. But not only for peace of mind: she had put her trust in the centrist prime minister Papandreou, and when he stepped down, she felt it was only indicative of worse things to come. How much worse was still up for debate.

Dimitri bristled. "If that's true, they must be going somewhere else. Or they certainly don't need surgery."

"They're probably too afraid to seek help," Sophie said.

Irini turned to Eleni. "And you? You haven't seen anyone?"

Dimitri's eyes shot up, as if to say, *If she has, she hasn't told me about it.*

"No," Eleni said. "I haven't." That first week, Eleni noticed an increase in the number of patients she saw with mundane, nonthreatening maladies, those whose colds and stomachaches normally would not send them to the doctor's office. They seemed to come to her looking for some kindheartedness, a link to someone other than their families. A simple checking in, a nod from the store clerk, a tip from the pharmacist, could provide enormous relief, a momentary calm.

But the patients Irini asked about and Dimitri had claimed no knowledge of—Eleni knew it would simply be a matter of time. A fellow doctor had whispered to her of a woman with lacerations in places you didn't want to imagine, and when Vangelis had been released the expression on his wife's face, when she came to see Eleni, suggested he had not been spared.

As doctors, they had been told that treating any victims of possible torture was illegal, in the same breath that they were told that the regime was not using torture. Immediately after the coup, the colonels had issued new decrees, one of them stating that medical treatment provided to anyone released was illegal if not declared within two hours to the nearest police station. It was like some kind of child's nursery rhyme or funhouse game. Inferred: *If they've done something that would induce torture, it's not up to us to remedy it. We are only doctors.* How the irony of those implications stung.

But Eleni didn't say any of this. "I think we'd both agree it would be hard to turn someone away," she said.

Dimitri didn't say anything, and Eleni was surprised he didn't immediately concur. She turned toward him. "Wouldn't you?" she asked.

He folded his arms in front of him. "It's not that I'm not compassionate," he said. "It's for my family. Why endanger my family for a stranger?"

This reaction shocked Eleni, his single-mindedness. *Because you're a doctor,* she thought. Was she naïve to think they'd be more aligned on such matters? She didn't want to assume his conservatism excluded him from humanitarianism. His rationale was logical but unsettling. Precisely because she had a family *would* she do such a thing. She remembered her own mother telling her, when she was a little girl, *Everyone has a mother.*

Then again she too had modified her politics for her safety and her family's; she had learned, for various reasons, to abandon idealism. She had been arrested in her younger years for suspected leftist activity, but mostly it had been Christos and Mihalis who moved in and out of jail. Christos's death had silenced a part of her, the young romantic with whom he had fallen in love. Not just because she was so bereft, but if she were arrested, who would take care of her children?

Eleni studied the room. Irini looked as though she might stand up and leave. Anna, silent this whole time, excused herself to use the bathroom, fidgeting with the bangles on her wrists. She had the repression of a Protestant.

"I just can't believe they've banned miniskirts," Taki finally said. "What good is that?"

Mihalis laughed, a sort of sudden snort, but both he and Sophie looked frustrated. They were used to Taki making a joke in order to change the subject. Irini held her glass of wine in front of her lips, as if to restrain the words that would otherwise come tumbling out. Sophie had that look on her face, the one she reserved for things she found reprehensible, the class of which all fell under the title of "fascists." Eleni could almost hear her saying it under her breath. *Fascists.*

But Eleni knew Dimitri was no fascist. He was also no progressive. His views were definitely right of center. In her younger years, she never would have thought to date someone whose views were different than hers politically, not this much. It would have seemed a breach of ethics, a moral flaw. Now perhaps this was one of the things that attracted her to Dimitri. He was solid, not extreme in any way. Extremes had only gotten her into trouble.

Eleni glanced over at Dimitri now. Although Taki's miniskirt remark momentarily defused the tension, Sophie wasn't going to let the conversation dissipate. "People are being jailed for being seen with certain newspapers. And the liberal papers aren't even being sold in the smaller cities. Not that it matters. It's all censored, anyway."

Dimitri leaned back in his chair. "Let me ask you something. Would you find it disturbing if this had been a communist takeover, and the fascist papers were not distributed? If the right-of-center was arrested?" He was trying to stay levelheaded, but Eleni could see his anger flaring up from beneath his finely tailored shirt.

"Yes," Sophie answered without pause, even though it was obvious Dimitri was directing the question at Mihalis. "Besides, members of the right were arrested as well. No rhyme or reason." Dimitri, with his three sons, was not used to such discourse with women. His late wife had been strictly concerned with raising the children and keeping the house and hadn't paid close attention to much else, to things she had referred to as the affairs of men. "I would," Sophie said. "But these colonels are no better than the Nazis. That's who's in power now, and it's no use navel-gazing, hypothesizing what our situation would be if the tables had turned."

Now Taki spoke. "That's what the rumors were," he said. "That the communists were ready to stage a coup; these colonels beat them to it." Eleni wondered if he was repeating Dimitri's words or had actually heard this on his own accord.

"Oh, honestly, Taki. You really believe that?" Mihalis asked.

"That's what they *want* you to think," Irini added. "It's easier to blame the left for everything. The civil war is still alive."

"And what better way to get the U.S. on your side than to mention communism?" Sophie asked. Her oldest daughter's cheeks were turning pink, and Eleni didn't think it was just the wine.

Irini looked around the table. "But these colonels are against everything the center stands for, too. That's their biggest threat, though they would never say it."

Eleni stood up to clear some plates. She had never been comfortable with the idea of the men arguing politics while the women sat back, submissive. In fact, though she and Christos held similar views, the two had debated the finer philosophical points of everything long into the evenings, after the children had fallen asleep. She knew few couples who interacted that way. What she had loved about him, from the very beginning, was the way he had spoken to her, the way he listened so intently before responding. The connection of both having been involved in the resistance against the Nazis, when they had been very young, had bound them in an intense intellectual and emotional way. She could see that kind of electricity in Sophie now, the discovery of ideas, the way she spoke with that unbridled look in her eyes, like a wild mare. From the black stockings of the Lambrakis Youth she began wearing years ago to her general resistance to anything, she was her father's daughter, her uncle's niece. That much was certain. No wonder her daughter was staying out all night. It was all-encompassing, exhilarating.

Eventually the conversation began to dwindle and her family members one by one found ways to disengage themselves. Taki peeled an orange, Sophie went to the kitchen for coffee, and Irini and Mihalis stood up to take a walk, united in their anger.

Eleni sat at the head of the table, next to Dimitri, across from Taki. But her uncomfortable role here—mother, sister, *friend*?—paralyzed her. She didn't know what to say. From the other end of the table Taki tossed Dimitri an orange. Dimitri caught it and thanked him. After he peeled it, he offered Eleni a slice, and she accepted.

Late in the night, after Dimitri had left, Eleni sat on the veranda alone, trying to relax. She overheard her girls on the roof, talking about Dimitri.

"Fancy," said Anna. "The clothes, the nice wine."

Sophie laughed. "I think he's a spy. A double agent."

"Too obvious," Anna said. "Wouldn't a spy be bearded, with old clothing, like a poor student?" Her tone, though, was serious, as if Sophie's observation were to be taken seriously.

"*That* would be too obvious," Sophie said. And then their voices grew too quiet to decipher.

Strewn about the ground, a few tiny pieces of colored paper caught Eleni's attention. They blended into the terrazzo tile, and she picked them up, startled by the typed protest slogans she read there. She could tell herself they had simply been dragged in on a shoe. But it was undoubtedly Sophie and Mihalis—her daughter's politics left a colored trail right to their red front door. Taki had left his Zippo on the table, and she lit the neat, bright strips on fire, one by one, and placed them in the large glass ashtray. She watched them hiss and burn.

12

Those weeks since Easter, each time Mihalis left Halandri he did so with a duffel bag, thinking he'd go home not to his sister's basement but instead to Irini in Kifissia. Irini had been living there over one month now and had asked him to *join* her, just as she had asked him to come join her in Thessaloniki. She hadn't said "move in" nor had she simply given him a key. They both realized such gestures were far too emblematic; were they back together or not? Had they ever *really* split? After three years of estrangement, where did one start?

Kifissia greeted Mihalis with its intense aroma of night-blooming flowers. It was late—he'd arrived on one of the last trains—but one lone taxi idled at the station, and Mihalis signaled to it. Though as a younger man he'd enjoyed the long walk from the station, tonight he wasn't in the mood. He had spent the evening in the back room of a friend's print shop, writing copy to send to international news organizations and printing up flyers. Athens stirred in him an intense, unrestrained anger. To watch the stunned populace going about its business, content with dinners out and strolls through the squares, made him crazy. If those brightly colored reminders that the country was under siege were enough to give someone pause, to consider what exactly was happening, then they were doing something. If anything, they proclaimed that at least some of them were not going to politely bend over.

As they neared Irini's house, Mihalis thought the driver was eye-ing him strangely.

"You can let me out here," Mihalis said. "I want to stretch my legs." Mihalis got out and the driver shrugged and sped away. He knew he was being paranoid, but no one needed to know exactly where he was. He was glad he hadn't given an address.

The large yard was surrounded by a cement whitewashed fence, about twelve feet high, her own private walled compound. Beyond the yard were groves of lemon and orange trees. He entered the gate and took the large stone path, the way he had when the place belonged to Irini's aunt and the back door was always open. The house was dark now, and the door was locked, so Mihalis called up to the second-floor balcony. "Hey," he said. "It's me. Are you home?" Irini was a night owl, but maybe she was sleeping. Her small black hatchback was parked in front, but he knew Irini preferred not to drive, which Mihalis of course didn't fault her for; he himself had never even learned. She could have still been out. He hadn't mentioned he'd be coming.

And why had he chosen this night? Or rather, what had held him back all those other nights? Fear? Pride? Sheer stubbornness? He wasn't sure. Athens and even Halandri seemed too much to him. After hanging a protest banner over the Acropolis, no small feat, a few younger friends had come back to the print shop breathless, reporting that there had been some more arrests, and Mihalis didn't let them see his fear. Mihalis would not admit it to her, but he suddenly yearned for the comfort of his wife and the pleasant disconnect of Kifissia. Although it was only some twenty miles from Athens, it felt far away from everything.

For one, there was no telephone. Irini had not yet applied for a line, and even if she had, it could take months and months to actually get one. She had thought it prudent to not announce her residence in the house, and Mihalis knew it was more for his benefit than hers. As far as the colonels knew, she was still in her Thessaloniki apartment on Manolaki Street, two hundred miles away from Athens and her poet husband. The absence of lines of communication, then, surely added to his feelings of security; whether these feelings were well founded or not was another story.

Mihalis went to the front, which was open. He let himself in, locking it behind him. "Hello?" he called out again. He stopped in the kitchen to pour himself a glass of *ouzo* with ice and went upstairs. The three bedrooms were small but airy, with large wooden wardrobes and simple desks, and even though it wasn't on the water, the white walls, pale blue bedsheets, and wispy curtains gave the house an island atmosphere. Irini's bed was neatly made.

Taking advantage of Irini's absence, he snooped around. He opened the linen closet in the foyer and held a soft, well-worn blanket to his nose. He couldn't articulate the scent exactly, something like laundry soap and old wood, but it was calming and redolent. One room looked unused, with two twin beds pushed together and a simple nightstand topped with a reading lamp. The other room Irini was apparently using for an office. There was a large desk covered with papers and books and also a vanity strewn with lipstick and some hair curlers. He'd forgotten this domestic detail. Irini had always been a little messy.

He walked through her bedroom to get to the veranda, which was lined with clay pots filled with healthy plants of parsley, oregano, and sage. How long before that night at Evan's *had* Irini started living here? Two chairs were pulled out around the table, and on the table-top was a bottle of scotch, the taste for which Irini had apparently acquired while she was gone (from whom Mihalis did not want to consider). There were two glasses, almost empty. Light-colored lipstick had rubbed off onto one of them. A large, fat candle sat next to a lighter. He lit it and then sat down there with his drink.

Half an hour later, he heard a car door shut and Irini arrive. He didn't want to startle her, so he leaned off the veranda. "I'm here," he said. "The door was open." He went downstairs to greet her.

Irini wore a bright green dress with white piping, definitely too short for the new junta standards, and a white crocheted cardigan over it. Her hair had been the same all these years, shiny and straight and just past her shoulders, like a university student. She wore it tied up in a twist or a bun when she taught, though now it was down and off her face with a thick white headband.

"You weren't expecting me, I know," Mihalis said.

"I never expect you," Irini said.

"Where've you been?" Mihalis asked, trying not to sound like a jealous husband. He thought of the two glasses up on the veranda but said nothing. He glanced over at Irini again. Were her cheeks flushed? It was too dark to tell.

"Out," Irini said. "How long have you been here?"

"Not long," Mihalis said.

She glanced at his bag in the foyer. "Do you want to stay tonight?" Irini asked.

"If that's okay," Mihalis said.

Irini went upstairs and out to the porch and he followed. She picked up her glass and flung the remaining liquid off the side of the balcony; for a moment Mihalis thought she was going to throw the glass. She poured herself a fresh drink.

"I didn't know you were coming," she repeated.

"Do I need an invitation?" Mihalis asked.

Irini looked up suddenly, a small, ironic smile on her lips. "I don't know. Do you?" She lowered her chin and narrowed her eyes, and her smirk turned to something a little darker, more pensive.

Oh, how he knew that look! She propped her smooth, bare legs up on the balustrade, and Mihalis wondered if she had sat like that with others there, her lovely limbs in full view.

"What do you mean?" Mihalis asked. She wanted to know where their marriage now stood, where it was headed, all those things women wanted to incessantly discuss. Was it too much to have the comfort of marriage without its constraints? Of course Irini would say it was.

"If it wasn't for this business"—Irini waved her arms, like the coup was something palpable and obtrusive, right in front of her— "we might not have even spoken yet."

"You did write, though. You said you were coming back to Athens. *Before* all this." Mihalis waved *his* arms in front of him now, teasing her. "Remember?" But she was right; he didn't know if only the calamity of the coup had brought them together again, or if it would have happened sooner or later. But what Irini wondered he wondered too: were they together yet? Of course, they were still legally married. But was that it? Should he have already moved into

the house? Did she want him to? Part of him couldn't imagine feeling so far away from everything, and the other part of him found it
wonderfully appealing.

"You think I was coming back for you?" Irini asked.

"You weren't?" Mihalis replied. But he knew she wasn't. At least,
not entirely.

On Easter, Mihalis had asked Irini how long her university leave
would be, and she had looked at him blankly. She had assumed for
just a semester, initially, but it was rumored that the junta would
soon dismiss most of the current faculty. Mihalis had told his niece
and nephew to take advantage of these last several weeks of university classes because undoubtedly the following year would show them
government-chosen replacements. Taki had grumbled something
about not being around to see that—he was leaving soon for the
States—and Sophie had simply looked at Mihalis as if he were utterly
fey. How could he know that in five months' time there wouldn't be
some other sort of revolution? And why, she also wanted to know, was
he behaving so nonchalantly?

Irini sighed and stood up. "I had the semester off," she said, "and
had planned on coming in January."

For a moment Mihalis was confused. Then he realized she was
expanding on why she returned.

"And suddenly it was April. I missed Athens. Athens is my home.
I wanted to be here for Easter. Not the village, not an island. Athens."
Her voice sounded muffled, garbled, thick with emotion. But Mihalis could have imagined it, because then her tone was matter-of-fact,
practical. She turned to him. "Are you scared they're looking for you?"
she asked.

He was quiet, staring at the slight curve of her hips. "No," he
lied. "You?" It occurred to him at that moment that maybe Irini had
thought that he'd be arrested long before this and that she may have
expected an intimate, brief encounter, a good-bye, a reconciling,
which was turning into something she hadn't planned. Maybe she
had even been coming to ask him for a divorce. He supposed if that
was indeed what she wanted she would have mentioned it by now. He
was irrationally projecting. It was true that while politics always inter-

jected itself into their relationship, matters of the heart never took a backseat to anything. Ultimately, he realized, they were all interested in self-preservation.

Mihalis pointed to the second empty glass on the table. "Did you have company?" he asked.

"Evan was here earlier, yes."

"Just Evan?" he asked.

"Yes. *Just* Evan."

Irini seemed to be bracing for an outburst but he gave her none. He did not necessarily believe in the sanctity of marriage, the idea that there was one person who would fulfill all your needs. This he found juvenile and ridiculous. The idea of monogamy throughout a marriage, a lifetime, was preposterous. Not because he didn't see any point to it; on a purely philosophical level, he concurred it might be wonderful, in a romantic sense. He tried hard to determine what it was, actually, that bothered him so much. So what if she had slept with someone else while she was gone? He certainly had. But it was decidedly not the act of sex or romance. It was not another man holding his wife's breasts or watching her naked back move away from him. Well, partly but not completely. It was the way the secret made him look, a stupid cuckold, a man without knowledge, someone being laughed at. It was slightly worse if it was Evan laughing at him. He had felt this his entire life, his friend's quiet mockery. Was it because he was a writer and Evan was a critic? Or did their personalities simply drive them to their respective careers, and these clashing personalities were what made their relationship so volatile?

Irini flipped her head up and wrinkled her brow, another one of her habits. Mihalis wondered if his marriage with Irini could only exist with some sort of conflict driving it and when there was nothing for them to argue about, there was not much of a marriage there at all. It fed on drama.

When they crawled into bed together that night it was as if a strange ripple in time had separated them, and the coup was a second wave that had thrust them back together. Those years apart seemed insubstantial. But in another way, it felt like they were starting over, like a newlywed couple in a new house, each amazed and bemused at the other's movements, habits, a time before revulsion and resentment. Whether it was this strange feeling of seclusion, the familiar comfort of his wife, or the simple rediscovery of her body, he slept that night more soundly than he had in years. They slept with the windows wide open, letting the night air in, far better than the cave of a basement as at his sister's.

The next morning, though, Mihalis was restless; he tried to ignore the feeling, make it go away. He woke to find Irini standing in her underwear in front of her closet, thinking about what to wear. Already he could tell the day would be hot. From the bed he watched Irini dress in a pair of loose-fitting linen trousers—the kind you could find in tourist bazaars in Plaka—and a cotton button-up shirt. Loose and light, she would say. She hated to feel fabric against her skin, Mihalis remembered.

She put her hand on one hip, jutting the other out. From the time he had been nine until he would be ninety-nine, the vision of a woman getting dressed would never cease to stir him. She looked over her shoulder at him and saw he was awake, watching her.

"Come here," he said.

"I'll make us breakfast," she said.

It took him most of his life to realize the most basic thing: comfort was certain, and passion was not. It was why when they had first married he was always out and about. He unquestionably had not wanted comfort then and felt he had no time for a wife. For him it would probably never go away, wanting the rush of flirtation, of danger, of newness and romantic and intellectual possibility. Yet unlike Evan, who saw extramarital affairs as a natural by-product of marriage itself, Mihalis rarely followed through on his obsessions. Often the energy they gave him was enough. Now he wondered if he needed any of that energy at all, which was difficult to admit or accept. Kifissia calmed him down. After a single night, it felt good. And this troubled him.

Downstairs, Irini handed Mihalis some coffee. "How'd you sleep?" she asked.

"Very well," he said. It was true.

Her face was open, giving, and Mihalis felt for a moment he'd never leave the house again. He smiled at her and went out to the porch. But when she followed him shortly after with a tray of orange juice and toast and butter and honey, he felt a little panicked. It had been so long since he'd had the comfort of domesticity and again it felt like a trap.

"I have to go back to Athens today," Mihalis announced. "I've got things to do."

"Oh," Irini said, trying to mask her disappointment. "I can take you. I have to go anyway."

Mihalis stared out over the orange trees. "No," he said. "I'll take the train."

"All right," Irini said. She didn't ask when he'd return. The rest of the breakfast they ate in silence.

When he was finished eating, he went upstairs, zipped up his bag that he had barely unpacked, and found Irini on the porch, where she was smoking, her bare feet propped on the railing.

"I'm sorry," he said.

"Don't be," she said. He could tell she was fuming.

Two hours later, when he was once again in the basement in Halandri, he felt he'd just dodged a bullet. Yet he felt more miserable than ever.

Two mornings later, Eleni appeared at the foot of his bed. She had left the door to the outside open, and the morning brightness tumbled down the stairs behind her.

"What?" he asked.

"This," she said, "is enough. I just talked to Irini. You're the worst I've seen you."

Mihalis grunted and covered his head with his pillow—as he had done as a little boy when Eleni would wake him for school.

"Listen." Eleni paced around the room like an interrogator. "You can't keep doing this."

"She was gone for three years," Mihalis said.

"And she always asked you to come with her. You wouldn't leave your rich life here in Athens. For all she knew you had found someone else. You were the one keen on the separation."

"Hmph."

"I know. *Hmph.* Who else would have you?"

Mihalis kept his head under the pillow and banged his arm on the nightstand fishing for his cigarettes. He drew the pack in, beneath the covers, and emerged with a Pall Mall in his mouth. Eleni turned to leave.

"Where are you going?" he asked. Maybe he just wanted permission—from whom?—to retreat into the ease of life in Kifissia with his lovely wife. He knew Eleni was growing wary of his comings and goings; he knew his unhappiness rose from the basement and scraped the air around her. He knew he was behaving like a child.

"You can stay here again tonight," she said from outside the door. "But tomorrow I'm driving you back. Either divorce her or commit to her. It's not fair to just barrel down the middle, blocking both lanes."

Later that afternoon, Mihalis took the train back to Kifissia. When he walked in the back door, Irini was washing vegetables from the garden in the sink. He sat down at the kitchen table, and Irini handed him a glass of water. For now, a truce.

13

Though Anna did not feel particularly unsafe, she didn't feel completely safe either. Most of her unease came not directly from this junta but from its resulting effect on her household. Taki's ranting about the state of the country—*Eight military coups in fifty years! A new government every time you blink! This is the birthplace of democracy?*—put her on edge, and Sophie's continued sneaking out and careless, come-and-get-me demeanor kept Anna's insomnia kicking. Matters were worsened by Taki's upcoming departure to the States, which until that June had only seemed an abstraction. Though he had not kept his plans a secret, most of the time to Anna they felt more like a threat than an actual plan. He was going to study, and this was a good thing, but something about the way he talked about it made it seem that he was never coming back.

And after his final examinations at the University of Athens School of Physics ended, the date loomed, and details of his new life were hard to avoid. He would be moving to Michigan to attend the university; he would live with their cousin George, whose father, Yiannis, was Christos's younger brother. Anna had met Yiannis only once, after their father's death, and all she could remember of him was that he had requested they have waiting for him an American-style mattress with springs, one Eleni had nearly killed herself going to find, all while mourning the death of her husband. It was called Stromatex, it was expensive, and when Yiannis arrived, even six-year-old Anna could tell by the look on his face that it was inadequate.

One late June morning, one week before Taki's departure, Anna sat at the kitchen table and watched her mother unwrap new underwear, T-shirts, and socks and toss them into the washing machine. Here was Taki, about to leave home, and here was their mother buying him bright, new things that she would surely later iron and press into his new suitcases. Already, Anna thought, their mother was beginning to take the same role with Taki as she did with her brother-in-law: wanting to impress while resenting that very desire.

Taki stood in the foyer watching, not quite entering the kitchen. For a moment he looked sad, but then this sadness flickered to annoyance and then quickly to anger. He blurted, "What, did you think I'd live in this house forever?"

Their mother looked up, startled, and closed the lid on the washing machine. "No," she said. "I didn't." She pushed past Taki in the doorway and went upstairs. She heard Taki walk out the front door. Anna stayed in the kitchen alone, listening to the violent swish of her brother's new clothes. When the cycle was finished, she removed them and hung them on the porch, and when they were dry, she placed them folded on Taki's bed. She didn't want her mother to iron them; it seemed, somehow, too much.

From the window in Taki's room, she could hear her mother and Dimitri talking on the veranda below. She was surprised at how clearly their voices carried and wondered how many nights Taki had sat here, or on the balcony, and listened to their conversations. Taki seemed to like Dimitri fine, though when he was around Taki usually was not, as if there were only room for one man in the house at a time. When Dimitri and Taki were both around, Anna thought their mother behaved like a frazzled cocktail party hostess, hovering over Taki one minute and then flitting to Dimitri the next. Instead of just letting Taki go about his usual business, she'd leave Dimitri in the living room and stand over Taki as he studied or read the newspaper, an unnatural sense of nervousness buzzing around her, as if she were trying to tell him, *See? My new friend isn't going to change anything.* But this bizarre, uncomfortable behavior showed them all just the opposite and reminded Anna of when their mother would force them to say nice things to older relatives: "Say thank you," their mother would whisper in their ears. Still, it seemed the latter held *some* merit, an instilling of social graces and niceties, while her current behavior was just unpleasant. Anna wondered if Dimitri was made just as uneasy by her mother's blustering or if he was simply in love and oblivious. Men complicated everything.

To Taki, their mother said only the minimum about his move— she focused mostly on the logistics, in the same way a bereaved person focuses on details of a funeral or the affairs of the estate. Anna wasn't sure if Taki found this complacency annoying or relieving. She talked about it to Dimitri, to her friend Eugenia, to the neighbors. It was hardly a secret. Though she had heard her mother say, "Well, it's not the Ivy League," Anna knew her mother was proud that he'd be attending the University of Michigan. Anna couldn't bring herself to mention it; to utter anything about his upcoming departure felt somehow disloyal. She felt if she acknowledged it, her mother would be angry at her, but if she didn't acknowledge it, would he just slip off to the airport, as if he were simply leaving for Piraeus, to board a ferry for an island weekend? She couldn't imagine that they wouldn't have some sort of send-off, a dinner, a party. It seemed horrible luck not to, and yet the idea of broaching the topic with her mother made her feel guilty. And she wasn't even the one leaving.

Could it be they were all motivated by guilt? Their mother felt guilty for bringing a man into the house. Taki felt guilty for leaving. From a young age, Anna felt guilty for just about every emotion she experienced. Was it something learned or something innate, inescapable? She didn't know, but she spent a lot of time thinking about it.

The next day, Anna noted her mother's relatively good mood. Whereas she had seemed on edge those past months—they all were—that day she seemed relaxed and relieved to have a day off. She watered the plants on the veranda and hummed. Anna joined her there, sitting quietly with a book. Her mother absentmindedly smoothed Anna's hair and then sat down next to her.

"Maybe we could have a party for Taki," Anna ventured to say. "A going-away dinner, or something like that." She expected her mother to balk or roll her eyes, but instead she looked pensively at Anna's face. Then she reached for Anna's hands and examined her fingernails, the way she had done when Anna had been a child, and then her wrists. She looked down at Anna's bare feet, and Anna expected a reproach, to be told to put on her slippers or shoes.

But instead she looked back up at Anna's face again. "A party," her mother said. "Yes. That would be nice."

The night of the party, the garden had been transformed. White embroidered tablecloths covered the rickety loans from neighbors, and atop them sat oil lamps that lit up the yard and the grapevines that climbed the trellis and the canopy. With the smell of sausage and *sou-vlaki* on the grill, the garden felt like a mountain taverna. The cicadas chirped, ever present but invisible; the night was warm. Anna liked this feeling of transformation, of being at home but feeling as though she were someplace else entirely.

If Taki was scared about his upcoming venture, he drank this fear away quickly, as every friend he had ever known seemed to be stopping by that night, and he'd do a shot of *raki* with each new arrival.

The blue solemnity that had been following her brother for weeks had lifted, or been masked, and he slopped from seat to seat, corner to corner, saying hello to all those there in his honor as if he were a groom at his own wedding or a young prince entertaining the villagers. Their mother was in good spirits too. On the front porch she sat around a table with Dimitri and her other friends.

While waiting in the foyer for the bathroom to be free, Anna peered into Taki's bedroom, where his suitcases stood erect in the corner, his traveling clothes laid out neatly over his chair. Many guests had arrived with small gifts, and Taki had whispered in her ear that she could have them all. She adjusted the sash on her dress, in which she felt at turns grown-up and childish. Her hair hung in her face, and she had resisted her mother's prompting to braid it. She liked to hide beneath it.

The toilet flushed, the bathroom door opened, and Anna was still fiddling with her dress. For some reason, she had expected a girl to emerge, one of their friends. Instead when she looked out from under her hair, she saw her uncle's friend Evan smiling at her, as if she were doing something amusing. She averted her gaze and tried to sidestep him, but as she passed he playfully brushed the dimple in her chin. In the bathroom Anna put her face close to the mirror and stared at it awhile.

When she returned to the garden, Spyro was playing the guitar. Taki, whose cheeks glowed red from the alcohol, put his arm around her. "Come with me, little sister," he said.

"Where?" Anna asked.

The crowd around them laughed; Taki had meant to the States. If only he knew how often she had whispered to herself, *Let me come with you.* But what she really meant was, *Please don't go.* Around them stood Sophie and Nick, Anna's friend Stella, and her mother's friends from the hospital and neighborhood. They all seemed happy, laughing, tossing back drinks and singing and dancing. Mihalis and Irini stood nearby with Evan and his wife, Simone, who Anna only at that moment realized was pregnant by the way she held her hand atop her belly. Mihalis put his arm around Anna. "You'll be able to visit him, you know," Mihalis said. "And he'll come back in the summers." He kissed her forehead.

When Spyro began to sing a favorite from the year before, cheers and claps broke out from the party, as if they were at a huge concert. His voice was rich and smooth, despite all the cigarettes. Taki's friends toasted one another and sang with their arms draped around each other, like characters in some sort of American cartoon. It was as if Spyro had transported them to another time. Anna didn't know if it was the wine—she hadn't really ever had more than a few sips before—or the bittersweet reality of her brother's plane ride the next day, but when she did a shot of *raki* with Taki she had to act as if it were the liquor that had made her eyes water. She set her glass down on the table with a flourish, exaggeratedly waving her hand in front of her face as their mother did right before she broke down in tears.

The party grew louder and more boisterous, but for Anna then, the world had slowed. She was aware of the moment so acutely that she knew she'd remember not only what was happening but the heightened sense of awareness itself. The hair at her crown felt attentive and erect, her skin prickled with goosebumps, and her chest heaved with her breath. She was alert to her every fiber, the folds of skin on her fingertips, the tautness of her stomach, the brush of her eyelashes on her face, the taste of wine on her tongue. And everything a picture, a photograph of their life in Athens, where everyone was suspended in a moment of elation, this pocket of contentment, where nothing seemed to stray, or drift, or careen forward at a great speed. Yet Anna felt as if Taki alone had already sprung from the scene, grown from it exponentially, unable to fit back in.

Later, when all the guests but Spyro had gone, when their mother had retired to bed, the three siblings and Spyro moved to the roof. Sophie was drunk and smiling—Anna had just watched her and Nick kissing good-bye in a frenzy at the gate—and Spyro was twirling her around. She knew they were all avoiding saying good-bye, avoiding the loaded emotional repercussions. Anna herself was not drunk. She felt exhausted, but going to bed would make her feel as though she were missing something important. She lay on the chaise longue, closed her eyes, and replayed bits from the night in her head, the sound of the crowd singing, the look of contentment on her mother's face, Evan's amused gaze.

Earlier in the party, some of their friends had played music with Taki's portable on the roof, and Taki now riffled through his stack of records.

"Hey, you taking those with you?" Spyro asked.

"Leaving them for Anna," Taki said.

Sophie pirouetted twice and then plopped herself onto the chair with her sister. "Taki *mou*," she said. "Don't you want to do one more radio show? Before you go?"

"Now?" Taki asked.

Spyro agreed it was a great idea. A farewell.

"It's almost four in the morning," Taki said.

"All the better," said Sophie. "Anna, go get the transmitter."

Anna knew Taki had told their mother he had thrown it away. She also knew where he had hidden it after he'd suspected Sophie had been using the radio. Their house was not large, and there were only so many places to hide something. And because this was the relationship the three of them had always had, Anna agreed without protest. She also was sure radio shows had been banned.

Inside, all was quiet; the kitchen had been cleaned, and Eleni slept. Since their father died, their mother slept with her door wide open, keeping one watchful, constant ear and eye on the house. Her shutters were not closed either and Anna wondered how their noise wasn't keeping her awake. The moonlight drifted in the window, through the white gauzy curtains, and in it her mother looked ghostlike, almost transparent. For a moment, Anna was transfixed, moving away but not taking her eyes off her. The hallway, though, was dark, and Anna smacked into Taki's closed bedroom door. She opened it, shut it behind her, and searched through his closet. Beneath the clothes and books and other things he had not packed for the States she recovered his transmitter.

This time, Anna went out to the veranda from Taki's room and up the wrought iron staircase. When she emerged onto the roof, Taki was laughing loudly and then shushed himself. He took the transmitter and untangled the extension cords for the record player. He held the small microphone close to Spyro's lips.

"Go ahead," Taki whispered, signaling they were on the air. Spyro settled back in his seat and closed his eyes, too drunk to reason with the even-drunker Taki, and pushed the mic back in Taki's hand. "It's your show," he said.

Had someone been tuning their radio at that moment, they might have wondered at the stifled laughter and strange sounds. They would have heard the beginning *bouzouki* of the song he knew would be his last, the one Spyro had sung earlier, the one they had all sung together.

"Play it louder," Sophie said. "Come on!"

And as the unique, unmistakable voice of Grigoris Bithikotsis rose up over the neighborhood and out into the airwaves, they lay down on the roof and stared into the starlit Athens sky together, the last time they'd do this for many years.

Only a few hours later, the Hellinikon airport was impossibly muggy, pregnant with cigarette smoke and the smell of sweaty bodies. It was only six in the morning and none of them had slept. The day promised to be hot, and it seemed fitting to Anna that Taki would leave on a day of oppressive heat.

She stepped away from her family for a moment, walking backward. When no one seemed to notice her movement from the group, she sat in a chair close enough to her family that she could observe them but far enough away that if they noticed her absence, they'd have to search the crowd for her. Tourists speaking languages Anna did not understand hugged friends good-bye or sat forlorn in the smooth, hard chairs, waiting. A British woman sat in a short white skirt, seemingly trying to get into a position in which her legs wouldn't stick to the seat. Her companion, a blond man with round, wire-rimmed glasses, read a book called *The Quiet American,* which Anna found oxymoronic and ominous. Then again, she didn't know what title would have made her feel any better. Toward these visitors Anna felt ambivalent. Many had called for tourists to boycott Greece, to boycott the colonels, yet they kept crawling in. They would give the summer a sense of rhythm, yes, and wasn't it flattering that they still came? But it left a bad taste in her mouth.

Anna had driven to the airport with her mother, Dimitri, and Irini. Taki, Spyro, and Sophie went along in Spyro's father's car. Mihalis, who had said good-bye to Taki the night before, was slowly withdrawing from regular Athenian life: airports, busy city centers, theaters. He had even forgone his beloved cafés for the peace and quiet of Kifissia. Anna worried that he was becoming too paranoid, but who was she to say anything? Sophie told her it was something else, a sort of self-imposed boycott of Greek life, and Anna simply did not understand such pompous functioning.

Anna knew Taki most likely had a horrible hangover, but he wore an expression of distaste, as if the family was something sour or bitter that he had to hold in his mouth indefinitely before swallowing. He looked angry at all of them, which made the situation uneasy and hurt Anna's feelings so much that she could barely look at his face without the uncomfortable knot reappearing in her throat. Where was the solidarity of only hours before? It was characteristic of Taki to choose such an early morning flight, like maybe the time would curtail his family from coming to the airport. *No such luck,* Anna thought.

She regarded her mother and Sophie carefully, looking for cues as to how to behave—how did one act when saying good-bye to a brother or a son? Irini seemed to be acting as their mother's support system; she stayed close to Eleni and tried to keep the conversation moving.

When it was time for Taki to board, the family froze. Anna was sure Sophie would be the one to release him, or Spyro, but everyone sat mute and uneasy. Finally Anna broke the silence. "Okay," she said. She stood on her tiptoes to hug Taki good-bye. He kissed both of her cheeks but didn't meet her eyes.

"Okay," he said.

And then they all followed, one by one, until it was back to Anna again, who gave her brother one last desperate hug before he disappeared into the gate door, down the stairs, and out to the plane.

Their mother, in shock no doubt, stood at the window waving her white handkerchief, an absent expression on her face. If from the plane Taki couldn't distinguish the blurs of his family standing in the window, maybe he would see her white flag. Her surrender.

14

To Eleni, though the party had been a fun distraction, Taki's whole departure had been anticlimactic. Maybe Taki had imagined, even hoped for, more crying, more show of emotion, but her own response had been rather brusque, which she knew enraged him to the point that he had threatened to not go at all. Perhaps this was exactly what she hoped for. Mothers, unfortunately, often knew their young sons better than anyone, an infuriating and sometimes even revolting fact of life for any twenty-year-old male.

Taki had always been fascinated with America; from the time he was a very young boy and his uncle would write him letters and send pictures, Taki pored over them, kept the American stamps in a book in his desk, saved the various trinkets Yiannis sent him, things that Eleni saw now were still in the top drawer of his desk: a sew-on Mickey Mouse patch, a small pin from Mount Rushmore, a key chain from some American theme park, a tiny replica of the Washington Monument. When JFK was assassinated, Taki was inconsolable. It was the only time she had seen his teenage self cry. She'd ask him if he was hungry, and he'd burst into tears. Yes, he had always been obsessed with the States, and looking back, Eleni should have assumed this was coming.

But there was another part of her that still wondered if Taki had scared himself out of Greece. He clammed up at any mention of anything remotely political, and she was sure she had heard him use the word "intellectual" as a pejorative. That's why his behavior with the transmitter was so out of character. She'd expect it from Sophie, maybe even Anna. Or Mihalis, of course. Taki himself was always complaining that her brother's conduct and activities would get the entire family arrested.

Those first few days Taki was gone the house felt interminably quiet, and Eleni and the girls interacted with a forced enthusiasm. Sophie was the most adamant that Taki's absence should not change her life, and Eleni found it tiresome just watching her insist they eat dinner together, or see a movie, or converse on the roof. Her eldest daughter was looking for proof that Taki would not, under any circumstances, mess up their happiness or the rhythm of their lives. To Eleni, Sophie's actions seemed perfect proof that he would.

In the same way the arrival of the dictators simply changed the air, so had her son's departure. At first. Time distended and compressed. Some days felt like weeks and some weeks felt like days, and Eleni sometimes recalled a trip to the grocery that morning, or a patient at work that afternoon, and thought to herself, *Was that really today?*

Regardless, days became weeks, and weeks months, and after three months she found that the most noticeable change was so obvious and trivial it surprised her. Less of a mess in the house, less laundry, less ironing. Less noise. She and her girls fell into a sort of daily, soothing rhythm.

Almost soothing, anyway. Taki's departure seemed to further unleash something in Sophie. Her brother's disdain for any sort of protest or political engagement had kept her a little more careful, or at least discreet. Sophie would never admit it, and Eleni never would have imagined it, but it was her brother keeping her in line. Without Taki to balance her outrageous radical claims, she was tipping farther and farther. Eleni often had trouble sleeping, waiting for the sound of Sophie's footfalls and her safe return to bed.

One late-September evening, the early autumn sunset bathed everything in a hazy glow, the intense green of cypress trees the one bright color on an otherwise muted canvas. Eleni walked from the hospital to her car. Across the street, she saw three young university women fighting with some police officers over what seemed to be the length of their skirts. She was shocked at the way the officers threw them against the wall, handcuffed them, and marched them away. In the tussle one girl had fallen to the ground, and even from across the street Eleni could see, when she stood up, that her forehead and knee were bleeding. The brutality was no surprise to her but in the softness of twilight it shocked her. The entire way home she replayed those girls' faces in her mind: young and open. Like Sophie. Eleni couldn't believe she had just kept walking. What was wrong with her? Then again, what could she have done?

In her garden, the *mousmoula* tree was blooming—white flowers with a hint of yellow—and bees buzzed around it. She felt relieved to find Sophie sitting on the porch, reading something in French and translating it into Greek. Eleni gave her a hug, and Sophie didn't resist, and Eleni could only imagine *Sophie's* face, *her* knee, *her* body being whipped around and thrown. It just as well could have been. All she ever wanted to do as a mother was keep her kids from harm; wasn't that any parent's goal? And the worst part was the realization that no matter what you did, their hearts would get broken, their elbows would get scraped. Even these small realities of life were sometimes too much.

"Sophie," Eleni said. "You need to be safe. All these meetings, this protest, whatever underground things you're doing. It's not worth it."

"I know what I'm doing," Sophie said. "Don't worry."

"These people are dangerous, Sophie. You think because you're a woman you can't get arrested? And tortured?"

"No," Sophie said. "Of course not. But that's why they stay in power. Everyone's too scared to make a peep. Even Mihalis has grown quiet, retreating into some bourgeois version of himself, in his country home like a British lord."

"It's for the best," Eleni said, though she wondered if her daughter really thought this was true or if Sophie was already paranoid, protecting Mihalis from his own sister. Maybe not. Sophie was still at an age where she didn't yet see one choice as an immediate closing down of other options. "You don't know what we went through," Eleni told her.

Sophie seemed to consider this. "You're right," she said. "But I can imagine." She looked back down at her work. "You can't stop me, if that's what you're trying to do."

The last New Year's Eve Christos was alive, they'd had a big, loud party that went until daybreak. How the house had pulsed with Eleni's colleagues from the hospital and Christos's from the Agricultural Bank; there were cousins and friends and a large representative sample from the universities of Athens. Eleni clearly remembered her burgundy silk dress, Christos's dark gray suit, the way he moved through the party with a bottle of wine propped on his belt, always ready to pour, ignoring when guests held their hands above their glasses.

A houseful, and their children, too, who inhabited the under-world of adult parties, orchestrating an elaborate war game. Sophie led one group and Taki the other, and some disagreement resulted regarding who exactly were the bad guys and who the good, but Sophie, already speaking a diluted and simplified rhetoric of the left, had the advantage of age and lipstick war paint, so soon the group split along gender lines with Taki leading a group of testosterone-riddled cowboys. As their leader, he wore a guest's Russian-style fur hat, the incongruity lost on him. Anna, reluctant to take sides, played per Christos's suggestion the part of journalist. Even at the age of six, she knew that loyalties were complicated.

In the kitchen, a group gathered around the radio and listened to the broadcaster announce lottery winners. Each ticket began with a leading letter, and each time that first letter was announced, the guests either cheered in anticipation or groaned, already eliminated. The New Year winnings ranged from small amounts of cash to the biggest prizes: apartments in Athens. Years before Anna was born, Christos had won an apartment in the neighborhood of Victoria, which Eleni still rented to a young family, distant relatives.

For a moment that night, Christos and Eleni watched the party together, near the record player. A colleague of Eleni's snapped their photo just as Anna rushed by with a tiny notebook and a pencil, covering her head as if dodging a bomb. He laughed, he lifted his leg to stop her, but she quickly scurried into another corner, her large eyes serious, darting. Someone had dimmed the lights, and a nearby candle cast a strange glow on her small face. They had watched as Anna opened her notebook and furtively pulled out her own lottery ticket, and Christos nodded in her direction and smiled, and Eleni knew his heart broke with the wonder and anticipation on her face.

By midnight, when the guests clinked glasses, the smallest had fallen asleep in both likely and unlikely places: Anna curled up in an armchair next to the cat; another boy on the floor beneath the kitchen table, a piece of *baklava* wrapped in his tight fist; another's small body spread over a *flokati* rug. Three boys, siblings dressed in identical outfits of dark navy and red, lay across the width of a white bedspread, like the horizontal stripes of a flag.

Sophie, her face covered in lipstick and wearing a mink stole, stomped through, berating the sleeping children: "You can't fall asleep! We're not finished!"

A guest had laughed and looked warmly at Christos: "There's no question, this one definitely belongs to you." And Christos beamed in the way men can only beam at their daughters and twirled Sophie around. "Dance with me, my little girl," and Sophie shone back at him, crazy joy spreading across her face, a whir of fur and braids and red party dress, spinning around as if she were the most important person in the room.

Now Sophie stood up with that same determined resolve and headed to the kitchen for more coffee. She stopped in the doorway and spoke, her voice even-keeled and determined. "I thought you, of all people, would understand." And somewhere beneath her words Eleni heard the insinuation of something else, of Christos: *Because he certainly would.*

15

Anna was at the kitchen table studying when Sophie came in the side door, kicked off her sandals, and slung her heavy satchel on the table with a thunk. For late October it was hot, and Sophie wore a royal-blue cotton shift that was so short it could get her arrested. Her hair was piled high on top of her head and held back with a lilac-print scarf, and little strands fell out and curled around her face from the heat. Her mascara had run a bit under her eyes. She leafed through the mail, stared out the window, opened the refrigerator. "No juice," she mumbled. She looked to the counter. "And no oranges to make it. Want to come to the store?"

Four o'clock, and much of the neighborhood slept. Some sat on their shaded porches, wishing they were on breezier islands. They fanned themselves and poured glasses of water from opaque glass pitchers.

Next door, Mihalis sat on Vangelis's side veranda. The two men played chess, each in a white sleeveless undershirt. She hadn't realized her uncle was even in the neighborhood; she thought he was in Kifissia.

"Mihalis," Anna said, pointing and waving.

Sophie nodded politely at the two men and kept walking.

"You don't want to say hello?" asked Anna. Though she knew sometimes Mihalis still slept in the basement when he didn't want to make the trip back to Irini's, she rarely saw him. Sophie, on the other hand, seemed to always know his whereabouts.

Sophie glanced over her shoulder. "Too hot," she said. "Let them finish their game." She seemed unusually quiet.

Anna didn't know if it was because Sophie and he shared the same sense of humor, the same indignant attitude toward the world, that overinflated sense of entitlement, or if it was simply because Sophie had been the first and therefore been given prime dibs at everything, from clothes to people to books, but Anna was envious of the way Sophie and Mihalis could joke like peers instead of uncle and niece. Mihalis learned about children from Sophie, and each age she reached he reached in knowledge, too, but by the time Anna climbed to that age herself, Sophie was long past it. When Anna was nine, if he had at some point understood how to talk to a nine-year-old, Sophie was by then fourteen, and so Mihalis eyed Anna with a bit of apprehension, as if she would scatter into pieces in front of him like a disassembled marionette kicked across the floor. It was unfair, she thought, the way Sophie's age alone, her birth order, made the world present itself to her first.

She wondered now if Sophie's closeness to Mihalis somehow related to her way with men, how she could carry on a conversation, would say the right things and know when to lean in, when to smile, when to compliment and when to tease. Sophie was a natural predator, their mother often said, and Anna assumed that implied that she herself was prey.

Or at least someone who got taken advantage of. Anna was already certain she'd be the one who would care for her mother in her old age, and Mihalis too, for that matter. Left behind and responsible.

She remembered a saying from her American cousins, from some game they had played in their garden. "Last one there is a rotten egg." Like something that had stayed too long, or failed to choose one thing or another, decaying from the inside out.

When they turned the corner, Anna noticed two familiar young men behind them, men she had seen in the neighborhood recently. Students, unshaven, both in worn white T-shirts and with long hair. One had slung an army surplus jacket over his satchel, as if he were expecting the temperature to suddenly drop. Sophie, always aware of the men around her, noticed them too. But she didn't acknowledge them, or toss her hair, or smile in their direction, and Anna sensed an unusual self-consciousness. Then, as if getting ahold of herself, Sophie flipped her sunglasses onto her head and opened the door to Luxe, the small neighborhood market.

The men lingered outside. Sophie was horrible at making decisions—and Anna noticed one of them come inside, look at the selection of chocolate and chewing gum, and walk back out. From the window she could see the two of them conversing, both smoking.

Anna chose an ice cream, and Sophie bought cigarettes and two small pots of yogurt. She settled on a carton of strawberry juice; the store was out of oranges to squeeze. When they left the store, back out into the glaring sun, Anna nodded to the men in recognition. She wanted her nod to be somewhere between a friendly acknowledgment and an *I see you there, watching us.*

"You know those two?" Sophie asked. She put her sunglasses back on.

"Just by sight," Anna said, which was true. But she had not thought much of them until that afternoon, when they seemed to be on her sister's heels.

"So you've seen them around," Sophie said.

Anna said she had. She turned around but the men were no longer there. Sophie led them home the long way so they didn't pass Vangelis and Mihalis but instead approached the house from the other side.

Anna didn't know exactly what was going on, but she was no idiot. Despite Sophie's claim that their uncle had retreated, Mihalis and Sophie were definitely involved in something. Yet another thing that brought them closer together and shut everyone else out, something that had slowly been accelerating since Taki's departure several months earlier. Sophie's skittishness was uncharacteristic. Usually, in Anna's opinion, she and Mihalis were too brazen, too sloppy—the two of them dove headfirst into trouble and laughed when they emerged, scratched up and bleeding, like unaware, injured drunks. And now there were people following them around because of it.

That night, it took Anna hours to fall asleep. Those two men at the grocery—or, more pointedly, Sophie's reaction to them—had unnerved her. She tried relaxing one part of her body at a time, the way Irini had taught her, but when she got down to her feet, her shoulders and neck had already tensed up once more.

In the morning, when her mother came in to wake her for school, Anna stuffed her head in her pillow and shook her head. "I'm sick," she said.

Her mother had never been one to argue with her children about this, particularly Anna, who loved school. If they said they were sick, she took their word for it, though Anna surmised it was less about respect for her own decisions and more the exhaustion of raising children alone. Their mother had long ago lost all energy to argue.

Anna slept the entire day without incident, and when her mother came home for her afternoon rest, Anna finally got out of bed and ate some fruit.

That night, she slept some more, a heavy, dense sleep she normally associated with a nap. But this time, when she woke, she felt the distinct sensation of someone or something at her bedside. She could feel it there, atop her, and when she tried to hoist her legs up and off the bed, they wouldn't move. Her mouth was parched, and she couldn't make herself speak. She closed her eyes and tried to relax. After a few moments, the paralyzed, leaden feeling was gone, and she got up to get some water. Downstairs, Anna stood in the kitchen a long time, staring out the window. The smell of the night-blooming jasmine in the garden was overpowering, and it made her feel better.

After her father's death, she would have dreams about his sitting on the edge of her bed, talking to her, smoothing her hair, reading to her from a book with colorful illustrations. But from these dreams she always woke with a peaceful, happy feeling, and sometimes she had trouble distinguishing her sleep life from her waking one, and secretly, she hoped it really was her father coming to her that way. Would that be so preposterous? As a child she had once blurted at the breakfast table, unaware, unself-conscious, that she couldn't find the book he had read from the night before, and her mother and siblings looked at her strangely. Sophie had rolled her eyes, Taki got up from the table and peeled an apple, and her mother looked at her with a lot of pain in her face. Anna corrected herself immediately. "I mean, in my dream. He was there in my dream."

Sophie had softened, then. "You're lucky," she said. "I never dream about him." Anna knew this wasn't true—once, years after his death, she found Sophie in the bathroom in the middle of the night, crying. When Anna asked her what was wrong, Sophie didn't say anything. She splashed water on her face and brushed her teeth. Anna watched. Then Sophie sat down in the bathtub in her pajamas, which were all white, and flowy, and Anna remembered thinking she looked like some sort of angel. Anna crawled in the tub, too. They sat there like that for a while until Sophie said, "Do you ever worry you'll forget him entirely?"

Anna didn't answer, and soon they had both fallen asleep in the dry basin, only to be awakened by the startled yelp from their mother when she came in the bathroom, half-asleep, and sat down on the toilet before she had noticed them.

Now, on her way back to bed, Anna peered into the bathroom. Of course Sophie wasn't in there. She pushed open Sophie's door. She wasn't there either, and Anna stared at the rumpled covers and the pillow shoved beneath them, as if this would somehow approximate a body.

Where was her sister going these nights? Obviously to some sort of resistance activity, but Anna didn't know what that entailed. No wonder she was so anxious. For as long as she could remember Anna had been worrying about her older siblings. When they began to go to school and she did not, she'd wait nervously on the porch until they returned, chattering about a world she could barely imagine.

And when they began to stay out late at night, Anna, still too young to come along, lay in bed until she heard the back door open and swing shut.

But this Anna knew: if she herself were ever to sneak out of the house, she'd at least go through more effort. Even she knew to be more careful.

16

Three o'clock in the morning and the streets were quiet, save for the sound of the occasional motorbike. Nick was uncharacteristically late, and for a moment Sophie wondered if he had since come, grown impatient, and left. In most cases, he arrived prematurely, looking annoyed that the rest of the world was not ready for him. What they were doing was small on the scale of things, small on the scale of the student protests going on around the world, the rallies, the civil disobedience, but it was an act of quiet revolution, and for this she felt pride and a little bit of fear.

Sophie, dressed in black, walked down to the old church and then back, in case she had misunderstood where they were to meet. But she was just killing time; they always met at the old ceramics factory. Earlier that day, he had gone to Corinth to visit some friends, and she imagined his not having returned to Athens but instead having driven beyond—to the port, onto a boat, off to Italy—in some impetuous burst.

She knew rationally he wouldn't go without her. They had grown close. But what reason really did he have for staying in Athens? Couldn't they fight for Greece better outside its borders? More than anyone, Nick talked of getting out. And Sophie, too, had liked to discuss it in the abstract because it seemed such a romantic thing to do, to leave their city, their country, together, alone, unmarried but living on some surge that would propel them forward in one cohesive stream.

It went beyond just idealistic patter. Nick, through elusive connections on which Sophie did not want to spend much time dwelling,
had procured them each a false passport. He was involved with a small
group that was helping certain dissidents leave Greece covertly. For
her and Nick, this would be their story, if they ever were in a position to relay it: They were siblings, with a Greek father and French
mother. Their hometown was Thessaloniki, but they spent the school
year in Paris. And why not? People often confused them for brother
and sister anyway, and this way they'd only have one story to remember between the two of them. Sophie's French was good, and Nick's
was fairly decent. Sometimes, when they were out together, walking,
Nick quizzed her. "Our mother's name?" he'd ask. "Agnès," she'd say.
"Father?" "Sotiri." Date of birth? Hometown? And so on.

Slipped in between his record albums were those passports; she
wondered now if only hers remained. The deepness of the night was
starting to frighten her. Didn't only the cowards flee and find a self-
righteous voice from afar, safely nestled away? When the wailing
screech of cats pierced the darkness, she thought maybe she'd keep
walking, put up the flyers that were nestled in her shoulder bag by
herself. The night before, they had mimeographed copies of one of the
colonel's pompous speeches replete with sarcastic, mocking footnotes.
She remembered Mihalis's admonition about not shitting where you
slept, all those months ago when this began. Part of her back then
thought it would all be over so quickly—with enough resistance how
difficult could it be? The colonels' rule was so farcical to her it seemed
a joke. Yet now, half a year later, there were times she forgot what it
had been like before. Partly because she'd been working so hard with
student groups, partly because it was easy to forget the world could
change. Or that it could change back.

After twenty minutes, Sophie debated going home. Each time she
turned to head there though she imagined Nick pulling up moments
afterward. She had waited this long. Still, she was getting so tired.
She thought about walking back to the old church and lingering in
its shadows. When she heard the hum of his car she'd emerge from
behind it. She was growing worried. What if he'd been in an accident?

Instead of going home, she moved toward a particularly dark place and sat down on a bench at the bus stop, below a broken streetlamp, picking at a hangnail until it bled. She didn't realize until the young man spoke that she was not alone. When the sound of a male voice startled her she took it to be Nick's. But then the man came out of the darkness and sat down at the opposite end of the bench. He, bearded in the style of a Latin American revolutionary, offered her a cigarette. "The bus doesn't come for hours," he said.

"I'm not waiting for the bus." Sophie glanced at his shoes, brown and worn. She noticed his army-green jacket and realized she had seen him days ago, one of the men from the grocery.

"No?"

"I had a fight with my boyfriend," she said. Though she was not sure why she felt she needed to explain herself, this was not completely a lie. She had been fighting with Nick in her mind for the past hour. "I'm out to cool off." She accepted the cigarette, and, leaning across the bench, she let him light it for her. She noticed his matchbook, adorned with the junta's bird. Of course, every matchbook in Greece seemed to be printed with the phoenix, but there, in the middle of the night, her boyfriend nowhere in sight, it gave her the chills.

He glanced down at her satchel but said nothing. She was dressed as if she were going to class, not as if she had just run off in the middle of a bedroom quarrel. She should have been in pajamas, not her slim black pants, a black sweater. At least she had by now pulled her long hair from its neat ponytail and it hung messy and disheveled around her face.

"And you?" Sophie asked. "What are you doing, wandering around this late?"

He smirked. "I'm having girl trouble myself."

Prior to that afternoon with Anna, Sophie had never been followed, though many of her friends had. Yet she hadn't heard of anyone actually being engaged in conversation. Most likely this guy knew where she lived, at least the general vicinity, because he had been trailing her to the grocery days earlier; if not, he had found out on their walk home. Sophie had tried to lose them by taking a circuitous route, stopping again for chewing gum and pistachio cookies, and when she turned back, she hadn't seen them. But that didn't mean anything. She wondered how often they came around and of which workings of her household they knew.

Here she had the anti–Che Guevara—clad too perfectly student-like to be real, dressed from some leftist's fashion handbook—sitting beside her, pretending to flirt as if they were indeed waiting for a bus. These "pimps," these men who would follow the suspected subversives, Sophie thought would not harm her. Their business was obtaining information, and, of course, psychological intimidation.

She wouldn't let him succeed at either. Nick wasn't coming for her, and at this point if he did perhaps they'd both be implicated. Sophie stood up. She did not want to look suspicious.

"Back to your boyfriend?" the man asked.

Now she was sure of it. She had to leave, if anything for him to follow her and not wait around for Nick to show up. "I'm going to sleep," she said. "Good luck," she added. Instead of walking home, though, which seemed too risky, she walked in the direction of the square. It was late, but she was happy to still see signs of life. And when she saw Vangelis's cab idling near a late-night taverna, in front of the movie house, she moved quickly toward it and slipped inside.

The man was not far behind her. "Come on, doll," he called after her. "Take me with you."

Vangelis flipped off the roof sign to indicate his car was occupied. "You shouldn't be out like this, this late, alone," Vangelis said.

"I know," she said. She asked him to take her to Psychiko. "I've got to check on something."

Vangelis sighed.

"It's important," she said. He pulled out of the parking spot and did a U-turn. He knew the way.

Once at Nick's, the adrenaline rush and fear from being followed not yet subsiding, Sophie felt like a clumsy criminal as she shuffled to the back of the house, tripping twice, and used the hidden key to open the side gate, which creaked when pushed open. Her hands trembled slightly. She took a deep breath.

Nick's bedroom light wasn't on, but the lights in the den were. She could see his mother seated at a desk, as if it were morning and she were beginning the day, except she was staring into space. Sophie knew there was a door at the other side of the house that Nick sometimes left open for her or for himself so his keys would not wake his parents. She checked it to see if it was open, and it was.

This entrance was near the back stairway to his room, and the thrill of ascending those stairs to find him never seemed to fade. But it was different that night, with his mother downstairs instead of asleep in her bedroom at the other side of the house.

Nick's bed was still made. She flipped through the shelf of his LPs, and inside an old kid's record of Greek folk songs she found both their false passports. Wherever Nick was, he hadn't yet left, and she felt a wave of relief. But where was he? She had the urge to ransack his room, looking for what, she didn't know. Now it wasn't sexual jealousy, or even general suspicion. She was afraid. Who really knew what he and his friends, with their chemistry degrees and evasive language, were up to?

She stood up and went for the stairway, then, thinking again, went back for her own passport, slipping it inside her pants.

On the way home, she asked Vangelis to stop and she darted out of the car and dumped the entire stack of flyers in front of a closed kiosk. By the time she had stolen back up her own stairs to the terrace and slid into her bedroom, by the time she had crept into bed, she was filled with what she could only describe as terrified emptiness. She had a sense that none of her explicit fears had come true—Nick hadn't left the country without her, nor was his body mangled from some gory accident—but instead, the unarticulated but omnipresent one had.

The next morning found Sophie in a state of near-dreamlike confusion. She had slept with her shutters open, and the pallor of the early morning light, along with her mother's voice, woke her. She had a visitor.

She sat up in bed. Nick? She recalled in bright, glaring detail her interaction with that young man on the park bench, her conversation with Vangelis, the way she had snuck into Nick's house and then carelessly riffled through his things, like a first-time burglar. She brushed her teeth, washed her face, and put a bra on underneath her nightshirt, an oxford-cloth shirt that had been her father's.

Her mother appeared in her doorway.

"Who is it?" Sophie asked.

"I don't recognize him," she said. "His name is Giorgos." Then, she glanced at Sophie's bare legs. "Get dressed, please."

Sophie pulled on her pants from the night before. She couldn't remember a friend named Giorgos, but then when she saw him sitting on her veranda drinking a coffee, she recognized his face.

But as she sat on the porch with this other friend, she realized she was not the only amateur. Nick and Giorgos and another friend had been caught urinating on a junta poster on their way to meet her. This side of him—the wilder, careless side—was one she only saw in small glimpses. She recognized it because she had that side herself. The Nick she *knew* took himself so seriously, sometimes infuriatingly so. Maybe she did, too.

"You were with them?" Sophie asked. She had assumed Nick was coming to meet her alone, and this wounded her a little bit.

"Until I saw the police," his friend said. "And then I ran in the other direction."

"Lucky you," Sophie said.

"For now," he said. "I suppose."

But it didn't matter. When he left, Sophie felt immobile and remained on the veranda for hours. When the phone rang, she yelled for someone to please answer it, but she didn't move. She watched the neighborhood go about its business. Vangelis kissed his wife and took off in his cab. Another neighbor, whose husband had been arrested and released, hung her laundry and fed her cats and snipped herbs from the potted plants on the terrace. Her mother set a demitasse of coffee next to her, insisted she eat some breakfast, and then left for work. Anna went to class, returned, and sat with Sophie while she smoked a cigarette. Then Anna disappeared inside to study.

Later, Sophie called Nick's mother, who only indicated a trace of recognition. Her voice seemed far too calm and mellifluous, as if she were heavily medicated. No word from Nick yet. His father had gone to the station, but they would neither confirm nor deny Nick's presence there. Sophie couldn't concentrate, and when she tutored two of her charges that afternoon, she had to ask them to repeat everything they said three times. They obeyed, taking it as requisite language-teacher drilling, but it was simply because she had not been listening.

That evening, when she got home, Anna was waiting for her on the porch.

"Well?" Sophie asked. "Any news?"

Anna looked terrified. Her eyes were red, and she was fiddling with the bangles on her wrist.

"What?" Sophie asked, again.

"Two men came by, looking for you," she said.

"Those men from the other day? The shaggy students?"

Anna seemed surprised at this. "No. Police."

"What did you tell them?"

"I told them no one was home."

"What did they ask you?"

"Just where you were. I said you were tutoring. I didn't know where."

"Why did you say that?"

"What was I supposed to say? I didn't have a sister?"

Sophie wanted to scream. She knew it wasn't Anna's fault, of course. "What else happened? Anna, *what else*?"

"They waited around awhile on their motorbikes. Then they left."

"You've been alone this whole time?"

Anna nodded and began to cry.

"Listen, Anna." Sophie grabbed her sister's shoulders, which startled her. "You have to pretend you never saw me come home, okay? If they come back, don't tell them where I am." She ran into the house and began throwing things into a duffel bag: clothes, a toothbrush, her glasses. She grabbed the false passport and all the cash she had and shoved it in her purse. Anna followed her, wrapping her cardigan tightly around her like a shield. She wiped her eyes with her sleeve.

Sophie zipped up the bag and threw her arms around her little sister. "Don't worry," she said.

Then she took a cab to the train, and the train to Kifissia.

17

Mihalis, over the years, had accumulated all sorts of disguises and cos-
tumes, some of them believable, some of them preposterous, collected
for a series of poems he had been writing but never finished, a series on
camouflage and doppelgängers. For years, these disguises had been in
his sister's basement in Halandri, in an old dusty box, along with the
manuscript, but now he had brought most of them to Irini's house.
He had given some to Sophie on Easter, not to wear when they hung
flyers but mostly for fun—there were, for instance, the giant round
sunglasses that she insisted were simply so in vogue. They covered most
of her small face and made her look like a cicada. And then there were
reasons he'd rather not think about. He was torn between fostering her
activist aspirations and telling her to run the other way.

Early evening and Mihalis sat on the back terrace, reading. He
took another sip of his drink and looked out over the trees, then
walked to the side and peered out over the dusty road.

Irini came outside, pulling her hair back. "I've got to go now,"
she said through lips pursed around a bobby pin. She had plans for
dinner. They had not been reunited quite long enough to fully merge
into the shared existence of coupledom, even immediately after sex.
Mihalis had been invited, but he didn't want to go anywhere.

"Do you want a ride to Athens?" she added. "To Evan's? Or to
Halandri to visit Vangelis?"

"I just feel like staying here," he said.

Irini shrugged and kissed him on the cheek.

In the house, long after Irini had left, he tried his disguises: a dark red
knit cap that matted his hair down like a fisherman's; a fake mustache;
heavy, dark, plastic-framed glasses; a wire-rimmed pair that he thought
made him look English if worn with a tweed cap; and various types of
sunglasses, including a pair he'd kept in case he ever had cataracts. The
beard he left in the box, since the colonels had banned beards, apparently the trappings of communists and intellectuals. He had other more

ridiculous garb, such as a long blond wig and a straight, floppy brown one; a pair of purple women's reading glasses trimmed with rhinestones and shiny stars; and a Groucho Marx ensemble, complete with nose, brows, and mustache. He wondered where he could buy a suit to make him look fat, for instance, or something to make him taller.

It was this daft sensibility, his fascination with the absurd and his proclivity to make scenes in public, that frustrated Irini in their younger years. And also perhaps had intrigued her, the horrible irony of attraction. What she reacted to was the way Mihalis could some-times be ridiculous and exhibitionist while at others he was brooding and serious, misanthropic, even. That is, she never knew what she was going to get. She often came home and greeted him as if asking a question, *What do we have today?* He knew as well as anyone that dur-ing courtship this sort of unpredictability could be exciting, but in the context of a serious relationship, it could be maddening, even scary.

His wife had not meant to, he didn't think, or maybe she did, but she had often emasculated him for not having work. And once, dur-ing a particular dry spell where it seemed he could not finish a poem, let alone publish one, which translated into a dry spell in the bed-room, Christos helped him find a job for two days selling Bic pens on the street, outside his bank. It was miserable work, and demeaning, and nobody wanted to buy the silly pens from him. That day, Christos had left the bank for lunch, and Mihalis had watched him slink away, not even saying hello to him or checking in to see how he was doing.

The second day, he was out there again, this time wearing that fake mustache, the red knit cap, and a heavy, cream-colored cable-knit sweater. For whatever reason, he did much better; perhaps it was the city dwellers' fascination with village fishermen, which he thought he resembled. The only person who glared at him was the chestnut ven-dor, who felt his turf was being compromised.

When Christos exited the bank that day, he looked at his getup, bought a pen, and said, "This is a travesty." On the third day, Mihalis returned the pens to the distributor, and that was the extent of his sales career.

Once, he had said to Irini, "You knew I was this way when you married me."

"*What* way?" she had replied. "I thought it was youth."

It was the agreed-upon attitude, after all, that a man was supposed to make money and that without it, he was useless. Agreed upon, of course, by the general populace, not by Mihalis. Mihalis couldn't care less what society wanted him to do as an individual, or as a man, or as a poet even, but it hurt him when his wife, as progressive and educated as she was, fell prey to these pigeonholes.

Maybe this was why he considered this house *her* house, not theirs. But had she not come from some means, he would never have been allowed his privileged artist's lifestyle; had his sister and brother-in-law not supported him all those years, he obviously would have done something besides compose poetry. He had too much dignity to live on the streets with the vagrants and the cats, and although he often ranted about the duty of a city to support its artists, it was not really the city supporting him at all, save for the free coffees here and there and a guaranteed table in their cafés. It was his family, all of them working, and most of the time handing him money, unblinking. They had not all come from money, either, but his sister was an excellent physician and also owned an apartment that she leased; Christos, in his short life, had been a well-respected banker, mostly assisting farmers; and even Irini had worked as a tutor through her graduate studies before she became a professor.

Irini saw his decision to stay in Kifissia, Mihalis gleaned, as an act of true manhood, a loyalty to her instead of some cause or maybe a signal that he had finally grown up. He didn't quite agree with this assessment but he liked to make her happy. Of his political engagement Irini voiced neither approval nor disdain, though she made it clear that she did worry about his safety. Her worry aside, the truth was, he was having trouble summoning enough commitment. When he had the energy he participated in clandestine meetings at the print shop in the center of Athens, perhaps for Sophie's sake, who in his eyes needed a mentor, and sometimes those nights he'd stay with a friend there, but he suspected if it were not for his niece's bright, admiring eyes he would have retired to the country completely. He also suddenly felt very protective of Irini and worried his actions might implicate her. For the first time in his life, he was worrying about others besides himself.

If only he could write there—it was the most tranquil living arrangement he'd ever had—but not one worthwhile word had materialized since he'd been in Kifissia, and these days Irini seemed a little indifferent to his writing altogether, the thing he thought had attracted her to him in the first place. Perhaps he was done with poetry. Maybe he had written all he had to write. He thought about taking up gardening, about planting some tomatoes. He wondered if he was finally satisfied. Was this the first time he had been such? At least consciously so? And what was more authentic, the self-conscious assertion of happiness or unaware bliss? Was it wrong to be content, to feel pleasure, when the country was in such shambles? He voiced this once to Irini, and she had only looked at him strangely. Sometimes, he got the vague sense that Irini treated him like a crazy person, but, at least now, a crazy person with balls.

Late that night when Irini returned, Mihalis, having realized he hadn't eaten since breakfast, was cooking eggs at the stove, wearing the blond wig and a pair of large, women's sunglasses. He grinned at her. She studied him for a moment and then picked some egg from the pan and tasted it. Then she adjusted his wig and cocked her head to the side. "Needs more salt," she said.

18

When Sophie exited the platform she noted the air in Kifissia felt softer, less thick, as if she had entered another country entirely. When she began the long walk to her uncle's, the charged adrenaline of her system, the fight-or-flight response, that had been telling her to do one thing suddenly signaled another. She knew she had put herself in danger, but it wasn't until the moment she saw her uncle's and Irini's house in the distance that she realized perhaps she had endangered her family too. She tried to banish the thought of poor Anna, alone, having to speak to the policemen.

But that didn't do much to tame the huge rush, the almost sick feeling of excitement—not unlike that of an intense crush, but with more danger—that seemed to be pulling her forward from her chest. It was this intensity, she was certain, that caused people to give in to forbidden love affairs, a complete disregard for the rational or right because at the time it was the only thing that actually felt rational and right. She knew what inspired people to jump from airplanes or climb mountains.

As she neared the house, she could see her aunt and uncle sitting on the back terrace. Only their feet, both propped up on the balustrade, were visible from where she stood. As she got closer, they must have heard her shoes shuffling on the dirt road because Irini stood up and peered around the corner.

They didn't reconvene on the back terrace but instead in the kitchen. She did not know what she had expected but the place felt unbearably blithe. Mihalis had almost been in a giddy mood, but behind her trailed the reality of the city, and she knew Mihalis sensed it. He seemed transfixed by something on the wall and then dusted some bread crumbs off the table into his hand, tossing them into the sink. Irini set a glass of water in front of Sophie and pulled some leftovers from the refrigerator: a tomato salad, some *spanakopita*. She poured a bit of white wine for Sophie and then a larger glass for herself.

Mihalis sat down next to her. And then Sophie blurted it out, first about the police who had come to the house when only Anna had been home.

Mihalis threw both hands into the air, as if someone had flipped a switch. "And?" he asked. "Police? Back up, Sophika *mou*."

"I have to get out of here, or go underground, or something." She knew she wasn't making sense but she couldn't figure out where to start. Then she told them about the men who were following her—this further distressed her uncle and she assured him no one had been on her tail on her way to Kifissia. She told them about Nick's arrest, explaining what she could.

Irini looked straight at her with her saucerlike eyes, but her fingers fidgeted, tracing the blue embroidery on the tablecloth. Sophie could tell that although her uncle knew what she had been up to, of course, Irini did not. Mihalis exhaled. He lit a cigarette, Irini followed suit, and Sophie continued her story, lighting a cigarette of her own.

"*Vreh,* Sophie. Didn't I tell you to be careful?" Mihalis asked, but when he realized how frightened she was he softened. The sheer dread of what was happening to Nick, not knowing where he was or how he was being treated, was terrifying, and saying it out loud made it more so. There were horrors that she could imagine and there were the horrors she could not. She knew from her uncle's timorous expression that he *could* imagine them, was all too familiar with the indiscretions of war and incarceration.

"It's not going to be easy either way," Mihalis said. "Whether you stay or go." He looked up at his wife and smoothed his unruly eyebrows. His eyes were red and watery and he waved his hand in their cloud of smoke. Gone was his sense of slight wildness, the untamed quality that she sometimes glimpsed in his face. Was this the same man who published poems in journals and when they were revised by the editor, followed them up the next week with an angry rebuke? The man who saw absurdity even in catastrophe, who came to the house on Easter to retrieve a bagful of ridiculous disguises from the basement? Was it just the quiet, domestic setting that made him seem so altered? At this moment, he was no different than one of the tired, middle-aged fathers of her friends, like rice pudding or bland soup. Why had she thought that maybe he'd be proud of her?

Mihalis continued. "You have to understand that. Listen to me. Sophie. You have to be prepared."

"I'll drive to a friend's to use the telephone," Irini said. "Your mother will be worried." Sophie wondered what Irini would tell her mother. She had always looked up to her aunt and wanted for her to see her as Sophie believed she was—a grown woman, not a child. But the expression on Irini's face, the vein that seemed to pop from her forehead like a creature trapped underground, warned she had seen far worse than had Sophie, had already lived through a distressing time, and she simply refused to do it again. She saw Sophie's actions, and maybe thereby Sophie herself, as reckless and stupid. Mihalis disappeared in his den and returned with a few phone numbers written on a scrap of paper. He held it out to Irini, who was standing by the door.

"On second thought," Mihalis said, "I'll need to make a few calls. You show Sophie where everything is, help her get ready."

"Fine," Irini said. "But let me be the one to call Eleni." Sophie's

mother and Irini had always been close, and often when a younger Mihalis drove Irini nuts she'd end up in their kitchen, discussing him and
his motives. Irini was pragmatic and sweet, a woman who rarely raised
her voice, though when angry she was apt to smolder for days, whereas
Mihalis could erupt and relax within the span of a cigarette. Her mother
always said they were the perfect example of opposites attracting, of seeing something in the other that one didn't have in oneself.

Irini showed her to the bathroom, where she gave her a towel and
an extra toothbrush. She drew the water so Sophie could take a bath;
her feet were grimy and blistered from the walk, and Sophie sat in
there until the water grew cold.

Later, Sophie heard a car and had the urge to climb onto the roof. Instead,
she went out to the terrace—it was dark now—to see who it was. Vangelis's
cab. Mihalis and Vangelis stood in front of it, talking. She couldn't make
out what they were saying. There was so much she didn't know about Mihalis's political world, even though he'd opened some doors for her. It was
a subterranean world, one to which she felt she wouldn't truly have any
access, though she hovered around its portals, like a child trying to catch
an adult conversation. She wondered if Mihalis had really dropped out of
engaged, public life, or if he was only trying to appear that way.

Irini must have been watching out her window as well, because
she asked, "What are we running here, some sort of fugitive palace?
Who will come up the path next? Mikis Theodorakis?"

In the guest room, Sophie lay down atop the bed's white, nubby
coverlet. The room was growing into Mihalis's office. Plastered up in a
random way above his desk were various pictures: he and Irini on the
beach, laughing; he and Evan at a taverna; Vangelis and Mihalis sitting
on the steps of someone's house; and so forth. One of herself and her
brother and sister. Sophie had a large bow in her hair and a serious, almost devious look on her face. Taki, five, reluctantly held Sophie's hand,
and Anna, barely one year, sat on the ground next to them. Both looked
apprehensive, the way all younger siblings look when left unattended
with the eldest. Sophie turned it over to see when it had been taken

and was startled by the message on the back: *To Theio Mihalis, so he sees how we're growing.* She remembered, then, that Mihalis, and most of his friends whose pictures dotted the wall, had at that time been in exile.

She couldn't stay there much longer. Not at home in Halandri, not in Kifissia, not in Greece. She felt suffocated; perhaps she had exhausted her options and the only way to breathe was to leave. She had begun to feel it the night of the coup, and a small hint of it even when she pasted up flyers, and it worsened when she had waited for Nick that night. When she discovered Nick had been arrested, that feeling had grown too big and was clamoring to get out of her chest, rising up through her throat. But then why did everything suddenly feel so panicked and spur-of-the-moment, as if this all had been sprung on her? She heard Mihalis calling to her up the stairs.

Sophie set the photo down and walked out to the terrace. The sun was setting, and the light held violet, murky beauty.

19

Early the next morning, after Sophie had been delivered to the port at Patras and, as far as Vangelis could confirm, had safely and without incident boarded a boat to Italy, Eleni's Fiat came rattling down the road at full speed. She halted fifty meters away from the house, which made no rational sense, as theirs was the only house on that stretch of road. If someone had been following her, she certainly wasn't dodging him.

Irini gave Mihalis a look but said nothing. How the old life he was partly subconsciously, but to some extent intentionally, trying to evade kept persisting, seeping into his new-cum-old world. Irascible bachelor, financially irresponsible little brother, politically enraged poet, all identities that to him had always seemed incongruous with that of husband, an attitude that Irini insisted was the main problem of their marriage. But this was another matter entirely. If Irini found his niece exasperating in all her drama, she would at least sympathize with Eleni, who had just slammed the door to the car and stomped to the front porch, her hair loose and messy around her collarbone instead of in its usual, neatly styled twist. It was a warm morning, and a few strands in front were matted to her forehead.

Mihalis opened the front door.

"And for how long does she plan on being gone?" Eleni demanded.

"If you think I've put her up to this, you're wrong."

"She idolizes you, Mihalis. She wants you to think she's a radical."

"She's doing a good job, then," Mihalis said.

"Where, exactly, is she?"

Eleni had refused to discuss it over the telephone the night before, when Irini had called her from a friend's. Probably Eleni had thought Sophie would disappear for a while, into one of those underground networks of hiding: people's basements, extra rooms, moving around just enough to not be tracked but also careful to not stay in one place too long. Eleni's basement in Halandri had once been part of those networks, and Mihalis himself had spent many of his earlier years moving among them.

Mihalis told her the plan, that they had packed her a bag, sent her with money, made arrangements for her with his old friend Angelo in Paris. Though Eleni had been hurt by her son's departure, he remembered the way she had fussed, buying him new clothes and packing his suitcases neatly, much to Taki's distaste. For her daughter she wasn't even able to send a toothbrush.

"She doesn't even have her passport," Eleni said. "How is she going to get into Italy? Into France? How can she just leave the country?"

Mihalis had thought the same thing. When Sophie had informed him that she had a false passport ready, if need be, he had been both surprised and impressed. He admired her planning and the self-importance of her youth. "She's taken care of that," Mihalis said.

Of course Eleni had no idea. Mihalis realized that his niece's movement from adolescence into adulthood was as foreign to Eleni as it was to him.

"They're already suspicious," Eleni said. "The police have been at the house. And two men were lurking around last night, trying to nonchalantly walk up and down the street."

"Well maybe it's good she's gone, then," Mihalis said. He studied his sister's wary, desperate face, and he knew she was reliving it all, her husband's arrests, her arrests, and his; the fear with which they had lived and the conflicting desire of wanting to make a past disappear yet all the while feeling proud and undeserving of punishment. He regretted giving her such a hard time about her relationship with Dimitri. Dimitri was a bit hidebound, of course, but *Mihalis* wasn't dating him. It struck him now that his older sister must have been horribly lonely all those years and that each loss was a reminder of such. He always thought it was simply grief, that despondent look in her eyes, which it certainly had been at first. But at some point the grief had lifted and perhaps that was another loss in itself. An emptiness.

"For her!" Eleni said. "What about us?"

"Do *you* have reason to be scared?" he asked. "Do you think you're being watched?"

"Honest to God, Mihalis. You well know that anyone who *thinks* at all is being watched. Thinking alone puts you in danger."

Mihalis conceded this point. He walked into the kitchen and pulled out a chair for his sister. Then, despite the early hour, he offered her a drink, one she did not hesitate to accept.

20

How could some decisions be debated for days, months, years even, while others, often the most important, were made in a split second? The gravity of her choice didn't hit Sophie until the boat pulled away from the dock: it always startled her, no matter how many boat trips she took, the way there were rarely any announcements, any last calls, any voice over the loudspeaker saying, *We're leaving in five minutes. Are you sure you want to come?* She was on the middle deck, trying to decide on a place to sit, when she felt the boat begin to move away.

And in the early dawn, the mist coming up from the water, Sophie watched the rocky terrain retreat further and further in the distance. Except she had to keep reminding herself that she was the one moving away; she was the one in motion. She had left everything behind—even most of the clothes in the bag were Irini's because she had only thrown in underwear and a few shirts, one pair of jeans. She could barely pull herself away from the railing, and it was not until her feet began to ache from standing that she found herself a seat.

At the port of Brindisi a weary Sophie was followed by two leering men, and they would not have unnerved her so had she not spent the past few weeks in Athens constantly glancing over her shoulder. She remembered Mihalis's warning of junta agents disguised as traveling students and to not talk to anyone. But these men were older and Italian. To be followed only because she was attractive and young seemed the least of her problems. Still, she was happy to have not much time between the arrival at the port and her departure on the train.

The next day, at the French border, she handed over her passport with nonchalance and was surprised when the officer barely looked at her. She thought of Nick quizzing her on all its information and felt a stab of sadness. Had she betrayed him by leaving? Would he have wanted her to do this without him? She didn't know.

Two days after her departure, when she, exhausted and grubby, stepped off the train into the grim Paris metro, she was hit with unfamiliarity. She had studied France's literature and history for years, immersing herself in its culture, but only from afar. How little she really knew the French character. How much more familiar Athenians looked to her in general. At the Italian port she heard Greek mixed in with Italian and Albanian, and it had comforted her, that transition. Now the sounds of French, once to her melodic and pleasing, surrounded and intimidated her. Regardless of how well she knew the language, its onslaught and ubiquity were overwhelming.

She adjusted the strap on her shoulder and tugged at her skirt, which was being pulled upward by the duffel rubbing against her hip, threatening, she now realized, to expose too much of her. No wonder she had been followed. She balanced her bag on her feet, so as not to get it wet, and retrieved a sweater. In her pocket was Angelo's address, a street not far from this metro stop. She took out the worn, over-handled piece of paper and stared at it. She surveyed the street, the restaurants and shops. This was where she would live.

The city she had left had been blazing brightly. Here, it must have rained earlier, because the streets were dark and wet, and the traffic lights were not working. It was cold, and Sophie was grateful Irini had insisted she take one of her coats. Policemen directed traffic, their white raincoats aglow in the headlights. The sight of them made Sophie uneasy until she realized she didn't have to evade them. In Paris she was a different person; even her passport said so.

Nearby, two young women wearing wool jersey minidresses with long, blond, well-styled hair stood beneath an umbrella, whispering to each other. A drowned-rat-looking man took photographs. A woman waited for a taxi at a stand, and when one stopped, another man stealthily slid in. When the cab drove away, its light changing to "occupied," the woman shouted out after them.

Everything was different: the faces, the taxis, the insults, the secrets. Even the puddles. This much Sophie knew from the moment she trudged up the subway station steps and emerged onto the street: She could mimic French women's clothing, their hairstyles, and even their demeanor. She could perfect her accent, her inflection; she could pepper her speech with trendy French argot. It didn't matter; she would always appear to be from somewhere else. Foreignness was simply in her face. It was always in their faces, those indelible stamps of nationality.

She thought of all she had left behind and stepped carefully into the street.

Part Two

November 1968 to April 1969

This silence which I've nurtured
between four walls
was destined early on
to become a song.
A deep, dark song
like water in a wishing well

—JENNY MASTORAKI, "TOLLS"

They were lovely, your eyes, but you didn't know where to look
nor did I know where to look, I, without a country,
I who go on struggling here, how many times around?

—GEORGE SEFERIS, "MYTHISTOREMA"

21

After one year in Paris, Sophie accepted she would never get used to the weather. November came around again and the city was taken over by a torrential rain deity, which everyone said was unusual, but Sophie did not believe it. It had been the same way when she first had arrived, at least as she recalled it. Rain pinged on awnings and slid down the arcades and ruffled up the Seine. It dripped down overcoats and umbrellas and brows. Never had she seen such a sustained downpour of water and the rain made her imagine Athens, its shining sun so far away.

Nonetheless, in the same way she became inured to the cold and rain, she resigned herself to being in one place and thinking of another, and Paris was beginning to feel like home. She had studied French literature, after all, and doing so had given her the sense of being united with the city. After a few months staying with Mihalis's friend Angelo; his wife, Monique; and their two-year-old daughter, Katerina, to whom Sophie served as a part-time nanny, Sophie moved upstairs. Monique's parents owned the building, and she persuaded them to let Sophie rent the small attic studio that was serving as a storage area, for practically nothing. She found a bed at a flea market, and Angelo, Monique, and a few others helped her wheel the bed the ten blocks back to the apartment, like some sort of parade. The ceilings of the studio were slanted, and Sophie squeezed the bed into a small space cut out beneath a window, the only place in Paris where she found the rain comforting. And when it wasn't raining, the tall, narrow windows let in a surprising amount of light.

The apartment had a hot plate and an electric teakettle but no stove or refrigerator. Clustered in one corner beneath a window were a small clawfoot tub, toilet, and sink, which Sophie boxed off with Asian-themed room dividers, also from the flea market. She painted the walls a deep lavender, a color she found soothing though quite different from the cool, airy white of her room at home. Old wooden crates held her clothes and lined one side of the room.

Monique's parents occupied the entire ground floor and believed in lowering the thermostat to a ridiculously low temperature at night. So each morning when Sophie woke she waited beneath her covers for the bang and snap of the radiator, which stood next to the door and was painted bright red, a fine contrast against the lavender of the walls. Beneath that red layer of paint, the radiator had been a minty green, and beneath that, a sort of fleshy pink that Sophie had not yet peeled back. When it engaged, she stepped out onto the white *flokati* rug her mother had sent and draped the Hudson Bay blanket from Taki over her shoulders. Sophie was sure his girlfriend, Amalia, had been the one to suggest the gift—it wasn't like Taki to send bedding—but still, when she had opened the box and seen the bright stripes of the wool, she fiercely felt her younger brother's absence.

Then she'd heat the water for coffee and scamper to the radiator. She folded her legs up to her chest and pulled her nightshirt over her knees, covering the thin fabric of the pajama pants. *How strange we are when we live alone,* she thought. She had become more primitive, hovering beneath the tent of her blanket, sipping her coffee, staring at the floor, and letting the heat slowly thaw her out.

Mornings were quiet. Monique and Angelo kept late hours. Often they'd fall asleep with Katerina and then wake up again around midnight. Sometimes when Sophie went to sleep she could hear the murmur of their voices and the hint of their music coming from the floor below. The combination of the muffling effect of those old, heavy walls and the strain of hearing a language not her own didn't allow her to register much beyond a *yes,* a *what,* a loud, sudden laugh. At times the sounds of their relationship were soothing, the way when she had been a child and tucked safely in bed she was comforted by her parents' low voices downstairs. And other times a groan of pleasure or a cry of relief embarrassed her and she'd bury her head in her pillow, hoping not to hear more, and at these moments she'd remember Nick, his body, the way he left her breathless and elated. And the next morning when she'd see Monique and Angelo she'd try not to think of how they'd spent their night, which only made her imagine it in vivid detail.

Nick was now studying medicine in Germany, where he had quickly moved after the three weeks he had spent in jail. They had written and talked of visiting one another but they always placed the possibility in the future (after exams, after the winter, yes it would be nice) until they no longer mentioned it. If he wanted to, he would have by now. Then again, she could have too, and maybe they both were letting go, because eventually the letters turned to postcards scrawled with something funny he'd seen, or lines from poems he knew she'd like, or a carefully copied drawing from his anatomy book: the bones of the foot, one lung, a diagram of the eye. Playful but without yearning. While Sophie was charmed to receive these notes, as random in interval as they were in content, she didn't waste time pining and recognized she had loved him once or maybe the idea of him, but he wasn't a part of her daily life. She had been the one to leave after he had been arrested, a betrayal whose severity was balanced by *his* carelessness. The levity of their communications was a mutual, unspoken apology.

She told herself her life was in France now. Paris was full of attractive, interesting men, and even a glance on the street or a moment of nimble banter left Sophie flushed and alive. Simple phrases such as an invitation to sit down for coffee, when delivered in French, exploded with sex, and she didn't know if it was the cliché of the language of love or because it simply wasn't Greek. There had been a few men but nothing serious, as if in the back of her mind Sophie felt as though she were just passing through. So what if she broke a few hearts along the way? Though she was sometimes shy in French, the otherness of the language and anonymity of the place also freed her in a way she wouldn't have imagined.

To be unattached romantically added to this freedom—everything was a possibility, open and fresh—but she did find stability in other aspects of her life. As Mihalis had promised, Angelo was well connected in Paris and she had been handed a job in a café. She had imagined herself with her hair pulled back with a pencil, wearing

glasses and black clothing, walking across an energetic office filled
with the *takou-takou* of typewriters—a girl Friday of sorts. She was
starting graduate school the following fall—finally she had gotten
around to it—and needed something with flexible hours. The café
was in the Ninth Arrondissement near the Palais Garnier, but despite its chic neighborhood, which he usually avoided, Angelo liked
it and its owners, Charlotte and Etienne, self-described Helleno-
philes who were as appalled and upset about the current regime as
anyone. Sophie found it strange to talk about the junta in regular
voices in a public setting, without paying attention to who walked
in the front door, to who might sit at the shiny marble tables. Charlotte and Etienne had a reputation as politically engaged, and the
café attracted many artists and student types even though it was not
a typical student neighborhood. The tall walls were decorated with
famous people who'd visited and sipped their coffees, who sat to be
seen or forge new philosophies or solve the problems of the world.
She spent her days waiting tables and making morning café crème,
and she ate more brioche and croissants than she probably should
have, but she loved the place's energy.

Charlotte had spent her childhood summers on Corfu, where
her nanny had taught her Greek, though she spoke the Greek of
a six-year-old, which Sophie found endearing. Charlotte's overall
demeanor was quite childlike for a woman somewhere in her early
forties. She held her eyes wide when she spoke, and when she got
excited, the cadence of her speech sped to such a pace that Sophie
had to always ask her to please slow down so she could follow. When
Charlotte listened, she leaned in close, as if watching a magic trick,
and Etienne, several years Charlotte's senior, looked just like the cartoon narrator of her French grammar book—floppy hair, a long, thin
nose, well-tailored clothing. Sophie had warmed to them right away,
and Charlotte and Etienne had taken her in like a skinny, pouty-
mouthed kitten, while she, Sophie, lapped up the dishes of cream
they set in front of her. She was grateful for their kindness. There
were plenty of political exiles and refugees in the city and Sophie did
not feel poor, as most of them were. She ate for free at the café, she
went out at night, she was able to buy books when she felt like it.

She worked, and her mother still sent her money. Maybe this pleasantness made her complacent, or maybe it was the absence of both Mihalis and Nick, the audience for her engagement.

On a chilly day in early December she received a letter from Mihalis, addressed to Angelo but obviously for her, an act of caution that almost seemed ridiculous now, but when she read it, she felt a homesickness so strong she had to sit down. Along with most of Athens, Mihalis had attended the former prime minister George Papandreou's funeral. Mihalis had written: *For a moment my faith in Greece had been restored. We were so many, shouting and brave and alive, and I thought,* Yes! This is it! *But our uproar was bigger than we were and we disbanded, just like that. People went back to their homes, their quiet, unobjectionable lives. We could have taken them down. We could have taken Greece back.*

Sophie and Charlotte had listened to the funeral over the radio, and for the rest of the day she had been shaky and unsettled with thoughts of the roar of thousands and their subsequent silence, crushed by images of her Athens overflowing with humanity. When she brought a customer a glass of white wine instead of whiskey, the customer politely corrected her, and she nearly broke down in tears. She realized she had not heard from Nick in a while—and suddenly missed him, a sharp blow of emptiness, and wondered if he had been listening too. They had met marching in support of the Old Man himself. And when he had been forced to step down, her mother had told Sophie it signaled something ominous. Now, some three years later, his death was emblematic of despondency. Was there anything worse than to have no hope? During the events of the previous May she had thought of Nick and wished he'd been there with her. She'd written him about it, the way she'd felt both an outsider and comrade to the fight and had watched the situation unfold with a mix of reverence and anxiety. The marches, sit-ins, and demonstrations she felt unworthy of and unentitled to join, as if this were not her fight.

She liked to think that the dictators would destroy themselves soon, if no one else could, and she'd be able to return home without incident or worry. If she wanted to. One part of her thought she would one day return to Greece, but another part of her was angry at the country that had betrayed her. Within Greece's borders she'd had a rebellious urge, a sense of right and good and duty. Yes, there was the concurrent thrill of Nick, but more than that politics had given her a sense of self to grow into, a way of being in the world, and after the coup she was intoxicated by the energy derived from the struggle against it. She wondered if this somehow made her complicit, her need for the junta to define herself. Because without Greece's borders, though she had the freedom and safety to remain even more politically engaged, the urgency was gone, as distant as the blaze of that hot sun.

Bits of Athens reached her like that letter or radio broadcast, in inchoate blips. She felt her native land was hurling ahead at a great speed, that every day she was missing something. She expressed this once to Angelo, who seemed to understand, but he had replied, "The only thing you're missing, Sophie, is torture, imprisonment, and oppression."

And this was not just conjecture or an attempt to make themselves feel better for living away from their homeland. They knew the situation was not good, and international awareness of it was building, making their exile feel all the more warranted. At a recent music festival in France, for instance, a Greek composer had dedicated the world premiere of his work to Greek political prisoners. With more and more stories of torture coming through the wires, with the Amnesty International reports being published in magazines around the world, Sophie's previous small acts of protest offered her a little peace of mind. She remembered the exhilaration from a simple act of defiance, something like distributing flyers, that gave her such satisfaction, such a rush.

She had wanted so badly to be a revolutionary, to be part of a protest movement, to *do* something. She knew now this might have been a naïve sentiment. Whereas she had once seen politics as a way to *empower* the people, she had begun to view it as a way to obtain power, and then to use it to do whatever one wanted. Ethics and responsibility had nothing to do with it.

But what was she doing now? She was safe from the regime, completely removed from it. Monique and Angelo were involved in an international movement of resistance, and they always invited her along to meetings. But she never went. She thought of Mihalis alternating between attending late-night resistance meetings and lounging on the terrace in Kifissia, where he was safe and hidden. Only now from Paris could she understand his contradictory spurts. Maybe it was exhaustion. Or simply a need to not make everything so difficult. But he had already done his time, in more ways than one. She hadn't. Sometimes, a stretch of days would pass during which she didn't give her life in Greece as much as a passing thought. Some days, she liked it that way. Now a new year had already begun, the old one gone forever, and she was beginning to take her life in Paris almost for granted.

Memory, she knew, was so much about desire. If she would allow herself, it might be easy to forget entirely.

That second winter passed quickly, and Sophie's work gave her a predictable, pleasant rhythm. She brought *pommes frites* and salads to the eclectic mix of patrons. At night she served Greek coffee, to her delight, and glasses of wine, snifters of cognac, and tall, tapered pilsners. She liked the mix of students and shabby artists and well-heeled opera goers and tourists. Sometimes, visitors asked her for directions, which more often than not took Sophie by surprise. Maybe she was really beginning to fit in there, as much as anyone. But could she really know a city that wasn't hers by birth, by nationality, by legacy? Charlotte and Etienne knew only the Greece of travelers: the blue and white islands with their all-night clubs and glorious beaches, the grit and dignity of Athens. She wondered if her perception of Paris was one-dimensional and, more gravely, if with time she too would distill her home country to such clichés.

She wasn't always lost in such introspection. She enjoyed work and the company of Christophe, the other waiter, though he never said much when working, more his affected persona than an actual shyness. In fact, it was his confidence, his arrogance, that allowed him to stalk around the café as he did, keeping his front section and the outdoor tables that still filled on sunny cold days in order and well served. When it was slow, he'd pull out two bar stools, hand Sophie a cigarette, and ask her about herself. When she came down with a cold or flu, he insisted she drink scalding hot scotch. His wife and two small, adorably tangle-haired daughters sometimes visited and drank hot chocolate, the girls grinning wildly at their father. Sometimes, if one of her tables would become obnoxious, Sophie would feel his gaze—avuncular, not lecherous—making sure she didn't need help. He was her ally, and this also gave her a sense of belonging.

Yet Sophie still assumed, as most outsiders might, that everyone else belonged more than she did. And this feeling lent her a certain apprehension. In Greek, she was witty and talkative; in French, though she enjoyed banter, her attempt at it sometimes came off unintentionally literal, serious. The more comfortable she became with the language the more intimidating speaking it became. It appeared the more she learned the less she could express, and the longer she was in Paris the less she felt she had an excuse. When alone with Angelo, she spoke Greek, but she was not often alone with him. With Angelo and Monique she spoke French, and although she had taught beginning French to children and could read and understand almost anything, intellectual conversation was still trying. Her lack of nuance in French made her say things too simply, or just as they were. Which was not always a good thing. Once, a regular customer said to her, "Oh, you're Greek! I thought you were just rude."

Sophie could pass an entire shift saying hardly a word, appearing silently, receptive to each table and ready to bring the customers simply what they wanted. Language was an alienating tradition, and Paris was transforming her into a quieter version of herself. To live in another country and to always be outside your language was emotionally exhausting. It took all her mental energy.

One late Saturday afternoon, after her post-shift duties, she pulled a sweater over her head and bunched her apron in her hands. She said good-bye to Etienne, who was reading the newspaper behind the bar. Whether they were slammed with customers or completely empty, Etienne had one pace: slow. Christophe nodded from the table where he was serving two Americans café au lait. It was late in the day, and she knew he would find this choice of beverage distasteful. One of the students, baby faced, brown eyed, smiled back at her, and this startled her.

The other two at the table engaged in universally typical young male behavior, and Sophie heard one say, "Ha! The silent one likes you." Stoic Christophe, who was now bringing them another round of coffee, actually laughed out loud. Not at what they said, but *how* they said it, because he hadn't understood a word. What was so surprising about this exchange was that *it took place in Greek.*

Sophie glanced over her shoulder at the boys, who were still watching her, and walked out into the spring twilight. This was a glimpse of her Greek self: coy, flirtatious. Hearing Greek in Paris was not unheard of—once, she had stood a few places behind a beautiful Greek film star and her filmmaker husband in a bakery—but always jolted her. Not simply because she was homesick, but because she had been privy to an otherwise secret conversation. Yet hearing it from these two raffish men while she was at work was exhilarating. Despite their vestigial adolescent behavior, she wanted to go back and sit with them, to be able to relax into the fluency of her own tongue.

She considered it but didn't, even stopped in the street and stood, thinking. The lure of her own language and fellow expatriates was not enough to overcome her new French hesitancy, and apparently all the energy that went toward daily life in French had eclipsed her carefree Greek self. To keep one foot in each culture would be not only strenuous but would maybe drive her insane. Once in her apartment, though, she felt remorse at her decision. That group of students had always stood out to her. Sometimes they came with women, sometimes not. Their conversations seemed heated and lively. They were always bundled up, bohemian style: scarves wrapped around their necks; ratty sweaters and fingerless gloves (easier to smoke); big, warm coats. She didn't assume they were all French—from their frequent talk of Chile and Allende Sophie thought some were Spanish—but she was fairly certain they spoke French or once in a while English. Certainly never Greek—this she would have noticed, for sure. For the rest of the night, she thought about them and regretted that she wouldn't be back at work for a few days.

Because she had the same days off each week, Sundays through Tuesdays, Sophie saw time passing in clumps, time off strung together in one cohesive unit—days off, days worked. One more week until. Until what? Wednesday afternoons, when she arrived at the café, she felt happy.

But she did also love her Tuesday nights, when she felt her week really begin. Since her arrival in Paris, she had been attending Advanced French Conversation to help with her confidence. And the class was liberating; each week she looked forward to that ninety-minute period, where she could test things out before she said them in real conversation.

What intrigued Sophie most was the sound of each individual accent superimposing itself over the new language they shared. There were people who came and went, and there were those, like Sophie, who attended religiously. Their dinners together afterward at nearby brasseries or at someone's home were the highlight of her week. She wouldn't have imagined that most of her friends from Paris would be from somewhere else or that there seemed to be an etiquette to disclosing it. No one was ever asked to reveal their reason for being there or what they had left; it was only discussed if they offered to. Paris was filled with transplants that stirred through its underbelly. They were there because they were, and for this, Sophie was grateful.

And she had made some good friends. There was Lena, who the previous week had entertained them with a giant Polish feast; Maria, the thirty-year-old Italian who had left her husband and with whom Sophie had immediately clicked; Petr, a gay Czech writer who fled after the Russians crushed the resisters. Sophie and Petr, at first, had approached each other carefully. How different their experiences were. Sophie had left Greece for fear her leftist beliefs would eventually get her into trouble, and Petr had left a country under a leftist regime where he didn't have the power to speak or act freely. Both of course were censored but Sophie felt a little sheepish around him, like a child with unreal expectations.

Sophie was running late one night and when she arrived at her class it was packed. It was a beautiful, misty spring night, and after the long, dismal winter it made sense that people were ready to emerge from their apartments, to better themselves. Spring in Paris seemed to turn over a new cast of characters.

She found a seat near the door, next to a young man in a dark gray sweater.

"You're from the café," he said in Greek. He was the cute one who had smiled at her. Until then, she had been the only Greek in the class. "Sophie," he added, "right?" Of course Christophe had told them her name.

He continued: "I'm Alex. Why didn't you ever introduce yourself?"

Their instructor, a sweet, amiable, smooth-haired woman who also taught contemporary poetry at the university, interrupted them, prodding them to continue their discussion in French. "Unless it's private, of course," she added. The class laughed and resumed their conversation about calling the landlord about the broken heater, about explaining why the rent would be late. The teacher knew among the émigrés money was tight.

Sophie slumped in her chair. She scratched on the corner of her notebook, writing in French that she hadn't noticed them before.

Alex rolled his eyes playfully but turned his attention to the instructor, who had just asked him a question. He spoke French slowly but well. When the instructor called on another, he leaned in toward Sophie. "We hadn't noticed you either," he whispered, but in Greek. He smelled like warm, wet wool.

After class, Alex and some of their classmates headed to their usual café, a small place with large, round booths and cheap wine. He was twenty-three, like she was; he grew up in Thessaloniki; at the time of the coup he had been studying in London. He'd been in Paris only three months and worked as a draftsman for an architectural firm, one of whose partners was also Greek.

As the night went on and more friends crowded into the booth, Sophie tried to stay focused on the conversation, always a little hard to follow as they communicated in French and English with bits of their native languages thrown in when the right word could not be accessed. Later, outside the café, after they said their good-byes, Alex hung back. "Come out with me," he said. "I'm meeting friends."

*   *   *

Down a narrow, tree-lined street, with every car seemingly parked halfway on the curb, the sounds of *bouzouki* filled the sidewalk, and nostalgia bowled her over. Nonchalantly Alex led her down a tight staircase and into a dank, smoky bar. The familiar throaty sounds of Greek song surrounded her, but something about it flustered her; she was more comfortable where Paris felt like Paris, when her preconceived notions were lazily confirmed.

The place was small and crowded. Near the front where they entered, two men sat on stools and sang. A willowy woman danced alone before them, oblivious to the crowded space, the bodies up against hers, as if they were in some sort of avant-garde film. Alex took Sophie's hand, more utilitarian than affectionate, and they navigated the crowd. Seeming to recognize everyone they passed, he led her to a large, round table toward the back and, while shouting in her ear over the music, told her she might recognize some of his friends, which she did. She was often surprised, when out and about, how many people she recognized from work, and though she liked the attention, the one-dimensional identity of "the Greek waitress from Charlotte's" was a stab to her ego.

It was too loud to be introduced, so Alex motioned to her as if she had just jumped out of a cake, and a few acknowledged her warmly. Before he disappeared into the thick crowd of bodies to get drinks, a gamine woman with cropped hair and heavily made-up eyes stopped him, and he kissed her on the lips. He had been in Paris less time than she yet he already held more entitlement to the city's cavernous world.

In fact, Sophie was so used to being the outcast that even there, in a café listening to *rembetika* and popular *laika,* the idea that the bar might be teeming with her compatriots was a particularly surreal notion. Next to her, two pretty, sandy-haired women shouted amicably in French. This relieved her. To suddenly hear Greek all around her would have been far too disorienting, as disorienting as the French she heard when she had first arrived and stepped off the train. Still, she watched some of the others at the table, their gestures, the way they moved their lips and nodded their heads. Language was so much more than just the audible. There was no mistaking it. She had stumbled into an entirely new world, as if she had gone to open a closet door in her own apartment and instead discovered an enormous room, full of people smoking and drinking and listening to music, and all of them turning to coolly consider her a moment, as if their living in her closet was not strange at all.

While waiting for Alex to return with her drink, someone grabbed both her hands and kissed her cheek, but it had surprised her so much that she had to back away from his face before she understood who it was.

Before her stood Loukas, Nick's cousin, whom she had not seen since the day after the coup. She cried his name with excitement. He looked thinner, much longer haired; those smooth, shaved cheeks had now grown over. She remembered how intrigued she had been by him then, how aware she was of him at that party and the day after. Now, again, there was that same jolt of attraction.

"How's your cousin?" she asked, immediately regretting it. Didn't she have anything else to talk to him about?

Just then Alex returned with their drinks; he handed her the sweaty green bottle, and Sophie had to pull one hand away from Loukas. "Oh," Alex said. "You've met each other."

For a moment Sophie wondered if they too were related. She thought of Taki's recent letter, where he told her all the people he met in Ann Arbor assumed he knew every Greek in town, and in nearby Detroit, too, as if they were all one big, large tribe. Here, that really seemed to be the case. Who would walk in next, her former nanny? Mihalis? The bar was hot, she was thirsty, and everything felt hazy like a dream, as if soon she would be able to fly or a herd of giraffes would prance across the bar stools, carrying umbrellas. She took a long drink.

Alex said, "Loukas and I work together."

"I thought you worked in Lyons," Sophie said.

"I did, for three years. Until this past January." Loukas smiled. "And you?" he asked.

"You know each other, then," Alex said.

"We have a history," he told Alex coyly. Alex raised his brows and walked away. Sophie could have corrected Loukas but she allowed the mystery of their past to hang suspended between them.

"So," Loukas said, turning to Sophie. He was smirking.

Sophie tilted her head to the side and waited. She liked the flirtation.

"Nick's doing well," Loukas finally said. "You haven't talked to him?"

She didn't bother telling Loukas about their letters, the once-in-a-while postcards. It felt insubstantial, and that time in Athens seemed so far away. "Not for a while," she said.

A friend of Loukas's approached and pulled him away by the elbow, something about telling a story to a group of friends. Loukas kissed Sophie on the cheek. "The highlight of my evening," he said.

"Well," Sophie said, smiling. "The night is young."

Throughout the evening, Sophie's and Loukas's eyes met several times. When she was talking with a musician she had just met, an older man in his forties, she glanced up to find Loukas carefully watching her. She blushed and looked away. On her way from the bathroom, she saw him standing near the bar with two other men, and he raised his eyebrows and smiled. Later she watched him dancing closely with a dark-haired woman, and when he left with her, their hands intertwined, Sophie thought she saw him glancing back to scan the bar. She wanted to imagine he was looking for her. Sophie and some of Alex's friends, French women, were bent closely together at a small, round table, engaged in the kind of raunchy dialogue that women who've had a bit to drink engage in, the kind of which men think only themselves capable. Sophie didn't always understand the nuance, the slang, and the way things were explained to her usually resulted in more laughter. When one of the blond women she had listened to speaking French earlier asked if she had come with Alex, Sophie didn't know how to answer. "Yes," she said, "but we're not together." The other, with round green eyes, laughed. "Oh, but you should be. He's got a huge—." This, of course, Sophie understood, and the table erupted with laughter again.

Another woman asked her how she knew Loukas. Sophie told her she had dated his cousin. And quickly added: "A while ago."

"It's too bad he's off-limits," said the woman. "He and Estrella, you know."

Clearly they were referring to the tall brunette she'd seen him dancing with.

"It's surprising to see them out," one of the women said. "Since Loukas returned they've been holed up together."

"In their misery," the blonde added.

What did she really know of him after a few loud exchanges in a bar, a few glances across a room, a reminiscence of the way he had squeezed her shoulder, years ago, at a party? Sophie was no stranger to light flirtation, but these things did mean something.

When Alex joined their table and asked what they were discussing, the women did not tell him their conversation had devolved to pointing out two men in the bar and analyzing which might be better in bed, or that the game had gone beyond the bounds of the bar (Che or Fidel? McCartney or Lennon? Montand or Gainsbourg?) into the silly and surreal, all of them with their eyes watering from laughing. It felt so good, to laugh like this.

When Sophie was ready to leave, Alex was talking intimately with the women who'd claimed to know details of his body, and Sophie did not want to interrupt them. She said good-bye to some of the others and walked toward the stairs. But on the dark stairway, just before she opened the door into the night, she ran into Loukas.

"I thought you had left," Sophie said, and immediately wished she hadn't given away her awareness of him.

"I had to take Estrella to her mother's. They're leaving early tomorrow to visit her grandmother, in Nice."

"Estrella is . . . ?" Sophie asked.

Loukas hesitated until he realized Sophie was teasing him. "I wasn't ready to go back home," he said. He touched her hip lightly. "You're not leaving, are you?"

Was this inquiry mere politeness, or had his comment implied that he'd come back to see her? Her friends at the table made it clear Loukas was unavailable. She wondered if he was one of those men who saw monogamy as a bourgeois social construct, and while this could serve her well that evening it would probably not work in the future. "I have to work tomorrow, early," she said.

"So do I," Loukas replied.

She liked the way his body felt so close to hers in that dark stairwell. She realized how nice it was to speak Greek with this man who was connected to her past and also here in her present. She realized it had been months since she had been touched and wished he'd put his hand back on her hip.

"Well," she said. "It was nice to see you again." Their faces were inches apart, and Sophie pushed past him and opened the door. The outside air felt wonderfully cool.

Loukas touched her shoulder and stood in the door, letting the music from below spill into the night air. He followed her outside. "Let me walk you back to your place," he said.

Sophie hadn't thought about how she would get home. She rarely took taxis, to save money, and was confused as to the nearest metro station. Perhaps the walk would do her good—she'd had a little too much to drink. Besides, she certainly liked the thought of spending some more time with him. So she agreed.

On the walk home, neither spoke of anything to do with the present: not their work, not Estrella. Loukas didn't ask if Sophie was seeing anyone; neither of them mentioned Nick. They looked farther back, talking of their childhoods. His mother had been an actress but died young, in a motorcycle accident on a windy mountain road in the northern part of the country, he told her. That he had lost a parent too drew her to him even more.

"It's strange to think most of my life she's been gone," Loukas said, and Sophie touched his hand then. Her own life was divided into equal-length segments with and without her father, something she had only recently considered, and it leveled her with sadness. She found herself walking slowly, stopping to look in windows so she wouldn't get home so quickly.

At the front door of her building, Loukas made no motion to leave. She fumbled with the large precarious key and then they both stood in the foyer, their bodies close, their hands touching. She began the walk up the echo-y stairwell. "You want to come up?" she asked, as almost an afterthought. He was already following her.

Inside her apartment, she dropped her bag and sweater on a chair, and she glanced back and watched him remove his own jacket. "Would you like a little wine?" she asked.

"Would love some," he said. He was looking at her books.

She tidied up the small table and as she reached for the highest shelf where she kept the glasses, she felt him behind her and then both his hands on her hips. He brushed away her hair and kissed her ear. She laughed, half out of nervousness, half out of delight. She turned to face him.

"I was wrong," Loukas said, kissing her. "I think *this* might be the highlight of my evening."

She started to unbutton his shirt, and there was first a look of delighted surprise and that smirk again, and she was aware of the feeling of undressing him and the pleasure in his face and knew that she would recall this image over and over. "Once again," Sophie said. "Speaking too soon."

When Loukas left the next morning, she heard Angelo pass him in the stairwell. Later, when Angelo knocked on her door, Sophie would put on water for tea and tell him it had been nothing. She'd lie and say Loukas had simply walked her home and slept on the floor. She would ask Angelo to please keep this quiet. And that would be that. But all day, she would relive every detail: the way Loukas had murmured her name, the pressing weight of his body, his smell of sweat and smoke and the excitement of such urgency.

One night two weeks later Sophie had just rounded the corner to the café when she noticed a crowd outside. She was cranky and didn't feel like pushing through the customers, out for a fun Saturday night. She wasn't in the mood to bring people coffee after coffee, to rush around, to be relatively pleasant to the cute, foreign businessmen in ties who flirted with her, who wrote their phone numbers on the linen napkins in an attempt to appear audacious, like bawdy sailors. She didn't care to better all her customers' inexplicable amount of leisure time.

Charlotte noticed her come in the back, through the kitchen, and when she appeared behind the bar Charlotte pounced on her, grinning, her ropey, honey-colored hair swinging in a ponytail. Etienne was behind the bar, fiddling with the sound system, and looked at them both, distracted. Charlotte pushed his glasses back, closer to his face.

"Your new friends have been asking for you," Charlotte told her as Sophie gathered her notepad and some pens. "Handsome ones. They came to hear the poet's address."

Sophie looked around the café.

"George Seferis. He wrote something against the dictators."

"He's here?" Sophie asked.

"Honestly, Sophie. How is it I know more about your country than you do? You're becoming too French. It's going to be broadcast at any moment." Then she hurried away to greet several women who'd just arrived.

Sophie tied her black apron around her hips. Next to her, Christophe filled tumblers of water and stacked them on a tray. "For your little friends."

"I've heard," she said.

She had been trying to remain nonchalant about Loukas ("We'll talk, okay?" was all he had said when he left), but she spent most of her shifts with one eye on the door, and the longer he didn't call her or drop by the more sullen she became. Christophe, whom she had told, began narrating her behavior in the third person as if giving a voice-over. "The female waits quietly for the male to return to the den," he'd say. Or, simply, "Sophie waits." Sophie shushed him first but then laughed. He was on her side, doing it to distract her. Earlier, when she had expressed to him she felt a little guilty for sleeping with someone else's boyfriend, he had looked at her as though she had said it in Greek.

Now she stood strategically behind a column and peered at their usual table, where Alex and Loukas indeed sat. "The female stalks her prey," Christophe said. "You can wait on them, if you'd like. I'm sure they'd prefer it." She blushed but continued to watch the group, which included Petr and Maria from her conversation class. Normally she would have rushed over to say hello. What unnerved her more than Loukas was Estrella, gorgeously suntanned, talking animatedly. As far as Sophie could remember, she'd never seen either in the café before, though when she'd told Loukas she worked there he said he knew the place and she'd been hoping he'd seek her out ever since. Why would Loukas bring her there, after what had happened? Then again, how would he tell his girlfriend not to come? Sophie would feel *worse* if he were avoiding her altogether, but she wished he had visited first alone, to break the ice. It was ridiculous for Sophie to feel betrayed, but she did. And was almost seething.

Christophe was waiting for her to respond. "I wouldn't like," she said.

He shrugged, picked up the tray of drinks, and carried it to the group. Sophie quickly braided her hair and washed her hands. When at the other side of the café at a table of four well-dressed women her mother's age, she had the distinct, self-conscious feeling that she was being watched. With them there she felt unzipped.

"*Dis-moi,*" Christophe said the next time they passed one another. "Which one is he? The one who keeps looking over his shoulder at you?"

Sophie looked him in the eyes, and he nodded. He already knew her so well. She sighed and shrugged her shoulders.

"Complicated," Christophe said, glancing over at their table. "Of course."

After thirty minutes—her section now full and her tables well tended—Sophie stood in an unobtrusive corner behind the bar and lit a cigarette. She watched Loukas stand up to use the WC, which was on the other side of the bar, near her tables. When he exited, though, he walked straight toward her. She crushed her cigarette out and quickly tried to look busy.

"Everyone wants to know why you won't say hello."

"I'm sure *everyone* does not," Sophie said.

Loukas was smiling and standing too close. But when he noticed Sophie was aloof, his lips moved into a pout.

"It's very busy," she replied. She set out two wineglasses.

"Seferis is going to speak any minute. Today we've brought more Greeks than French with us! Please join us a moment?"

Sophie just looked at him, a little incredulous.

"Don't worry," he said.

She poured wine into the glasses and handed them to him. "Can you bring these to the table in the corner? You can tell them I'll be right there."

Loukas, bemused, took the glasses. "I'd like to see you sometime," he said, which crumbled Sophie's sardonic façade. But she didn't want to show it. How could she be thinking of silly infatuations or her irrational anger at the situation? With all else going on in the world, matters of love and desire seemed almost insignificant. She watched Loukas deliver the drinks to the confused patrons. *Such nice shoulders,* she thought. Almost insignificant, but not completely.

The music had stopped and the sound system was crackling now, and the din of the café lowered to a thoughtful murmur. Even those unaware of what was going on were quiet, curious.

Charlotte poured Sophie a glass of wine, and Sophie took a sip before setting it down on the marble-topped bar. She delivered two omelets to a father and daughter near the window and two cloudy glasses of pastis to a couple in the corner who sat with hands entwined. They barely noticed as she set the glasses down, and Sophie was reminded of not only her intense loneliness but that she had discovered this world of people who back in Athens lived minutes from her home. And now they were gathered to hear a Greek poet speak out against the repressive regime. She picked up her glass of wine and walked to greet her compatriots. Alex pulled a chair out for her. She would sit with them, and she would listen.

Sophie and Loukas's flirtation continued for months but went nowhere. Sometimes she'd wonder if it was simply in her mind, wishful thinking, the charge she detected from a simple kiss hello or a smile across a room. Estrella was often by his side, and when they appeared together at the café or one of the bars Sophie had begun to frequent with Alex and Maria and their friends, Sophie found it jolting and would realize again the extent to which she thought of him.

Once, at a crowded party in a small apartment in Saint-Michel, Sophie pushed through bodies to get to the bathroom. As she inched past a crammed couch, stepping over bare legs and denim, platform shoes and sturdy boots, a corduroy-clad leg propped itself up on the coffee table, blocking her path entirely. Before she could recognize the worn leather boots, their owner had grabbed her hand and pulled her to his lap.

"Where you headed, so determined?" Loukas's face lit up in a grin. He leaned in and kissed her on the cheek. The girl next to him barely noticed and refocused her attention on the guy to her left. Was Estrella here too? She glanced quickly around the room but didn't see her.

Sophie's dress had hiked up a bit when he plopped her down, and she was aware of the soft, worn fabric on her bare thighs, which he ran the length of with the back of his hand, as in appreciation, and then up again with the front of his palm. The frisson of his touch made her jump with pleasure. "Where've you been?" Loukas asked.

"I could ask the same of you," Sophie said, and Loukas smiled and kissed her cheek again. He was a little drunk. Sophie wanted to stay there but desperately had to empty her bladder, so she excused herself and said, "Find me later, if you like." When she stood up he pulled her back down, and she rose again, enjoying the attention. Loukas then stood with her and in that close space between the couch and the table, their feet entangled and his hips were planted firmly against her, and she lost her balance, falling into him. Then he grabbed her face with both hands and kissed her once more. "I'll walk you where you're going," he said.

"We know where that's led us," she said, and he grinned. For a second she thought he was going to follow her to the bathroom and they'd have sex right there, up against the sink. But on the way some other friends started talking to him, and when Sophie emerged only moments later she spotted not Loukas but Estrella, walking through the party with her long neck craned and alert, an obvious goal in mind. Sophie didn't talk to him again that night, but as she was leaving with a group of friends, she glanced back to find him watching her, wiggling his fingers in a truncated wave.

Her crush was large and terrible, and Sophie knew not to expect much beyond stolen conversations in the backs of bars once in a while. That's what she told herself, but below this directive lingered something else. Though she and Nick had spent much time together she never really knew how he had felt about her. She and Loukas spent no time together yet for some reason Sophie felt he thought of her just as often as she thought of him. Of course there was attraction, but maybe because he was unavailable it felt more exhaustive, more profound. Their connection was undeniable; she could feel his presence at a distance, and when their eyes met Sophie felt as usual embarrassed for the bystanders, like they had witnessed something more intimate than appropriate for public display. She didn't know how much longer she could take this, the soar and inevitable plummet. While Sophie fell asleep after these flirtations filled with heat, she still woke the next day in her apartment alone, so cold she could see her breath.

Loukas had once asked her whom she was seeing and why she kept him so secret. She had quipped that she didn't want to torture him, but the truth was she had been remarkably startled. Was he fishing for information or was his inquiry into her love life a blatant signal that, despite evidence that may have pointed otherwise, he strictly saw her as a friend? When she told Charlotte, Charlotte had laughed. "Did you tell him that he *is* the secret?" Sophie had told Charlotte everything about Loukas, the ongoing drama, at least on her mind's stage, and the divulgence had brought the two of them closer, less mother-daughter and more sororal. Sophie had always wondered what her life would be like with an older sister, and she liked having someone there to confide in.

Sophie and Charlotte began to refer to him as such: *the Secret.* Did I mention the Secret is a magnificent lover? Or, the Secret came into the café today, wearing a gorgeous sweater. Later that week, as Charlotte and Sophie walked out of a shop together, they spotted Estrella climbing into a cab, folding up her umbrella. She was an elegant woman, the kind whose limbs seemed to also fold up neatly around her. "There she is," Sophie had said. Later, Charlotte had referred to her as Lady Umbrella, which stuck. Once, at a dinner party at Charlotte's, Charlotte had slipped, using the names, and their guests of course had been confused. "What are you talking about?" one of them asked. "A children's book? Marionettes?"

"Yes," said Sophie. "Puppets." Many of Charlotte's friends were from somewhere else, and each one's collective cultural consciousness that included knowledge of nursery rhymes and children's shows belonged to other countries.

But the joking, the silly childish obsession, made it somehow more bearable. If this were only an unattainable crush, why did it fill her with turns of ecstasy and despair? Charlotte was beginning to worry about her. "You're too much of a loner," she said to her one slow afternoon at the café. "You need love. Or at least sex. It's not good to go this long." She acted as if Sophie's chastity was doing irreparable damage to her body. This was not far from the truth. Sometimes, when she fell asleep at night, the longing for a warm body was so strong it made her cry.

"You don't need to tell me about it," Sophie said.

"What, are you saving yourself for him? That's ridiculous. Another man will take your mind off him a bit. And the worst that will happen? You begin to want someone else."

But then Sophie propped her elbows up on the table and leaned in closer. "Do you think that's all this is? Unrequited lust?"

Charlotte laughed. "As opposed to what?" she asked.

Sophie made an exaggerated gesture of burying her face in her hands. She didn't want to want someone else. She liked wanting Loukas.

Charlotte continued: "Actually, no. Lust and desire aren't exactly the same. But I never understand when people say something is *just* sex. And I don't mean that in a prudish way. But sex is everything. It's everywhere. How can anything be *just* sex? It's *all* sex."

Sophie laughed and admitted she had never thought of it that way before. She supposed it wouldn't be hard to *just* have sex. But Loukas took up so much of her longing, she had trouble even considering others: the handsome musician who came into her café, for instance, or the older professor whom she often ran into in the local bookshop.

"To make things worse, I'm just so irrationally jealous of Estrella," Sophie said. It was hard for her to even utter her name. "If I could only get over that. She has what I want. And I have no right to want it."

"Let go of all your analyzing, your attempts at logic," Charlotte said. "Really. Is there anything more agonizing than sexual jealousy? Just allow yourself to feel it."

Sophie had agreed, then, that there was not. But Loukas was not just sexual jealousy. That beast she could handle. She agreed Loukas was not an option, and she needed to be more open, to respond to the attentions of others. Easier said than done.

In the fall of 1969, Sophie started graduate school in comparative literature, and all the reading, the classes, and her job kept her busy. She was meeting many new people and she had taken Charlotte's advice, gone out with fellow students with whom she shared dinner or wine, a kiss or a bed. But she was still not interested in anything serious, and neither were they, and she kept thinking about Loukas anyway. Then one snowy afternoon in what was unbelievably her third Parisian December, wasting time she did not have, she browsed in one of her favorite bookstores, an eclectic place that specialized in literature and politics and had an impressive selection of foreign magazines, most of a leftist nature but some popular ones as well. "Candy," Marc, the owner, called them. Marc was a friend of Charlotte's and often came into the café, and Sophie spent many of her free afternoons in there, chatting and reading. That particular day, he had shown her an article in *Look* magazine. In a small section entitled "World," Sophie read about her country. When she read about the torture of a member of the Lambrakis Youth, an organization to which both she and Nick had belonged, she had to stop reading. Everything inside her felt wavy and uneasy, and her body grew hot. She was about to go outside, but it had now begun to sleet, and others were pouring in, stomping their feet and pulling off their hats. She wandered again to the back of the store, where there were a few reading chairs and some small tables where various groups often held their meetings.

Though impulsive, Sophie was fairly rational, and those strange moments that others might have seen as destiny or providence she simply saw as mere coincidence, though she granted that this distinction may have been a matter of semantics. But just as she was winding her scarf back around her neck and pulling the hood of her duffle coat over her head, ready to brave the awful weather, Loukas came walking around the corner.

He kissed her on both cheeks. "Long time no see," he murmured. He took her hand, a warm greeting, but he didn't let go. They walked like that for a moment, their hands touching, perusing the shelves.

"I heard you started graduate school," he said.

She told him she had. Had it really been nine months ago that he had slept in her bed? She hadn't even seen him at all in over a month and was glad he thought that was long, too.

"Where've you been?" he asked.

"Have you been looking for me?" she quipped, but then noticed how sad he looked.

Loukas shrugged. "You studied the French in Greece and the Greeks in France," he commented. His eyes didn't meet hers but instead scanned the shelves. She was happy he remembered. In Greece she had read the French poets and novelists and essayists, but once in Paris, she turned to Seferis, to Ritsos and Elytis, poets whose work she had overlooked simply *because* they shared a homeland. Even Cavafy, though he to many Greeks was more Western than Greek, or too Eastern, depending on whom you asked. Like many things, she had taken them all for granted. "Distance, I suppose, is nice," she said.

He smiled, halfheartedly, and Sophie asked if he was okay.

"Estrella's moving out," he told her. He was killing time so she could pack her things, which, as he said, were everywhere. How envious she felt of his sadness, and how far away from him then. In all their encounters they had rarely spoken of Estrella, and Sophie had naïvely ignored that he cared for her. Or perhaps it wasn't naïveté or ignorance but self-preservation; she didn't want to imagine the workings of their life together. Her relationship with him existed on another plane, at a remove from the rhythm of their everyday lives. Sophie remembered the silly names for them, the Secret and Lady Umbrella, but it was her own relationship with him that might as well have been in the confines of a children's magical show.

Later that evening, Sophie saw him sitting in a café, alone. She didn't acknowledge him, but as she passed the large window, she felt his eyes on her back. And because she did not want to know if he was the kind of man who could so quickly move from one relationship to the next, even if it were to her, she ducked beneath her umbrella and pretended not to see him.

But two weeks later, when he showed up at her door with a bottle of wine, a pack of cigarettes, and a bar of milk chocolate, she said, "Okay." Sophie smoothed the old lace tablecloth and invited him to sit. She handed him the corkscrew, and he poured two drinks. Loukas started to say something about Estrella, but she stopped him. "We have pasts," she told him.

"Fair enough," he said.

Much later, they fell asleep fully clothed, but when they woke the next morning and removed each other's clothing, Sophie felt euphoric. Any rational being would have told her to be careful, that this was a rebound, a bad idea, that desire was clouding her senses. She didn't care. After they dressed again and walked peacefully through the fresh, quiet snow to have breakfast, her judgment felt sharp and keen and not clouded at all. *Maybe more return than rebound,* she thought.

22

Taki's departure Eleni had thought to be inevitable, and Taki had been talking of a move to America since he had become aware of its existence. When Sophie left, quickly, recklessly, completely unexpectedly, it had distressed Eleni far more. Being home with those two empty bedrooms made her uneasy, and she spent much time out of the house: perusing bookstores, meeting friends, seeing movies, shopping. The first Christmas and New Year's without both Taki and Sophie had been difficult, and she and Anna had spent some of the time with Mihalis and Irini, some time with Dimitri and his sons, and the rest of the time they traveled to the north of the country together. It was the first time Anna saw snow.

But once the days grew longer and both Easter and the first anniversary of the coup came and went, once the days started to warm and the angle of the light and the smell to the air signaled spring, Eleni's sorrow about her two missing children began to lessen. She liked the thought of her daughter in France, though she had never been there. In May 1968, when she read in a British paper (she didn't bother with the Greek ones since they were all censored) of the Paris protests it riveted her, to think that a movement could spring up like that. Her daughter's presence there made it feel closer to home, made the situation in Greece feel less hopeless. She wondered how Sophie had experienced it; her letters covered only safe topics, such as descriptions of what she ate or where she visited, something she was reading if it wasn't too provocative.

One afternoon that May, Eleni and Dimitri ate a leisurely lunch outdoors at a café near the hospital. There was a bright, benevolent sun, and the day was so beautiful that Eleni seemed to forget—momentarily, anyway, because she, they, never really forgot—the rumors of torture, the censorship and the propaganda and the military officers with their smug, disgusting faces.

Dimitri, though not a proponent of the regime, was offhand about it: whether it bore down on the everyday comings and goings of daily life was debatable, he said. And certainly many things remained unchanged. Mihalis was now living with Irini in the house in Kifissia. Irini still joined Eleni and the girls for their Saturday lunch, though Mihalis, always a little bit single-minded, thought his sharing the house in the country somehow precluded him from his old haunts, as if they'd rub off on him and remake him into a bachelor. Eleni's home in Halandri was a bit too reminiscent of his *poet engagé* life. He seemed, finally, or for now, content with the quiet hum of the domestic.

But there was more to life than the ordinary details of domestic affairs. Foreign papers were for sale but fear made you reconsider buying them; the press continued to publish, though so severely censored as to make most everything pointless; you had alleged freedom of speech as long as you said the right things; and the threat of the nighttime arrests hung over you as you brushed your teeth and applied your face cream. These things *did* change your life. The worry alone could kill you.

And that afternoon, when Eleni went back to work, it hit her as hard as the cold antiseptic smell of the hospital contrasted with the warm, breezy day.

In the examination room, two men waited. They had similar eyes the color and shape of kalamata olives, and they were both thin and sinewy. Neither was of an age that would require a companion to the doctor.

The older man's wavy hair was matted below a newsboy cap; his face was not quite clean shaven, but his clothes were well pressed and fit him nicely. His eyes were bright and he didn't look sick. He was younger than she was, maybe by five years. On the patient's intake chart the nurse had written, *Bowel distress*. At first she wasn't sure which of the two was the patient.

The boy held her glance a second but then averted his large eyes and stared at the tile floor; he fidgeted with his left earlobe. He ran his hand through his buzzed, dark hair and carefully hoisted himself up on the examination table. He held his body still, as if she hadn't yet entered the room. Though he said nothing, she recognized that look in his eyes, across his face. She didn't know what it was that gave it away, exactly, nor had she ever treated one of these men or women before. She had heard of the detention center on Bouboulinas Street, with its purported motorcycle engine running all night to muffle the screams of the detainees; she had heard all sorts of murmurings about the brutal, unreal tortures, but they seemed just that to her. Unreal. And this man: it was in his movements, edgy and distrustful like a dog who had been abused.

"Maybe you should undress and put on this gown," Eleni said in the gentlest, most soothing voice she could muster, the one she usually only used on children. "I'll wait outside."

In the hallway, Eleni looked around. The hospital was busy, and nurses and doctors buzzed past her on their way to attend to their own affairs. No one looked suspicious. Then again, these were doctors and nurses, not soldiers. She pretended to be engrossed in something on the patient's chart; he had given his name only as Y. From one room, she could hear a baby crying. A young man on crutches walked by her, cringing with each step.

She knocked on the door, but the boy still jumped when she came in. He kept his eyes focused on his bare feet, two deformed-looking, swollen stumps. Foot beatings, she knew, were a common form of torture.

"They've already healed up a bit from the *falanga*," his friend said in a voice so low that at first Eleni thought she was imagining it. "He couldn't walk before." Eleni thought of the man on crutches in the hallway.

"My entire leg was swollen," Y said, still looking at his toes. "I pissed blood for days."

"They called him a homosexual communist and shaved his head," his companion informed her.

The boy looked up then, right into Eleni's eyes this time. "I'm not either," he said, in case Eleni had been wondering. She was relieved that the two men began to relax around her, but she wished they hadn't said quite so much. *What if the rooms are bugged?* she suddenly thought.

"Never mind," Eleni said.

The bruises on his arms and legs alone made Eleni, hardly faint-hearted, recoil, but when she lifted his gown, she had to take a deep breath to hold herself together. His genitals were swollen and practically indecipherable. His pubic hair had either fallen out from the damage or, more likely, been pulled at and pulled at until it tore out. The other man stared politely at the wall.

There was not much she could do for him except send him home with anti-inflammatories, strong painkillers, and some ointment. But when they were leaving, the older man, as much to her surprise as his, took her hand and kissed it. He drew his head up and looked at the clock on the wall. "Is it okay if I come back?" he said.

"Of course," she said. "I'd recommend a follow-up. Just to be sure he's healing."

"No," he said. "There are others."

Later that night, when Dimitri touched her waist, her hips, she flinched.

"What is it?" he asked. He regarded her with his strange gaze of curiosity that drove her mad. Her bra strap had slipped down her shoulder, from underneath her blouse, and he reached to adjust it. He'd meant it as a tender gesture, but she recoiled and readjusted the strap herself. They were alone in the house, and Eleni opened the refrigerator door, looking for something to cook for dinner, ignoring his advances.

"I had a long day," she said. "And I'm hungry." Dimitri leaned against the sink. She couldn't tell him about the young man, as if even speaking of it, however generally, would violate the man's confidence. But it wasn't only that. Dimitri, she knew, would not understand. She clearly remembered the opinion he'd voiced at that Easter dinner, only days after the coup. Suddenly, she ached for Christos, the ultimate humanitarian. He would advocate such a thing. He would have probably pushed her farther.

Some late nights when she could not sleep, Eleni, working herself into a fit of anxiety, worried Dimitri was somehow involved—an informant, a collaborator—and it made her more than nervous. In another way it made her feel guiltily safe.

That night, Dimitri left early. The next morning Eleni slept very late.

Several weeks later the man returned. This time he was with two women no older than Sophie, and they were in the office, talking to Eugenia. Eleni stood behind a door, listening.

"You're patients?" Eugenia asked.

No one said anything a moment. "Yes," one of the girls said.

When she heard Eugenia direct them to Eleni's office, Eleni pretended to be walking down the hall, and she bumped right into one of the girls, the taller, black-haired one. She looked familiar—was she one of Anna's friends? Sophie's? She motioned for them to come into her office. She looked at the man, and he didn't avert his eyes.

It moved Eleni, the way he put his hands between their shoulder blades and led the girls inside. He still seemed hesitant, as though he had found an ally in her but didn't want to push it.

He excused himself from the room. It was a busy floor, and she hoped he would just go unnoticed.

The girls had been raped. The tall one, though her bruises had been carefully covered with makeup, had been also hit hard in the face. Afterward, their captors had released them onto the streets like stray, pesky dogs. While gynecology was not her specialty, Eleni was trained to do the basics, and so she gave each girl a pelvic exam. She offered each of them the option of waiting outside while the other was checked, but the two girls didn't want to be separated.

After, while the girls were getting dressed, Eleni found the man sitting in a chair in the waiting room, leafing through a newspaper. "The girls should be ready now."

"Thank you," he said. There was nothing else he could say with the hospital staff and other patients moving around them.

Eleni felt suddenly awkward, not sure how to transmit what she wanted to say. "It's nothing. Anytime, okay?"

He nodded, his eyes grateful. "Andreas," he said, as if it were another word for *thanks*.

After they left, Eleni went back to her office, realizing she didn't tell him her first name. Eugenia wasn't there. She shut the door and called home. When Anna answered she was relieved, and she asked her daughter if she would please meet her for dinner, any place she wanted. Then, she sat down a moment, laying her forehead flat on the desk.

An hour later, when Anna arrived at the café rosy cheeked and smiling, Eleni was happy; with moody Anna, you never knew what each day would bring. She wore pale blue jeans, tight and low-cut in the hips, large and flared at the leg, like a British rock star. A sheer red scarf held her hair out of her face. And, as she did with everything, she wore bright red clogs that Sophie had sent her from France. Eleni jumped up and took her daughter's face in her hands; she inhaled the scent of her clean hair. Anna's small body tightened and then squirmed, but Eleni held on to her until the waiter stood at the edge of the table, ready to take an order.

"You're okay?" Anna asked.

"Of course," Eleni said, and sat back down.

When the waiter set a lemon soda in front of her, Eleni delighted in the way her daughter drank it through a straw, her eyes wide. Only once in a while would Eleni get a glimpse of Anna's child-self.

Eleni wondered if Anna realized as much, that her adolescence was slowly but surely falling away. Not gracefully, but in large, stone-like parts, like a statue that has been cracked to reveal something underneath. Unlike Sophie, whose adolescence billowed behind her like gauzy curtains or a cape, whose childhood seemed still affixed like so many bracelets and hair ribbons. Sophie was built and cluttered, but Anna simply transformed. And it was always with shock that Eleni regarded Anna's transformations; something about her being the last child had always blurred the various stages of her life with those of Taki and Sophie, which Anna surely could sense and accounted for her slightness, an apprehensive quality, a sketch rather than a finished product. But that had all changed. Anna was as solid as any of them. Even her profile, always regal, had lost its childlike softness.

That night, while she lay in bed, to her surprise and embarrassment, she imagined Andreas kissing her face, her hair, her body, her hands, completely quiet. But each time, in those fantasies in between sleep and wakefulness, when she'd try to imagine him naked, she could conjure nothing between his legs at all, just skin as smooth and inhuman as the strange Barbie and Ken dolls her brother-in-law once sent to Anna and Sophie.

Her daughters hadn't been too interested in the dolls, anyway, but Taki had tied handkerchiefs to the toys and hurled them off the roof, howling with laughter as they landed in shrubs, in flower beds, or next to the cat.

One week later, when even Anna had uncharacteristically risen before noon and already disappeared, Eleni drove to the center of Athens to the department store, where she shopped for lingerie. Her nightgown was threadbare, her robe stained and worn, and her bras had lost their support. She could not remember the last time she had purchased underwear.

As she turned the corner around a display of aggressive girdles, she heard a vaguely familiar voice, a man's. She was facing a woman in her late sixties, dressed in black. The woman held up two bras and examined the seams. A man stood across from her, holding a slip. Eleni walked behind a stack of cotton briefs and eyed him.

It was Andreas.

His hair was not combed back neatly but rather unruly, beneath a cap, and he was unshaven. Were it not for that distinct, dry voice, one that implanted itself in her mind more firmly than she cared to admit, she would not have recognized him. His demeanor threw her off; in this setting he seemed much younger. Nothing remained of the confident self-assurance he had displayed in her office. He appeared the way all men appeared with their mothers, regardless of age: a bit shameful, a bit impatient, and a bit endearing, always with a disposition that hinted at the remnants of a mortified adolescence. Then again, what man wanted to consider his mother's unmentionables?

Idling now amid the bathrobes, Eleni watched them from afar. She wanted to say hello, to reintroduce herself. They'd had an understanding, she thought. But something held Eleni back: his being with his mother, for one, and she worried that the change in context might jar him. So after they had paid for their purchases and emerged onto the street, Eleni continued her shopping. Just as the cashier was wrapping up her sturdy bra and beige, sensible underwear, Eleni added a matching top and bottom set in flimsy pink silk.

For the rest of the day he didn't leave her thoughts. She lay on the couch and pretended to read but instead daydreamed. Could it be possible to miss someone you didn't know, someone who only entered your life for a few moments? If not, why, when she heard his voice again, did she feel completely overcome with melancholia?

Two weeks passed with no sign of Andreas, but it was too late. He had been reintroduced into her consciousness and she couldn't stop thinking not only of him, but those he might have been helping; perhaps he himself had been a victim. She felt bound to, even proprietary of, those hypothetical patients. Where had they been going before? How many were there? Maybe Andreas had found another doctor, younger, more forwardly sympathetic. Eleni wished she had been more assertive, had told the man she would help, even wished that she had met his eyes over the racks of underwear. Being at work made her anxious; the muscles between her shoulder blades tightened as she'd walk into each examination room. She scanned faces.

But more anxious-making was being at home, away from work. What if he returned and she wasn't there? She woke each morning with neck pain. Once, after a few days off—which she had spent staring out off the terrace or at men of a certain age in the square—she asked Eugenia if she had seen anyone interesting. When Eugenia wanted to know interesting *how,* Eleni dropped it. She had mentioned Andreas and his charges to no one and decided she should keep it that way. That Eugenia was just as disgusted wasn't enough. What years of political turmoil had taught her was this: people behaved strangely if they felt threatened or implicated, and it often was best to remain silent.

Summer grew quieter and Athens grew hotter, and the city flooded with tourists, pouring from hotels, wearing shorts and squinting at signs—vacationers who either ignored the pleas of expatriates living abroad to boycott a Greece under the rule of the colonels or who had simply not heard them. Junta or not, anyone on the streets in midafternoon in midsummer was surely a traveler, slogging through the hot air and peering around corners at churches and ancient rock.

Perhaps Andreas had gone away for the summer, Eleni thought, and she was filled with a moment of hope that the tortures had stopped, the arrests had ceased. Maybe the man wasn't coming back because he had no victims who needed his help. And this would have been a good thing.

In July Eleni took one week off work to go to Paros with Anna and another two weeks in August to go to Kea with Dimitri while Anna stayed at her friend Stella's place in Hydra. Each time she returned to the hospital, she asked Eugenia how things were, and Eugenia said they were fine but that she was happy Eleni had returned because now she'd take her own vacation. She didn't mention anyone who had asked after her, and Eleni didn't bring it up herself.

In September of 1968, you couldn't walk two meters without seeing the phrase *YES to the constitution!* plastered somewhere: every kiosk, every utility bill, every streetlight and mailbox. If it wasn't the phrase, it was the emblem of the dictators, the phoenix or the bird. In one week Greece would go to the polls to vote on this new constitution, which Eleni thought was simply a way to force them to accept their oppression. The constitution, which one could buy at any kiosk for five drachmas, on the surface stressed the importance of human rights, of education, of peaceful protest. It declared that personal liberty, one's home, and the secrecy of correspondence and freedom of expression were sacrosanct. But then, only if these freedoms were not exercised in opposition to the regime. Everything hinged on the subordinate clauses. And, of course, the subordinate masses.

On the day of the referendum, Eleni felt uncomfortably self-aware. Everyone was watching everyone. If the rumors had been true and there were cameras at the polling place, Eleni didn't see them, but before she entered the small booth where she would mark her vote—booths, as if they had a right to a private, anonymous vote—she took a deep breath. Around her stood the already defeated, hands in pockets, faces blank, waiting in line with an unusual degree of politeness to endorse what was surely a predetermined outcome.

In the booth, she stared at the ballot in front of her. She could feel her lungs emptying and filling; she could feel blood pumping to her heart. Predetermined or not, the thought of marking "Yes" on the ballot, affirming the constitution, made Eleni sick. But to vote against it could get her into trouble, as could no vote at all. At her feet she noticed discarded "No" ballots. At first, she assumed they had been cast by others like herself, people who wanted to vote their hearts but then became afraid. Then she considered something else. These "No" votes were probably bogus, planted there to dissuade those who entered brave and proud, to show them that yes, others had also thought like you, but see? They made the "right" decision after all. The thought of this maddened her, such an engineered provocation, the futility of it all.

When she arrived at home, Mihalis and Irini were there, sitting at the table with Anna, and Eleni was surprised to see them. She supposed they had driven into the city to vote and stopped back on their way home. There had been a call for no alcohol on the referendum day—if there was any day Eleni needed a drink, it was this one—and Mihalis was making a big show of drinking *retsina* from a teacup.

Together they listened to the radio for the referendum results. "If ninety-three percent of Greeks could agree on anything, it would be against this constitution, not for it," Irini said. But the sobriety of her voice was tinged with shame that they had passively gone through the motions. It seemed the best choice. Mihalis hadn't wanted to vote at all—to vote would verify the regime's authority—but Irini had convinced him to just do it, it was mandatory, and he did not need to draw attention to himself.

"Well," Anna said. "There is that seven percent."

"It's rigged, Anna *mou*," Mihalis said, not realizing she was being sarcastic. He still saw her as a child. "They just throw in something so it doesn't look too obvious."

Rigged, yes. But in what direction? Eleni couldn't help but wonder if there had been others braver than she, others who had voted against the constitution and left the polling place with that frightening rush, like being a child and forcing yourself to look in the mirror in the dark, but running out screaming and excited before you even saw anything.

Eleni refilled their wineglasses. Mihalis downed his teacup like a shot and motioned to Eleni for more. She handed him the bottle.

The vote had removed the sense that everything was somehow temporary, and she began to think that Sophie would never come back. One night weeks later she dreamed she was constantly trying to find her. She'd hear her footfalls and her voice but in the dream she couldn't open her eyes. She woke terrified and spent much of the night staring at the blackness. When she finally fell asleep, she slept hard, and when she woke she could tell by the angle of the light that she was late to work.

At the hospital, Eleni quickly dropped her things off in the office and washed her hands. When she passed the intake station, the receptionist asked, "Nice morning?" and smiled passive-aggressively.

"Sorry," Eleni said. Outside the examination room Eleni grabbed her first patient's chart and hurried in.

There he was again: Andreas. She hadn't seen him in three months, since the department store. This time he was with a boy who seemed even younger than the others. It was possible he was still in high school.

At first, Andreas was hesitant, as if he wanted Eleni to be the one to ask, *Another one released?* But then he spoke, very quietly: "Bouboulinas. Thrown down a flight of stairs. Kicked in the stomach."

"When did this happen?" Eleni asked. "How recently?" She couldn't help but wonder if it had to do with the referendum.

"Last night," the boy said. "They said if I saw a doctor I'd regret it."

Eleni gently moved his hospital gown aside and checked his knee. It was gashed open and mangled. She drew in her breath. "I'll need to clean that off, get you some stitches."

He nodded, holding the pain back in his face.

"Does it hurt when I do that?" she asked, though she felt the flinch of his hip muscles the moment she touched him.

The boy's shoulder was also darkly bruised. Luckily, it wasn't dislocated. Eleni stepped out of her door and called for a nurse to bring her some ice. She told the boy to hold it on his shoulder.

As she got a suture kit, she spoke briefly to Andreas. "The wound on his knee is superficial. It won't require surgery."

"How can you tell?" Andreas asked.

At first she thought he was questioning her authority, and she prickled. But the open look on his face showed he simply wanted to know. She remembered how much she liked him, how impressed she'd been by his demeanor.

As Eleni numbed and cleaned the boy's knee, she explained that none of the ligaments or connective tissue had been damaged. And after numbing the area some more and having the boy lie back on the table, she irrigated the wound to show Andreas what she meant. As she worked, she kept talking. Andreas watched her intently, and the boy seemed calmed by the discussion.

"There are two types of stitches," she said, and explained that one looked like Frankenstein and the other, for deeper cuts, was sewn in an S-shape. "See?" she asked.

Andreas nodded. "I see."

It took her only a few minutes to finish, and she was pleased by the result. Her stitches were neat and even, and there was no puckering of the skin. To the boy she said, "I can send you to an internist. But you don't seem to have internal bleeding." She took the boy's hand and gently placed it on his own abdomen. "If it's rock-hard here, underneath, then you know something's wrong."

The boy pushed down on his own stomach. He winced.

"Still, it can't hurt to have a more thorough examination. I can have the receptionist call him for you, if you like." She was thinking of Eugenia's husband; she knew he wouldn't turn the boy away.

But the man looked worried. *But is he with us?* his eyes seemed to ask. Eleni wasn't quite ready yet to identify anyone as this or that. She pretended to miss his silent request.

"Do you play sports?" Eleni asked the boy. She was well familiar with soccer injuries, not only from her day-to-day work but from Taki and his friends, who played in the empty lot across the street. When they had been younger, someone was always running in with a busted-up shin, a twisted ankle, a fractured rib. She remembered the way Taki would announce to his friends, with pride, "She's a doctor!"

"Sure," the boy said. "Soccer."

Eleni wondered about his mother, if she had seen him like this, if he told her what had happened or tried to hide it instead. "There you go. You slid into a kick, and the opponent's foot hit your stomach. That's why you need to see the internist," Eleni said. "Don't worry," she added, one hand on the door. "He's a great doctor. One of the best."

Andreas and the boy nodded, like obedient schoolchildren.

"You're going to be fine," she couldn't resist adding. Mother, doctor. It was hard to separate her roles, especially when her patients were young.

As she was about to leave to let the boy get dressed, he looked her right in the eyes. "Whatever you've heard about Bouboulinas," he said. "It's worse than that."

She could tell the boy was trying not to cry. Andreas looked at the floor. They all shared his humiliation.

"You're going to be fine," Eleni repeated.

In the dispensary, hands shaking, she filled a small bag with morphine, bandages, and various ointments and solutions to clean wounds. When she came back into the room she handed it to Andreas without a word. Then she helped the boy rig up the sling for his arm and escorted the two out.

Her next two patients were routine and required little more than reassurance. It wasn't until a six-year-old arrived with an ear infection that she needed her prescription pad. When she wrote the instruction for antibiotics and tore it off to give to the mother, she found a note on the pad's second page. It was simple, direct: a thank-you, Andreas's name—only his first name—and a street address.

As the relieved mother left with her sniffling daughter, Eleni imagined how easily she could have torn off both sheets, how this simple communication could have been lost. She also realized that Andreas could have stolen the pad and written his own prescriptions but hadn't. But all these thoughts followed her realization that he lived only blocks away from the apartment that she leased to the young family in Victoria—Lottery Place, they called it, because Christos had won it in the New Year's drawing.

She remembered living there with a two-year-old Sophie and an infant Taki, and they quickly outgrew the place. Then again, Christos's mother had also been alive and living with them, which was bound to make even the largest space feel just a bit smaller. The current tenants, a young couple with two children and a third on the way, distant cousins of Christos, didn't seem to mind the close quarters. They often had large gatherings, people in and out, meetings and parties and sometimes friends just staying there. The previous month of rent was still due, and now they were late on this one as well. The last time she had dropped by to collect the rent, one month earlier, only the grandmother was there with the children, and she apologized and said they didn't yet have the money. But they were good tenants, and sometimes she had the urge to tell them they could stay there for free. After all, the apartment had been a win, a bonus, not something they had paid for, and they were related in a way Eleni couldn't exactly remember but she regarded them as family nonetheless. Even if they weren't, she liked them, and they reminded her of Christos and her younger self. She would stop by and see them soon, see if she could do anything to help.

Later that night, Eleni thought again of Andreas. If not for her, where would he go? Where *did* he go? What about more serious cases, those who needed surgeries? He seemed very grateful for all the information, the supplies, and had left his address—though no phone number. Was he worried about the line being tapped? Eleni wondered if her handing them all those supplies was taken as a gentle warning to *not* return, a way of politely letting him go, of saying, *I've helped you now, but I can't do much more.* That had not been her intention. Not consciously, anyway. But why else did she rattle off all this medical information? And did she really think the boy needed an internist, or was she trying to send them elsewhere for another reason? Even if she didn't acknowledge her fears, they manifested in all sorts of ways.

All night she was plagued with the feeling that she had done the wrong thing. Not as a doctor, encouraging someone to play the role of one without any training, but as a woman, as a human. She should have been more clear that she was there for them. After the earlier visits, she had desperately hoped that he'd return. She wanted to help. Then he did, and she however inadvertently may have sent him away for good, armed only with superficial medical knowledge and a paltry sack of supplies. What occurred to her next was a sick thought: that he would be too desperate to take her rebuff seriously, that he would have no other recourse but to give her one more chance. She remembered something—was it Dostoyevsky?—Christos used to always quote: *Everyone is responsible to everyone for everything.* Her selfishness embarrassed her.

Three days later, before work, Eleni stopped in the neighborhood of Victoria. Though the rent was late, she was visiting more out of concern than anything else. She had been calling for days to no answer.

She knocked on the door and waited. Nothing. She went to the front of the building and called through the not-quite-closed shutters. When she heard no sounds at all, she let herself in the front door.

Save for some furniture, the living room was empty. No cups or newspapers littered the coffee table's surface, no coats hung on the rack, no small shoes cluttered the entranceway, and the couch was free of dolls and books. A glance to the kitchen, clean and empty, was all

Eleni needed to confirm that the family had gone. She had no right to feel abandoned but she did anyway.

She did have reason to be concerned, certain that their departure had been much like Sophie's and arose from either a real or perceived threat. These days, people seemed to be coming and going all the time, and the less said, the better. At dinner that night, she almost mentioned it to Dimitri but something held her back. She didn't want to hear him talk about irresponsibility and she worried he would grow angry at their negligence and try to persuade her to involve the police or courts. It was just another thing she didn't care for him to know.

Then, one Friday morning a few weeks later, with Anna at school and Dimitri in Thessaloniki with his sons, Eleni felt a sense of peace and elation she hadn't felt in a very long time. The day was unseasonably warm, more like late spring than late fall, and she had the day off and nothing planned except to clean the vacated apartment. She had no new tenants and she hadn't had a chance to even advertise, though part of her wanted to keep the place open in case the former ones returned. She remembered the way Christos had always said he wanted Sophie to have it when she was old enough. But Sophie was in Paris and Eleni imagined Anna would be living at home with her for a long time to come. She would have offered it to her brother, but he seemed more than happy with Irini in Kifissia.

Eleni let herself into the apartment, which of course seemed so much larger with no one in it. Eleni missed those tenants. She had fallen a bit in love with their young optimism and hope for a certain sort of world. She loved the way Yianna, the mother and wife, could carry on amid all the chaos. Eleni could still picture the two toddlers hurling themselves off the coffee table onto the floor, naked and squealing with delight, and Yianna lounging on the couch, reading the newspaper, as if this were the most normal thing in the world. Eleni couldn't imagine anyone else in that flat.

She was filling a bucket with soapy water when there was a knock at the door. She immediately knew it was Mrs. Triantafillou, who had lived two stories up since even before Christos and Eleni had lived there. When her husband was still alive and her children lived at home, she was slightly less preoccupied with her neighbors, but once she was alone she began to bother Eleni's tenants about this and that—noisy children, garbage collection, water bills.

Mrs. Triantafillou had strangely supersonic ears that could detect the slightest movement of keys in the door. She'd wait for them to return home and she'd descend. Yianna had told humorous stories of shutting the door behind her as quietly as possible and peering out the peephole to see if the elderly woman would emerge. If she didn't within a few minutes, to be safe, Yianna would open and slam the door again, to pretend she had come and gone.

Eleni was not so lucky. When she opened the door, Mrs. Triantafillou craned her short neck to see over Eleni. "People moving in now, finally?" she asked.

"Nobody yet," Eleni replied.

"They were dodgy, that family," she said. "Communists, definitely."

In her socks, Eleni slid across the tile floor to shut off the faucet. Mrs. Triantafillou, not having been invited in, spoke loudly from the doorway. "I've the bill here for the elevator," she said. "You owe me for the entire past year."

"We don't use the elevator. Split it among those who do. That's how it's always been."

"I don't use it either. I take the stairs. But I still pay for it."

"You should have brought that up with the tenants," Eleni said. She walked back to the door now and put her hand on the handle, ready to close it.

"I did," Mrs. Triantafillou said. "They refused."

"There's your answer," Eleni said. "Talk to the building manager, if you must."

The woman harrumphed and turned to go back upstairs. Eleni watched her as she almost unconsciously pressed the up button, then caught herself and disappeared into the stairwell.

Eleni scrubbed the counters and mopped the floors. She polished the stove and took a brush to the refrigerator door, which was covered with the handprints of Yianna's children and evidence of Yianna's less-than-stellar cleaning habits. Then again, Eleni's standard of clean was elevated, as Sophie had often pointed out to her. She certainly didn't clean the house daily, like Vangelis's wife, who always seemed to be engaged in some sort of housework, but when she cleaned, she *cleaned*. Sophie, like Yianna, was equally lackadaisical; when she volunteered to clean the kitchen Eleni always breezed through to finish the job, and Sophie would say, "It's just going to get dirty again," a comment so ludicrous it always made Eleni laugh. Sophie would usually wryly add that if she knew her mother would be performing surgeries at home, she would have cleaned accordingly.

And with this thought Eleni straightened from her position scrubbing the floor. She walked to the front door and surveyed the place, and the two twin beds in the bedroom, the small double bed in the second bedroom. The bathroom, like the apartment, was old but white and clean. She thought of the building's other tenants: In the apartment below was an elderly man who only ever seemed to go out for church. Above was an apartment of students, intellectual, quiet types who attended the Polytechnic. She didn't know the other tenants, but they seemed to keep to themselves.

She thought of Andreas coming to her office, to the hospital, hoping to get help for those who'd been beaten, tortured, or who were simply trying to stay off any sort of public-record radar. She had kept his visits off her personal record. She left the mop water in the bucket, her cleaning materials on the floor, and walked quickly back to her car. She rummaged through her purse until she found the note Andreas had left her with only his name and where he lived—a dare, a clue, a lure to something else. She had looked at it many times but could never think of an excuse to visit. Now she had one. It was only a few blocks away. Her pulse galloped and she started the car.

After Eleni rang the bell she had the urge to dart away. What if his wife came to the door? Did he have a wife? A child? But Andreas answered wearing worn jeans and a light-blue T-shirt that looked, if she reached out and touched it, like it might disintegrate. His hair was wet, a smudge of shaving cream lingered by his ear, and he smelled strongly of soap. Eleni was sure her hair frizzed around her forehead, and she felt beads of perspiration dripping down her sides.

She couldn't bear to glance down at herself and what she was wearing, fit for cleaning an apartment and not for stopping in on a younger, handsome man she did not know. She could still smell the Ajax on her skin.

"Well, it's about time you visited," he said, smiling. He didn't seem to notice her disheveled state.

"I'm sorry to drop in like this," Eleni said. "But you didn't leave your telephone."

Andreas motioned for her to follow him inside. "I haven't gotten around to one yet. Shall I make us some coffee?" he asked, as if she stopped by every Saturday. "Sugar and milk?" Eleni said yes, though she usually took neither.

While Andreas stood at the kitchen counter, shaking frappés, Eleni studied his profile. His skin was smooth and clear and only a few lines had formed around his eyes when he smiled. Definitely younger. His hair was brown and his eyebrows were thick but neat. Then, aware that she might have been staring, she looked nonchalantly around the room. She had imagined him to live very spartanly, but she was surprised to find so much art on the walls, nice old furniture that looked like it had come from a much statelier house. A gray cat sat atop a footstool, gazing at her with interest. Eleni joined Andreas in his small but bright kitchen. She had no idea what he did or if he lived alone. She looked for signs of a woman—a scarf draped over a chair, a pair of shoes, the scent of perfume—but she didn't detect any. Andreas noticed her glance at the table, which was covered with books and papers.

"I'm correcting student exams," he said. "I teach history at Athens College."

He handed her a drink in a tall, cool glass, and she sipped it. So cold and so sweet, like a child had made it.

"Look," she said. "I have an idea."

Later, when Eleni walked back to her car, the tranquil city in the November sun hummed with possibility. She returned home for her midday rest and collapsed onto her clean, white sheets, smiling with her secret.

23

April again, and Anna and the rest of the city's high schoolers assembled as was required of them in the stadium to celebrate the two-year anniversary of the colonels.

Though the idea of all the high school students converging in one place did not bother Anna, the reason behind the meeting could not have been more depressing. One, celebrating such an event even though not by choice made her feel like a traitor, and two, the stadium in pasts both distant and recent had been used to round up and detain prisoners. Anna, with an eighteen-year-old's propensity for the macabre, couldn't help but wonder if they were being taken hostage, all those young, idealistic minds, captured for brainwashing or something far more menacing.

But if her friends had felt this sense of foreboding, they hadn't let on. Most around her, upon their arrival at four o'clock, had used it as an excuse to survey the rest of Athens's adolescent population. But now they had been waiting already two hours—who did these men think they were, the Beatles?—and still no sign of Papadopoulos or Patakos or any of the lunatics who, somehow, still managed to run the country. The flirtatious energy was waning, and most of them sat carelessly. The boys slouched with their knees apart, the girls nonchalant, staring off or pouting with their heads in their hands. The initial excitement of all that youth had faded.

Anna wanted to be back at home where she could curl up in the late-afternoon sun, Orpheas the cat at her feet. Though she would never admit it, she wished she could listen to the comforting sounds of her mother in the kitchen, cleaning up, or the low timbre of her voice when she spoke on the phone. She slept best while the rest of the world was awake and engaged. Anna felt she was the only person in the world for whom sleep was difficult, and the only time she felt she got any real rest was after school, when she dozed on the sofa. She had been experiencing those strange sensations again: waking up remarkably alert while her entire body remained immovable for minutes at a time. And suddenly it would seem that some lever was released and her body's movements were restored. It was unsettling, to say the least, but since it did not grow any more disorienting, she was able to calm herself, to trick herself into just waiting for it to pass.

She tried to do that now, calm herself, and watched a boy named Panos, who smoked a cigarette even though it was prohibited and crushed the butts out at his feet. "We've been summoned here so Papadopoulos can pick a lover," Panos said. He pretended to closely scrutinize the girls around him, and Anna liked the feeling she got when his eyes rested on hers. "Which one of you will it be?"

"Maybe he wants a harem," said a tall boy.

"Maybe he's an admirer looking for a young, virile male," quipped Stella, Anna's best friend, who always seemed worlds ahead, as if she were an adult placed in a teenager's body as some sort of spy. Stella pointed at Panos: " 'You, so smooth skinned,' he'll say"—she turned to the tall boy—"or 'You, so slim hipped.' "

"Touché," Panos said, and leaned back in his seat, helping himself to a chocolate cookie from Stella's bag.

Anna was intrigued with the way Panos slouched, at ease and bright-eyed, as if he indeed *were* waiting for a rock concert. She wanted to follow his lead but still found herself at the edge of her chair. She grabbed hold of the seat in front of her and let her head dip below her arms, her long mane draping down to the cement floor. She took a deep breath; she stared at her red clogs; she closed her eyes.

Still she did not feel relaxed. The hairs on the back of her neck prickled, the sensation of being watched. She pushed her hair out of her face and sat back up, just as she noticed Panos eyeing her with a look that was half curiosity, half concern. He asked if she was okay.

Anna shrugged. She felt self-conscious, but no one besides Panos was paying attention to her. His eyes were large and almond shaped, his face fine-featured like a Tatar.

"We could take over this stadium," he said. He attempted a flirtatious wink, but it came out more like a squint.

"Is that a challenge?" Stella asked. While she was her usual, cynical self, Anna could tell she was disturbed by this gathering, that it had stirred something inside her too.

Behind them, a group of girls from an exclusive private school (Anna could tell by their light blue uniforms in contrast to her own navy one) sighed almost in unison. One of the girls filed her nails while another plaited her friend's hair into a French braid.

Soon, though, from the front of the stadium materialized a roar—they themselves were up high. Colonel Papadopoulos and his cronies had finally arrived, and all those adolescents, restless and punch-drunk, shouted out sounds for the sake of releasing noise from their bodies, the way Anna and Taki used to when their mother would for some reason or another leave them alone in the house.

Papadopoulos approached the podium with its microphone and raised his hands in the air like a deranged fanatic. He shouted back at them, "*I am your father!*"

"Daddy!" Panos yelled, standing. "Daddy!"

Anna laughed. Such self-importance, Anna thought, among these men in power. But could mockery be the only way around such a thing, the only defense of the weak and powerless? And if mockery were misread as sincerity, was there any point to it at all?

Some of Anna's friends took up Panos's joke and began to shout *Daddy* in unison. Wild, angry, euphoric chaos, this overcompensation of the oppressed spread like an uncontrolled burn, and soon the noise of the crowd was indecipherable and totally nonsensical. Though like the rest of their citizens, with a few stern commands the crowd settled into submission. While they listened to Papadopoulos and his platitudes, they laughed but also felt a little afraid, though none of them would admit this to the others. How could so few have such power over so many?

After, when they exited the stadium, the energy deflated. They walked quietly, filled with a sort of posthysteria calm or the comatose stillness of a wild animal, postkill, postbinge, but with far less satisfaction, with far more hunger.

She didn't want to go home yet, and she didn't want to be alone. It was anticlimactic. Their snickers and shouts were no more effective than a child's orchestrated tantrum that only resulted in more uncontrollable sobs; heavy, exaggerated breathing; and the need to finally soothe herself to sleep. More importantly, Anna wanted an excuse to stay with Panos, to somehow find herself alone with him, if only for a few minutes. She liked him. He had attended primary school with Stella, and their parents were friends, but she had never met him before. It was strange to her, how her world seemed so complete, how it seemed she knew all of Athens, and there, earlier, where tons of her peers were packed together, she recognized almost nary a face.

To Panos and Stella she said, "Let's go back to my house." They agreed, probably as relieved as Anna for the night not to end. Anna rarely had friends back to her house, a habit left over from two more overbearing siblings, her uncle, and all their friends taking up the space. When Sophie left the first thing Anna had done was burn everything—flyers, pamphlets, membership cards, notes from friends—out of fear, but maybe she was trying to make more room for herself. At nearly the same time, Mihalis had retreated as well, retired to the old country house in Kifissia just like the old cowboys in American Westerns hung up their guns. But the cattle rustlers were still in power, and Anna had been left behind.

When they arrived to an empty, quiet house, they blared the banned music of Theodorakis out the open windows until a surprised Vangelis came to the porch and asked her what she was doing. She didn't know, she said. She just felt like listening to music. What she didn't say was that it was April again, and things had not seemed to change except in terms of what was lost, and if winter was a time to keep silent, spring most definitely was not.

Part Three

June 1971 to June 1972

Are you for or against?
Either way, answer with a yes or a no.

—MANOLIS ANAGNOSTAKIS, "THE DECISION"

My crippled generation, see in me
Your wretched plight as in a mirror and
gesture as I do; without hands,
without shield, without tomorrow

—LEFTERIS POULIOS, "THE MIRROR"

24

Anna had been only eight years old in 1960, but she had been a particularly sensitive girl, and the change of the numbers from fifty-nine to sixty troubled her. She didn't like that year, with its terminal zero, and she didn't like the fact that her father and his memories had been left in the decade before. But then the movement to 1961 had been a relief, the safety of being solidly entrenched in a decade, impenetrable.

The arrival of the seventies brought on that same ominous charge; she felt the earth shift, as if the whole world were balanced precariously on a high, steep rock and might hurl itself into hell at any moment. The unease from a decade earlier came back with amazing clarity. And while she wasn't sure she was ready for them, she knew the new decade would bring her other things: grown-up, adult things. She had once, late in the night over too many drinks, confessed all of this to Panos, who had looked at her with bemusement and said she was a very strange girl. Since some island hopping together with Stella and other friends the summer before, they had spent much of their time together. But besides one kiss one late night at a party—which the next day they didn't mention, nor the next, nor the next, and after a while Anna wondered if she had imagined it—their relationship was not romantic. But they were close, and Anna sometimes felt a wash of jealousy when Panos paid attention to another girl. Did she want him, or did she just not want anyone else to have him?

After high school, she had not been ready for university and had blown off (read: not taken) her entrance exams, sure she would not do well. So the year after, while Stella and Panos and most of her friends began university, Anna hung in limbo, thinking about what exactly it was she wanted to study. She read a lot, sometimes preparing for

her exams and other times reading things that had nothing to do with
exams—comic books, novels, books of poetry Sophie or Mihalis had
left behind. School seemed pointless to her. Mihalis declared that any
professors worthy of note had been removed by the junta and replaced
with those deemed more sufficient. Particularly in the humanities,
where the potential for subversive ideas was higher. And maybe she
could just learn on her own.

But one year later, Anna, to everyone's surprise, did remarkably
well on her exams, physics and math especially. She joined Panos at
Athens Polytechnic and worked very hard. Now her first university
year was coming to a close, and she was busy studying for her examinations, looking forward to the summer that stretched before her.
Even though as a child she had been saddened by the end of the
school year, now a summer ahead with nothing to do but relax and
swim and spend time with friends made her giddy.

Mornings, she rose early, fresh from dreams. To sleep through the
night was new for her, something that began that year off. Each morning she drank her coffee on the veranda, savoring being alone. She
imagined living completely by herself, she imagined hosting large dinner parties for her friends from the university, but her most frequent
fantasy involved living a solitary, adult life—playing records, cooking,
reading, weekend trips to the islands. These ideas thrilled her, too,
perhaps more than anything else. As much as she had thought as a
younger woman that she wanted everyone to stay in one place—and
she still did, in a way—she was realizing that she wanted a life more
private than most. That is, she wanted the security of knowing her
family was all in Athens, nearby if she needed them, but she wanted
space. She didn't want the obligation of family but she did want family. Was that possible? It was selfish, yes, but why was selfishness necessarily a bad thing?

She envied her sister wandering around Paris alone, able to do
whatever it was that pleased her. Though Sophie was never really
alone. She had a boyfriend, a Greek, no less, and spoke of her friends
there as if she had known them for decades. Leave it to her sister to
fall in love with a Greek while in Paris; even Taki, in Detroit, had a
Greek girlfriend. Neither of her siblings had yet returned home. Not

once. Sometimes, she had to stop and think: had it really been four years since they had lived underneath the same roof?

One June evening, Anna studied at her desk after her classes, listening to the rustle of keys, the shuffling of shoes—sounds of departure. Her mother called up to Anna that she was going to Dimitri's for dinner, and did she have enough to eat, and there was stewed eggplant and salad in the refrigerator. Anna came downstairs to make coffee and closed the heavy front door behind her. Mihalis was supposed to come by; something about wanting to retrieve more books from the basement. Though he lived with Irini, he treated the Halandri house like his own.

She was surprised to hear a faint knock on the door; Mihalis usually just let himself in, and her own friends used the back entrance, the one off the kitchen. Her mother's friends just called through the open windows. Only Dimitri still used the front door, a habit her mother, perhaps for the sake of appearances, did not discourage. Perhaps he and her mother had crossed signals and he had come to pick her up. She opened it slowly.

It was not Dimitri nor Mihalis but Mihalis's friend Evan. Something about his height and impeccable neatness—the starched white shirt, the thin tie, the pressed cotton trousers—made her feel unsuitably sloppy and small in her bare feet and jeans and T-shirt. "I'm supposed to meet your uncle here," he said, more interrogatively than declaratively.

She invited him in. Her uncle wasn't there yet, she told him, but he could sit and wait in the living room. She blew her too-long bangs out of her eyes. He smiled.

"You're at university now?" he asked.

Anna told him she was studying civil engineering. Her favorite class was geology. She was almost speaking by rote, like a child with scripted, appropriate comments for her elders.

"Rocks?"

"Earthquakes."

Evan perused the tall shelves that lined the study, turning his head to the side to read the book spines. He asked her if she had read many of them.

"Not really," she said. She had started many, during her year off, but finished only a few.

"Why not?"

Anna wasn't sure. Her mother enjoyed a novel now and then, but all those dense Russian volumes, some in their original language, had been her father's.

"Would you like some coffee while you wait?" she asked, ignoring his question.

"*Ouzo,* on the rocks, would be nice," he said, continuing to look over the books. He treated her so casually it was almost startling. She turned for the kitchen, found a bottle in the cupboard, poured some into a short glass, and dropped a single ice cube into it as her uncle did. She didn't bother with the coffee but slipped on a pair of shoes and glanced at her reflection in the kitchen window.

When she came back with his drink he had pulled down *Anna Karenina.* "You should start with this one," he said, and offered it to her, adding, "Anna." She traded him the *ouzo* and turned the heavy book over in her hands. She had read the first thirty pages, twice, but that was all.

"I tried," she said.

"You didn't like it?" He seemed shocked, even wounded. He put his hand on his hip, which pushed his jacket back at the waist, exposing the front of his well-tailored pants. He assessed her like this, and she imagined him standing before his students in a lecture hall the very same way, waiting for their responses. The gesture was half-serious, half-chiding. Then she remembered Mihalis mentioning that Evan had lost his position at the university.

"It wasn't that . . . ," she said, though she couldn't remember now why she'd put it down. She did recall that Sophie had loved it, which could have accounted for why she'd picked it up as well as why she'd abandoned it.

Mihalis arrived then in his usual, plodding way, stomping into the room. He glanced at the dusty novel in Anna's hand, then up at her, then at Evan. He handed her the stack of mail he had brought in. On the top was a postcard from Taki, and while usually she'd stow it away to read carefully, she just tossed it and the rest of the mail onto the desk, the Tolstoy next to it.

"How long have you been here?" Mihalis asked his friend.

Evan raised his glass to indicate the state of his drink.

Irini walked in then, carrying a box of sweets, the cat stalking behind her, interested in the sudden activity.

Anna peeked into the box of sesame cookies and decided again to make some coffee. She headed back into the kitchen, wishing Evan would follow her but knowing of course he had come for Mihalis. Instead Irini did, chatting about why the cookies from this bakery were better than that one. Anna glanced over her shoulder. Mihalis and Evan were standing at the desk, poring over something together, but right at that moment, Evan looked up and caught her eye, just for a second. It was a short exchange, but she would play it over in her mind for days.

25

Mihalis set the manuscript on the sideboard and followed his wife and niece into the kitchen. He poured himself a drink and brought the bottle into the den, where Evan was on the third page of his manuscript. "A story!" Evan said, not looking up. "Finally."

Mihalis shrugged. "It's not that I haven't been writing," he said. "I haven't been *publishing*. There's a difference."

"Is there?" asked Evan. "What's the point?"

"You would say that. Critics without writers would be useless. You *need* us to publish."

"Not necessarily," Evan said. "We'd just riffle through your personal papers after you died. Besides, they've lifted censorship."

"How many times are we going to hear that?" Mihalis asked.

Evan ignored him and kept reading. Mihalis watched him. He both loved and hated to watch people read his work, but suddenly he wanted Evan to stop reading. "How's the baby?" Mihalis asked.

Evan looked up and smiled. Aliki, almost four, was their first child, born only months after the coup. And though Evan liked to joke that she was a worse tyrant than the colonels, Mihalis knew he was completely entranced with her. "We can barely call her a baby anymore. As difficult and intense as her mother. But even more charming."

Evan went back to reading, though he wore a slight expression of amusement. "The first line is a little heavy-handed, don't you think?" he asked. "Maybe start more subtly?"

From the kitchen came a burst of laughter. Evan glanced in the direction of the other room, a little bit distracted.

Mihalis snatched the manuscript away from him. "On second thought, I want to give it another draft. Then I'll let you see it."

"Suit yourself," Evan said. He put the story down and wandered over to the couch. He picked up a magazine from the coffee table and flipped through it. Mihalis sensed he was trying to wait him out, but Mihalis could sit in silence on the other side of the room for a year if necessary, sipping his clouded *ouzo* as the ice disappeared into his drink. He would show his cagey friend.

Mihalis wouldn't even consider publication anyway; the thought of some dim-witted editor censoring his work was unfathomable, and publishing under a repressive regime, whether literature of protest or otherwise, seemed to validate the dictators in a way that Mihalis was not interested in doing. Then again, he wondered what good this cessation of art would do. He didn't want to sound elitist, but surely those boneheaded army colonels had no interest in the arts whatsoever, so his publishing strike, as it were, was virtually ineffective.

Instead he and fellow writers exchanged their work on mimeographs they passed among themselves, different colors of ink signaling whose comments were whose. Sometimes, they exchanged work just for the pleasure of reading new work, of new work being read.

Mihalis sat down on the chair across from Evan. "So what occupies your days?" he asked.

"This and that," Evan said. "Translation work, mostly. A book contract with a UK publisher about Elytis."

Mihalis wasn't really listening. He already regretted allowing Evan to read the small amount he had. Truthfully, he had never been one for feedback. He liked to share his work with others but the moment someone said, "Perhaps you don't mean *apartment,* but *high-rise;* perhaps you mean to break the line *here,*" he drifted off. He had made-up arguments with others in his head, or he imagined fucking the said critic's wife. It was his work, and though difficult to admit he well knew that the purpose of sharing his work was for the desired reaction of "Bravo! Splendid. A masterpiece." Any writer who told you otherwise was a liar or a fool. He needed readers to simply answer his *Is this anything?* And then if they said, *Yes, this is something,* he would go on. And if they said, *No, it is nothing,* he would go on too, with more resolve than before, cursing and having imaginary fights with them in his mind.

Mihalis absentmindedly thumbed through the pile of mail that sat on the desk. He looked toward the kitchen, where Evan was now talking with Irini and Anna. He had never felt good showing Evan his work; he always left the exchange feeling angry or defeated. Perhaps because Evan was a critic, a career choice Mihalis found to be a little repugnant. At least fellow writers understood the work that went into the piece, the inability to ever make something perfect. Art, to him, was inherently imperfect. He simply wanted to make something authentic.

He also stopped showing Irini his poems. When they had been younger, first married, he had read them to her or would leave a stack of them on her high-backed chair, and she would delve into them and make small notes in the margins. He had loved to read those scribbles, those little bits of encouragement and admiration, those small, curlicue flower doodles. It was one of the reasons he had fallen in love with her, for the way she made him feel about his writing, and in turn, about himself.

Since they'd reunited, she was generous with but more discerning in her comments; she questioned the metaphors and scrutinized the themes, she wondered if the choice of verb tense was most effective. It drove him mad, this analysis, and it was to the point that if he were writing and she came into the room, he'd stare into space and place a blank sheet in front of him, furrow his brow and look deeply troubled, as if the words inside him would deform or abort if he so much as looked up at her.

But the minute Irini announced she was going out, he wanted to persuade her to stay. He was beginning to need her there in order to work. He knew those strange habits of writers: his friend Aris could only write in a certain café, at a certain table, with a certain pen and an artist's sketch pad. Haido, a novelist who lived on Andros, wrote only on a typewriter at a small desk next to her bed. He had stayed with her once during Irini's estrangement and she had kicked him out during the day so she could write. He knew how her day had gone based on whether they were intimate later that evening, and whether it was gentle, or rough, or absentminded. It had been a short-lived affair. Sometimes, in the bookstore, he'd pick up her latest novel and stare at her face, wondering which characters were based on him, which of the words had been composed when he wandered around the *hora,* which she had written as he stared, distracted, at the work in a small gallery or hiked up a rocky overlook.

Yes, Mihalis found *he* could only work if Irini were in the house *with* him; the moment she left he felt defeated or forlorn or anxious and would hold one key down on the typewriter in frustration or put his paper and pens away—unlike some writers, his medium varied, depending on his mood. He couldn't express this to his wife, though. She'd say, "I'm going for some groceries," and he'd say, "Could you get some nectarines?" instead of "Will you please stay here, *please*?" After all, she had her own life, her own work, things to do; he couldn't expect her to be his obedient muse.

An editor he trusted had asked him and various others to write a humorous piece, a riff on the theme "If I were a dictator." This, perhaps, was something he could get behind. But each time Mihalis began he grew angry, and the result was not a satirical essay or a poem but fiction, the opening beats of which Evan had read, and the deadline blew past and his piece had not been included. No matter. He had been rereading the Russians and Eastern Europeans lately, mostly books taken from his sister's living room and den—like the one his sly friend had been pressing on his niece, so predictable it made him sick—and they had inspired him to write a short story, his first.

The story was set in an unnamed Latin American country under an unnamed dictatorship. In the story, the townspeople began, one by one, to lose their hands, their feet, a random limb or organ. They woke up crippled or paralyzed. One man woke to find his liver sitting atop his dresser, another woman stumbled out of bed to her alarm clock and found smooth, worn stumps where her feet used to be. Others lay in comas. To satirize the colonels' demand that all contents of a book be announced in its title, he counted words. Currently, the story was called "Five Thousand Four Hundred and Twenty-nine."

He wasn't sure where the story was going. And he had no sense if it were any good. One friend, Dino—who only wrote in the mornings, before the sun—said you never knew if your work was good but despite all the doubt you loved it anyway. It was like having children, he said. Dino had five children, and Mihalis took his word. The draft was unfinished, and his intention in giving it to Evan was for suggestions on how to end, but as he saw Evan's eyes tracing over the text, he knew he wasn't ready to hear from him. He couldn't pinpoint why exactly, but he knew it had to do with the perfectly cheerful conversation Evan and Anna were having when Mihalis walked in.

26

Dimitri did not want to leave his place in Filothei, and Eleni was happy in Halandri, so they were like two goats face-to-face on a narrow mountain path. Eleni was relieved at this standstill, as much as she was that the idea of marriage was politely, nonchalantly shirked. Neither was interested in marrying again. As much as she cared for Dimitri, she couldn't rid herself of the thought that if they did indeed live together, she would be miserable. Not to mention the various levels of judgment she'd have to deal with; the woman across the street alone, with the way she'd watch Dimitri leave some mornings, was enough for her. And now that she had been running the underground medical clinic out of the Lottery Place apartment, she was happy for the space. It wasn't that she had become so set in her ways, her habits, that she couldn't welcome someone else into her home. But if he moved in, it would be Dimitri's house, in the same way that the plural noun, when any males were involved, took the masculine form. Besides, Dimitri's house in Filothei was beautiful, far more grand than their modest place, and she couldn't imagine him giving it up. And for this she was grateful.

Fridays, when Andreas was done with classes he came by the Lottery Place clinic, where Eleni had begun to give him a crash course in medicine, trying to suppress the nagging sensation that perhaps this violated the Hippocratic oath. Andreas was a natural, an incredibly quick learner. While at first his role had primarily been to direct those in need to her, after a few months Eleni noticed he was interested in hands-on work, so she began to show him the basics: how to check a patient's blood pressure, how to determine if a person was in shock, how to check for signs of a concussion. He listened to their lungs, he checked for internal bleeding. Teaching him gave her great satisfaction. In fact, Andreas said to her one afternoon, "Maybe you're the one who should have been the teacher."

"And you the doctor," Eleni answered, blushing. It was true. He had such compassion, such heart. Eleni didn't doubt he was an excellent teacher himself, but he was a natural healer. He put people at ease, he put *her* at ease, and when the day was over she felt sad to leave him and looked forward to the following week. Their effortless conversation reminded her of her rapport with Christos, the only other man with whom she could so easily speak. Even their disagreements were splendid. If she was not careful, Andreas could capsize her heart, and though sometimes she missed the sort of passion she had with Christos she feared it like no other danger. So she would focus on their working lives together.

About their underground clinic word had spread quietly, hopefully among those *with* them, and on Fridays from three until six they took walk-in patients. It wasn't just those recently released from prison and in need of medical care whom she saw, but also those who had either evaded being arrested or had long ago been released. Many were simply afraid to visit any hospital where their names might be noted, worried they might be rounded up and taken away.

So much energy, she realized, was spent just trying to stay under the radar. Young women her daughters' age came to her for birth control; other women came needing abortions. While she could often help with the former, for the latter she did not have the resources. But, along with Andreas, she was able to refer them to someone who did, a whole network of people underground. He was unbelievably connected and seemed to become more and more so each day.

And then there were those who had been arrested and released because they had grown too sick. To no one's surprise, they were given shoddy, minimal care while incarcerated, only to get worse and return to their normal lives sicker than ever. Patients with TB and pneumonia, asthma and viral infections.

A too-damaged patient, though, made the colonels nervous; Eleni had heard they also employed doctors to see just how much torture a prisoner could take. Someone emerging in too bad of shape would be a testament to the torture the colonels were adamant was not occurring. Eleni couldn't imagine what sort of doctor would agree to such a position. If *this* was not a gross violation of the Hippocratic oath, Eleni didn't know what was.

Some weekdays, after work, Eleni stopped at Lottery Place to drop off more supplies she had taken from the hospital, robbing Peter to pay Paul. She'd phone Andreas and the two of them would have a glass of wine or beer on the back porch together, enjoying the spring night, talking about their days. She learned, for instance, that he had a son who lived with his mother, in Nea Smyrni. He was six and wanted to be an astronaut. Eleni didn't ask when Andreas had gotten divorced or if he had been married; she tried not to think of it too much.

For the neighbors to see some sort of everyday, relaxed activity there was good. Once, Eleni overheard Andreas telling Mrs. Triantafillou that he was separated from his wife. This gossip was enough to keep the old woman satisfied and not too suspicious, though it did further pique Eleni's curiosity. Had the statement been for the old lady's benefit or for hers, to remind her that he was single? He also told her Eleni was his cousin, and Eleni wasn't sure how to take this. What to call a man who was neither a lover nor husband but something just as significant? Andreas knew about Dimitri but usually didn't mention him. Some Fridays he showed up looking polished and pressed, as if he were going somewhere else afterward. Eleni couldn't entertain the idea that he had dressed up for her. She tried not to think of it too much. In that apartment the workings of their regular lives were suspended.

They shared a secret, a new context, and that alone was rife with possibility. And there was delight in such a secret, something that was not shared with her children or her brother or Dimitri, something independent of their histories. But it was not merely about having something of her own. The tentative, promising friendship between herself and Andreas brought something more profound: a release from sadness. Since her relationship with Dimitri began, they were rarely apart. Though they kept their separate residences, they saw each other almost every day. She realized she sometimes felt lonelier after having met Dimitri than she had felt before, and the contrast of the high she'd feel around Andreas made her time with Dimitri feel a little flat, but to do anything about it seemed far too complicated and exhausting. Dimitri was a good man, stable, reliable. She didn't want to hurt him. He cared for her. She cared for him. Wasn't that enough?

27

Evan had taken it upon himself to oversee Anna's literary instruction—science was fine, he said, and necessary, but she would be unwise to overlook the humanities, and each time he'd see her, usually near the university, he'd present her with a novel, most often by a foreign writer, or a collection of poems, almost always by a Greek. "The English, the Russians, the French—they do the novel well," he said. "But poetry belongs to Greece." Evan rarely suggested women writers, a fact Anna had challenged. She liked to argue with him if for nothing more than to defuse the burgeoning sexual tension she insisted to Panos was not there. Of course, those frequent meetings were coin-

cidental. She was a university student, and she had every right to be
there, more than he, in fact, since he had taught not there but at the
School of Philosophy—he always claimed to be visiting a good friend,
a colleague, he had an office nearby. Still, it did seem each time she ran
into Evan he had something for her.

It had always been like this. The ones who captured Anna's interest treated her with a cool intellect. Men took on a protective, almost
sacred adoration with her, and she had mixed feelings about it. Even
Panos, who Stella insisted was in love with Anna, treated her more like
a sister, though this was fine with Anna. She liked Panos but she didn't
lie in bed thinking of him. While some of her friends complained that
men didn't take them seriously enough, Anna wished she'd be taken
more lightly. Would it kill one of them to not give a damn what she
thought? To only want her for her body?

It was a nice body, she thought, slim hipped and narrow in the
way that was fashionable. Her hair was straight and long; she supposed she was pretty enough. But by the time Sophie was her age she
had seemed to accumulate far more crushes and boys calling for her
attention and whistling to her on the street, gestures at which Sophie
would roll her eyes, but Anna could see, below the artifice, that she
had been pleased.

Panos was skeptical; he saw the man's interest in the Education of
Anna, as he called it, to be a thinly veiled attempt to get her into bed.

"Why do you insist men only want one thing?" Anna asked him.
They were having coffee together near the university. She spoke slowly
and carefully. In a way, it's exactly what she wanted Evan to want, but
she wondered if he actually made a move in that direction whether
it would be disappointing, or worse, scary. They were in a safe place,
though admittedly teetering there.

"Because it's true," he said. He carefully tapped the last bits of tobacco from his pack out onto a rolling paper, crumpled up the green
package, and shoved it beneath the table leg to steady it. They were
both quiet for a moment as he rolled his cigarette. Then he licked the
edge slowly and sealed it closed, meeting her eyes midway.

"You want to know what I think?" Panos asked.

"You'll tell me anyway."

"Your professor friend," he said, blowing smoke off to the side, "is one crafty *kamaki*."

Anna opened her bag for some money to pay their tab and ignored Panos's comment about Evan knowing how to "spear" women. Evan wasn't exactly using erotic seduction techniques on her: inside her bag was Kafka's story "In the Penal Colony," which Evan had been shocked she hadn't yet read. "He's known me since I was this tall," she told Panos, holding her hand up to the height of the small coffee table.

"Exactly," Panos said. "He's had plenty of time to rehearse his plan."

Anna laughed. She took a drag of Panos's cigarette and blew smoke across the table at him. He leaned back in his chair.

Panos was more perceptive than Anna would have liked. True, her feelings for Evan had started as a silly crush, something to think about; he was an object of affection that seemed too unattainable. Not only was she the niece of his friend, but he was refined and educated, well dressed, such a beautiful, tragic face. Not to mention more than twenty years her senior. It was not as if she were so naïve as to think marriage precluded him from relations with other women—just with her. With a city full of beautiful women, women more experienced, more interesting, more gorgeous and elegant than she, the whole idea had seemed amusing.

At first.

Crafty or otherwise, he stayed in her mind like the remains of a dream. Anna found herself looking for him at cafés or going to places she thought he might be, and when she'd be lucky enough to run into him, she'd affect a sort of surprise or banal disinterest, depending on her mood, and she wondered, worried, really, if this were obvious, because once he smirked at her in a way—perhaps she had imagined it, but it was a very brief but very knowing glance—that suggested she had been caught. On the rare occasion she had use of her mother's car, she drove by his house, or made Stella drive by while she ducked down and shouted, "Do you see him?" Sometimes, they wore cowboy hats or wigs, things pilfered from the basement, strange costumey things that had accumulated there. Panos did not know about this; such antics were not to be revealed to the other side.

Once Anna had finished her coffee, she stood up and straightened her skirt. "I'm going shopping," she said. A spontaneous decision. "Want to come?"

Panos rolled his eyes, then heaved himself to his feet dramatically.

"You're really something today," she told him.

"Shopping? Really?" Panos asked.

"Yes, Panos. Shopping. It's not so strange." For her, admittedly, it was.

It was a beautiful June day, and Ermou Street, which ran from Syntagma Square to Kerameikou Park, was crowded with shoppers. The shady cafés tucked in the small perpendicular streets were full of people enjoying their Saturday morning.

Anna tried on clothes. Since they'd left the café, Panos had wanted to know when she'd become interested in what she wore. He was annoyed, almost offended. He himself was boyish and distracted and seemed to dress in anything available to him, mostly things off the floor, a fact that Anna knew drove his mother crazy. In his closet were finely pressed, beautiful cotton shirts and well-cut trousers. His mother said he found his clothes in the garbage, discarded off the boats in the port of Piraeus. Once, Anna had admired a gray wool sweater he wore, new and thickly knit, and the next day he gave it to her. "I have dozens of these," he said. Anna wore the sweater often.

But again, Panos was right. She had always regarded Sophie's preening and dressing as some sort of character flaw. Anna preferred things comfortable, soft, and usually men's: her father's old sweaters, co-opted by Sophie, abandoned, and now for Anna to wear. Taki's old button-up uniform shirts. Panos knew this. Often he joked at her choice of outfits. "Did you dress in the dark?" he'd ask. So to see her trying on short, knit dresses and tall boots threw him off. And, for some reason, made him hostile.

"I like your oxfords," he said. "With the scuffed tips. And I like your clogs."

She motioned to the salesclerk to bring her size in a tall pair of tan boots, similar to a pair Sophie had left behind, a little too big for Anna, and a pair of platform sandals. She bought them both. Suddenly the thought of looking more feminine, more sexy, more adult, did not sound so bad.

A few days later, dressed in a lavender-gray dress and her new sandals, Anna met Evan for coffee at a café in Kolonaki. It was only part coincidence this time because Evan had made it clear that was where he'd be. Anna liked the café, and she liked sitting there with Evan. As with each of their previous meetings, he began by asking her about the most recent book she was reading for him. That day, the Kafka sat between them. She picked it up and turned it over in her hands as she talked. She wasn't really aware of what she was saying, though; she was waiting for him to take the book from her, brush her hands as he did, wanting to find a passage to read to her. But as she talked on, Evan seemed distracted. He kept glancing over his shoulder.

Immediately Anna was sure it was Simone, or perhaps another person Evan knew. And part of her wished it would be. Though nothing had happened between them—*"Yet,"* she heard Panos say in her head—part of her wanted some sort of outside recognition of their relationship. Not Simone's of course but from a friend, a colleague. She felt bad about this impulse; it could only lead to trouble.

But it wasn't Simone or a friend but Mihalis, who circulated the café as if looking for someone, pausing beside the tables to size the patrons up.

Anna snapped her gaze back to Evan, expecting to see some unease in his eyes. Instead, he simply looked curious, almost bemused. If anything, Anna thought he might walk over to her uncle. But he kept watching from their table.

Mihalis pulled a chair to the center of the room, the dragging legs making a horrible sound on the tile floor. He climbed atop the chair, his hands in the air like a conductor waiting to start, the orchestra's attention on him. Some waiters had even stopped moving, balancing large trays in the air. When he had the attention of the entire bistro, he drawled, his voice full of sarcasm and scorn, "You pigs. Eat." Then he said it again, slower and louder: *"Eat. You pigs."* After, he turned and left.

The restaurant murmured; some people seemed uncomfortable (*Yes, we are bourgeois pigs, aren't we*) and some laughed (*Silly poet*). Anna wanted people to stop laughing at her uncle. She worried the restaurant owner would call the police. She realized those who had laughed at first had done so out of shock or discomfort. No one was laughing now. In fact, the entire place seemed embarrassed, like children reprimanded by someone other than a parent.

Evan raised his eyebrows. "He's seemed unstable lately. That is, more than usual."

"No," Anna said. "He's always been this way." But she was aware that perhaps Evan knew him in a way she never had. The situation had flustered her, and Evan had subdued his charming flirtation a bit, so she felt again as if she were with an uncle or a tutor.

After they finished their drinks, she and Evan walked together awhile. She wondered if Mihalis had seen them. She hoped not. She didn't think she was necessarily doing anything wrong, but she didn't feel particularly open about the whole situation. Whatever it was. On the walk Evan explained to her that the café had been shabby and comfortable, and when the owner decided to remodel, the clientele grew more upscale. He covered the tables with white tablecloths, and the food was suddenly more expensive. The owner was often photographed with men with whom years before he never would have considered keeping company. When Mihalis had pointedly asked him what he had done, the owner had replied, "You can still write your poems atop white linen. But I, my friend, have got to make a living."

Soon, they found themselves outside Evan's place, a beautiful old neoclassical house in Kolonaki. She had never been inside before, though she had passed by many times. "Why don't you come in awhile?" he said, his voice low. Just like that.

It was strange to be inside. He went to help her remove her trench coat, also new, but she shrugged it off quickly; he hung it on a rack in the foyer. She lingered in his library, one hand delicately fiddling with her earlobe or pushing back her hair, the other tucked behind her back. She admired the art on his walls, the shelves packed with books. She ran her fingers softly across the spines; she took one volume down and held it in front of her to examine, exposing one very fine wrist. Inexperienced, maybe, but she was no fool—and she felt him moving across the room to her. Then, maybe thinking again, he disappeared into the kitchen to fix something to drink.

She was demure enough to ease herself into a frenzy of flirtation but not quite deft enough to know what to do once she was deep within its ranks. She was old enough to lure the man to the bedroom but not sophisticated enough to know what followed, like a cat who catches a mouse but has no idea what to do with it afterward; paws it back and forth awhile, and, uncertain of the next step, leaves it there, trotting away to something else. No killer instinct. She didn't have the skill to back out tactfully, or maybe she didn't want to, but when she heard the unexpected rattle of keys in the door and the sound of a little girl crying, she cringed.

Evan reappeared quickly, empty-handed, to greet his wife and daughter. His expression was no longer relaxed or flirtatious. The muscles in his face had tightened, his eyes narrowed. Anna stood awkwardly by the bookshelf. "You know Anna," he said. "Mihalis's niece." Anna wished she could disappear beneath the rug. "She's picking up some books for Mihalis."

Simone was distracted; her light hair fell from its bun, and her own trench coat, certainly from London and of which Anna's looked like a cheaper imitation, fell off one shoulder, as if she were in too much of a hurry to take it off. Her dress was a blue Liberty print. Anna could have been standing there naked for all she cared; already her own short dress made her legs feel suddenly too bare. "Aliki is sick, and I have to get back to the school. I was hoping you'd be home." Simone taught English at the British day school.

"I was just on my way out," Evan said. "I've got a meeting. I was going to drive Anna home and say hello to Eleni."

Simone looked desperate. "I also need to go to the pharmacy and the market. Then a meeting at Aliki's school." She stopped and took a breath. "Aliki has a fever. She's exhausted. She's burning up."

Anna, feeling some need to atone for what might have happened there, spoke up. "I'll watch her," she blurted, and of course immediately regretted it. Was she insane? She had never babysat in her life. And what was Evan talking about? He'd said nothing about a meeting, let alone driving her home.

"Really?" Simone asked. Her face brightened, and for a moment Anna thought she was going to kiss her. "You don't mind? I'll just be gone a few hours."

"Sure," she said.

The little girl looked up at her through large, watery eyes. "Can you read stories?"

"Of course," Anna said.

Evan kissed his daughter and his wife and walked out the front door, his hands in his pockets, barely giving Anna a glance. "Talk later," he said to no one in particular. Evan ended their meetings this way: "We'll talk later." And Anna always wanted to grab him, to cry out, to shake him: "When's later? An hour? A week? A month?" But it would be admitting too much.

"You don't know how grateful I am," Simone said. "I'll be back as soon as I can. Help yourself to anything." Then she too was gone.

Anna led Aliki up to her bedroom, all the while listening for Evan to return. After she'd read her the same story four or five times, she realized he probably wasn't coming back. Was this his way of asserting that indeed nothing was going on? To her, or to himself? She put her hand on the little girl's forehead, which was hot. She brought her a glass of water, which she drank with her eyes closed. Soon, Aliki was asleep.

When Anna went back downstairs, she didn't let herself glance into Evan and Simone's bedroom. She didn't like seeing these more intimate, quotidian details of his life. She knew nothing of Simone. Was she nice to him? Did they make love every night? Downstairs, she looked around the kitchen. She saw two wineglasses Evan must have retrieved to pour them each a drink. She had the urge to smash them. Instead, she wrapped one in a napkin and put it in her bag. She telephoned Stella, but her father said she was out. She could take the bus, but the thought seemed exhausting, all those people, and she needed the reassurance of a familiar face. So she tried Panos. "Listen," she said. "I'm going to need a ride home later. Will you come get me?"

While Aliki slept, Anna sat on the back porch and stared out at the small but well-tended garden. After two hours, Simone returned and thanked Anna profusely. "Evan's not back yet?" she asked.

Anna shook her head. When Simone tried to give her some money, Anna refused.

"Next time, then," Simone said. "If we can call you again?"

"Sure," Anna said.

When Panos arrived in his older brother's car with the loud muffler, she dashed out of the house. He looked at her, incredulous. "Babysitting?" he asked.

"Please," she said, tugging at the hem of her short dress. "Don't ask."

They were quiet for several blocks, moving out of the neighborhood to the main street back to Halandri, but Anna could tell Panos had not dropped the issue. "What exactly is going on between the two of you?" he asked.

"Nothing," she said.

"Seems like nothing," Panos said.

"Why does everything have to be defined? Spouse, lover, boyfriend, mistress. Why can't it just be what it is? Uncategorizable? Complicated."

"Everything is categorical. Complicated things."

"Not true. Stop treating me like I'm naïve."

"Believe me. I know you're not naïve."

"I should have called Stella for a ride. Or taken the bus."

"Then why didn't you?"

"Why are you so angry at me?"

He lowered the window and let the warm breeze fill the car. He tossed his cigarette butt into the street. "Nothing good will come of this. You know that, don't you?" Then a car cut in front from a side street. "*Ela, malaka!*" Panos yelled, throwing his hands up.

Anna stared out the window. Of course she did.

Panos didn't bring up the incident again, and neither did she. Weeks later, she and Panos met with friends to talk about summer holidays. But while her friends wanted to stay at Stella's family home on Hydra, Anna couldn't help but wonder what Evan was doing, and she grew anxious at the thought of a long summer without him. When they'd meet, she always meant to ask him of his plans, but then somehow the question seemed too personal, or she feared obtaining more information than she would like. But she hoped he would be on Hydra; she knew he often went there, and with its proximity to Athens, its chic, artsy vibe, it was a definite possibility.

Since she was fourteen she had been invited to spend a week with Stella's family on Hydra, but this would be the first time she would travel alone, only with friends. Her mother didn't like the sound of it, but finally she just told her to be careful and to not come back pregnant. She had heard her mother say something similar to Sophie, years before, when she had gone to the islands; she had heard her tell Taki, before a trip to Kyparissia, that if he got mixed up with a village girl he'd be sorry. It was always related to travel. Meanwhile, they could have sex in all the corners of Athens, in broad daylight, and no one said boo.

Except she wasn't having sex in all the corners of Athens. It had happened only twice, a fact of which she was sure her mother was unaware. She was fifteen, in the back shed of her own garden, after school, her siblings not yet home and her mother still at work. The boy, S., had been a few years older, a friend of Taki's, and he and his family had moved to Thessaloniki soon afterward. It was neither enjoyable nor unpleasant, and Anna remembered both times being over very quickly, though S. certainly acted like he knew what he was doing.

But Anna had been young, probably too young, and it wasn't that she lost interest in boys but nothing after that seemed to progress beyond a friendly good-night kiss. It hadn't been until recently that she began to experience fierce, incessant arousal, and now she often called to mind those moments with more nostalgia and revision: instead of her school uniform and braid, she wore a dress she didn't own but had only conjured in her mind; her hair was long and unkempt; she led him into the house, loosening his tie and kissing his neck. There were no grumblings and fumblings nor the sounds of the neighbors preparing dinner in the distance but instead complete, impenetrable silence. And soon his face was not that of the neighborhood boy but the dark, brooding face of Evan.

Not even Stella knew the extent of their association; by the day it grew more inappropriate than she wanted to admit. Such things often moved exponentially, not linearly, and she had felt a gain in momentum. No one knew that late afternoons, for instance, while her mother was still at work, she and Evan had begun to talk on the phone. First he'd called to apologize for the babysitting, though whether he had indeed had a meeting he didn't bother clarifying, and Anna didn't ask. Did it matter? And then, once he'd made that first call, the others just began to come. Sometimes, they'd talk for an hour, until Evan would quietly say, *I should go.* This usually meant Simone had suddenly appeared. Anna would always say, *Okay,* and she'd wait for the gentle click of the receiver on his end. After a few of these conversations Anna realized it was too difficult for her to say good-bye to him, as if each conversation were a continuation of the last, each replaced receiver simply a pause. She imagined him behind the closed door of his den, behind his desk, which faced the doorway, his back to the large windows that overlooked the garden. She remembered that cognac-colored chair with the brass studs, the rows of bookshelves, the way atop a small, antique table sat a wooden tray and a crystal decanter of whiskey. Most of her fantasies involved that den, the desk, the chair.

While the first call had been spontaneous and taken her by surprise, now, in the laziness of summer, a few days without hearing from him was excruciating. Sometimes she rushed home in hopes that this might be a phone day, and when it wasn't, and she had abandoned her friends somewhere swimming or seeing a late-afternoon matinee, she grew angry at herself. But not enough, because she found herself doing it again and again.

At the end of July, on the feast of the Dormition of St. Anna, one week before she'd go to Hydra, she was sure he'd call. But when the afternoon turned to evening, she was hit with the sinking sensation that he wouldn't. She knew *his* name day was March 25. Surely he knew other Annas who celebrated on this day? How could he not be thinking of her?

Though she usually observed her name day in December, she had been sick and unable to celebrate. Her mother proposed they would have a party in July. As they were preparing, she called Evan at home, something she had never done. In fact, he had never even given her his number, but she obtained it easily enough by looking through one of Mihalis's old address books he had left in the basement. When he answered, it sounded as though he had been laughing, in the middle of a conversation, a joke, and she could hear the sound of merrymaking in the background: music, voices, clinking glasses.

"Hello?" he said again. Anna quickly hung up the phone. She had not seen him in over a week, nor had she heard from him in days, and she told herself to simply get him off her mind. Obviously she was not on his.

That night, as many of her friends began to arrive, Anna found herself missing not Evan but her siblings. Sophie's birthday was in late October, when the nights began to get cool, and they had always held bonfires in the empty lot across the street. Their friends would gather until late, drinking coffee or beer, listening to music, telling stories. It was a rite of passage, a farewell to the summer. Spyro always brought his guitar, and another his *bouzouki,* and they'd entertain the neighborhood. How a younger Anna had loved to wander through the crowd, entranced by the behavior of teenagers, as if they were some other strange breed. She would comb the field the morning after, finding abandoned packs of cigarettes and chewing gum, barrettes and hair ties, cardigans left draped over rocks. And for some reason, becoming a teenager to Anna meant these things: a bonfire and a large group of friends, singing songs, couples sneaking off to dark places and abandoning more than their sweaters.

But the threat of fires and the intense heat made a bonfire impossible. So instead they lit up the garden once again, as they had done when Taki had left, and her mother prepared trays of *mezedes* and later scooped out bowls of melting pistachio ice cream. She wanted to call Evan again and invite him, but one phone call was enough. And, already, he was celebrating something else, away from her.

Soon, neighbors came from their houses, and other friends wandered over or arrived on motorbikes or in taxis. Even Spyro, who had since moved to Washington, DC, for school but was home for the summer, came by with some friends, and Anna felt proud as they paid her a lot of attention. She tried not to wonder why her own siblings didn't return for the summer. Stella's older sister had joined them, too, a wispy girl with straight, black hair and a doll's complexion, whom Spyro immediately zeroed in on. He played songs on the guitar and passed around a bottle of whiskey he kept in his jacket. One of them in particular resonated with Anna: it was called "April," by Mikis Theodorakis. Although the original song had an upbeat melody, the way Spyro played it in a minor key, slowing down the tempo, was haunting.

Later, she saw Stella's sister and Spyro kissing in the street, his guitar pitched carelessly on the curb, and Anna felt that tug underneath her belly button. She imagined Evan kissing her like that in some foreign city, away from all of this. She grew angry that he hadn't acknowledged her name day and didn't want to spend the next week in Athens, wondering if she'd see him.

When most of the guests had left, Anna sat with Panos and Stella on the roof, staring at the sky. Stella lay in the chair and drifted in and out the conversation, half-asleep.

"Let's leave tomorrow, instead," Anna said. "Let's do something different." But *Screw Evan* is what she thought.

"Like what?" Panos asked. Though he seemed game for anything.

Out of nowhere, she blurted, "I've always wanted to see Samothraki. Less touristy. We can still end up on Hydra."

Panos didn't miss a beat. "We can visit my cousin," he said. "In Alexandroupolis. And go from there."

The next morning she woke early to pack her bag. First she, Panos, and Stella would take the train to Alexandroupolis to visit Panos's cousin Kostas. It was a long trip, but the idea of a train ride with friends sounded fun and new. They'd continue to the island for a few days and eventually, even though it was close to Athens and not Samothraki, they'd end up on Hydra as originally planned, to stay in Stella's family's home. They had plenty of time. The summer was open with possibility, and Anna felt at turns anxious and delighted and perhaps a mixture of both.

On the train, they sat in a compartment with a table between them, Anna and Panos on one side and Stella on the other. Anna tried to concentrate on her book—Chekhov's short stories, which she found boring but Evan had gone on about—but mostly she daydreamed, staring out the window at the blurs of pink and white oleander, of olive trees, poplars, and cypress. When the sun set she closed her eyes and tried to sleep. Panos covered her with his sweater.

Somewhere near Xanthi they were startled awake by a passport check. The train slowed and stopped, an eerie cessation of motion that woke Anna immediately. Her head was on Panos's shoulder, and his threadbare white T-shirt was soft on her cheek. Anna handed the guard her passport and tried to smile but the officer didn't return the gesture. Instead, he descended from the train into the darkness.

"What's going on?" Stella whispered. She was a confident, even arrogant girl and had already spent two nights in jail for playing banned music. In Halandri, the night after the big stadium gathering, they'd been lucky. But Stella lived in a more densely inhabited neighborhood, where more space was shared and communal living space could betray you. She was Anna's only friend so far who'd been arrested. Now, startled from sleep, she looked frightened, which in turn frightened Anna.

"I think he just stole our passports," Panos said.

"Come on," Anna said. "It's just a routine passport check. Happens all the time." Truth was, she had never witnessed anything like it, but she wanted to appear slightly more experienced than she was. Her words seemed to reassure her friends even if they didn't actually believe them, and they slouched back in their chairs, waiting. They were near the Turkish border, and the Bulgarian one, too, and it seemed as good an explanation as any.

When the guard finally returned, he handed back their passports without a word. When he came to Anna, though, he held hers in his hand and looked squarely at her face. "Come with me, my girl," he said.

Stella looked at her with surprise. Panos futilely asked, "Where are you taking her?"

The guard stepped off the train, and Anna followed him. It was dark, and save for the background buzz of the cicadas, silent. There was no railway platform, just a dusty, gravelly road running along the tracks. The night was cool. He walked quickly, and Anna had a hard time keeping up with him. The ground was uneven, and pebbles kept lodging in her shoes. She thought for sure she would twist her ankle. She concentrated on not losing her clogs. She had no idea where they were going. Had others been pulled off the train as well, or just her? She kept glancing back, wondering if her friends could see her out the train's windows. But of course they couldn't; beyond the soft lights of the train it was pitch-black.

Finally, they reached a small cabin, and Anna followed the guard inside. Behind a desk lit only by a dim pharmacy-style lamp sat a large man in an unbuttoned military shirt, untucked, his undershirt showing. It gave the appearance of pajamas. When he saw her, he ran his hand through his hair, clearly recently woken for this interrogation.

"Are you a student?" the pajama man asked. He cleared his throat.

"Yes, sir," said Anna.

"University?"

"Polytechnic."

"Impressive," he said. "A girl at the Polytechnic."

"I'm not the only one," Anna said.

"You look too young." He stood up and came around to her side of the desk, staring at her. *Too young for what?* Anna wondered. Then he leaned close and tucked her hair behind her ear, brushing her cheek with his fingers. Anna flinched at his touch. "Sit down," he said, pointing at the wooden chair facing his desk. She did.

He began to ask her more questions, as if her youthful appearance were a very covert disguise. Did she know this person or that person? (No, she didn't.) Had she ever been to Kavala before? Alexandroupolis? (Yes, both, when she was a toddler). She thought maybe this interrogation had something to do with Sophie or Mihalis, maybe even Stella, who was waiting on the train, but they didn't ask about any of them, and she was grateful. But they asked about her siblings, generally. She lied and told them both were studying in the States.

The man circled her, never quite staying in one place. She didn't know where to look. She felt at any moment he might strike her. Her body felt rigid, and she found herself clutching the wooden seat of her chair with both hands.

After a pause, he asked, "Your father?"

She didn't know how to respond. Were they asking who he was

or what he did? They didn't seem to know or care who he was. They were looking for someone specific, and it wasn't her. "Deceased, sir."

"How long?"

"Fourteen years."

When the two men stepped to the other side of the room, mumbling to each other, Anna had the urge to run. But where? Back to the train? Then she would really seem guilty. She couldn't hear what they were saying, but it was clear they were disagreeing. She strained to hear, sitting up straighter and cocking her head slightly, and she somehow threw herself off balance and the chair creaked. Then the man came back to her and placed a rough hand on her shoulder.

"Stand up," the man demanded. He nearly knocked the chair out from under her.

Anna was small and felt even smaller as he shoved her across the room, nudging her in the shoulder with the butt of his rifle toward a narrow door. Her first thought was that it was an interrogation room, but when he opened the door she saw it was a small broom closet. He shoved her inside and she had to jut her hands out to catch herself. She collided with the brooms and mops leaned up against the wall. She froze like that, her hands up against the coarse wood wall, the man in the doorway behind her.

Anna thought she knew what was next and wondered how she could shove past him, a man more than twice her size. But he didn't touch her.

"Bitch," he said through clenched teeth. Then he shut her in the tiny closet, in the dark. She slid to the ground. Beyond the door, she could hear his boots stalk back and forth across the floor. Someone leaned back in a chair and she heard the springs squeak.

Finally, both men opened the door. The guard who had found her on the train said, "Not the one we're looking for. A *synnonymia*."

The officer jerked Anna to her feet. He held the passport next to her face to compare her photo. "Now," he said. "You'd better hurry back to the train." He dropped the passport on the floor, at her feet. "Or you'll miss it."

Anna scrambled to pick it up. The two men laughed, and Anna dashed out the door into the dark.

As she ran, she kept slipping out of her shoes on the uneven ground. Finally, she took them off and ran barefoot over the sharp gravel, toward the lights of the train. It hurt, but it was better than being left behind.

When she climbed back onto the train, Anna didn't know if it had been waiting only for her or for others as well, or if its idling was sheer luck. She let out a burst, a sort of compressed sob, and then pulled herself together. She was sweating, despite the cool night, and could barely catch her breath. As a child she had had horrible asthma, and she could feel her lungs tightening, unable to expel enough air. Back at her compartment, she saw the grave looks on her companions' faces before they saw her. Anna stood in the doorway, her chest heaving, her shoes still in her hand.

When they asked her what had happened, Anna was too exhausted to recount the whole experience. She would tell them the story later, or most of it anyway, when she caught her breath and the sun rose and the early morning light filled their cabin. At first even imagining herself retelling it made her feel ashamed, as if it portrayed some sort of weakness. And then, as the train began to move only minutes after she had boarded, Anna went over the experience in her mind. She grew enraged at the humiliation.

The simple awareness of the dictators stealthily altered both public and private space, and every so often, it burst out like this: a frightening lump, a jagged edge, an eerie, alarming wail.

Anna stared out the window at the blackness, wondering if she would ever again see any of the towns and villages through which they had passed. Anna thought about the way she had lied about Sophie. Why had she said her siblings were both in the States? What if they had known otherwise? She thought of what she and Evan had talked about after Mihalis had come into the café and berated the diners, about the way everyone, herself included, was always trying to escape culpability. Involvement in one cause alleviated disinvolvement in another. If you help the old woman carry her groceries, you can ignore the beggar in the street.

Across from her, Panos, his longish black hair drooped over his face, seemed to move in and out of sleep, restless and uncertain. He often jumped or twitched, and sometimes he'd stretch his leg out and place his stockinged foot next to her hip, as if to make sure she was still there. When he opened his eyes, he'd look at Anna a moment and then close them again. Anna now felt too guarded to sleep on the train; she knew Panos would understand why. His family, mostly from Crete, remembered the bombings by Nazi planes, hiding underground and hoping they wouldn't be blown to pieces. Panos himself had been born after the war, but his family stories had imprinted in him a sense of urgency. But though his presence soothed her, it didn't make her feel protected. She closed her eyes and imagined Evan, which calmed her down awhile.

After arriving in Alexandroupolis and having lunch with Panos's cousins, they took a boat to Samothraki, supposedly a hiker's paradise, unspoiled beauty, not many tourists. Panos and Kostas napped on a bench in the shade, and Anna and Stella sat on the top deck of the boat, the sun warm on the tops of their heads. In the distance, she could make out the faintest outline of land.

At the youth hostel, Anna opened the doors to the tiny balcony and stood outside. Purple bougainvillea spilled violently around the railing, and she could smell the sea so close. She looked out at the port, the smattering of lights. People ate at the tavernas below. She was hungry and soon they'd go for dinner. Somewhere in the distance she thought she heard the low beat of a discothèque.

Were they all visitors, like she was? It always surprised her—even though she knew it shouldn't—that people actually lived on these islands, that these beautiful places had a role beyond a summer vacationing ground. Perhaps some felt that way about Athens.

Early the next morning when she and Stella woke, Panos and Kostas were in the small downstairs sitting area, drinking fresh orange juice and eating anise-flavored cookies; they must have gone out. They were bent over a travel guide—if the island was so untouristy, as Panos had claimed, why was there a travel guide for it?—planning a day hike into the town on the other side of the island, six kilometers away. Anna was not dying to hike through the intense heat that already radiated from the sky, but she did not want to spend the day alone.

The town was nestled in the hills, among dense woods of pine trees. Kostas had a small map he'd check every so often to make sure they were going the right way, and on the rutted dirt road he kept a steady pace, stopping to identify various plants; he was studying biology. Panos was in a hurry and kept forging ahead. Stella was unusually quiet and content to just be outdoors, walking. Anna trudged behind, trying not to drink all the water in her canteen at once. For a short while, a few small, dusty orange butterflies followed them along.

When they finally arrived at Hora, it was midafternoon, and the town seemed deserted. But the red-tiled roofs and cobblestone streets lent the town a quaint, pure feel, a sense of things going on behind closed doors. There were policemen sauntering around but few others. "Where is everyone?" Panos asked.

"It's afternoon. People are sleeping," Anna said.

"What's with all the cops?" Stella's relaxed demeanor immediately shifted.

"We're near Turkey," Panos said, as if that were enough of an explanation. But Anna could tell it made him uneasy. She certainly did not like it. They had run out of water and were hot and cranky, and Anna wished they were back at one of the beaches for an afternoon swim instead of wandering around an unknown village, one from which they now had to hike back. Anna saw what looked like a bus stop, but when she scanned the area for signs of buses or taxis, she didn't see any.

"I'm starving," Kostas said. "You?"

"Let's sit down someplace," Anna said.

They stopped in a small square, across from the statue of the winged Victory, the goddess elegantly descending to her triumphant fleet. "This one's a *gift* from the French for the real one they took from here," Panos said.

Anna knew this, of course; she had heard her uncle rail against the British for taking away "half the Parthenon," against what Greeks called "the foreign finger." She had grown inured to such tirades. Thinking about it now, though, incensed her, and coupled with the heat and the long hike, she was seething. As if they were careless children who couldn't take care of their toys. She began her own small tirade, but quietly, so no one but her friends could hear, about Hellenic art and culture, the theft of ideas and civilization, which led to the apathy of Western countries who sat idly by as fascist regimes persisted. "Didn't the U.S. fight the Nazis to end fascism? Yet now they're so afraid of communism that they look the other way, or better yet, supply these jackasses with guns and tanks."

"True enough," Kostas said. But her friends looked at her strangely, not because of what she was saying but because it was the most she had spoken the entire trip. "I think we need to get something to eat," Panos said, guiding Anna away from the statue by her elbow. "The little one's losing it." But there was something in his touch that indicated she'd impressed him a little bit.

They walked to the center of the village, where they found a small cluster of cafés. No one was sitting outside any of them, which Anna again attributed to the time of day. The island was not a popular tourist destination, and it was always the tourists who crawled around at all hours, their mouths agape and gazes directed everywhere but straight ahead.

But inside one, through the glare of the windows, they saw lots of people moving about.

"Let's go there," Stella said.

"Agreed," said Anna. "The others look closed anyway."

Kostas opened the door to the restaurant, but before they could go in, they were stopped by two men in their forties. Both were thin and wore glasses; they looked like brothers. "Can we help you?" one asked. His voice was soft.

"We'd like to have lunch," Panos said.

"Lunch?" the other man said. "Oh, *paidia*. You can't have lunch here." He said it like a father to his son. Around the room a few of the men at tables turned to watch them. The four friends stood quietly a moment, perplexed.

"We're political prisoners," he finally said. His voice was serious, but his expression seemed almost amused. "This is where they feed us."

Anna looked around the room, at the many gentle faces. They didn't seem like prisoners to her at all. They were just men eating soup. It could have been a university cafeteria, a *kafeneion* in Omonia Square where men gathered to argue and play backgammon.

From the corner, a uniformed man approached them, a rifle at his side. "Go across the way," he said.

"We're terribly sorry," said Panos.

"It doesn't matter."

The four sat down on a nearby bench. Panos rubbed his eyes and put his head in his hands, pulling his hair out of his face and leaning in toward Anna. He shook his head. "*Can we have lunch here?*" he said mockingly.

Anna felt embarrassed, too. She knew that some of the islands were being used as prisons, though she hadn't known this one was. Leros, Yiaros, or Makronisos were the ones she always heard about, and she told her friends how Mihalis had done his time on the latter two, years before. Stella's face grew very dark. She had never talked about being arrested, as if it had never happened. Anna thought of her uncle and wished she could call him right then to see if he was okay. But even if *she* could find a phone, Mihalis, with no phone himself, was unreachable. It was his way of staying off the radar.

And no wonder. What was the alternative? This? It made her feel a little sick. Here she was, gallivanting on an island used as a prison, sitting down for salads and bread at the open taverna farther away. Anna had no appetite. The prisoners probably lived in barracks nearby, but she imagined them all sleeping on the ground, outside, and being rounded up once or twice a day to eat in the café-turned-mess-hall, dusty and achy and exhausted. She felt ashamed and hoped those two men who spoke so kindly to them would forgive her for her ignorance. If she could have gone back, she would have, to apologize again for their self-absorption. She would tell them that the junta was both everywhere and nowhere: people still traveled and went to work; shops were open, people got married and had babies and fell in love. She, too, had simply been living her life.

They stayed on the island that night but then went back to Alexandroupolis. And after days of island hopping, staying in one hotel room to save money, or sometimes with friends, they finally ended up at Stella's family's house on Hydra. Though the trip to Samothraki had been Anna's idea, she was immensely relieved to be able to settle and relax. And for the next three days she did nothing but nap and swim, swim and nap. Eat.

The fourth night, they met others at a taverna. The air had cooled a bit, but the heat of those days at the beach still lingered on her shoulders. She had chosen a blue sundress with flat, brown sandals. Her hair, the longest it had ever been, hung loose past her shoulders, wavy from the saltwater, the tips lightened from the sun, as if they had been dipped in honey. Stella said everyone looked better in the summer, on the islands: the air, the sea, the sun, the charge of it all. Anna agreed.

Their friends sat at a table in the back. She ordered a drink, and Panos did the same. She glanced around the table to say hello to everyone, and at once she saw Evan leaned back in his chair at the next table over. This Anna may have hoped for but certainly did not expect, and she had to focus a few seconds to make sure it was him. Oh, but how she had missed him. His skin was brown with sun. He wore a white linen shirt with the sleeves rolled up. He waved to her, nonchalant, as if they always ran into one another on the islands. A woman next to him, not his wife, spoke into his ear. In front of her was a drink with a little umbrella. Each time Evan caught her eye that night, a sensation shot up Anna's leg and into the pit of her. Sometimes she thought the desire alone would split her in two. She glanced around every so often for Simone, but she was nowhere.

Panos, who had noticed Evan immediately, was expressionless. "How convenient. Maybe you'll do some babysitting while we're here," he said.

Anna didn't say anything. Since that incident, Simone had called Anna once to watch their little girl. It definitely had felt strange, but Anna liked Aliki so much she didn't mind. She kept telling herself, *Nothing is going on.* When Simone insisted on placing some bills in Anna's hand, she didn't object. "Book money," Simone said.

Later, after they had eaten, Evan cornered her as she was leaving the bathroom and pulled her behind the kitchen. She leaned against the wall, and he placed his hands on either side of her shoulders, his arms enclosing her. He loomed over her; she realized here how much larger he was. She could smell his soap, clean and fresh, not the usual barb of his cologne. "Were you going to ignore me all night?" he asked.

Anna, a little drunk now, touched the bridge of his nose, where he had burned in the sun. "What were you expecting?" Here in the island air she felt less constrained, and he seemed much younger: his dress casual, his hair not quite combed, as if he had gone swimming and let it dry any which way. "It seems as though you're following me," Anna said.

"And if I were?"

Anna looked up at him from behind her bangs, which had fallen in her eyes. She smiled.

"I didn't know where'd you'd gone," Evan said. "I called your house, but there was no answer."

"There's a lot you don't know," she said. She was enjoying this. She wanted to stay back there with him, guide his hand between her legs, feel the heat of his skin on hers. This was what it meant to feel yourself losing control and liking it.

Evan had his hand on Anna's hip, sliding down; he had never truly touched her before. Not like this. He looked first at her body and then at her face. Then two of the dishwashers appeared to smoke cigarettes. They looked at them both like they saw this type of display there every night. One rolled his eyes, not impressed. "Bravo," he said, blew smoke in their direction, and they continued talking. Neither made a move to leave.

When she returned to the table, she saw Panos watch her as she sat down, and then she saw his eyes wander past her and notice Evan walking back to his table. "Don't worry, Anna," Panos said. "He'll need a sweet little trifle to finish off his meal." He didn't mention anything else about Evan after that, though he smoked cigarette after cigarette for the rest of the night and seemed particularly flirtatious with the other girls.

But Anna ignored Panos; she was having a great time. Each glance from Evan felt both wonderfully private and new. At one point, he came and sat next to her, and when she told him what had happened on the train, he put his hand on her knee and then her shoulder—not lecherously, but a little proprietary. He seemed more horrified by the incident than she had been. When she left the taverna, late, she and her friends poured out into those narrow streets, and she turned back to see where he was. She was delighted he was watching her, and he held up his hand, a half wave. Panos, who was going off with friends to another club on the beach, snubbed her. Kostas disappeared with the crowd, and Stella went back to the house with a bartender she had had a crush on for years. Had Anna been sober, Panos's snub would have left a knot in her gut, but she was not, and so she took it lightly. Her thoughts, after all, were elsewhere.

In her own room, after she had brushed her teeth and washed her face, she settled into her bed. She was glad she had chosen the smaller room; there was not a balcony with a view, but there were large, shuttered windows. She was happy for the solace, particularly with all the others staying in the house; she was content to sink into herself. Stella, with her parents not there, stayed in the large master bedroom with the grand balcony and separate bathroom; her brothers took a room with bunk beds, where they'd sleep all day. Panos and Kostas would stay on the couches downstairs. Anna had been sure she'd return to the house to find Stella's brothers playing cards at the kitchen table, noisily, but they too had left for a club, and besides Stella and her bartender talking softly on the back porch, the house was quiet.

Anna got up again to get a glass of water and when she was returning upstairs came a knock so light she thought she had conjured it in her mind. She opened the front door.

It was Evan. How had he found her there? Had she told him where it was? Then again, he had been coming to the small island for years, and so had Stella's family. Maybe he simply knew of the place.

She'd barely gotten him up to her room and shut the door before all the tension of the evening, of months and months, poured into the way his lips brushed her cheek and met her bare shoulder, then her neck, then each breast he pushed up from under her camisole. It was as if he didn't have enough hands, the way he was moving so quickly over her body. She unbuttoned his shirt, she kissed his chest, he groaned as she took a nipple in her mouth. Her drawstring pajamas fell to the ground, and he held her up against the ledge of the window a moment,

her legs wrapped around his waist, before he brought her over to the
bed. She didn't care about the others, about Stella and the boy downstairs, or Panos, or this man's wife and daughter asleep somewhere,
happily. She wanted the world to stay suspended like that for the night
and then to return to normal, to rewind, to be able to take it all back
and then do it all again and again, to bring him through the door like
this over and over. And even as she thought this, she knew of course it
was impossible. This was happening, all of it. "It's okay," he said, quietly. "We've been hurtling toward this for some time."

When Anna awoke to the sound of Stella padding through the hallway, Evan was gone. She hurried back into her pajamas just as Stella
thrust open the door. "Can I come in?" she asked, already standing at
the foot of the bed. "Don't think I didn't see from the back porch who
you led upstairs last night." She held her hands on her hips, a huge
smirk on her face.

Oh, God, Anna thought. More of his family were to arrive that
day, on an early boat. Simone and Aliki as well as Simone's mother
and some other friends from London. He had mentioned it at some
point early in the night. Anna took a sip of water from the tumbler
next to her bed and ran her fingers through her hair. "That wasn't supposed to happen," Anna said.

She looked around the room. The thin, white curtains covered
the window, but the morning sun announced itself. She wondered
what time it had been when Evan had left. She had glimpsed him
dressing in the blue morning light and started at the sight of his long,
bare torso, the line of hair down below his belly button, those defined
muscles pointing down in a self-congratulatory V. The perfect state of
his body had startled her; she didn't know what she had imagined, but
it certainly was not this. The thought of it now made her sigh, something deep and guttural. She rolled over onto her front and buried her
face in the pillow, which smelled wonderfully of Evan, and of her. The
both of them. She felt Stella sit down on the bed beside her. "Did you
hear us last night?" Anna asked.

Stella laughed. "Did you hear *us*?"

She hadn't, and this gave Anna a little bit of relief.

She lifted her head up off the pillow and felt a little dizzy. She looked at her friend. "Who else was around last night?"

Stella shrugged. She looked toward the shutters, the slats warm with light. "It's early. I think everyone is still out. I just heard the drunks ringing the church bells. That's what got me up."

Anna flopped over again. Each time she moved the blood pounded behind her eyes and she had to wait for her brain to settle.

Stella was waiting for something, too. Finally she said, "This is a small island, Anna." There was a bit of admonishment in her voice. Though Stella, of all her friends, was the least likely to judge, she was right; if she had run into him once, she was sure she'd see him the rest of the stay. "Come to the kitchen," Stella said, patting Anna's legs. "I'll make coffee."

Anna nodded. "In a minute."

After using the bathroom, Anna went downstairs. Stella's parents would not arrive for another week, and so they had reign of the house: swimming suits and beach towels hung from any available space; bottles of beer and unemptied ashtrays littered every surface. The wreckage of late nights hung in the air. Breakfast dishes, glasses of juice with the pulp sticking to the sides, and orange peels and containers of yogurt remained on the kitchen table. This, she saw now, was what she'd led Evan through on the way up to her bedroom.

"We'll clean later," Stella said. She shoved the mess on the counter aside with her forearm and retrieved the coffee from the cupboard.

Steaming cups in their hands, Anna and Stella went out to the back veranda, where they sat in blue canvas chairs, their feet propped up on the railing. They stared out at the glitter of the water and listened to the drone of the hydrofoils. They watched the large ferries leave and others come in. Stella offered Anna a cigarette. It was far too early for her to smoke but she gladly accepted.

Afterward, Anna felt a little dizzy. "I think I'm going to go back to sleep."

"You okay?" asked Stella.

"Of course," she said.

When Anna woke again it was already afternoon. There was a buzzing in her chest, and she wanted to shout. Someone ran water in the bathroom, but otherwise the house was quiet. Her mother always lamented the fact that when she went on vacation with friends they rarely enjoyed the seaside mornings. "We do," Anna always said. "We watch the sunrise. Then we go to sleep."

As her bare feet dropped to the cool, white tile, she was hit with the feeling that she had done something she would regret. But by the time she made it back downstairs, the feeling had dissipated. She drank a large glass of water. She found a plum from the refrigerator and ate it over the sink, letting the juice dribble down her arm. A girl she only vaguely recognized shuffled past and out the front door. "Morning," she mumbled. Her hair hung over her eyes, and she grinned sheepishly.

"*Kalimera,*" Anna said, mock-cheerfully. She rolled her eyes.

A few minutes later, Panos emerged from the bathroom, shirtless. *Of course,* Anna thought. Anna sat at the kitchen table and put her head in her hands.

"What's wrong with you?" Panos asked.

"I drank too much," she said.

"So," Panos said. "What'd you think of Roula?"

Anna shrugged, her head still down. She remembered talking to her a few nights before. "She has nice teeth," she said dryly.

"You're something else," Panos said. He poured himself some juice. When he tilted his head back to drink it, Anna could count his ribs. "When did the professor leave?"

"What?" asked Anna, looking up.

"The taverna. When did Evan leave?"

He didn't know. "I'm not sure," she said, and hoped Panos didn't notice the relief wash across her face. "When we did, I guess."

It was, indeed, a small island, and by some cruel coincidence both Anna and her friends and Evan and his family swam at the same pebbly beach a few days later. Anna saw Simone first, and Aliki spotted Anna immediately, running to her with arms outstretched. Anna hugged her. She looked up and saw Evan watching her, and she felt that knot of desire in her stomach.

Aliki grinned. "Will you swim with me?"

"Maybe later, sweetheart," Anna replied. The girl was disappointed at first but soon forgot, running over to her beach toys.

Anna and Panos stood with their feet in the water, talking, and she could feel Evan watching him closely, the way older men watch younger men with judgment, or smugness, envy, or disdain. Stella, who sat on her towel reading a book, lowered her sunglasses a moment and looked at Anna, who couldn't eject certain sensations from her mind: the look on his face, the feel of his hands, the smell of his skin. The wind had blown Anna's hair into her eyes, and Panos, as aware of Evan as Evan was of him, brushed Anna's hair behind her ear.

As Evan's family was leaving, Aliki asked Anna to swim with her the next day.

"We'll see." She glanced up at Evan, but he was busily packing their things. She didn't think he had heard his daughter's request.

Simone smiled at Anna then and picked Aliki up. "You'll see Anna back in Athens, okay?" She touched her tiny nose. "You've got to take a little nap."

Simone had been nothing but nice to her and treated her just as she saw her to be: the niece of a friend who sometimes babysat their child. Anna was the age of Evan's students. But any woman whose husband spent his days with admiring twenty-year-olds was no fool; she felt Simone's eyes on her with a twinge of sadness. Anna was horrified that perhaps he had told her, that perhaps their relationship was open and evolved and beyond petty jealousies. As Anna watched them walk up the craggy path, back to their place for a rest, she felt relieved but completely deflated.

Evan waved good-bye. She wondered if this was easy for him, if he was used to such double-faced behavior. Maybe he assumed they'd sleep together from time to time, nonchalant, noncommittal. But she was too young and too immature for such pleasantries; the entire situation was far beyond her level of experience. This much she knew.

She wondered if images of her body came to him while he had a coffee on his terrace with Simone, or if he heard her voice when he pulled down the shades.

28

Eleni emerged from the bus and began the short walk to Lottery Place. Slung over her shoulder was a shopping bag full of supplies that she had nonchalantly loaded up from the hospital. She was getting good at this routine, and it became such a part of her week that she often forgot she was technically stealing. She never brought her car there because she didn't want to be so easily traced.

When she reached her building, a man was standing in front of the door. "Excuse me," he said. "Do you know of a medical clinic near here?"

Eleni was about to ask him who had sent him, but something stopped her. He looked like a normal-enough man—brown hair, hazel eyes, clean shaven, and in his early thirties. He wore jeans and a blue shirt. Eleni pretended to seriously consider the question. "Yes," she said after a moment. "I'm sure there's something near the Polytechnic. Are you looking for a particular one?"

"No," said the man. "I've just got a flare-up of something." He touched his side lightly and smiled wanly. He did not seem to be in awful pain, but how could she really know? Maybe he was as distrustful of her as she of him, trying to downplay the gravity of his injuries. Still, there was something about him that felt wrong. She wished him luck and kept walking past the apartment, resisting the urge to look back.

Once she'd turned the corner, she exhaled with relief. Though she had been headed to the clinic, it was not one of the usual times during which she saw patients. She was only going to drop off some supplies and clean. But what if she'd been inside already and he'd rung the bell? Wouldn't she have buzzed him in? When she saw someone off her normal hours they usually came through Andreas and his complex connection with underground resistance groups. Then again, word of mouth was by definition not discreet, and who knew who this man could be?

She wished Andreas had been with her; experiencing this alone made it feel all the more ominous. Several blocks down, Eleni stopped into an old coffee shop, one where Mihalis used to spend much time. Inside, it was not full but still lively, mostly men, and smelled of eggs and butter and smoke. The owner, a stout, jovial man in his sixties, remembered her and approached her table, beaming. "My sweet girl!" he said. "It's been so long since I've seen you." He gave her a kiss and then returned to the table with a coffee, which she had asked for, and a pastry, which she had not.

The owner pulled up a chair and straddled it backward, leaning his elbows on its back. "You don't age," he said. "Me, I'm an old man already."

"Nonsense," she told him. But it had been years since she'd seen him, and his gray, thinning hair had surprised her. She was relieved he hadn't asked her what she was doing in this neighborhood, though she could easily remind him she had renters nearby, which wasn't too far from the truth.

"How's your brother?" the man asked. "I haven't seen him in a while." His dark eyes looked sad, expecting her to say the worst.

When Mihalis was younger, Eleni often showed up to pay Mihalis's weekly tab, the careful, conscientious older sister. Eleni looked into the owner's almost black, round eyes. "He's back with Irini," Eleni said. She found comfort in that coffee shop, its front windows open to the warm September breeze, with a man who called her "girl" and treated her like a daughter.

"As good a reason as any," the man said, laughing, as if that explained everything. When he returned behind the counter to help another customer, he glanced back at Eleni. She drank her coffee, and then another, and knew she should head back to the clinic. At least Andreas would be meeting her there, so she could recount the situation to him. She asked the owner to use his phone so she could call to warn him, but he didn't answer. She was probably overreacting anyway.

But when another man came in, Eleni, noticing his blue shirt, quickly averted her eyes. Could he have been following her? When he met a group already at a table and greeted the owner hello, Eleni was relieved to see it was someone much older.

She remained apprehensive, as if that man who had stopped her outside the apartment was on his way. For what? To follow, arrest her, turn her in? One's secondary life could eventually overturn the primary, she knew, and the vast consequences of this, private, public, political, she didn't want to imagine. She felt paralyzed and watched the door intently, willing Andreas to somehow think to find her there and walk her out, transport her to the safe space of their illegal clinic, where she could catch her breath behind a locked door, drawn shades, and the comfort of his voice as it filled up the room.

29

Meanwhile, Mihalis had just returned to Athens. He was headed to the Church of the Transfiguration, where the body of the poet George Seferis was being laid out. It was his first trip to Athens since the beginning of the summer. For the last three months he'd turned down dinner offers from Evan and Simone, as well as one from an editor interested in his work. He worried that what had started as a political gesture—withholding his work from publication—was becoming habit or laziness.

When he'd left that late September morning, Irini had been surprised. "You're going out?" she asked, and though there was no detectable annoyance in her voice, Mihalis knew her too well. He knew every intonation, every inflection. In her voice now was mock incredulity. It was not that he was going out that bothered her but that usually he wasn't. Of course, it hadn't always been that way. Those early years of their marriage, mornings after he had been out late, for instance, the way she asked if he wanted coffee was tinted with aggression: a *Do you want coffee, you bastard?* Because then, when the newlywed Irini wanted to spend time with her husband, Mihalis was never around. He preferred to spend his days in cafés, his nights in bars, and when he was home, he was struggling to write and usually in a bad mood.

Now Mihalis was content to sit on the veranda and look out over the trees; he was happy at home reading and doing not much else. Though he wouldn't admit it to anyone, any trip into Athens felt like an opportunity for arrest: on the street, on the bus, in the spontaneous raid of a *kafeneion*. The risk once had fueled him but more and more it simply frightened him. He still took his walks nearby, though they were evidently not enough because a soft, round belly had formed in spite of them. He found himself napping often, sometimes the entire afternoon and into the evening, and he liked it this way. Irini woke him by opening the shutters to let in more air and the last of the day's light. She'd poke his paunch and offer him tea and a newspaper. Even though the papers were being censored, Mihalis still read them, making sure to point out obvious instances of propaganda to her, the way she might show her students examples of figurative language. Sometimes, she sat down with her own cup of tea and asked him, "What did you do today?" But after a while, she knew the answer, and Mihalis imagined the blank look on his face—*What* did *I do today?*—was enough to keep her from asking. He hadn't been doing much. According to Irini, walking in the garden, or sleeping in the garden, did not count.

He fibbed and told Irini he was writing more than he actually was. She was happy when he was writing, and not only for the selfish reason that she knew it made him easier to live with. Irini knew all too well what a monster he could be when the words that floated around in his head couldn't manifest themselves on the page, and her interest in his productivity was as much self-preservation as anything else.

So today, she was probably relieved he was finally getting out. She got out all the time. She went to movies, something Mihalis hadn't done in months, or tutored students all across Athens, sitting in their kitchens while their parents sat in adjacent living rooms, talking quietly, the clink of spoons on stoneware as they drank evening coffee. She had lunch with former colleagues, many of whom had been fired but not arrested; she caught up with old friends. Maybe this was the key to their marriage working: an understood separate togetherness. He loved being with her at home but going out together made him restless. The only place they seemed to go together was to Eleni's for Sunday lunch. His one concession.

*   *   *

As he walked into the church, he made an obvious point of ignoring the pacing, smug police officers. Inside, a lone chubby officer stood next to the candles. (Why? In case someone didn't make a donation before lighting one? In case someone ran off with an icon?) The officer, full of a self-importance common among the police and the churchgoing, gave him a look but said nothing.

Few people were inside. Mihalis didn't know what to expect, exactly. But for one, he had imagined a long line of people waiting to get in. Hardly the case. As much as Mihalis liked to think the nation adored and thrived on poetry, the sad fact, he surmised, was that the nation was basically illiterate. Or more disturbing still, many of the poets and writers had already been locked up, sent away, removed from public life.

A few people sat in the front, staring ahead, while a small cluster (literature students?) sat in the middle, whispering softly. Mihalis recognized several writer friends whom he hadn't seen since immediately after the coup, when they had met with sincere intentions of toppling the silly junta quickly. But they had all fallen away from the movement—at least, Mihalis had—and seeing them was a reminder of how he had failed to meet any of his promises. Perhaps they, too, felt sheepish, and anyway, it was not a time to discuss these sorts of things. Mihalis felt ashamed for his inaction. He nodded at the others politely and sat far from them, keeping his head low and not looking back when he'd hear more shuffling behind him.

There was also Anastasia, the slightly deranged woman who was rumored to spend her days attending funerals, and on any given day in Athens you could find her somewhere near where someone had died. She was eighty years old and was the only woman perhaps in all of Athens who could hurl insults at the police with no repercussions. Once, years ago, Mihalis had struck up a conversation with her, one of the few times he had seen her lucid and taciturn. He bought her a coffee in Omonia Square and offered to buy her lunch, too. She had looked at him strangely. "I'm not poor," she said, tucking a loose strand of hair back into her bun. "Just crazy." She looked horribly sad at that fact—as if, given the choice, she would have chosen poverty. Later that day, Mihalis had seen her walk out of another church blocks away and sit down on a bench, her eyes squinting at the light. There, she pulled her knitting needles out of her giant bag and produced a very small sweater, almost complete: white with bright blue trim. The idea of this woman with a grandchild, or any family at all for that matter, was strange indeed. No one locked her up because no one wanted to deal with her; she reminded everyone of the most ugly aspects of their mothers: the yelling, the nagging, the obsession with death, the hairs sprouting from her chin.

After an hour, though there had been a lot of comings and goings, the church didn't seem any more full. Usually at this time he himself would be taking a nap; he figured the crowds would come later in the afternoon. He stood up, nodded disingenuously to the candle policeman, and left. He walked about in the small square. He realized he hadn't eaten anything all day, so he got himself a coffee and toast. He waited, watching the church.

While the church had been less crowded than Mihalis would have thought, the funeral procession that followed was huge and turned into one large, rousing protest. It was not enough, but it was something. Through the evening and into the night, the shops of the city displayed the face of the poet like so many dimly lit shrines.

30

One clear late afternoon in October, Anna and Evan lay in bed in the apartment in Exarheia he called his office, where, since their return to Athens in August, they met some weekday afternoons. Evan came there to work, and the large desk in the center of the living room was corroboratingly cluttered with books and papers and pens. There were two small bedrooms, and the one they used opened up to a pleasant balcony that overlooked a courtyard. Sometimes they kept the double doors that led there wide open. The bedroom itself was just large enough for a dresser, a nightstand, and a small double bed that always seemed to be made with fresh, expensive sheets, despite the relative shabbiness of the rest of the place. In the closet hung a few shirts and a pair of trousers. But the thrill of pressing the buzzer, of hearing him allow her entry, of the way he opened the door for her made her not think too much about his double life and what else might have gone on in that apartment, and she reminded herself that he was almost twenty-five years her senior, and his life had been firmly in motion before she'd even entered the world. Yet that thought alone made her horribly jealous.

They had been there one hour. Evan was naked and lying on his side, the sheet covering him from the waist down, his head leaning on his hand, and Anna had wrapped herself in one of the shirts from the closet in the way she imagined women who had affairs did. But the effect was slightly off; Evan was quite tall and Anna was not and his shirt went past her knees. Her own clothes were heaped on the floor. She, sitting cross-legged on the bed, considered him as he considered her.

"I think my mother is having an affair," she said. "I saw her the other day with this other man. A younger man. Handsome."

Evan smirked at the word *affair;* she had made it clear she didn't like that word, as if what she was doing was somehow different. A meta-affair. She reached for a cigarette. Evan placed the ashtray in front of her, on the bed, and Anna wondered if he'd do such a thing at home. It seemed dirty, the thing a wife simply wouldn't allow. But what did she know of husbands and wives? Or men and women for that matter? "Maybe he's a friend. A colleague," Evan said.

Anna thought about this. Her mother and the man seemed to know each other well. They hadn't been holding hands or touching; they had simply been walking through the square, talking. He could have been anyone. But another time, when she was walking from the Polytechnic to a friend's apartment for a study group, she saw her mother's car idling on a residential street outside an apartment building. The same man got out of the car and thanked her, smiling. One night, a few days later, Anna and Stella had walked past the apartment, nonchalantly peering in windows. She saw him at a table with a few other men, smoking and laughing and playing cards. She didn't tell this to Evan because it was too close to the way she and Stella spied on him, at his own house.

"I suppose. I'm not used to seeing her with men. Particularly men I don't recognize."

"Anna *mou*. Life gets more and more complicated, the older you get."

"You don't say," Anna quipped, but she blushed at his reproach of her naïveté. "I was just getting used to Dimitri."

"And how is *your* boyfriend?" Evan asked. Panos hadn't talked much with her since their trip, blaming his reticence on being busy with school. Anna's usual reply, *He's not my boyfriend,* was beginning to tire her so she just said, "He's mad at me."

"Perfect," he said. He slid one hand beneath her shirt and with the other removed the cigarette from her hand. He placed it in the ashtray, still burning, and moved the ashtray to the nightstand. He took her breasts in his hands. Soon, they were kissing. Then again their bodies slowly moved together.

Later, the sound of neighbors arguing woke them. Someone had thrown something: a plate, a vase. Outside, it was already dark; they had not meant to stay so long. While Evan often dozed after sex, Anna usually could not, always aware of the noises in the courtyard, an imagined phone call or sudden knock on the door. This time, Anna had fallen into such a hard nap that looking at Evan with his thick hair messed up and his eyes wide open made her want to collapse back into him again. The more they were together, the more she wanted. But instead, she stood up, not touching him at all, and walked around to the other side of the bed to check the clock on the nightstand. Already nine o'clock. She put her watch and bracelets back on. The smell of grilled meat drifted up from the *souvlaki* shop below.

Anna gathered her things and disappeared into the bathroom. When she returned, Evan was dressed and talking quietly into the phone. She sat down in the small kitchen.

After he hung up he used the bathroom. When he emerged, he was smoothing his hair. "I was supposed to meet your uncle an hour ago," he said.

"Oh," said Anna. "That was him you called?"

Evan ignored her question. She knew it wasn't. "Ready?" he asked.
"You want to leave *together*?"

"It's fine," Evan said.

When they walked out, the men in the *souvlaki* shop eyed her.
Sometimes, when Evan was late, she sat on a stool in the shop's window, drinking lemon soda through a straw and trying not to watch
the clock. Evan waved at the owner, who responded with a lecherous
grin. Anna was rarely there after dark, and the street felt a little shady,
the kind of narrow street that she was nervous to walk alone. When
they turned the corner and no one was in sight, Evan gave her a swift
kiss almost on the mouth. "Good luck on your exam," he said.

Her exam. She had forgotten. She, too, was supposed to meet
classmates an hour ago to study. She watched Evan walk off, smoothing his shirt and trousers. Luckily for her, the university was only a
few blocks away.

31

Several days after the poet's funeral, Mihalis had heard from his
sister that Vangelis had been arrested following the march. And
whether out of anger or solidarity, for the next few days Mihalis
returned to his city, to his old cafés in Omonia, where many people
recognized him. And with these old Marxists and journalists and
poets who still remained free to walk the streets he would beat
tabletops and rail against the colonels, almost as if daring them to
come find him there.

One rainy afternoon, his favorite café was quiet. Using the owner's phone he had called Evan, whom he had seen at the funeral, but
before that, had not seen since the early summer day at the house
in Halandri. Evan wasn't home, so he spoke to Simone instead, who
despite their brief interlude years before—or perhaps because of

it—treated him with a cool indifference. She told Mihalis she'd have Evan get back to him, though she did not bother to ask him to leave a number.

So Mihalis went to the movies. He couldn't even recall what film he had paid to see, because as the requisite, short propaganda films began—to warm up the crowd indeed—he became so full of rage that he could barely remember his own name. He looked around, wondering who among them was an informer; then, at the same moment, he thought, *Who the fuck cares?* There was probably a stupid policeman among them, those *hafiedes,* just waiting for someone to speak out of turn or make a wisecrack at the ridiculous newsreels of Patakos, his shiny bald head, his swollen face taking up the screen.

It had been cold in the theater and he pulled his sweater around his shoulders. In a more carefree time, the theater had filled with chatter until the actual feature began: people called across the rows to their friends, discussed politics and weekends and other films. During the newsreel, most were deathly quiet, and though a few brave ones muttered under their breath they were motionless, at attendance, waiting politely like children at Sunday school. Nobody cared about anything beyond the personal. Everything was fine if you didn't think about it. Hadn't that been what he himself had been doing? Not thinking about it?

Papadopoulos was on the screen now and a few people clapped. Miserable ass-kissers. This was it for Mihalis; this, indeed, was simply too much. He threw a handful of his salted pumpkin seeds at the screen. A few landed in a woman's hair, and she turned around and scowled at the teenagers behind her.

Four years had been too long. The junta had broken down doors, crashed through walls to get in, but once they were there, they lingered in the room, forthright but unassuming, just innocuous enough not to rouse any protest. And Mihalis was tired of it. Seferis's funeral had shaken something loose in him.

"Applause!" Mihalis shouted, standing up. "You assholes." He began to clap in an exaggerated, stupid way. A voice yelled for him to sit down. Mihalis spun in the dark to face the man but had no idea who it was or where it had come from, and the coward certainly wasn't going to identify himself. "Go to hell," Mihalis said finally, to all of them. He threw the rest of his seeds in the air.

Then he turned and pushed out of his row, stepping on toes and tripping over feet. When he reached the aisle, he pointed his finger at the image of the colonels on-screen. The film reel was still going and the pompous, patriotic images whirled on. "How can you all sit here?" Mihalis cried. And then he shouted the words of the poet Seferis: "Out of stupidity!"

He stormed up the aisle toward the lobby. "Out of stupidity!" he said again. Then he walked into the bright outdoors, where two police officers waited calmly to arrest him. "How much longer before somebody does something?" he yelled back at the glass doors.

At the Security Police headquarters, Mihalis was taken into a room with two other officers, who circled him. An unusually fat man in a sweat-stained shirt began the questioning.

"You're a poet?" he asked, smirking.

"I am," Mihalis said.

The man snorted, as if he'd said he were a ballerina.

"Write us a poem then." He handed Mihalis a ballpoint pen and a sheet of paper. "Let's see what sort of poet you are."

Mihalis took the pen in his hand. He stared at the black pen against the single, white sheet of paper before him, the white of the paper against the scarred wood.

When he didn't begin, the second man prompted him. "Write us a poem about what happened in the movie theater."

Mihalis began to draw the dictator's phoenix. He hummed while he drew: banned music, Theodorakis, songs they had sung in the funeral procession, in the protests. Whether it was the drawing or the humming that angered them, Mihalis wasn't sure, but one of the men—he didn't look up to see—grabbed the pen and laced it between the fingers of Mihalis's left hand.

Then he pressed down until Mihalis winced. It was a warning. "You have a family?" the man asked, increasing the pressure on his hand.

"Everyone has a family," Mihalis replied.

"Perhaps we should bring them in," the other man dryly suggested. "Perhaps they'd be more cooperative."

"Yes," Mihalis said. "Bring them in. Bring every Greek, every poet, every man and woman who walks and eats and breathes and fucks—"

The man stopped him by bringing his fist down hard on his hand. Mihalis heard something snap, whether the pen or his fingers he wasn't sure. The pain was agonizing, but he'd learned long ago that that was what they wanted—to see you hurt. So despite the fact that he felt like a refrigerator had dropped on his hand, he simply smiled. Grinned, really, like a lunatic.

What did these men want from him, anyway? Names? They seemed to want nothing except to hurt him, to intimidate him. A part of him was shouting, *Finally!* inside. Ready to confront these bastards head-on. What had he been waiting for? The city that had slept in him and he in it all those years had finally been roused, and Mihalis would not slip back into somnolence. Let them break his fingers.

He began singing now, songs he knew they knew. "Shut the fuck up," the fat one said, hitting him in the back of the head. "Stop the goddamned singing." But he didn't. Enraged, the men threw him out of his chair onto the concrete floor.

"We have you for public disturbance. We have you for insulting Greek nationality. Do you want us to also add resisting arrest?"

Mihalis stared at the light on the ceiling. His hand burned, but he'd detached himself from the pain. Inside his chest he felt fire and when, once more, they told him to be quiet, he stood up, raising his arms as he sang. He was halfway through a Tsitsanis song before they whacked him on the back of his head with a pistol. He began to leave his body even before he fell to the floor. He witnessed, but he hardly felt, the pain. When they tied his ankles together they beat the soles of his feet—first with a whip, then with an iron rod. Even then he felt a strange peace because he saw that they couldn't win. He didn't know if he was singing anymore or if the words were only in his head. But then a line came to him—his own, someone else's, he didn't know—as he heard himself say aloud, "Here's a poem, here it is," just before he lost consciousness.

When he came to, who knew how much later, he thought he was in the room alone, but then he noticed two men in the corner, a guard and another. He was a military doctor, apparently. Though frankly Mihalis had been through much worse. It was rumored that the young ones had it the hardest; their bodies could take the most. The doctor handed him his shoes, and Mihalis tried to stuff his swollen feet into them, but he couldn't get them on.

"You shouldn't buy such small shoes," the guard said cruelly.

"Jump up and down," the doctor told him.

"I'm not a monkey." His head was pounding. The pain had come to him now.

"Do it," demanded the doctor. "It'll restore circulation."

With his shoes in his hands, Mihalis followed the guard to his cell. "They say you're a crazy one," the guard said.

"Do you have any cigarettes?" Mihalis asked.

The guard surprisingly gave him one and lit up one for himself. In the cell were two other men, a few benches, and nothing else. Mihalis shared his cigarette with the other two and the guard gave him a glass of water.

And then in came the prostitutes, seven rounded up and tossed into the same cell.

"What," Mihalis asked the women, "were you on strike again?"

During the time he was detained, Mihalis was allowed the occasional visitor, and only because of a sympathetic guard. Eleni and Anna and Irini brought him food, and without this allowance he would barely have eaten at all. Though not in solitary confinement, he couldn't have any writing or reading materials in his cell. The worst part was listening to the screams of the others. In fact, one of the colonels' favorite methods was to force a husband to listen to his wife being beaten.

Because they were also not allowed combs or towels, Anna sometimes smuggled in a wet washcloth sudsed with soap. Despite his often bohemian lifestyle, Mihalis liked to be clean. He liked to be well dressed, too, even if he only owned one suit, but she couldn't help him there.

Sometimes, in conversation, he snuck in lines for poems and she memorized them, rushing back outside to write them down. One, she said, she had painted on the side of a building; he knew this act should worry him but instead it impressed him, such daring from the smallest one. It was a new relationship for the two of them: With Sophie he'd had an intellectual connection, almost like mentor and student. With Anna it was purely emotional, and he had felt fiercely protective of her, as if she might snap in half at any moment. Sophie he always had wanted to teach, and Anna he'd always wanted to hug.

Anna visited with Evan, which incensed Mihalis, but he was glad at least someone was watching out for her. People had abandoned Anna one by one: her father, her brother, her sister, and now he, Mihalis, had done so too. Did he blame her for the way she beamed up at Evan as she would at some sort of movie star? No. Did he blame Evan for allowing it? Absolutely.

32

So very far away from Athens, Sophie spent the morning babysitting Katerina, who was home sick from school, and when Monique returned Sophie rushed back upstairs to her apartment to grab her notes for class, holding the mail in one hand and her keys in another. She didn't stop to look at what had arrived until she noticed Anna's careful script. Anna's letters were infrequent and always a pleasant surprise; usually, she just tacked on a few words to her mother's letters, a "hello" or a small note written in French to show that she was keeping up with her foreign-language study. This was fine with Sophie because this way she could just address her letters to her mother and Anna together, and she didn't have to admit to her relationship with Loukas. Her mother never cared much to know of her love affairs, and she was sure Anna would find it distasteful, to date an ex-boyfriend's cousin. Anna had always taken the high moral ground with everything and wouldn't understand the complexities of the heart.

But this was a full letter, written on blue stationery (Sophie's). Sophie could imagine Anna sitting down at Sophie's desk—it was much larger than Anna's—and choosing from her stationery. Blue, yellow, or lilac? She could picture her writing with her tongue sticking out, a habit she had had since she first held a pencil. She imagined her struggling to get the words right—Anna hated composing and often grew impatient before she ever finished anything. But when she read the letter, Sophie knew why her sister chose to write. While her mother probably was composing a letter with the same information, she would try to tell her gently.

Anna told Sophie of Mihalis, his arrest. Then, maybe to make the situation feel less grave, she wrote her the gossip of Athens. This juxtaposition felt strange to Sophie (Mihalis was arrested, Spyro had been home for a visit, and so-and-so had a huge fight with her boyfriend in the middle of the coffee shop, and Anna thought love was just a vehicle for getting your heart stomped on). But this was how they had to live. Her uncle's arrest had not surprised her though it upset her all the same. Sophie frankly couldn't believe that he had managed to evade arrest all that time—Loukas's theory was that they kept a few prominent figures circulating, so they could say, "See? Our poets are here, sitting in cafés! Our artists are going about their business!"

She read the letter over and over. The way she received her information here, the way the letters reflected a past already, the way they were a bizarre recording of life that she read with a ten-day lag, always filled her with a disturbing sense of remove. Where would she feel more helpless, she wondered, here in Paris or back in Athens? The last time her uncle had written her more than a few scratches on a postcard had been years before, after George Papandreou's funeral, about how moved and inspired but helpless he had felt. Maybe the death of the poet Seferis three years later set off an outward, angry mania.

Sophie remembered how Radio Paris had broadcast Seferis's statement two years before. She recalled the way the entire café had quieted, the French patrons, the Greek and other expats, even the American tourists, to listen, the way they had been both roused and deflated. But that famous line of the poet's hadn't meant much to her until that very moment, when she read her sister's letter: "*Wherever I travel, Greece wounds me.*"

She couldn't get those words out of her mind, nor could she shake the feeling that she had grown far too complacent. Her uncle had been shaken awake, though to disastrous results, and it was time for her to be again, too. She had the shield of another country's borders. Loukas attended regular meetings and he reported back to her. The network of Greeks abroad was huge. Their involvement, and specifically Loukas's, allowed for her passivity. With Nick political engagement had been so intertwined with their romance, but they had also met through politics. Everything was about timing. She also wondered if in some way it had been vanity, or a showing off, or an assertion of her identity that here in Paris, years later, felt too commonplace. Since those May '68 demonstrations, resistance groups had risen and converged around her. A group of women she knew ran an underground women's clinic, for instance; another group of Loukas's friends worked on Salvador Allende's election campaign, many of them with no native ties to Chile whatsoever. Another acquaintance, a fellow architect whom Loukas had helped find work, had fled Greece after being suspected of bombing the American embassy in Athens. When Sophie asked him one night at a bar after too many glasses of wine if the accusations were correct he simply said that two of his friends had died. "Something was wrong with the bomb, after all," he said, and his nonchalance was condescending, intimidating. Two Americans were sitting with them, and Sophie thought perhaps this would disturb them, but one, a pretty redhead in a green sweater, said in clear French that it was no matter, the embassy deserved it. "Aren't they the ones behind your country's coup?" she asked. Americans seemed to be arriving in Paris as if they were shaken from a bag, young men recently drafted and who surreptitiously escaped, into Canada and beyond. Dissent and political engagement were in the air. It wouldn't be too difficult for her to, if nothing else, raise some awareness about the situation in Greece. Greece *should* have been wounding her.

Through the café, Sophie knew some siblings who ran a printing press, and shortly after receiving her sister's letter she stopped by their shop, only blocks away from the café. Without much persuading—they, two sisters and a brother, loved the idea—Sophie convinced them to help her produce a small booklet in exchange for her doing some office work for them a few hours per week.

So one month after her uncle's arrest, Sophie spent all the spare time available to her compiling information: Amnesty International reports, articles in foreign magazines, press releases from resistance groups within and outside of Greece. Perhaps what had been missed individually would be noticed collectively. In addition, she included translations of everything, from French or English into Greek, or into French in the case of the Greek press releases. She knew that the Greeks were hungry for information about their own country, information that within its borders was being censored. This small detail made her feel better about being away: from Paris she could do what would be near impossible in Athens. Monique and Angelo, who knew people coming and going from Greece all the time, would help her disseminate the multilingual packets. Marc, the owner of the bookstore where she and Loukas had met that rainy winter day, helped her compile and lay out information; he read more than seemed humanly possible and knew of things she had never read, never seen, never been aware of. She even included typed-out statements from the composer and activist Mikis Theodorakis, whom she had waited on several times and to whom she had wanted to say, "You know my uncle! I once sat on your lap!" In those difficult years after the civil war, her uncle and Theodorakis had spent a week hiding in the basement of her very house in Halandri. She had been only a little girl then and now felt too tongue-tied to mention it to this famous man, but when he asked her where she was from, her reply gave him pause. "I know Halandri well," he said, and for the rest of the evening Sophie had felt his gaze on her, curious, even speculative. She vowed the next time he came in she'd tell him, but since then he hadn't been around, and Sophie wondered if he was still in Paris.

After the first week, Marc had run out of copies of her newsletter and her friends had agreed to make more. Charlotte and Etienne kept a few on the bar, which customers leafed through with their morning coffee. The women who ran the clinic stacked her booklet next to various other bits of activist literature they carried, strewn across a large table in the center of the room. Hardly light reading, but people seemed interested.

Sophie didn't know if her small project made much of a difference. Doing anything outside of Greece made her feel like a coward, like a child teasing a barking dog trapped behind a fence. But Charlotte disagreed. Any act of resistance was better than no act, she often said, and each time Sophie thought of her uncle, languishing in some prison, each time she heard another story of torture or ill treatment, she found relief in the fact that at least she was making sure they, and the thousands of others like them, were not forgotten. And that, to her, was something. If nothing else, it was her penance.

33

One Friday afternoon in December, on her way to Lottery Place, Eleni saw Anna strolling with a group of friends, walking in the middle of the group, her books held in her arms. Anna had been staring at her feet like she did but listening intently to something her friend Stella was saying. Eleni knew that Stella had been arrested but released, and she had the affect of a girl who could not be broken. Now Stella tilted her pretty head back, her long hair tied in a high ponytail, and she was laughing. For some reason this thought flashed through Eleni's mind: *Anna's lover?* And she didn't know why; she had no reason to believe anything of the sort except that by this age Sophie had been brazenly boy crazy, giggling with her friends, sneaking out at night, and writing names across notebooks, whereas boys held no interest for Anna at all. Despite her delicate features she sometimes seemed boylike herself.

Eleni continued to watch the group. As they entered the campus, Anna turned back and met the stare of a stern-looking police officer.

She flipped her bangs out of her eyes and spit in the street. Then she turned back and smiled at him, a sweet-sarcastic smile that Eleni would never imagine coming from her youngest child. It wasn't even for the benefit of her friends; they hadn't noticed the gesture at all. Perhaps it wasn't a boylike demeanor she was noticing in her youngest daughter but simply a new, aggressive one, slightly sexual, decidedly provocative.

Before this incident, when Eleni had imagined Anna at the university, she still saw her in her white shirt and navy-blue smock, with her hair long down her back, maybe a ribbon tying it up, and a satchel strapped at her nonexistent hip. She imagined her timid and obedient, raising her hand politely, completing all her assignments. And white bobby socks, which she couldn't even remember if Anna had ever worn at all.

Eleni didn't think Anna was attending many of her classes. Eugenia, at work, had told her her own son was attending school on paper, taking his exams, and mostly passing, but that most of them had found everything to be a joke. While some professors had by then had their positions reinstated, few professors whom they respected were left. But Anna seemed voracious in her reading: Eleni found all sorts of books scattered about the house, most likely all banned by the junta, taken from the bookshelves and from crates Mihalis had left behind.

Anna had always spent much time in her room, claiming she was studying—reading, studying, daydreaming, who knew?—but lately often materialized looking rather beastlike, her hair tangled and her eyes wide, as if she were out foraging. In the fridge she'd rummage until she'd find something that seemed appropriate; usually it was filled with large porcelain dishes, as Eleni only found the energy to cook on her days off. Sometimes, Anna would eat *pastitsio* or salad right from the refrigerator, one bony hip holding the door ajar.

As the months passed after Mihalis's arrest, Anna more often emerged onto the first floor of the house, and soon they began to spend so much time at that large, round white kitchen table with its chrome edges that the other rooms in the house felt foreign. They even moved the small television—a gift from Dimitri—from the living room onto the kitchen counter. They had gravitated toward each other, each feeling more vulnerable. Taki's and Sophie's departures had stung, but Mihalis's arrest hung over them like a fog. Eleni, now far too aware of what was going on at Bouboulinas Street and beyond— that Friday at Lottery Place had been particularly full—could barely entertain the thought of what might be happening to her brother, let alone imagine what Anna was getting herself into. She had begun to add extra hours to her clinic to keep herself busy. Sometimes, even if no one came, it felt good to be there.

That evening when Eleni returned from Lottery Place, she was happily surprised to see Anna sitting at the kitchen table, reading and popping olives into her mouth, lining up the pits in a neat line. As was often the case, Eleni left the clinic so abuzz that she couldn't concentrate, the face of each patient flying through her mind, the snippets of her interactions with Andreas. She was full of restless energy. In contrast, Anna seemed engrossed and surprisingly calm.

"I don't feel like cooking anything," Eleni said. She wanted to go back out.

Anna looked up, distracted. She pointed to the tin of olives that sat in front of her. "I'm eating."

"Why don't we go downtown and eat something? It's been a while since we've gone together." In fact, Eleni remembered the last time to be the evening after she had treated the two girls who had been raped. She had vowed then to reach out to her daughter more, not only to protect her, but also simply to not let the last years of her youth disappear; but patterns had been set and it was easy to stay in their rut.

Anna stood up. Around her mother she was diffident, a little morose even, not at all the young woman with the swaggering walk and tight trousers whom Eleni had glimpsed on campus. Lately, Anna reminded her of something, someone, but Eleni couldn't quite articulate what or whom.

"I'll go change," Anna said, and she reappeared minutes later in a navy shift that hit at the knee—something else Sophie had left behind, Eleni was sure. She wore a heavy beige cardigan and flat, tall boots, and she had pinned a small red barrette in her hair to keep the bangs out of her face, anticipating her mother's scrutiny.

"You look nice," Eleni said.

Anna curtsied, a sardonic smile on her lips. This was not her shy little girl, and this new, untamed quality, the leaned-forward and determined walk, made Eleni vaguely uneasy. Though her youngest daughter had the features of a princess, she had the unbridled energy of a revolutionary, and Eleni wondered why she was only noticing it now.

"How about one of those cafés in Kolonaki?" Eleni suggested. "We'll watch for actors." It was frivolous, but it made her happy, such a silly activity.

Anna's face clouded, and Eleni thought that perhaps her ragtag daughter found the area too posh? But then Anna agreed. When they parked the car, they walked along quietly. Eleni stopped every so often to gaze in some store windows, Anna glancing around as though she were being followed. The normalcy of this world never ceased to amaze Eleni and often she'd almost forget there even was a dictatorship. They went to work, they bought new shoes, they curled their hair. Anna walked politely at her side, stopping to examine what Eleni looked at, as if she were a colleague she didn't know too well from the hospital. Eleni put her arm around Anna and squeezed her toward her, briefly, a quick sideways hug.

Anna leaned into her a bit shyly, her old self again. The youngest child never knows the feeling of being alone with her parents, and then, eventually, that is all she knows. Anna turned to face her. "When do you think Mihalis will come home?" she asked. "How long will they keep him?"

Eleni took a deep breath. After having to explain death to small children, to try to make sense of what had happened to their father, few questions had fazed her. What *would* happen to Mihalis, who had been gone almost three months, now transferred to an island prison? She didn't know. If it had been Sophie who had asked, Eleni would have been frank. Maybe she would have even told her of the patients she had seen, girls like Anna, of the way people came to the apartment and she sent them home with medicine she had stolen from the hospital. She wondered if she would ever be able to treat Anna like an adult.

"He'll be fine," Eleni said. And while such a lie seemed disingenuous, Eleni felt better saying those words. *He'll be fine he'll be fine he'll be fine.*

At the café, they ordered more food than they could ever finish: fava, salad, fish, eggplant.

Eleni, wanting to talk about lighter things, was going to ask Anna about school as soon as Anna finished chewing a large forkful of tomatoes. Unlike Sophie—yes, she was comparing the two again, she couldn't help it—Anna rarely mentioned her classes. Anna rarely mentioned anything at all.

But instead, Anna spoke first, through a mouthful. "Do you want to marry Dimitri?"

Eleni put her fork and knife down and studied her daughter's face. She wondered if Anna had heard her last conversation with Dimitri, wherein he brushed off Eleni's worry about Mihalis's arrest: *He'll be taken to some island, where he'll live like a man on vacation.*

"No," Eleni said. "I have no intention of marrying again."

"But do you *want* to?"

"No," Eleni repeated, interested in the way her daughter separated desire and intention.

Anna seemed neither relieved nor surprised. "I don't want to marry at all. Ever."

Eleni laughed. "You'll change your mind," she said.

"No," said Anna. "I don't think so." Her voice seemed so confident, so adult, so *knowing*. But then she looked down at her shoes. A certain motion, an unintentional gesture, would suddenly reveal her children's younger selves—that upward blow of the bangs off the forehead, an involuntary frown, a surprised look of joy—like a flash on a movie screen, a quick projection of a photograph from years before.

Back at home after dinner, Eleni read a magazine and listened to Anna's Joan Baez record. Anna lay on the couch, already in pajamas, staring at the wall in that existential way only young people could sustain. Eleni had never imagined Anna ever wanting to move out or away. Until now. Maybe Anna was afraid not of leaving her mother, but of leaving her mother alone, which was why she had asked if Eleni wanted to marry Dimitri. Eleni watched her twirl a lock of her hair and then start when her hand brushed against fabric. Sometimes, Anna caught her watching and met her eyes, somewhat blankly, or in midthought.

"You're not going out tonight?" Eleni asked.

"I feel like staying in," she said. She seemed sullen now, as if she had forgotten something while they were at dinner but it had come crashing back. And when the phone rang a few moments later, Anna pounced for it. She spoke in a low voice, twisting the cord around her finger. When she hung up, she approached Eleni, her arms extended as if she was going to hug her, but then changed her mind and lengthened her body into a deep stretch, yawning loudly, exposing her impossibly flat belly. "I'm going to go meet some friends after all," she said. What a mood shift. She was trying to keep her tone cool, Eleni could tell, trying to suppress a smile, leaving Eleni to suspect that she also had a secret. She wondered who it was on the phone, but before she could ask Anna ran into the bathroom and closed the door behind her.

A cat, she thought. That was it. Her daughter reminded her of a cat. Not in the predictable, slinky way nubile girls were often compared to them—not a sleek, pampered apartment cat who rarely went outdoors and had a name like Athena or Sultana, and not even a cat like Orpheas, who stalked through their neighborhood and home as if he were king. But rather, Anna reminded her of the scruffy, stealthy, nameless felines you saw around Plaka, the scrappy ones who weren't afraid to fight, to yowl, to get dirt in their eyes.

After Anna left, back in the boots and dress, her hair freshly brushed to a sheen, and her eyes rimmed with a smoky gray, restless Eleni drove to Dimitri's, and to his surprise as much as hers, they made love with the gracelessness of said alley cats. After, when Eleni was getting dressed, she asked Dimitri if his boys ever went through such a moody stage. If anything, they would have been self-righteous and arrogant. She certainly couldn't imagine any of them as temperamental teenagers, and this made her hope that they had been, that they had been horribly difficult and had simply outgrown it. But Eleni hadn't seen this extreme petulance in either of her other children, and it worried her a little. Sophie, although sarcastic at times, was affable even when arguing.

She lay back down on the bed next to him and put her head on his chest. "Not moody," Dimitri said. "Argumentative, yes. Horny, yes. But not particularly moody."

Eleni sighed, and the two of them lay quietly for a while. Then Dimitri arose and left the room. She heard him turn on the television. "We were once five," Eleni called from the bed. "Five, then four, then three, and now two."

"You're being dramatic," he said.

Eleni got up and followed him into the living room. She turned the television off and stood in front of it. "And then one." And what was one? she thought. Almost nothing. Invisible. Disappeared.

34

There were things in Paris that reminded Sophie of Athens: the way the street signs were mounted on the sides of buildings, a mark of some sort of collectiveness between the world of the street and the world inside; the way different neighborhoods had different smells and the way she could almost assign colors to them. The early-morning farmer's markets, solid women scrutinizing the fruit.

But there were things about Paris that were nothing like Athens, and these were the things Sophie was drawn to the most. Everyone talked about Paris in springtime but Sophie found it the most amazing at Christmas. She loved the tree outside Notre Dame, the lights, the skaters in front of the Hôtel de Ville, the shoppers and the carolers. It was hard to believe it was her fifth winter in Paris; it was hard to believe that she had lived her adult life in France. That year, Loukas had promised to teach her to glide across the ice, and now, as another Christmas passed, and spring was close, they, along with seven-year-old Katerina, headed to the outdoor skating pond.

The other skaters made it look so easy, and little Katerina flew across the ice as if someone were pulling her by a string. But Sophie's limbs were everywhere, and she'd never felt so out of control of her body.

"You look like a rag doll," teased Loukas, who wore a tight brown sweater and a blue knit cap over his curls and appeared as though he had grown up skiing and skating and doing cold-weather things. He twirled around her, showing off, and then kissed her on the head. "My adorable rag doll."

"How is it you know how to do this?" she asked him. She was shuffling along, and he skated smoothly, in control. From time to time, she gripped his arm.

"I learned in school," he said, gliding past her and then turning around quickly, stopping cleanly. "Besides, it's just physics." Katerina, who had found friends from school, skated by effortlessly in a gaggle of girls. Two young boys raced and whipped by them, and the girls screamed in delight. He punched Sophie playfully on the arm. "They get it," he said, pointing.

"I *understand* the physics," Sophie said. "But it doesn't mean I can do it."

Loukas rarely talked about any part of his life before university. His childhood in Greece intrigued her, as did the thought of him at some Swiss school. He was the type, like so many of his friends, who went to all the right schools and let it emerge in the most calculated, nonchalant ways. Sophie herself had had a fairly privileged, middle-class upbringing compared to many in Athens, but she remembered feeling out of her element the one time she had dinner at Nick's house, with his parents. For some reason, she hadn't equated Loukas with this sort of privilege, even though Nick's mother and Loukas's father were siblings. Perhaps the boarding school had been his bereft father's only way to deal with being left alone with his young son.

"Boarding school," Sophie said, "is also why your French was so good, even when I first met you. And why you never joined my conversation class." While Sophie had become more fluent, she still enjoyed those weekly meetings. Her class was fairly advanced now, and she was learning all sorts of slang, and at home she and

Loukas spoke a confused mix of Greek and French. Sometimes days would go by when they wouldn't speak any Greek at all, and then as if only realizing it themselves they'd suddenly switch back into Greek.

"Alex only took it to meet girls," he said.

Sophie laughed, mimicking him: "Oh, you poor fragile foreigner, let me show you around Paris." She tripped then and fell.

Loukas helped pull her up. "It worked, no?" And then he took her hand and patiently coaxed her to mimic his movements, trying to convey in words what his body did naturally. How simple such instructions sounded when articulated precisely. Sophie remembered the way a French teacher many years ago had told her to try speaking from the front of her mouth and how then the words began to flow, as if her own mouth was the obstruction, not the knowledge.

She was more skilled in language than in sports, however; but after an hour with Loukas Sophie began to get the hang of gliding, or at least pushing, across the ice, and her concentration was so focused that she ignored Loukas and their friends who had joined them. Luckily, Katerina was entertained by her friends, and Sophie kept one eye on her whereabouts. The rink was becoming crowded, and Sophie could see Loukas off on the sidelines now, talking with some others. Her thighs were burning and sore, but when she skated by him, he waved, smiling.

She was finally learning to ice-skate perhaps because she sensed that it might be her last winter in Paris. She was in her fourth year toward her PhD and could finish her dissertation—*Writing, Wandering, Death by the Rules*—in Athens. Lately she and Loukas had begun to reminisce about island holidays, about places they both had been to—a certain club in Mykonos, a quiet beach in Kythnos, the splendor of Athens at night from a point up above. They wanted to share those places with one another. The draw of their native land was becoming too strong to ignore, and some days the nostalgia was overwhelming. Plus, there had been talk of liberalization, of releasing all the political prisoners, of more lifts on censorship, and if Sophie had been on any sorts of lists, those had faded away, been lost, misplaced, ignored for larger problems, those more urgent voices from within the country. She doubted the small booklets she had made had been traced back to her. Or at least, this was what they told themselves. Talk of liberalization was often a ruse.

Sophie thought of Mihalis often, sometimes daily, which meant she had to push the guilt she felt for leaving down to a place where she couldn't readily summon it. Still, Mihalis had been the one to help her leave; she told herself he could have as easily left, with all his connections, too. She tried not to think about her uncle suffering in an island detention center, but it was a hard thing to forget, even here, among the skaters and their bright colored scarves and mittens. She looked up at Loukas, who was listening amusedly to something Katerina was saying. Oh, how she loved him. Maybe forgetting was harder when your home country was far closer than its physical distance.

Sophie skated over to Loukas and rested, and Katerina bolted at them at full speed, her limbs a whir of pink and red, running into Sophie and hugging her tightly around her hips. The three of them sat down on a nearby bench, and Sophie helped Katerina unlace her skates. She sat on the bench, her legs dangling, her skates about to fall off, smiling, content. Loukas sat next to Katerina and put his arm around both of them. Sophie leaned over the little girl and placed her head on Loukas's shoulder, and the three of them watched the other skaters awhile. Sophie had grown so close to Katerina and knew Katerina thought of her like an aunt. In some ways they were putting down roots. She and Loukas had already been talking of moving in together when Loukas's lease was up in a few months, which gave Sophie a certain comfort, a sense of commitment, though neither had initiated the search for a new apartment. They could live in Sophie's little attic but it would be cramped. Did a new place have to be in Paris? Though neither had expressed it so blatantly, Sophie and Loukas agreed on one thing: Paris was wonderful. But it wasn't quite home.

35

They had come of age in such places, those island prisons—during the Nazi occupation, during the civil war, throughout the fifties, and today— and now some were growing old there. "We were wondering about you," many said when Mihalis arrived. "About how long you'd be spared."

After twenty-five days of detainment (and beatings, and torture) he had been sent to an island. "How auspicious," he had said to the officer who had come to collect him. "I've spent time on several, but the detention center of X—— I haven't yet seen."

Once there he found many artists and writers and the rank-and-file of the left and center, people he had known before and with whom he was now reunited. That was not surprising. Still, out of all the possible people he might have known at the island detention center, he had not anticipated finding Vangelis, whom Mihalis had not seen since Seferis's funeral procession.

"Why are you here?" Vangelis asked when they found one another. "We already have several more famous poets." The two men embraced, happy despite it all for the coincidence.

Mihalis waited for Vangelis to ask of news from Athens, from Halandri. When he didn't, Mihalis mentioned that he had seen Vangelis's wife just a month before, walking home from the girls' school where she taught. Vangelis scanned the room where they ate. Finally, his gaze settled on a skinny girl, no older, it seemed, than Anna. Later, Mihalis would learn her name was Nefeli. She sat alone, sketching, the long drape of her hair, black with hints of red, covering most of her face. If lice were a problem at this camp, she didn't seem to be afflicted.

"She's well, I hope?" Vangelis asked. He drew his spoon to his mouth but didn't take a bite. He glanced again over at the girl.

"Who's that?" Mihalis asked.

Vangelis took a bite, moved his soup bowl aside, and lit a cigarette. "What?" he asked.

*   *   *

They slept in barracks left over from the Italians. Some days, they were allowed to swim and walk on the shore; other days they were not. They rarely knew what was allowed because it seemed to change from hour to hour. Sometimes they ate fish, sometimes only broth. Things were inconsistent; how they were fed depended on who was in charge from day to day. They talked about food often. When they lay in their cots or double bunks at night, the room would be quiet, until someone would cry out: "*Soutzoukakia!*" And another would answer: "*Galaktoboureko!*" And another "*Spanakopita!*" and they would continue like that, shouting out favorite foods, until they'd fall asleep. Other times they called out names of women: "Irini!" "Melina!" "Sophia Loren!"

Yet they were better off there, they knew, than on some of the other islands—some prisons festered at the bottom of ravines, enclosed by twenty-foot-high barbed wire and locked in with iron doors—and surely better off than in previous times of exile. This Mihalis knew firsthand. But it didn't make it unobjectionable, and it certainly didn't make it morally excusable, so many people exiled simply for having a voice. It was still absurd. It was like paying someone one cent per day for his labors and then arguing that at least he was receiving that lousy cent. Or a man claiming he only beats his wife occasionally, on Sundays and holidays.

When it rained for stretches at a time, everything grew moldy and damp. The drinking water was sometimes brackish. Mihalis, though always a little thirsty, felt he would never be dry. He wrote poems he did not finish, a whole notebook of unrefined work. They'd surely take it from him if and when he was released.

When they were not working, cleaning the camp, doing laundry, or preparing their meals, the detainees busied themselves taking walks or studying the flora of the island. They read or wrote or sketched. Many, even if they had not arrived as artists, would leave at least as craftsmen: they created delicate worry beads and nice sitting chairs and tables they could gather around. Something from nothing, something in nothing.

A few boys from the village hung around the barbed wire fence that enclosed them, at first to observe, like curious anthropologists, and then to provoke. But soon the prisoners had become used to them, and they to the prisoners, and for a fee they'd bring chocolate or cigarettes, or simply provide amusing conversation. One boy's father was a guard, a less severe one who seemed as unsympathetic to the regime as they were. He had not asked for this, his look seemed to say; he was only doing his job. But that was why, of course, fanatical regimes prevailed. Too many people doing their jobs, not wanting to make a scene.

Though they ate their meals together, the men and women were lodged separately. The women's sleeping quarters were a short walk away, separated by a paltry, unintimidating fence. Near the back of the camp, someone had slashed a hole through it, and they passed through as nonchalantly as if ducking beneath a low copse of shrubs on a path. The guards, or people keepers, as the prisoners called them, either didn't notice or didn't care. Perhaps they too conveniently used this entrance.

During the day, when they were not working, Vangelis and Nefeli were suspiciously absent, a detail that most of their fellow prisoners took as matter-of-fact. The two seemed to always appear for their mess duties together. Sometimes, at night, Mihalis heard Vangelis rise from his bed when the guard had disappeared for a moment to relieve himself. Once, Mihalis woke uncharacteristically early to find Nefeli sneaking from their barracks, like a child at scout camp, barefoot. On the top of her delicate, tanned feet were splatters of paint: crimson and gold, like the marks of the stigmata. "Hi," she said. And then she shrugged, as if to say, *How much more can they do to me?*

Plenty, Mihalis thought. She was young, this was her first prison, and Mihalis hoped she would not have to learn the things he already knew.

One day in the barracks, Mihalis and Vangelis sat in their beds, beneath blankets. Outside fell a cold, miserable rain. Mihalis asked about Nefeli.

Vangelis waited. "What about her?" he finally asked.

"You're very covert, but our quarters are small," said Mihalis.

"Has it been so long since you've been with a woman that you can't recognize the act? It's something else entirely."

"You've got a creature like that sneaking into your tiny cot, and you're telling me you're not having sex?"

Vangelis smirked. But then his face changed; he grew quiet. "You don't think there could be something between a man and a woman besides sex?" he asked.

"Yes, of course there can," Mihalis said. "But in addition to sex."

Vangelis drew his legs to his chest and set his chin on his knees, rocking back and forth, the same way Mihalis knew Nefeli sat when alone, staring out at the water. "I came here with a good marriage, you know."

"And I came with one patched together like a quilt," Mihalis said. It was true. Irini wrote him countless letters, some of which he actually received. "These separations are doing wonders for it." Through their letters, they began to communicate even more than they had since her return to Athens, like yearning, adventurous teenagers, but like teenage love their relationship would never be easy. He missed her and wanted to talk with her now, wondering what she would make of Vangelis's newfound friendship. He hadn't mentioned it in his correspondence, not sure if she would be angry or sympathetic.

Vangelis managed a smile, though absentminded. "Come on," he said, standing up. "Let's go for a walk. I'll show you something."

Mihalis dressed in the raincoat Irini had sent, and he gave Vangelis a heavy sweater. Along with the letters, Irini sent packages filled with supplies: two wool blankets, soap and toothpaste and cigarettes and tins of fish, sleeves of crackers. Even a set of flannel pajamas, for which the other prisoners mocked him but of which Mihalis knew they were jealous. In this cold, dreary spell, Mihalis was happy to have all of it.

Vangelis held above them an almost-broken umbrella that threatened to snap down, and Mihalis then recalled a day when they were much younger men, ambling around Athens. A downpour had begun, and they ducked onto a parked bus, jumping off just as it was about to leave and darting onto another, all the while maintaining their conversation. Two middle-aged men had glared at them, and Vangelis and Mihalis had laughed.

Now they themselves were middle-aged, and they walked, their hands held behind their backs, through the wet, fragrant pines, the thick shrubs of eucalyptus, until they came upon an old husk of a church, the outside visibly neglected, overgrown with weeds.

"Don't tell me. You're taking me to church?" Mihalis asked.

Vangelis opened the front door, a large, creaky wooden gate, and motioned to Mihalis to follow him.

There were only a few rows of wooden chairs; the rest, Mihalis realized, had been removed and now served as the seating for their mess hall. Vangelis seemed impatient. "Well?" he asked. He pointed at the frescoes that covered the walls and, so far, some of the barrel-vaulted ceiling. It was a work in progress; Mihalis felt dizzy from the fresh smell of plaster and paint.

It was truly spectacular. One image melted into the next, a continuous Byzantine dream: Saint Nicholas, and around him small, crude, brightly rendered scenes of his miracles; the raising of Lazarus; Saint Peter with his staff and a scroll tied up not with a simple string but with an oversized red ribbon. It brought to mind the bright red bows Eleni would tie in his nieces' hair when they had been little, and how once they had come home sobbing, saying the teacher had taken them away. A symbol of communism. He remembered the way his sister had put her hands in the air, calling the accusation ridiculous and the offense completely unintentional. But beneath her incredulity he had detected insolence. The girls, from then on, demanded only white adornments for their hair.

Neither Mihalis nor Vangelis was a religious man but Mihalis found the image in the center, what appeared to be the Dormition of the Theotokos, to be stunningly moving. The Virgin lay atop a bier, and the faces of those who surrounded her, apostles, bishops, angels, were distorted with grief, and the emotion present in each figure's face was far unlike that of more traditional iconography. Some even appeared to be shouting. Where one would expect a Christ at the top of the image, holding the Virgin's spirit, there was only empty, blue space, like a cloudless spring sky. Mihalis could not tell if the omission was a statement or simply a matter of being incomplete.

Then, in the corner, Mihalis noticed a ladder and a scaffold, and above it, Nefeli. She was painting the sky a deep blue, a continuation of the previous image, and up there she seemed even more diminutive. She sat up and brushed her hair back with her forearm. Usually, she looked at Vangelis in a way that made Mihalis sick with envy. But this time her face didn't brighten.

"Why did you bring him?" she asked.

"You hate the rain," said Vangelis. "I assumed you'd be inside, sleeping."

Mihalis looked around. He felt he had somehow intruded upon a tender, intimate act. "*You* did this?" Mihalis asked.

"The two of us, together," said Vangelis. He stepped back toward the door and surveyed the scene. "All of it."

For two days following, a torrent of rain kept them all inside; most huddled in their beds with their thin, worn blankets. Vangelis, who for two nights had not seen Nefeli, was insufferably restless. He cheated at card games, not to win, but so they would be over quickly and he could return to his pacing. He looked out the window to see if she were coming up the path that linked their two quarters. "Why don't you just go find her?" Mihalis asked. "Maybe she's waiting for *you*."

Vangelis muttered something and flopped down on his bed, sulking.

Mihalis felt embarrassed at how much he had become fixated on Vangelis and Nefeli, but he couldn't help but wonder if they had fought because Vangelis had brought Mihalis to see the paintings.

The rain continued a third day, heavy and unyielding like some sort of biblical plague. Rivulets of water formed throughout the camp, tiny rivers going nowhere. The roof of the barracks began to leak, and the men busied themselves finding containers to catch the rain so the dirt floor would not be muddied. One of the more sympathetic guards arrived with coffee and cigarettes (for a fee, of course), something they hadn't had in days.

That afternoon, they talked of the rumor that had been suspended over them like a dead animal hung to bleed. Whoever signed papers of allegiance to the regime would be released.

"Never," said Vangelis. "I won't do it." Others agreed with him, though a few looked sheepish.

"Your intentions are less noble," Mihalis said. "Am I wrong?" Mihalis proposed that Vangelis was in no hurry to leave, that his stubbornness was not a matter of political conviction but one of simple emotion instead. That the make-believe life he'd created here suited him, that he liked being able to run around with a beautiful woman and throw paint and believe in artistic transcendence and the Platonic ideal and not drive his cab around Athens. "Meanwhile," Mihalis said, "your wife is at home, worried, broke. Alone."

And then Vangelis punched him, square under his left eye.

When Mihalis came to, he saw Vangelis's face hovering over him, closely, checking both his eyes and studying his cheek. Vangelis then put on his shoes and walked out into the downpour with his broken umbrella. Mihalis drew his hand to his throbbing face. He noticed Vangelis was wearing *his* raincoat. "Bastard."

When Vangelis returned, not long after, Mihalis was ready to punch him back. But Vangelis was sopping wet, visibly distressed: to hit him now would be like socking a child. "The women are gone," Vangelis said. "They've moved their camp." He was panting, like he had been running.

"To where?" another asked.

"The guard said he didn't know. More men are arriving today, and they needed the room."

"Maybe they've been released," Mihalis said.

"Or the guards want the women to themselves," another man added.

"No," Vangelis said. Mihalis wasn't sure to whose comment Vangelis was responding.

"Maybe they've all signed loyalty oaths," someone else said.

For a moment all of them were lost in their own verdicts. In quieter tones, one-to-one conversations, they talked of the women, how there had been rumors of their planning an intricate, mass escape, or some sort of insurrection. Perhaps, they thought, this was why they were isolated, and if so another testament to the bizarre reasoning of the powers that be. It was like throwing a match at a gas tank. Everyone knew that men left alone destroy themselves, and women alone flourish.

In the corner of the room, near the stove that blazed to seemingly no effect, Vangelis slowly peeled off his wet clothes, carefully hanging Mihalis's coat to dry. In his underwear, he crawled beneath his blanket.

Mihalis woke to another's gravelly voice, an older man who rarely said much at all. "Mihalis had a point, Vangelis. What he said earlier, about Nefeli. What is it, exactly, that you're doing?"

Vangelis said nothing, though he exhaled intently, as if he had been holding his breath. Mihalis knew he was, in spite of himself, thinking of Nefeli, wondering why she hadn't somehow come to tell him what had happened. Mihalis was wondering the same.

"*I* would sign something," another man said. "They're only words on a page."

"*Only* words on a page?" Mihalis blurted. "That's everything." But what he'd do to be back home with Irini. Shouldn't Vangelis have wanted this too, to be back with his wife? Mihalis wanted to wander through the square in Halandri, to drink coffee at Zonar's patisserie, to sit on his terrace and look out over the lemon trees. But he knew this was a dangerous way of thinking. *I'll get out when I get out,* he told himself. *This can't last forever.*

The next morning, the rain had subsided to a measly drizzle, and Vangelis asked Mihalis to walk to the church with him. This was evidently his apology for the deep-blue shiner beneath Mihalis's left eye. Mihalis shrugged and went along. After all, they had been friends for years.

On the way, Vangelis narrated to him the details of the paintings' creation—how they collaborated; the way Nefeli was allowed, with a guard, to go into the village and send for paint; the way another guard, a closet artist, had secured the scaffold and the paintbrushes in exchange for being allowed to add a few touches while pretending to keep an eye on them.

Inside, the two men sat in chairs, looking up at the unfinished ceiling. "I'm going to stay here a bit," Vangelis said. A few purple flowers, which grew all over the island, were scattered on the ground. Mihalis recalled having seen one tucked behind Nefeli's ear once, an embellishment both ironic and sincere.

"Don't wait for her too long," Mihalis said as he left, and Vangelis agreed. But when he wasn't back for hours, Mihalis assumed she had shown up, from wherever she was now being held. After Vangelis returned later that day, bleary eyed and glowering, Mihalis knew he hadn't had any luck. He couldn't help but marvel at their charged connection. Here in this prison camp Vangelis was more alive than Mihalis had ever seen him. He didn't paint sheepishly in the back garden the evenings he wasn't working, squeezing it in in the moments of free time available to him, as if changing a lightbulb or painting the shed. Mihalis first had wondered if it was Nefeli's youth or her art, and probably it was both, but Nefeli was also the first woman who had not only seen Vangelis as an artist *first* but as an artist *only*. Surely he had triggered something in Nefeli as well. They needed one another. Suddenly he thought of Anna and her natural rapport with Evan. Could he have been overly judgmental, of all of them?

After the transfer of the women came a new rule: they were not allowed to leave the immediate confines of the camp. They could not walk through the dense path to the church, not even with an accompanying sentinel. Many of the guards they had come to trust were being replaced. A new batch of freshly cut, surly ones was now arriving.

They began to welcome the presence of the boys at the fence; if anything, they might be able to bring them news. One day, they arrived excited and energetic. The oldest boy's eyes were wild, like an enraged horse. "The frescoes in the church," he said, out of breath. "They've transformed!"

"It's God!" said another. Mihalis noticed the large cross that hung around his neck, too big for his small body.

"It's magic!" said the youngest. His name was Niko, and his father was the one guard left whom they liked. "And one of them has your face," he said to Vangelis. "I'll be back with my father. He'll take you there to see." He turned and ran off.

As promised, Niko's father returned an hour later. "I can accompany you," he said to Vangelis. "I've obtained permission. He can come, too," he said, gesturing toward Mihalis.

"Why not," Vangelis said.

The boys were right. The frescoes had been transformed, some subtly, others in huge and glaring ways, and the tone had gone from mostly pious sobriety to unbridled drunkenness. Some of the faces looked more ecstatic than grief stricken. But the Virgin was now faceless, her features painted over to a blank slate, and instead of a blue robe covering her head, her hair fell down to the ground in thick, dark ropes.

The figure above her indeed had the face of Vangelis, the eyes exaggeratedly wide-set, the thick hair, an impish smirk. Another image bore the hairline, the large nose, and the unruly eyebrows of Mihalis. Some of the men in the painting were now women, modern-looking Greek women, the faces of fellow prisoners. Others drank from large wine jugs; others threw their heads back, laughing. It was almost bacchanalian.

"Nefeli," Vangelis said. His tone was sheer pride and joy.

"If it's indeed Nefeli," Mihalis asked, "how is she still allowed here? She must have some relationship with a guard." Mihalis knew this thought alone was maddening to Vangelis, the idea of she and a young guard coming here, to *their*—hers and Vangelis's—space, in the night.

"She's communicating with me," Vangelis said. "About the loyalty oaths. Whether to sign one."

"Well?" Mihalis asked. "Does she want you to?"

"That I haven't figured out." He climbed atop the ladder, grabbed a brush, and to the image of Mihalis added beneath the left eye a sizable bruise.

That night, Mihalis watched Vangelis rise from his bed and peer out the small window, looking for the guard. The old one, who got up frequently to use the bathroom and did not seem to care about Vangelis's moonlit meetings, had been relieved of night duties, and two younger, more fanatical ones took his place. There was never a moment without close watch, and although daytimes they were able to convince some guards to bend the rules, during the night they were draconian. Nights were the time of escapes.

The next morning the sun was shining and the air was drenched with warmth and wet. Spring was coming, and everyone's spirits lifted slightly. The guards allowed them to walk back and forth on the shore, a meager fifty-meter distance, but it was something. Vangelis convinced Niko's father and another guard to escort them back to the church. "One last time," they said. On the way, Mihalis tried to coax from them the women's whereabouts, but they claimed ignorance.

Inside the church, the frescoes had begun to resemble modernist painting more than Byzantine icons. The image of Mihalis now wore dark sunglasses, the blue of his bruise only a hint. The Virgin's face had been recast as that of Nefeli: the large forehead, sharp cheekbones, and heart-shaped lips were unmistakable. Her eyes looked like they were on fire.

Every one of the figures had one limb covered in a glaring white plaster cast. In the top corner, Nefeli had painted herself up on a scaffold, her arms stretched above her head as if she were hanging the entire fresco or holding up the sky.

Now Vangelis suddenly wanted out. He wanted to sign a loyalty oath, and he wanted to somehow communicate to Nefeli that she should, too. In fact, he was convinced that the plaster casts on the figures meant just this: *I surrender.*

Then what? Mihalis wanted to know. "Then you'll go back to Athens and live happily ever after? Is that what will happen?"

For the next two weeks, the guards received strict orders not to let the prisoners leave the camp under any circumstances: no walks on the shore, no walks to the village, no walks to look at the frescoes. The whereabouts of the women were still unknown, and the village boys were kept far away from the barbed wire fence. Once again they were cut off from everything.

One warm evening, Vangelis and some of the men played chess outdoors, in what they sardonically called their courtyard, a little area beside the barracks where they had some tables and chairs and rocks to sit on. Mihalis lay on the ground nearby, feeling the late-day sun on his face, dozing. He was startled by the crack of the loudspeaker.

A guard, in a typical self-important tone, announced that a batch of new prisoners was arriving from another island and that some of the current residents would be released. The boat was already waiting at the port, he said, and when their names were called, they should immediately assemble their things. Over the shoddy intercom, papers crackled and shuffled, and Vangelis stood up from the table so quickly he jostled the chessboard. The small wooden pawns scattered.

The first two whose names were called disappeared into the barracks immediately to pack their bags.

Another prisoner threw some pebbles in their direction. "Cunts," he called out after them.

"They've signed something?" Mihalis asked.

"They haven't said anything," said Vangelis.

The names were called slowly and erratically, sometimes two in a row, other times one, a three-minute pause, and then another. They were listed in no particular order. In itself it was a kind of torture, such lack of rhythm.

Then, they heard Vangelis's name, loud and clear.

"I knew it!" Mihalis said. "What are you scheming now?"

"I haven't signed a thing," he said. He looked distraught. Mihalis saw him as the man that he was: forlorn, emotionally devastated, and utterly exhausted.

And then Mihalis was called. The two men regarded each other but said nothing.

The same man who had thrown the stones called out to Mihalis, "You've barely been here six months!"

Mihalis thought about Irini, their bed, the clean sheets; he thought about what he would eat, the things he would drink, new poems he would write. Vangelis sat back down and put his head in his hands. Some of the younger prisoners, still full of bravado, sat at the other end of the yard, sharing one cigarette. They stayed close together—because their spirits had not yet been broken, they were treated the most brutally. From the looks on their faces, they knew they would not be among the lucky.

Inside, Mihalis gathered his things, spread them on his cot, and began to pack. Some whose names had not been called looked on in envy. To these men it did not matter who had or hadn't signed any-thing—they were traitors just by their fortune.

Vangelis came inside and opened his small duffel bag.

"She might be on the boat too," Mihalis said. He removed a sweater, a blanket, and a few cigarettes from his bag and placed them on another bunk.

Vangelis sat down on his bed and put his head between his hands. "This is a good thing," he said, his voice muffled. "Of course it is."

As they boarded, their bodies massed up against one another and spilled onto the narrow staircases and up to the ship's various decks. There were already other prisoners from other islands aboard, strewn like garbage on the benches and floor. Vangelis strained to find Nefeli.

Some women did mill around, though whether they had come from other islands or were from their camp was unclear. Mihalis followed Vangelis around the ship: the middle deck, back to the top, the middle again.

"Let's try the top one more time," Vangelis said. "We'll get the warmth of the sun."

"Maybe she's not here," Mihalis said. The boat was getting crowded, and Mihalis wanted to make sure he'd have a decent place to sit.

Vangelis was certain she was. He said he recognized one of the women from their camp.

Mihalis snapped, a new bout of frustration he thought he had overcome. "When, exactly, do you plan on resuming your real life? When we get off the boat? The first time you sleep with your wife?"

"Who are you to say what's real?" Vangelis asked. His face twisted in anger. "You've lived your entire life in some sort of ideological bubble."

"*I'm* the idealist?"

"Who can only have a real relationship with his wife through letters? And your false sense of importance—you were actually upset you hadn't been arrested sooner. It was a blow to your ego."

"That's preposterous."

Vangelis dropped his bag to the ground, as if he had forgotten he was carrying it. He kicked it along the floor to an open bench, and he used his jacket sleeve to wipe away the grimy water before he climbed onto the bench and laid his head on the small, dirty rucksack. Mihalis lay on the other side, feet to feet with Vangelis. They had taken these boats coming and going from places of detainment; they had taken them to the islands for vacation. But the former had long ago tainted the latter, and lying on those long, white benches would never be anything but gloomy and disquieting. If they used discrete boats to transport prisoners, he couldn't tell the difference. A boat ride to or from an island would always feel a certain way.

Then Vangelis sat back up. He brushed himself off, stood up, and walked away. He left his bag on the bench.

"Don't blame me if someone takes your seat," Mihalis said, wishing he could stop being so spiteful.

"Fuck you," said Vangelis.

And as Vangelis turned around, there stood Nefeli. Though they barely touched one another, their reunion was both poignant and bittersweet. There had been a great intimacy in their separation. From his bench Mihalis was able to watch them. They sometimes seemed to be talking, but mostly they were quiet. Later, when the wind picked up and the waters grew turbulent, Mihalis watched as Vangelis kept his hand on Nefeli's back while she vomited over the edge.

The trip was long; they stopped at other islands, sometimes for minutes, other times for hours, and more tired and mangy-looking men and women boarded, looking hopeful and exhausted and proud. Mihalis fell asleep, and when he woke, he didn't see Nefeli, though Vangelis stood nearby, staring out at the horizon. How bizarre that the outline of a mass of land, a rocky island, a narrow shore, could fill one with both dread and hope.

When night came, the weather calmed. They lay across benches or on the deck.

Mihalis looked out at the blue-black of the night sea, the frothy white of waves, illuminated by the ship's light. If we could film the workings of our minds, he thought, they would look like this.

They arrived at the port at dawn, the same port where tourists set sail for islands for vacations of drinking and screwing, and the browbeaten, skinny, and sickly prisoners materialized back into their own lives. Families milled about anxiously, craning their necks to see.

Mihalis noticed the way Vangelis and Nefeli disembarked, temporarily united, looking out together at everything else. Vangelis leaned in and whispered something into her ear, and Nefeli's long face lifted, just for a moment.

If someone had seen the two of them then, Vangelis and Nefeli, they would have been given away. But then they moved farther apart from one another so as to not cause suspicion. Only minutes later,

Vangelis greeted his wife. Mihalis hoped that someone, a husband, a boyfriend, a sister, her father, had come for Nefeli.

Nefeli brushed past Mihalis. Up close like this, the closest he had ever stood to her, he noticed her eyes were light, amber colored, and almost disarming—just like in the painting—unexpected against the black of her hair, as if they had been taken from another's face and planted there by mistake or afterthought.

She clutched her sketchbook close to her body and dragged her bag behind her, the curtain of dark hair covering her face. He watched her disappear into the crowd. What had Vangelis said to her, in her ear? What swift, gentle words? It drove Mihalis mad to think of it. Here was Vangelis, open to the experiences of the heart. And at his age. Even when Mihalis was young he had kept himself guarded, pushing Irini away when he wanted to let her in.

He recalled that first day he had seen Nefeli, that day in the mess hall. She had left her drawings on the table, and he had sifted through them when no one was looking. They were of long-faced, limp-haired women, almost featureless—cartoony, sad caricatures of herself. And this: they were without hands, or feet, or mouths.

Mihalis saw Irini approaching, lovely in a beige trench coat and red blouse, her hair tied back in a patterned scarf. Anna, whose delicate womanhood startled Mihalis, and Eleni followed closely behind her, the confusion of early morning still on their faces. Everyone looked so clean and Technicolor. Irini kissed his lips, and Mihalis was taken aback by the taste of her lipstick, so soapy, perfumed. Mihalis's hair had grown unruly, and when she tried to run her fingers through it, they became ensnarled.

Mihalis turned back to Vangelis, whose wife was glued to his side. Vangelis lifted his hands and shoulders slightly, a gesture of irrational defeat he didn't want anyone else to see.

Once, back in Athens, on a warm June day three weeks after their release, Mihalis and Vangelis were walking together when they saw Nefeli leaving the police station. They had to report weekly and were headed to do just that. Nefeli stepped out the door hesitantly, blinking into the blazing noon. Vangelis hid behind a kiosk and watched her, pretending to look at newspaper headlines. Mihalis bought some tobacco, and when Nefeli was out of sight, they continued to the station. Mihalis was about to mention something, but then he thought better of it. There was nothing to say.

Like he did each week, Mihalis signed in first and then recorded the time. He handed Vangelis the pen, but Vangelis was too preoccupied by the sign-in book. There was Nefeli's name and the time, 12:05, signed in only ten minutes before. He took the pen, he set it down, he ran his hands through his hair. Mihalis waited patiently. Was he looking there for some sort of signal? Some articulation of affection in her small, neat script?

The police officer on duty, bored and disaffected, sat with his feet on the desk. He sighed loudly. Vangelis picked the pen back up and painstakingly wrote his name in large, uncharacteristically legible letters. He stopped before he recorded the time, glancing again at her name. Mihalis looked at his friend and thought of the church and all those broken images, their emptiness pealing to no one, like the clamor of wooden bells.

Part Four

April to December 1973

Athens notice your poet
and put your submissive shoulder
to a new floor of madness

—LEFTERIS POULIOS, "ATHENS"

The times are all upside down, and yet
As water in a sinking
ship
Beauty pours in from everywhere

—YIANNIS PATILIS, "THE SONG NEVER STOPS"

36

In April of 1973, Loukas's father learned he had cancer. The course of treatment and prognosis were unclear and Loukas was going back to Athens. Sophie watched him pack, worry spread all over his face. He folded his underwear into a small suitcase and Sophie crawled out of bed, wrapped her arms around him from behind, and kissed his cheek. She let go to use the bathroom and from behind the half-open door she asked him if he was nervous.

"It will be okay."

A vaguely familiar feeling rushed over her, and at first she identified it as nostalgia, an almost nauseous ache. Then she thought it was the wash of sorrow she felt when she thought of her father's death.

"Why don't you come with me?" he asked, though slightly absent-mindedly. They had already discussed this, many times. The longer she stayed away, the harder it was to go back, and when she returned to Greece she felt it had to be for good. There was something too demoralizing about going back with the junta still in power. Besides, plane tickets were expensive. She told herself she just wasn't ready. Going back home would mean facing so much more than political uncertainty.

Oh, but she didn't feel well at all. She disappeared behind the bathroom screen and splashed cool water on her face. She drank from the faucet and brushed her teeth.

Loukas was sitting on the bed fumbling with his tickets and passport. "I'll miss you," he said. Sophie would miss him too. They had been living in that small apartment together almost a year. For a while they had talked of finding a bigger place, but this way they could save money, and how much space did they really need?

He looked at her curiously. "You look beat. Did you sleep?" He brushed her forehead with his hands, touched the damp skin around her eyes.

She told him maybe she was a little nervous, but no, she wasn't sick. It pained her to see his sad expression, and Sophie knew he was worrying about his father but undoubtedly thinking about his mother too, her death, the suddenness of it and the grief and shock that stretched out endlessly and what might now await him.

"I'll be fine," he said. He wrapped his arms around her and rested his lips on the top of her head.

Angelo knocked on the apartment door. He had offered to drive Loukas to the airport. "You coming?" he asked Sophie.

"She's feeling sick," interrupted Loukas. "You should stay here and rest," he said. As he walked out the door, he turned back to her, his large eyes looking both doleful and expectant. "I'll be home soon. Okay?"

After Loukas left, Sophie heated the water on the stove and looked out at the rain. When she scooped out the coffee, she retched, making it to the bathroom just in time. Had she not felt this before she would have assumed she had a stomach bug. *Oh, God,* she thought. She poured herself a mug of hot water and added some lemon instead.

She sat back down by the radiator, listening to the murmur of voices below. She was relieved to have something to redirect her attention. Over the past few weeks there had been a lot of activity at Monique and Angelo's, and Sophie wondered if it had to do with the anniversary of the junta. Had it really been almost six years since she'd been home? She was distracting herself. What seemed the more important question: When was that last time she had had her period? She couldn't remember. She felt another wave of nausea, but she took a few deep breaths, and it passed.

That first night with Loukas, when they had gone home together, giddy, drunk, and reckless, they had not been careful on any count. Sophie thought she was in a safe-enough time, but five weeks later, when she found herself vomiting in the bathroom at work each time she served an omelet to a customer, she had known. She thought this sort of thing happened to other girls, careless, stupid girls, and realized this had been an unfair assumption. She quietly went to the clinic run by some acquaintances, in an inconspicuous, large, fourth-floor apartment, and took care of it. Charlotte had driven her home and waited as she crawled into bed and fell asleep. "I've had one too," she had whispered in her ear when she hugged her. "You're going to be fine." They never discussed it again.

Sophie had imagined afterward she would feel great sadness, an unquestionable guilt, but instead she had felt a small amount of numbness and a whole lot of relief. It was something she could never admit to anyone. As much as she believed a woman's body was hers and hers alone, she couldn't imagine confessing the day-after's profound release. She could tell her closest friends that she had had the procedure, but she couldn't admit those subsequent feelings. The cramping, the bleeding; this was all tolerable. The physical they were comfortable discussing.

The whole experience had given her another connection to Loukas, but he knew none of this. It belonged to a time that did not belong to him, and she didn't think any good would come of his knowing, even now that they were living together. Rarely had they been separated; Loukas traveled to Lyon for work but each time only for a few days. Sophie, with her job as well as her graduate studies, was rarely in the apartment, but what she loved more than anything else was to come home late and find his warmth in the bed. When he left for a couple of nights she'd wake, reach for him, and be saddened to find only a blanket.

Sophie had the day off and planned to work on her dissertation. She threw open the windows, despite the cool air, and crawled back into bed, both grateful and wary to have the place to herself. She had to think, but she felt so tired. She laid her head back down and slept for three more hours, until Charlotte phoned and invited her for dinner.

While Monique and Angelo's place was delightfully chaotic, Charlotte and Etienne's felt like a sanctuary, and that night, as Sophie allowed herself to consider the immensity of her situation, it was just what she needed.

Charlotte handed her a cup of hot chocolate and showed her the stack of French and British and American magazines she had saved for her, all containing articles about Greece and the dictators. Sophie had been dying to slowly page through them, assemble them into another booklet. But now she wasn't in the mood. She just wanted to relax on Charlotte's couch and stare. Sophie sniffed her drink and took a small sip to see if it would engage any gag reflex. So far, so good. She looked to see if Charlotte was watching her but she was busy arranging herself underneath a blanket on a large chair, balancing her cup on her knee. Once she was settled she looked up at Sophie and asked her what was on her mind but then the phone rang and Charlotte untangled herself to answer it.

Sophie tried to recall who she had been when she had arrived in Paris, when she first met Charlotte. She was so much more spontaneous and passionate, also hotheaded and imprudent. Or did she just remember herself that way? That girl, real or imagined, was another person entirely. When Charlotte sat back down, Sophie asked, "In a few years, will I look back at myself and marvel at how young I was? Will I be exasperated by this current self?"

Charlotte thought about it a moment. "Maybe exasperated and sentimental," she said.

Sophie understood. Charlotte was right. A part of her liked her hotheaded, braver self, and another part found her silly and naïve, and she thought about how many selves she had and how this new, *pregnant* one might correspond with her idea of who she was, who Loukas was, who they might be together.

Charlotte continued. "You know, I never felt *less* like myself than when I was in my twenties. It's a difficult time. But marvelous."

Sophie, twenty-seven, could only begin to understand this sentiment. "Do you feel like yourself now?" she asked.

"Definitely," she said. "Except much younger."

Sophie laughed. "You've been so good to me," she blurted.

Charlotte shrugged, was lost in thought. "When I was a child, spending summers on Corfu," she said, "I had a nanny. Daphnoula."

"Yes," Sophie said. Charlotte often talked about her childhood summers in Greece.

Charlotte continued. "Now when I think of it, she was probably only your age, even younger. Her fiancé dropped her off at the house each day; she taught me Greek, she taught me to sew and to sing. She was just a young village girl, but she spoke in a way that I knew she had designs on more."

"Did you stay in touch?"

Charlotte shook her head. "When I was older and began to travel to Corfu alone, with friends for vacation, I tried to find her. Her father said she was gone, but that's all he would say. Later, I found out that she had ended up in Moscow."

"Self-imposed exile?" Sophie asked. This part of the story she hadn't ever heard.

Charlotte shrugged. "When I look back, she always did have a leftist sensibility." She rose from the couch and began folding a pile of laundry. "It's important to have mentors." She seemed to want to say something else but was quiet for a moment. "I always thought, if I had children, I'd take them back to Corfu, give them the same gift of Greek summers, of another language, another culture."

"You'll go back. With Etienne," Sophie said.

Now Charlotte smiled. "Yes, someday. We'll all go back." Charlotte had a sticker on her car that said DANGER, DICTATORSHIP: STAY AWAY FROM GREECE. The end had said IN 1968, and each year, as the junta persisted, Charlotte took a marker and changed the year. But Sophie could tell what saddened Charlotte even more was this mention of children.

"You can adopt me," Sophie blurted. "I'm a good daughter." As she said it, though, she wondered, *Am I?* This little statement alone felt duplicitous. And then the idea that she would have to worry about being not only a good daughter but a good mother crossed her mind; it was too much to think about. She wanted to tell Charlotte she thought she was pregnant. But it felt too soon, too uncertain. She wasn't ready to tell anyone yet. Not even Loukas knew.

"Haven't we already?" Charlotte said. "Adopted you?"

Gentle and nurturing Charlotte would have been a great mother. Years earlier, after Sophie had been working at the café a few months, a friend of Charlotte's had visited with her two daughters, slightly younger than Sophie. Charlotte seemed thrilled by their presence. "The girls have been studying in the UK," Charlotte said. "I've missed them. Their mother and I went to university together." Charlotte polished glasses as she spoke. "Your mother must miss you and your brother, no?"

Sophie had never thought then about being missed. Now, as she lay comfortably on Charlotte's couch, nested in blankets, she thought about that exchange again. Sophie knew her mother had reluctantly seen Paris as a measure for keeping her daughter safe. As something temporary, a year abroad, two years at most. How much longer could it last? And how often did they still ask themselves that question? Taki had already finished his degree and had begun his master's. He had even gotten married and had told his family only two weeks before the event. Now he had a baby: an entire life he was living away from home. But Taki didn't go to the States to study, no matter what he said. He went to the States to go to the States, and school just happened to be something he did while he was there. While Sophie fully expected to one day return, Sophie knew her mother could only hope Taki would come back for occasional visits, perhaps for the weddings of his sisters, the christening of their children.

Sophie had always wanted to ask Charlotte about children but the question seemed too intimate, even with Sophie's unintentional French bluntness. But she and Charlotte had become good friends. She could probably ask her now; the question, in light of Sophie's still-undisclosed condition, would have so much more weight. She thought of Charlotte's abortion and wondered if she regretted it. Charlotte only had said if she *had* had children, she would have taken them to Corfu, but entertaining the idea of something did not necessarily equal an intense desire, though it certainly could. Yet often it was a mature acknowledgment of life's array of choices. No thinking person didn't consider other paths; it was when the *other* became an obsession that there was a problem. But Sophie didn't bring any of it up. She could barely articulate it to herself. She was sleepy, and she sensed Charlotte was exhausted too. Sophie's eyelids felt heavy. She yawned.

Charlotte brought her an extra pillow, and Sophie settled into the couch. "You don't want the guest room?" Charlotte asked, but Sophie told her the couch was fine.

Charlotte stood over her a moment, as if she had reconsidered and wanted to keep talking. Her lips parted and closed. She sighed and a distant look swept over her usually cheery face. "Everybody wants to know why a woman doesn't have children. But does anyone bother to ask one why she did? To me, it seems the more obvious question."

The next afternoon, right before she was leaving for work, Loukas called as he had planned. His flight went well, though a bomb had gone off earlier in the Athens airport. He added this as an aside, as if talking about the almonds he had eaten on the plane.

"What? A bomb? Was anyone hurt?" Sophie asked.

"Only cuts and scrapes," Loukas said.

"How can you be so nonchalant?"

"Total commotion. But no one hurt. The bomb was in some sort of foam cushion."

"Clever," Sophie said. "But what's the point, then?"

"That's strange, coming from you," he said. "The point *isn't* to hurt innocent people."

"No?" Sophie asked.

They had different ideas about violent protest: Loukas felt sometimes it was the only way to get political attention; Sophie believed in peaceful negotiation. She didn't want to get into this circular discussion again.

She changed the subject and asked about home.

His father's surgery was the next day, he told her, and his father was upbeat, happy to see his son, trying hard not to act afraid. "I think he's relieved he's going to have it taken care of; at least after they see what he's up against, he'll have a better sense of where he stands."

"Not knowing is an awful feeling," Sophie said.

Loukas was quiet a moment. She asked him if Athens looked the same, and he told her it did. "The light is so bright. I forgot how intense it is. And it's so warm here."

He asked how she was feeling, and she told him better. She

didn't like keeping things from him. But he had enough to worry about without the added fact that he would soon be a father. It wasn't that she wasn't going to tell him, but she wanted to do it in person.

"Let's get married," he blurted. "Let's get married and come back here, to Athens."

"Romantic," she said. "A proposal over the telephone."

"I'm serious."

She was quiet for a moment. Did he know? She didn't want this to be about some strange masculine duty. "I love you," she said. "Take care of your father. Athens is making you sentimental."

When she hung up, she was shaken, but not about keeping her possible pregnancy to herself. About this she was amazingly calm, and she would tell Loukas when he returned. It wasn't like the first time, when she'd felt panic. In fact, she was excited that parts of them had merged and grown there again, that she hadn't done herself physical damage, that her body hadn't failed her. What unsettled her was the idea of going back to Greece. She could spend a lifetime traveling from city to city, country to country; she could fall in love with French and Italians and Moroccans and Japanese; she could travel through Africa and Asia and South America and the States, and Sophie knew that Greece would still pull her back. And for some reason, this filled her with heaviness.

But she didn't want to marry Loukas now. Someday, maybe, but not yet. She saw marriage at such a young age as a mark of the naïve, the innocent trying to appear adult. To Sophie, those who married young seemed more childish than ever, unfazed by desire or the possibility of failure or heartache. She acknowledged the beauty in this. She was twenty-seven, hardly a child bride, but she still thought of herself as the age she had been when she had arrived in Paris, twenty-one. Loukas had just turned thirty-two; each April they celebrated his birthday right before they solemnly acknowledged the junta's reign.

Two weeks later, when Loukas returned, it was late and Sophie was already in bed. That morning, she had gone to the doctor. Pregnant indeed, about seven weeks. Scattered around her were books for her thesis and a notepad filled with her writing and notes. She composed in longhand and only used her typewriter after she had a sense of what she was going to say.

He looked exhausted but happy to be back. His father's condition was stable. He crawled into bed. "Can you make room for me, or have you already gotten used to my not being here?" He took off his pants and swept off the bed with his arm, letting all the books crash to the floor. He kissed her and closed his eyes, put his head on her chest, and stayed there for a moment.

"I'm too hungry to lie here," he said. "Do we have anything to eat?"

Sophie motioned for him to rummage through the tiny kitchen. He dug two bottles of *ouzo* from his bag, the kind she had asked for, with the girl on the label, though she had never cared for it much while she lived in Greece. In France, it took on a nostalgic element, and she developed a taste for salty, briny fish and *ouzo*. But when Loukas opened a tin of sardines, Sophie jumped out of bed and came at him, disgusted. He was going for the olives when he looked up and saw her.

"Hungry?" he asked.

Sophie ran to the corner. Loukas stood at the counter and watched, bemused.

"What is that awful smell?" Sophie asked. "Those fish smell like they spoiled. Get them out of here." She darted to the toilet and hovered there, waiting for the next wave. "Please," she said. "Open the damn window or something."

Loukas did as she asked. Sophie slumped over the toilet.

"Sophie?" Loukas asked.

"What."

"When were you going to tell me?" But he didn't look angry at all. In fact, he looked pretty pleased with himself.

Sophie looked up at him. The smell of the toilet was making her sick.

"Sophie," Loukas said. "I wasn't born yesterday." He handed her a glass of water, and after she brushed her teeth, she drank it. "Are we having a baby?"

We, she thought. "I didn't want to tell you over the phone," she said. She crawled past him and splayed out on the rug because it was closer than the bed. He lay down next to her.

He wanted to get married, he said once more. He wanted to be a father, and no, they were hardly too young.

Sophie was always amazed at his resolve, his decisiveness. "I don't want this to be because it's the right thing to do. Some sort of macho-hero thing. Save the poor helpless girl."

"Oh, Sophie. Always with the women's lib."

"You know what I mean," Sophie said. "Is it a religious thing?"

"Of course not," he said. "I'm no more religious than you."

"Come on," she said. "Not quite. I *see* you, crossing yourself like an old, crazy widow when you witness an ambulance."

He laughed but crossed his arms in front of him and gave her a look of exasperation.

"Let's have the baby," Sophie said. "Then let's worry about getting married."

"That's backwards," he said.

"We already live together. We slept together the first night we met, when you were living with another woman. We live in a city hundreds of miles from our families. Now you want to argue for tradition?"

"Our own tradition," Loukas said.

She could see them having a life in Paris together, pushing a stroller through the parks. She could teach poetry at the university, and they could live in a large, chic apartment like Charlotte and Etienne, with turn-of-the-century damask furniture and large, beautiful windows. But when she really tried to imagine what having a child would be like, she saw herself in Athens, the summers in Kyparissia or on quiet islands, the long days at Sounion, family lunches on terraces or bustling cafés in Plaka. The idea of going back to Greece was more appealing than she wanted to admit.

Sophie was afraid to say all this out loud because she knew Loukas would agree. Had they had been waiting for this? They were both quiet a moment, lying on the white *flokati* in their Paris apartment as if Athens were splayed above them on the cracked plaster ceiling. Sophie turned on her side to face Loukas. His eyes were closed, but her movement startled him and he leaned up on his elbows.

"Where would we live?" she asked.

"We'd figure it out. Wherever you like."

Sophie imagined all the neighborhoods of Athens she liked: Mets, behind the Kalimarmaro stadium, or Kypseli, or the other places that were lovely but surely expensive: the area surrounding Lykavittos, or Psychiko, or the sprawling, pristine land of Kifissia. Her family's rental flat in Victoria or even the quieter streets of Halandri. "You really would want to?" Sophie asked finally, though she knew the answer. Maybe she was really asking it of herself. "Because I think if we left Paris, we wouldn't come back."

"We could visit. I want our daughter to be cosmopolitan."

Sophie laughed. Already Loukas was imagining a daughter? She could only in her mind think *baby*, and even that was a stretch.

"Yes," he said. "A headstrong little beauty, like you."

It struck Sophie, this discussion of Athens as a mysterious place, a young couple planning a move to the unfamiliar and convincing themselves they could make it work.

"I can start looking for a job tomorrow."

"Well," Sophie said. "At least we have some money saved."

As quickly as Sophie had decided to come to Paris she was deciding to leave it, and their plans to go to Athens progressed. Though Sophie insisted that if they were going to drive through the south of France and through Italy, and then take a boat to Athens, she wanted to wait until she didn't feel so ill. Those first months were the hardest, everyone said. They would wait another month.

"It's our honeymoon," Loukas told everyone.

"You got married?" came the reply.

"We're doing things out of order," he'd say.

Sophie also had to meet with her dissertation committee. She had plenty of work still to do, and conscientious Loukas did want to make sure he had employment in Athens before quitting his job in Paris. It wasn't that she couldn't continue writing in Greece; in fact, to start her thesis in France on the poetry of exile and to finish it after her return home seemed fitting. But she had to finish a draft before she gave birth, or else, she worried, she never would. And her family, she had to tell her family. The dissertation seemed easy comparatively. Not only would she be returning to her family that she had left when she was basically a girl, she would also return as a part of Loukas's family, and therefore Nick's. It was too complicated to think about.

One night in July, after a long, exhausting meeting with her adviser, Sophie took the metro to the café, where Charlotte and Etienne were throwing them a good-bye party. Even the dim, gritty subway filled her with nostalgia. In a way, Paris too was home, and it began to confuse her, picturing the two of them living in Athens. That is, she could see the two of them together, and she could sort of imagine a child, but she couldn't imagine the day-in-and-day-out of their lives.

Loukas had already secured a job, yet Sophie still had yet to tell her family about her pregnancy and return. Saying it out loud made it too final, and though Sophie was happy about the baby she was torn about the move. Perhaps being an expatriate suited her. In Paris, she felt different, important even in her distinction.

Who would she be in Athens?

At the next stop, a young couple boarded with a stroller that folded up like an umbrella. The man held a small blond boy in his arms, and the child, grinning, offered her his dingy stuffed toy. Oh! She loved this city; maybe she wanted to stay and take her own stroller onto the metro, a baguette under one arm and a baby's blanket under the other. In all the planning, the tying up of loose ends, Sophie had barely paused to accept that she would be saying good-bye to Paris. The city would always hold for them a sort of intense, romantic, idealistic pull.

At the café, Loukas and Monique and Angelo were already there, along with Maria and Alex and several others from her conversation class, Loukas's coworkers, her fellow students. Her life in Paris. Etienne waved from behind the bar. He was playing Greek music on the stereo. Charlotte greeted her at the door with a hug. She had already promised Sophie she'd visit. "I won't go with those maniacs in charge," she said again. "But I'll be there immediately after."

Charlotte continued, "It's different for you. It's your home."

Already Sophie was crying and couldn't respond. She wasn't sure what or where her home was anymore. At that moment it seemed it was right there.

"Okay," Charlotte said in the midst of a hug. "Maybe I'll come regardless, when the baby is born."

Even Christophe, in all his stoicism, gave Sophie a big hug and a kiss. She wondered if this was why Anna once said she never wanted to leave Athens. When in a new place, the looming reality of a good-bye always clouded everything. They had been saying good-bye for days.

"It's just the pregnancy," Sophie said. "It's made me emotional."

"You've been like this since the first day I met you," Christophe said.

Late that night, after countless rounds of good-byes, Sophie and Loukas walked home, carrying two large bags of gifts from their friends. Loukas was unusually pensive and careful, taking her hand when they crossed streets, hovering. When she asked him what was wrong, he said, "I need to talk to you about something. About our trip."

"What about it?"

"Promise me you'll listen to what I have to say." He set both bags down on the sidewalk and put his hands on her shoulders. He touched her cheek, then her belly.

"Of course," Sophie said. What was this? she wondered. Loukas looked so serious. "If you stop treating me like I might explode."

His face took on a strange cast then, and he studied her eyes as he spoke, all the while keeping one hand on her body. The night was warm and balmy, and Sophie would remember this, one of her last memories of Paris, as if it were a photo taken from a balcony up above.

The morning they were to leave Paris, Sophie woke before their alarm clock, before the sun, before the street below them came alive with cars and scooters. This was especially strange considering how little she'd slept, how through the night she moved from one emotion to the next. All the while, Loukas stuck to his promise that it was her decision. In many ways, though, this made it harder. He swore he would not pressure her, and he didn't. More importantly, he swore he himself had not been pressured.

"I feel like a terrorist," Sophie whispered.

Loukas put a finger to his lips and then hers.

"What, are we bugged or something?" she whispered, this time louder.

"You're not a terrorist," said Loukas.

"Define *terrorist*," Sophie said. "In what way does transporting explosives not fit the definition?"

As Monique and Angelo had convinced them, it had made perfect sense in an imperfect way. Sophie and Loukas wanted to travel through France and Italy before the baby, and a pregnant woman was probably the least suspicious of the bunch, a fact that Sophie found disheartening but reassuring. If they were to carry a box full of bomb-making supplies, hidden carefully in their car, they would not be discovered. Security on these ferries was insignificant, they were assured, and they would drive on and off it with no problem. When she'd resisted initially the others had seemed surprised. Hadn't she put out resistance literature? Hadn't she once plastered flyers over Athens in the middle of the night?

Yes, she agreed she had. But hadn't any of them noticed she was *pregnant*? Perhaps a younger Sophie would have found it all wildly and wonderfully revolutionary and seen it as a solid reentry in such a cause, but the pregnant Sophie felt neither young nor particularly radical. And where were these bomb-making supplies coming from? Who was making them? Had they been in Monique and Angelo's apartment below her? She couldn't help but think of the luckless but well-meaning who were injured, killed even, doing the same thing. But she wasn't sure what bothered her most, that explosives might have been assembled in her building or that she hadn't been included, until it was particularly convenient, in the project.

Sophie knew that she had encountered a world whose workings were already in motion and whose intricacies and interconnections were far beyond what she had imagined. It was amazing what you could miss when you weren't looking. She felt betrayed by Loukas, but he swore he hadn't known much before. Just that it made so much sense.

"Sense?" Sophie asked. "How does this make sense?"

In the end, though, she had been neither shoved into the plot nor convinced by ideology. Rather, she did it for that old Sophie, her old self. She had come full circle, having fled Greece as a dissident and now returning as one. And, as was usually the case, Sophie was torn between running in the other direction and hurling herself toward the eye of the storm.

As they drove through France, it took at least an hour of her cringing over each bump in the road before Sophie could lean back in the passenger seat. Her shoulders hurt from holding them so rigidly. To look in the back of the car would only reveal suitcases and over-stuffed shopping bags of their books and clothes, and things for the baby given to them by friends: a playpen, blankets and clothing, even a stroller. But what lay beneath it? What did a detonator even look like? She pictured a box of tiny watches, crammed together and ticking, sitting beneath blankets with satin edges; she imagined hundreds of little light switches or tangles of red and black wires. Loukas kept glancing at her, telling her to relax, resting his hand atop her knee; the whole thing seemed to charge him up. Once, after they had stopped for something to eat, he began kissing her outside the car, full of desire. If she had complied they would have had sex right there on the hood of the dusty little car, and rocked the car too aggressively, and dissipated themselves, the car, and all those baby things into the south of France.

They stopped that evening in Nice, where they would get some sleep and leave early the next morning. Nice reminded her of Greece and she felt a deep pull in her belly. But they were still far away. She was tired and quickly fell into a deep, heavy nap.

Two or so hours later, she was brusquely awakened by loud

noises—gunshots, bombs, she didn't know—and sprang up in bed. The sense of fear was astonishing; for a moment she couldn't move, and had it not been for the throbbing pressure of her bladder she wouldn't have. A note on the nightstand from Loukas said he had gone for a walk and some coffee and would bring her back something to eat, and maybe later they'd go out again. He had originally wanted to drive straight through the night and she had convinced him otherwise. But now he was acting as if they were simply on vacation.

Sophie used the bathroom and splashed cold water on her face. It was dark, and she peered out the window. Over the water she could see fireworks. Fireworks. Bastille Day. Of course. Traveling was so disorienting; she hadn't even remembered.

Still, the loud noises unsettled her and she crawled back in her bed, beneath the covers, and didn't emerge until Loukas returned to the room with a bottle of wine and two baguette sandwiches, a bar of chocolate. He sat on the bed and stroked her hair. "Hi, love," he said. "Did you sleep a little? You must be hungry."

"Where's the car?" she asked him.

He touched her forehead and then her cheek. "You're all clammy. Do you have a fever?"

"No," she said. She sat up and took a bite of the sandwich. She was starving.

Loukas looked at her strangely. "The car? Where we left it. Why?"

Another bang now, larger, perhaps shot from a cannon. Even Loukas jumped this time.

"And it's fine there, with all this going on? You think it's safe?"

"Baby," Loukas said. "Yes." He pushed her hair out of her eyes and pulled her toward him. "You think it will spontaneously combust?"

"I have no idea," said Sophie. "I have no idea about anything."

When they drove onto the boat from Brindisi, Sophie was certain their car would be searched. She felt herself not quite breathing as the dockworkers waved them on. Then, as they parked in the long line and stopped the engine, she was hit with an incredible sense of déjà vu. The smell of the diesel, the thrum of the boat engines, the squawk of gulls. The shouting people and the docks and their gasoline-fishy scent made her feel as though she had just taken that boat from Greece to Italy the week before, and not six years earlier.

When it was time to retire to their sleeping quarters—men and women slept separately—Sophie kissed Loukas good night and tried to ignore the nagging sensation that she would not see him again. It was anxiety, that was all, from the knowledge that they were transporting detonators. But just because she knew it was simply anxiety didn't make it any less tolerable, and she felt it covering her, a dark, gray cape.

In her sleeping cabin was a woman not much older than Sophie, and her four-year-old daughter. The Italians, Sophie had found, treated pregnant women with a stunning reverence; she had been beamed at, made to listen to stories of labor and child rearing. She didn't understand what they were saying but knew what they were talking about.

Barely five months along and already her belly gave her away. It was her narrow hips and small frame, they said. She had nowhere to grow but out. People had told her it would be a while before she'd begin to show, but Sophie swore her belly had protruded from the moment of conception. All of her seemed to be moving forward, stretching out to something ahead. When she looked at her profile in the mirror, she was stunned to see she was not C-shaped and curved over with her back concave. No, her ass was as full as ever. There was just so much of her.

The little girl, Antonia, seemed happy to have a stranger sharing their space. She taught Sophie a song in Italian, whose words Sophie didn't understand but was able to sing phonetically. She had a tumble of light-brown curls and eyes the color of honey, a mini version of her mother, and in that tiny cabin Sophie fell asleep wondering for the first time what her baby would look like; until then, the idea of an actual human had seemed abstract. It was still only a pregnancy. An extension of herself.

She could hear the little Antonia climbing up the bunk, to where Sophie slept.

"Yes?" Sophie said, in English.

The girl spoke to her softly in Italian, and the mother translated for her, into English. "She wants you to know that her father is Greek. He lives in Kalamata."

"You're going to visit him?" Sophie asked.

The little girl smiled, exposing her tiny teeth, like Chiclets. "*Buona notte*," she said. And she looked at Sophie for a minute, studying her belly, and then her face.

"Good night," Sophie said.

Her mother whispered something to her in Italian, and the little girl giggled.

"*Kalinichta*," she said.

"She's learning Greek," her mother said.

In the bunk below, Antonia sang her song once more, unmistakably a lullaby, and soon both she and her mother were still. Sophie, on the other hand, was distressed. Convinced that whatever materials were packed in their small, gray Deux Chevaux would vaporize the ship and everyone on it into the Adriatic, despite having been persuaded otherwise, or maybe just lied to for a cause for which she'd once willingly exiled herself, she wondered if she could go down to where the cars lined up in neat rows.

She got down from her bed carefully and slipped into her shoes.

On the ship's deck, Sophie stared out at the deep night. She walked down the stairs to where the cars were kept, kicking over an ashtray. It was eerie down there; she felt it in her chest and pelvis. Two men, smoking cigarettes and talking on the stairs, stopped her. They spoke in Greek.

"Where are you going?" They both looked at her belly.

"I wanted to get something from my car."

"Is it urgent?"

Sophie couldn't answer this. What *was* she going to do? Just look at the car? Listen for a ticking clock? She didn't even know where the things were hidden: In the trunk, beneath their suitcases? Beneath the floorboards? She hadn't thought to ask.

"I suppose not." She was suddenly aware of her thin pajamas, her messy hair. She wondered if they would follow her; this could be a bad idea.

"Go back to sleep, doll."

The other laughed. "Nighty-night."

Sophie climbed back up the stairs.

"Crazy women," she heard one say.

They arrived at the port and drove off the boat as if they were simply coming back from an island vacation. Ten kilometers in, they pulled over in the parking lot of a deserted roadside taverna. "We're meeting them here," Loukas said. He got out of the car and looked around.

Them? Sophie thought. When she noticed a small, black Citroën on the other side of the lot she was reminded again of the life she'd just left. A young man wearing sunglasses climbed out of the car and ran his hands through his longish hair. It was Nick. He walked toward them, smiling big and bright, and kissed her on both cheeks. "It's nice to see you, Sophie," he said, pulling her in for a hug. "Lovelier than ever," he said in her ear. With his face nestled in her neck she was reminded of sleeping next to him on her roof, a sudden, sharp but pleasant hit of nostalgia.

"Hi," Sophie said, pulling back. "Nice to see you, too."

He hugged his cousin, like they were just meeting for lunch, though Sophie supposed that Loukas had recently been back. Two young women also emerged, ponytailed, dressed simply but stylishly in wide-leg trousers and striped tees. Loukas unloaded their suitcases and the boxes of baby things onto the ground and then into the car Nick had arrived in. "Good cover," commented one of the sailor twins, pointing at Sophie's belly. "Nice disguise."

"It's real," Sophie said, touching her middle. With her other hand she wiped her brow. It was hot.

"Even better," the other replied. "You must be getting close." She climbed into the front passenger seat.

"I've still got months," Sophie said, though no one was paying attention. Two things came to her mind. Were these women so dedicated to their cause that they would assume any pregnancy was a disguise? And did she really look *that* pregnant?

"How'd the trip go?" Nick asked them.

"Fine," Loukas said.

She knew he was involved and that she'd see him very soon. She didn't realize he'd be the first person to greet them. But Loukas's father was living at Nick's parents' house, where they were headed, so she supposed she'd be seeing far more of him. And she couldn't go back to Halandri yet. Sophie had mentioned to her mother that she had wanted to come soon for a visit. She had not yet said they were moving back for good, partly because she didn't want to face a barrage of questions over the crackly long-distance call. And the other reason was that telling her mother was an admission that her life in Paris was over.

The only one who knew was Mihalis, and he had promised not to say a thing. So that night, she and Loukas would possibly spend the night in the house where they had first met, a place that had once felt if not intimate then familiar to them both: those spacious, airy terraces, the teak furniture, the Persian rugs.

Loukas had been the one to tell Nick of their involvement several months after they had begun dating, and Nick had been affable, and when Loukas came back to Greece to see his father the first time, he had told Nick that it was serious. That was all he mentioned about it, but Sophie kept wondering, *No, Loukas, what did he say? No jealousy at all? No feelings of betrayal or anger or disbelief?* Since Sophie, Nick probably had had dozens of girlfriends, and there had surely been many before her, too.

Sophie wanted to hear more from Nick, curious about who he had become, but she also was ready for the trip to be over. Fortunately Nick and his friends were focused and hurried. She noted there was something changed about him, perhaps simply maturity, and something that remained exactly the same. An earnestness. Even through medical school, he seemed to have remained true to the cause. He had been far more active in resistance efforts from abroad; he had been arrested, he had that badge of courage. With it came a certain level of purity.

Nick called to the two women. "Well?" he asked.

One of the women made the okay sign. "We're set," she called. "Everything looks good."

When had they checked, and what? Sophie wondered. Clearly when

Nick was greeting them, but was it all so easily accessible? She realized now that she hadn't wanted to know. Just like she didn't want to ask Nick about his life. She was happy with Loukas, but things with Nick had never been resolved or ended but simply faded away. And maybe that was a good thing, she decided, and stopped herself from the over-analysis. Now was not the time to expose herself to more emotion.

After a few brief pleasantries, Nick hugged them both once more, squeezing Sophie's hand. Then he threw his backpack into the car with the materials and climbed into the driver's seat. "I'll see you at home," he said.

They watched the car drive away, the women's ponytails waving out the windows. Sophie felt a wash of jealousy. She ran her hand over the Citroën's hood. "This is our car?" Sophie asked.

"You sure you don't want to go to your house?"

"My mother doesn't even know we've left Paris, remember, let alone that we're in the country."

"And you're planning on telling her when?"

"Soon, obviously." She looked at Loukas closely, and then their new car, and all of it flooded over her: the stress of the trip, her old boyfriend and whatever his new life entailed, the fact that they had just arrived in Greece and she had no idea where they were going next. Where would they even live? Sophie was thinking the apartment in Victoria, but she wasn't even sure if her mother had renters now or not. If she really wanted it, she could have given her mother some warning, plainly asked about it, and she realized she was still wary about stepping back into the familiar. The apartment in Victoria would make her feel settled, and "settled" was not a state she viewed positively. It sounded to her too much like "trapped."

Sophie strained to look into the backseat, filled with their things. "We're going to need to buy a crib," she said. "So many diapers." She laughed, a bizarre, guttural grunt. Until then, the enormity of what they had just done, and what they would soon do, had only struck her in quick, electric sparks. Now, in the warm Greek night air drenched with the smell of the sea, she let its vastness envelop her, and, safe and in a car of their own where a baby would soon ride in the backseat, she put her head in her hands and cried.

37

The next afternoon, while Sophie slept and Loukas accompanied his father to the doctor, Eleni, unaware that her oldest daughter was anywhere but Paris, came home from work in the afternoon haze and took a cool bath. She poured water onto a washcloth and folded it onto her forehead, closing her eyes and laying her head back. She was not thinking of her children or her patients or Dimitri or Andreas or Christos or any man at all. She was thinking about where she would go in August. Often she spent it in her ancestral village of Kyparissia—even the previous summer she had gone with Anna—but this year, she wanted to go somewhere she had never been. Anna was leaving in a few weeks for Stella's place on Hydra, and the house would soon be completely empty save for her.

Each year Eleni looked forward to that break. But this year she didn't want to leave her clinic, though things had slowed considerably in the summer, as if both human suffering and human cruelty had paused. Maybe she didn't want to leave Andreas. The two had become somewhat inextricable.

The phone began to ring. Anna—for whom the caller was probably looking—was out shopping for a new bathing suit. Eleni told herself she'd let it ring four times first. If it went a fifth, she'd answer it.

A fifth ring, and then a sixth. One more and she'd get up. No mother is able to let a phone simply go ringing. What if it was an emergency? She jumped from the tub, tossed her robe over her damp skin, and headed down the stairs to the foyer. As she reached for the phone she almost slipped on the tile, which resulted in her voice sounding more irritated than she was.

Her daughter. "Sophie *mou*! Is everything okay?"

"I woke you up?" Sophie asked.

"No," Eleni said. "I was in the bath. What is it?"

"Any time I call something has to be wrong?"

Sophie had been good about communicating with letters, but

long-distance phone calls were rare. Eleni had almost forgotten about Sophie's defensiveness; it was subdued in written form. She adjusted her robe. "No, of course not."

Sophie continued, but her voice sounded strange, heavy, a little guarded. "Everything's okay." Eleni didn't say anything, and Sophie, too, paused, and for a moment neither spoke.

"I'm coming back to Athens," Sophie blurted. "Loukas, too."

"You're kidding," Eleni said.

"No," Sophie said.

"When? Soon? For how long?"

Her daughter was silent on the other end, and then she heard her whisper to someone else. "Actually," she finally said, "I'm already here. In Palio Psychiko."

Eleni stared at the lace-patterned cloth that sat beneath the phone. Just a minute out of the cool bath and sweat trickled down her neck. She had thrown the front shutters open when she had come home and hadn't bothered to close them before her bath. Now she felt overexposed, standing there barefoot, dripping wet, her hair messily piled atop her head.

"Loukas's dad?" Eleni asked. She had known he was ill. Had something happened? She had gone to work that morning, she had seen two patients with high blood pressure, one with what seemed to be a thyroid problem, and one with heatstroke; she had taken a coffee break with Eugenia, talked to both Dimitri and Andreas on the telephone; she had soaked in the tub, hot and tired and empty-headed, a typical day. Now she stood dripping on the tile floor. And her daughter was only ten minutes away. Hardly a prior announcement, no news of travel plans, not even a cryptic postcard saying, *See you soon*.

"He's okay," Sophie said. "Are you still there?"

"Well, when are you coming *home*?" Eleni asked. "When will you come *here*?"

Later, after she had lain on top of the bed for a few minutes, ridiculously trying to close her eyes and rest, Eleni heard Anna crashing around and found her in her room, trying on clothes.

"Your sister is coming home," Eleni said. "Did you know about this?"

Anna looked up, her eyes widened. She blew her hair out of her eyes. "Don't tell me," she said.

"I'm serious. In fact, she's already here, with Loukas."

Anna looked around. "Here?"

"In Athens."

Anna, nonplussed, stood up and cleared her throat as if about to say something very important. But she didn't say anything.

"She honestly didn't tell you about this?" Eleni asked. She watched Anna slip her feet into a pair of sandals, and then another. Her toenails were painted red.

"Why would she tell me anything?" Anna asked. "Yes, I knew she'd been homesick. But that's all."

But there was something floating around her words that Eleni didn't quite understand. Was she hurt, or angry, or jealous? Had Anna spent so many of her formative years without her siblings that their return meant little to her, like the arrival of a distant aunt or cousin a few generations removed? She didn't know.

"Well," Anna said. "I'm going out."

"Sophie will be here tonight," Eleni said.

"She shows up after so many years and I'm supposed to drop everything? Let her work around me if she wants to see me." Anna tossed a tube of mascara and some lipstick into her purse and checked her watch before placing that in her purse as well. "Sophie has always done exactly what she wanted when she wanted and I'm beginning to think it's not such a bad idea." Anna checked herself in the mirror. She was wearing a royal-blue sundress printed with daisies. "Do you like this outfit?" she asked. Not bothering to wait for her mother's answer, Anna looked around the room, kissed Eleni on the cheek, and left her there.

On the phone, Sophie said she and Loukas would be there that evening, and this rankled, the way her daughter used *we*. *We'll be there this evening.* Her reunion with her daughter after six years and she had to share it with her daughter's boyfriend whom she had never met? He couldn't stay at home with his sick father? So Eleni invited Dimitri, as well as Mihalis and Irini. Perhaps a full house would make her daughter's sudden reappearance feel less strange.

She went out to buy some wine, chicken, and potatoes and items for a salad. She salted the chicken and put it back in the refrigerator. And then she pulled her hair back into a scarf and began to clean. When the marble counters and the terrazzo tile floors gleamed, when every surface was dust free, when the house smelled like citrus, she collapsed again into the bath. She still had another hour or so before anyone arrived.

At eight o'clock exactly, Dimitri knocked, the most shocked of them all by the news of Sophie's appearance. His sons were far more proper, and such last-minute antics were anathema. For her children, they were a fact of life, sudden catastrophes, sudden delights. Irini helped Eleni set the table, and Mihalis rummaged through the liquor cabinet. He and Dimitri drifted to the front porch, where Eleni had set out some *mezedes*, and they each had an *ouzo*.

The two men hadn't liked each other much before, and they didn't like each other much now, but the years had softened them both, so socializing together had become less painful but not without conflict. That hot evening, the two men were at it immediately: Dimitri had come with a dry white wine.

"Nemea? You brought wine from Nemea?"

"For a man of the people, you've certainly got some elitist taste," Dimitri said. He tried to say it jokingly, but Mihalis wasn't going to let it go.

"What's one got to do with the other?"

"I'd think a Marxist would shun such bourgeois indulgences."

"Please," Mihalis said. "I'm hardly a Marxist. Is everyone not a moderate automatically a Marxist?"

"My brother hates everything," Eleni said. "He's against everything," she added. She thought Mihalis would grow frustrated then, at her mocking, but instead he laughed. There was truth there, after all.

"Not everything," he said. "I like good food. Nice wine. Beautiful women." He smiled and pulled a chair out for Irini, who rolled her eyes. "I've spent too much of my life living in the dirt to not appreciate the finer things."

"Interesting way of looking at it," Dimitri said.

Eleni went back into the kitchen and continued the preparations for dinner. Having Mihalis and Dimitri in the same room had always been taxing, and she used to exhaust herself trying to control the direction of the conversation, always worried one would offend the other. She finally had accepted that the two men would exchange mild insults as a matter of communication and the friction was almost performance. Her younger brother, she had noticed since his release, had grown less disagreeable in general. There was something almost fatherly in the way he talked to her, not condescending but caring. Whereas he had always used conversations as occasions to correct people, to show them why they were wrong or misinformed or simply not as intelligent, he was now a little less combative, a little more relaxed.

Eleni heard a car and peered through the window so she might catch a secret first glimpse of her daughter but the trees were blocking her view. She felt a rush of adrenaline: what about this homecoming made her so nervous? The car doors slammed shut and Eleni dashed to the front porch.

Like an apparition Sophie stood framed by the garden gateway, her hair very long, down her back, and windblown. There were few times in her life when Eleni could say she had been speechless. This was one of them.

Sophie walked toward them, and Eleni hardly registered her daughter's boyfriend because of Sophie's round, protruding midsection. She remained frozen in the doorway, while Dimitri and Mihalis stood from their seats on the porch.

Mihalis embraced Sophie. "My little girl," he said. Sophie looked as though she'd been crying and might start up again any moment. "Don't cry."

Loukas introduced himself to Mihalis. "She's okay," he said. "She's been like this all day. For months, really."

Sophie stood with her hands at her sides, staring at her mother as if waiting for judgment. For a moment Eleni did not move or make a sound. Finally, mystified, she hugged her daughter, whose narrow shoulders were a stark contrast with her stomach. In fact, Eleni was stunned by the sensation of hugging her daughter at all; it had been so many years but felt as natural as when she'd inhale the powdery scent of her infant head.

Eleni let go of Sophie and watched everyone settle back in around the table while she still stood in the doorway. Two extra chairs in hand, Irini immediately invited them all to sit.

Dimitri remained standing. "Well, you'll get married?" The *you* was plural, but he was directing the question at Loukas. Blunt, judgmental, well-meaning Dimitri. No wonder his sons were still afraid of him. Not that Eleni wasn't thinking the same thing. Sophie looked at Dimitri blankly; she seemed to still view him as just a visitor, one who shouldn't involve himself in family decisions. Then again, Sophie seemed to view her—her own mother—that way, too.

Mihalis told him to let them settle in first, use the bathroom, have a drink. Now her brother as social mediator? "You! You knew about this, didn't you?" Eleni asked.

Mihalis didn't say anything at first and looked to Sophie for consent. "I have friends in Paris," he finally said.

"Don't feel bad," Irini said. "He didn't tell me either. Mihalis knew the Athens gossip even when he was detained on the island. It's like a sixth sense."

Her little brother, always one step ahead. But Eleni didn't just feel bad. She felt alarm and rage, the sort of vehement anger only one's children could provoke. Pregnant! "You should have told me," she said, to Sophie, to Mihalis, to neither, to both. It was all she could think to say.

"And ruin the surprise?" Mihalis asked. His sarcasm was undeniable, and Eleni knew she wasn't giving Sophie the welcome she had been looking for. It was painfully obvious. But what did her daughter expect? Not only had she arrived unannounced with only a previous hint that she might visit, but pregnant, too? And Mihalis didn't tell her? There were so many things wrong with this situation. Her children had pushed her before, but this was pushing too far.

She took a deep breath and didn't say anything, not necessarily because she had calmed down, but because she couldn't articulate her emotions. She looked at her brother then, who was wiping his eyes. His show of emotion not only moved her but settled her down for a moment.

"Well? You'll get married, of course," Dimitri repeated, as if no one had heard him the first time.

Loukas looked at Dimitri while he spoke. "I'd marry Sophie right here, right now, on this porch if I could. I've asked her twice already."

"It's better to be married," Dimitri said.

"I agree," said Loukas.

Five minutes there and they were already taking sides.

"Like this? So fat?" Sophie said, pointing with two fingers at her stomach. "And I'm only growing larger." Eleni should have guessed that to not marry was Sophie's decision. All her life she had wanted to do the opposite of what was expected of her.

Loukas shrugged and Eleni studied him a moment. So this was her daughter's boyfriend, this would be the father of her child. He had a warm, handsome face and deep voice and spoke as if he had rehearsed his words before he said them. The effect was thoughtful, though, not overly calculated. He seemed uncomfortable with the starkness of the announcement, the visual before the verbal. That too had been Sophie's idea, Eleni was certain. How typical of Sophie to do it this way, to use shock as a method of communication. How much easier it would have been if she had just told her over the phone, allowed Eleni to let it sink in, to accept it. Even a letter, which she could have read over and over until she believed it.

Oh, but her daughter! Her firstborn, pregnant! When Sophie was an infant Eleni worried about everything, hovering over the crib in the middle of the night, holding her at all hours because she refused to sleep. And now Sophie would soon experience that same overwhelming force. There she stood, pigeon-toed, her hair too long and in need of a good brushing. Sophie wanted her mother to be happy for her, she knew, and Sophie did look happy, albeit exhausted. Who had her firstborn become without her? Then again, she was still Sophie, just six years older. An unplanned pregnancy didn't seem to daunt her at all. Maybe it *had* been planned? Even among the youngest and most progressive, this simply was not done. Sophie was inventing all sorts of new rules.

"*Mana mou?*" she asked. "Will you please say something?"

Eleni looked up. Then the rush of all that missing, the void of having two of her children away, was suddenly amplified at the reality of one return, like a pain you become inured to until it's newly irritated or slightly changed. She took her daughter's hand and pulled her body toward her, wrapping her arms around her, smoothing her hair and remembering the way Sophie always loved to hug, bursting with affection like bright bouquets of flowers. She remembered the way she would look up and ask, "*Mana*, hug?" even if she had just been scolded. Eleni's anger softened and then she was crying, too, still holding on to her daughter.

"Where will you stay?" Dimitri asked. "Here?"

Sophie broke from the embrace for a moment and looked at Loukas. Dimitri continued, as if still discussing the matters of the men, "Your family's here?"

Loukas nodded.

How lives could change in a matter of an instant. Her daughter was back in Athens, and Eleni would soon be a grandmother again. She thought of how she and Christos had lived in the flat in Victoria and remembered so well the feeling of starting a small family while one war ended and another war raged, the strangeness of worrying about feeding small mouths and sleeping patterns while her brother remained somewhere up in the mountains to the north, and then in an island prison.

Finally, it was Sophie who spoke. "Where's Anna?" she asked. She had not yet stepped foot into the house, and she peered through the doorway as if Anna were hiding somewhere inside.

"Out with friends," Mihalis answered.

38

A few days later, Eleni was at the clinic, scrubbing it clean. When they had all lived there, Sophie referred to the apartment as *to spiti mou.* Not "our house." But "my house." "Are we going back to my house?" she'd ask, on their way back from a wedding or running errands.

"Yes," Christos would always answer. "We're going back to Sophie's house." Even though it was not unusual for a child to speak this way, Christos had been adamant that the apartment would go to Sophie when she was ready. To him it had become Sophie's place. And now, newly arrived in Athens with a baby on the way, Sophie should have been as ready as ever. Was she? She hadn't even asked about it. Eleni certainly wasn't ready, nor had she offered the place, half out of shock and half out of spite. Her anger had subsided a little but her hurt feelings had not.

It was not a day she saw patients, but she had asked Andreas to come over so they could talk. Sophie and Loukas were comfortably situated in Psychiko—for now.

Andreas arrived with a paper bag, which Eleni expected held some sort of supplies, and his smile when he walked into the kitchen lit her up from the inside out. But instead he stood at the kitchen counter and pulled out a dozen small oranges. "I'll make us some juice," he said. "I thought I saw a small juicer here the other day." He rummaged through the drawers, the contents of which they had never emptied, and found what he needed.

"So tell me about your daughter," he said. "Is she staying for good or going back to Paris after the baby is born?"

Eleni told him she assumed she was staying. She explained about Loukas, his father. "Her boyfriend wants to marry her. You can see how he loves her, the way he looks at her."

"But she doesn't love him back," Andreas said, half question, half statement.

"She *does*, I'm sure," she said, and found it interesting Andreas would assume that. She thought about his ex-wife and child but said nothing. "But she doesn't want to get married. She's stubborn. You know what she told me? She doesn't want to be typical. Doesn't want to be a cliché."

"I can understand that," he said. He mashed the oranges over the small metal juicer. "I suppose," he quickly added.

"She asked, '*What do you want me to do? Go away to a convent?*' As if that was such a crazy option," Eleni said. But Eleni didn't really believe that. She provided for women who came seeking birth control, she assisted women who needed abortions. She was not conservative on these matters at all. And yet, when it was her daughter, neither logic nor ideals seemed to matter.

Andreas looked at her carefully. "Is that what you want her to do?"

She shrugged. She didn't. But Sophie having arrived in Athens with her pregnant belly still angered her. How could she have been five months pregnant and Eleni hadn't known? Her own daughter, sharing her life with strangers in a foreign country: Easters, Christmases, name days. What had particularly stung was seeing all the bright baby things in the back of their car. So casual, so taken care of.

Eleni hesitated. "Last night she asked about this place," she said, waving her hand. It was a small fib. Sophie hadn't yet, but she knew that it was coming.

Andreas looked up at her, waiting to continue. "And?"

"I told her there were still renters. It's midmonth, after all, midsummer."

Andreas was quiet a moment. "You know, if you need to, we can think of something else."

"I haven't had quite as many patients lately," she said. "That is a good thing," she added quickly. "Maybe the worst has passed." Even as she said this, she wasn't sure it was true. The student protests that year had grown more numerous and frequent, and the police had reacted violently. Many she had just seen right at the hospital, along with released prisoners, some with bad colds, dozens of others with TB contracted in exile. No one seemed to worry about treating the detained anymore, or maybe no one cared about the stupid rules, particularly when they were so inhumane. "Maybe we could just send patients over to me at the hospital."

Andreas looked worried. "You think that would work?"

"Of course," she said.

"What about the people who know to come here?" he asked, and Eleni hadn't considered what Sophie would do if some poor soul appeared at the door, saying Andreas sent them. And what if someone else came looking for Eleni or Andreas and found Sophie instead? Years ago, she had worried that Sophie's actions would endanger the entire family. Now she had to consider the implications of her own.

"I don't know," Eleni said. They were both quiet. He finished the juice and poured it into their glasses. Eleni drank hers quickly.

"When is the baby due?" Andreas asked finally.

"Around Christmas," Eleni told him.

"And she has a place to stay now?"

"Of course." Eleni told him about Psychiko. "But she always has a place to stay. She could stay in Halandri, if she wanted." *Mana, hug? Are we going back to my house?*

"Okay," he said.

He was about to say something else, but Eleni interjected. "I was thinking to tell her maybe after the New Year."

Andreas nodded. "That will give us time to figure something out."

Eleni liked that, this *us*, this *we*. Though she wished Andreas would either tell her to keep the clinic or to give the flat to Sophie. She didn't want to make the decision alone. But Andreas wasn't this type of man. It wasn't that he didn't care or wasn't decisive—hardly. But like a good doctor who would never tell a person what to do, he also wouldn't make the decision for Eleni. She respected that. They were both quiet again. Finally, it was Eleni who spoke. "This heat. I have a taste for a beer."

"And I need some cigarettes," added Andreas. "Let's walk down to the kiosk."

Eleni agreed, and they walked out together.

"Is it that she's pregnant? Or that she's pregnant and didn't tell you?" Andreas asked.

It was a good question but she couldn't answer it. She was surprised that Sophie had decided to have the baby, she told him, though she would never convey this to Sophie. Then again, Sophie had always been a giant mass of contradiction. Taki did not surprise her. Her son would not be a part of the counterculture movement happening in the States, the hippies with their long hair and drugs and free love. He would be part of the backlash to the movement, the self-righteous ones. Though she had never visited the States, she envisioned—based on what she heard from friends, from television programs—a sterile suburb, his family the most ethnic of the bunch, among nice cars and green, green yards, trimmed just so; she imagined him driving to go to the corner store, if there even was such a thing. He would make a good living and take his children to theme parks for vacation; they wouldn't know the simplicity of the beach, and maybe they'd never see summers of Kyparissia, or Loutsa, or Paros. The word *socialist* would fall off his tongue like a four-letter word. He would view his old country as third-world, as barbaric, as corrupt and disordered.

Andreas bought the beers and cigarettes while Eleni went on, barely stopping to allow him to respond. "And doesn't this all make sense?" she finally asked him. He smiled and Eleni, aware of all the ground she had covered, smiled, too. She had moved from Sophie to Taki in one long, rambly sentence, giving Andreas a glimpse into her family dynamic.

"You're afraid Taki will find Greece backward and therefore his family, too. That he won't acknowledge his past, his roots. That he's turning his back on us."

She nodded. She imagined the past in America was filed away quickly and without incident; Monday's events were forgotten by Friday, and each week, month, year seemed to forge into the next. The past was regarded as a nuisance, an annoying little fact, a dirty secret that stood in the way of the new. People went there for the very purpose of starting fresh. But Athens was centered around history. Tourists visited ruins, and scholars fixated on the ancient and ignored the modern. People visited for what it had been, not for what it was. The graves of the dead protruded above the earth, and behind the new churches sat low, squat old ones, halfway in the ground but there nonetheless. Behind the nationalistic pride lay a deeper, shared sense of melancholy and heartbreak. History was inescapable, undeniable, and palpable: an acrid taste of ash.

Andreas and Eleni sat on a bench in the shade so Andreas could have a cigarette. Two children rode by on bicycles, and another man, most likely their grandfather, followed behind them, his hands behind his back, fiddling with his worry beads. "I'd like you to meet my son sometime," Andreas said. But before Eleni could answer, a middle-aged couple walked down the middle of the street, studying a map, and stopped and asked in English the way to the archaeological museum. Andreas stood and pointed them in the right direction. "It's not very far," he said. "Once you're on the main road, you won't miss it." The couple thanked them and went on.

"I tried to take my son there last weekend," Andreas said. "He told me it was boring and it smelled like history. I asked him if he remembered that I taught history and he just shrugged."

Eleni laughed and wanted to respond to his comment about his son but the moment seemed lost. Instead, she asked Andreas if *he* thought history had a smell, and he'd responded as if he'd just been thinking of it. "The earthy smell of archaeological excavation. And the exhaust-infused smell of rain," he'd said. Eleni agreed, and added the industrial smell of the ceramics factory blocks from her house, where her children used to play and dig for dishes, stoneware, porcelain.

As they were walking back, she told Andreas what seemed to be absent in the States was the collective past, a shared anything. "Everyone has their own *everything:* their own garages for their cars, their own swimming pools, their own histories. And in a way," she said, continuing, "I know Taki likes this."

"Probably," Andreas said. "But he's still a Greek. And part of him probably loathes it."

Back in the apartment, he opened a beer and poured two glasses. "Even the beer bottles in the States are single sized," Andreas said, and laughed.

Eleni felt warmed by their alliance, even in such a simple comment. "And what's worse is that Sophie thinks I'm judging her," she said.

"Okay," Andreas said. "We're talking about Sophie again?" She knew her thoughts were all over the place, pouring out any which way, but Andreas was attentive, waiting for her to continue.

Eleni laughed again, surprised how much she had laughed despite the topic. "Sophie, Taki, it's all the same! But yes, Sophie, my pregnant Sophie."

"Did you tell her this?" Andreas asked. "Any of it?"

She took a sip. The exhaustion of raising her children virtually alone still lingered; how could they now be having children of *their* own? She didn't mention this. "No," she said. She didn't care that she was ranting, and she wanted to stay there all day with him, all night, and keep talking. She wanted to lay her head in his lap. She realized he was the first person who had asked her about it. Mihalis had aligned himself with Sophie; Irini had told her to let her make her own decisions—as if Sophie had not been doing that since she could walk; and Dimitri just had shaken his head and said it was inappropriate, that this generation had lost all sense of shame. But Andreas was the first who had asked her how she *felt*.

This was not the first time he'd listened to her about her children. When Taki had told her he was getting married—only two weeks before the fact, hardly enough time to arrange to attend, which she assumed had been his intention—Andreas was the first person she'd told, and he had listened sympathetically and then given her a hug.

Years had passed since he had arrived at the hospital with that first boy. They talked about medicine, about politics, and while she knew him intimately well, she knew maddeningly little about his romantic life. Surely he had one but he was very private in this way, though if she asked, he would probably tell her. What would this information bring her? She would never admit this to anyone, barely to herself: he was the man she had trusted the most. She knew of the slogan "The personal is political" and of course it made sense to her. It had always seemed an obvious fact. Certainly politics had intruded into their personal lives before, which was perhaps why she was so reticent to let it in again. The way she lived sometimes felt the opposite. There was politics and domestic life; there was her work as a doctor and her relationship with Dimitri. Perhaps separating the two in her mind allowed her to date a man whose ideas were so different and was the reason she ignored him when he treated her belief system as naïve ideology. Andreas made up for what she felt she lacked with Dimitri.

Andreas placed his hand over Eleni's gently and she thought for a moment he might lean over and kiss her. Instead, he held his glass of beer to hers. "To our health," he said.

39

Twilight Anna associated with parting, and so each day when the sun set and the darkness gave some respite from the stifling city heat, she felt slightly more at ease. Late afternoons with Evan in that small apartment left her with joy and a shadowy ache, afternoons without which she felt restlessly empty, but either way, each completed sunset brought a temporary relief.

Afternoons, then, she associated with sex, and the neighborhood of Exarheia not only with her university but with Evan's small apartment. That day, the moment he opened the door he reached for her, and she loved it when his desire was so plain like this. Anna couldn't help but notice the strong smell of cleaning supplies and the three open boxes half-full of books that sat in the corner of the otherwise spotless living room. Evan's desk, usually cluttered, had two sealed boxes beside it and was shiny and clean.

But Evan was kissing her neck.

"What's going on?" she asked, pushing past Evan and walking into the bedroom. He was behind her still, their fingers intertwined. The closet was empty, the bed had been stripped of sheets, and a fresh set was neatly folded on the chair. All the windows were open, but they didn't do much except let in the city's hot, stagnant air, which was being blown around by a fan that sat on the nightstand.

Evan wasn't saying anything. He put his hand on her hip and slid it under her smocked halter. She wasn't wearing a bra—too hot—

and she could tell this excited him, which in turn excited her. She removed his T-shirt and unbuckled his pants. His skin was hot and clammy, and so was hers, and when he was on top of her, beads of sweat dripped from his forehead onto her face, her chest. The naked mattress was rough and hot against her bare back.

When they finished, they were both drenched—Anna, in her sugared girlhood fantasies, had never imagined sex could be so raw and vulgar—and Evan set the fan on the bed to dry the mattress.

In the cool shower, he let the water run over his face. When she leaned her head back and wet her hair, he put his arms around her. She opened her eyes, looked up at him, and let her face burrow in his chest.

"I've got to rent the apartment," he said. Anna heard his words but also was distracted by the fact that this was their first shower together. Usually she rinsed off quickly and modestly and rejoined him back in the bed. It was too hot for that anyway, and the bed was not made for lounging around.

"Oh," Anna said. "For good?" From the pained expression on his face, she had expected him to tell her someone had died or had cancer. But he might as well have told her that, the way her entire body felt like it were falling.

"I don't want to," Evan said. "But Simone says I have an office at home, and I should just work there." He seemed completely deflated, like he had spent the morning arguing; had he been more nonchalant about the entire thing perhaps Anna wouldn't have felt that knot welling in her throat. "And with Aliki getting older we have more expenses."

"She's suspicious, then," Anna said. *Simone says, Simone says.* What was she, his mother?

Evan touched her cheek with his hand.

"I understand," Anna said. She hoped she wouldn't start crying.

She stepped out of the shower and used the one towel that hung there. The rest had been newly washed and sat folded in the closet. When Evan stepped out he hesitated but then took a clean one. Anna wrapped the towel around her body and sat on the edge of the bed, in front of the fan, combing her hair. Evan collected his clothes from the floor. From a duffel bag that sat on the bottom of the small closet he retrieved a clean pair of underwear and a T-shirt. He put them on and sat on the bed next to her.

She wanted to say, *But this is our apartment.* She wanted to ask him, *What about us?* But she didn't. She told herself the apartment and she and Evan were not inextricable from each other. But, she wondered, were they to him?

"We'll figure something out," Evan said, and Anna felt relieved. He touched her shoulders, which were red from the mattress.

After they dressed, Evan collected their two dirty towels and placed those in his bag, which he carried out with them when they left.

While they had last parted on a sort of melancholic note, in Anna's mind that tone had changed and in his absence she had conjured a completely alternate reality, one in which they had bitterly fought, and as a result she felt rudely antagonistic toward him. On the phone she responded to his sentences with brief *maybe*s and *no*s, and when it was clear she didn't feel like talking Evan told her he had to go and that he'd see her on Hydra. The moment Anna hung up the phone she wished he would call her back. He didn't.

The night before Evan was leaving for Hydra, Anna found herself back in Exarheia for a party. The entire neighborhood to Anna became highly suggestive and fraught with emotion, and the rough white wine they had been drinking had made her at turns maudlin and combative. She rarely drank much at all, but that night she had had far too much, too quickly. The apartment had a huge terrace and everyone stood outside. The night had cooled considerably. She went inside to use the bathroom, but it was occupied, so she waited in the small hallway where a phone sat on a small stand. She pressed her face into the corner, covered her ears. First she called Evan's apartment but no one answered. She was marginally comforted to still hear the ring. But it wasn't enough.

She glanced back out on the veranda. She didn't see Stella, and Panos was engaged in conversation. He was chasing a black-haired dancer and she seemed to occupy much of his time. Stella thought she was only a stand-in for Anna—she and the dancer even looked alike. These days Panos rarely brought Evan up at all, and when Stella mentioned him, Panos usually retreated into a book or pretended to zone out of the conversation. He regarded the situation with a sort of agnostic indifference: it neither existed nor didn't. Much like Evan, she thought.

She dialed Evan's number at home this time and was shocked when he answered. She held the phone to her ear a moment and then placed the receiver back into its cradle. A rush of adrenaline made her walk out the door, into the night, and that was when the tears came. She walked and cried and tried not to make eye contact with the tourists in droves who crossed the streets looking confused.

She was a mess, a drunk sloppy mess. She was aware enough to realize this but not sober enough to do anything about it. She walked through Exarheia, past Evan's apartment, whose doorbell she held down for a good, satisfying ten seconds, until someone in the building opened the window and shouted, "Who's there already?" She traipsed down through Kolonaki and past the lively cafés and restaurants, bracing herself, cringing at the thought of running into Evan while all the same hoping for the possibility. She knew he was at home but by habit she scanned faces. The area was full of men his age, holding forth around tables. She turned down a narrow, residential street and began the climb to Evan's house. The air was redolent with cigarette smoke and jasmine and garbage, a sweet, sickly smell. She stopped behind a copse of honeysuckle and thought she might be sick, but the feeling passed and she kept going.

Anna caught a glimpse of herself in a window: her hair was tangled and too long; her mother had been threatening to cut it in her sleep. The mascara she had applied at Stella's now pooled beneath her eyes. Earlier that day she had fallen asleep at the beach at Sounion and her skin had gone from golden to burned. The strap of her sundress had fallen off her shoulder; her heel flapped out of her platform sandal, the discomfort of which she only registered when she saw her foot's precarious presence in it.

She adjusted her shoe and continued up the hill along the uneven brick. She stopped at a kiosk for something to drink and drank it in one large, beastly gulp. She was infuriated, she wanted to fight with him, wanted to grab him by the shoulders and shake him. She hated him, that moment, she hated the way she had fallen in love with him and felt this constant, mysterious weight. She hated the way he wanted everything to be here and now and not before and after.

When she got to Evan's, the reality of his place right in front of her gave her pause. But she soldiered on, tripped up the front steps, and climbed over the veranda wall so she could spy from behind an open shutter. She didn't know what she expected to see at this hour: a group of friends gathered around the kitchen table, a party of people dancing in the living room, or maybe Simone and Evan making love on the sofa while Aliki slept upstairs.

But there he sat in front of the blue glow of the television, alone, slumped in his chair. He wore a white T-shirt and trousers and slippers, as if he had begun to get undressed but hadn't finished. Maybe he heard her out there, or maybe he could feel he was being watched, but he stood up and walked right to the window. Anna could have touched him, and now she could see that he had noticed her there, aware of her bare legs and sandals that she had kicked off.

"Anna?" he whispered. He sounded surprised but not angry.

What else could she do? Sheepishly she appeared from behind the shutter. "Hi," she said.

She expected him to tell her to leave, to say *How dare you come to my house*. She thought at that moment he'd tell her he didn't want to see her again. Instead, he came out to the veranda and motioned for her to sit next to him on the bench.

"Sorry," she said. But why did it feel like she was always apologizing to him?

"It's okay," he said. "Simone is already on Hydra, with her sister and mother and Aliki. But—" He brushed her cheek with the back of his hand and smoothed her hair out of her eyes. "What in the world are you doing? Coming here in the middle of the night?"

She leaned into him. Simone was gone, and he hadn't called her.

"Oh, dear girl. You're drunk," he said. "Come inside with me a moment."

Anna followed him into the house. She used the bathroom and

scrubbed away her makeup. She got some eye makeup on the white towel and had she been totally sober she would have fretted about it but instead she just replaced it on the rack. At that moment, she hated Simone. Let her see the mascara-stained towel. Her skin was hot, sunburned, and the tears had exacerbated it. She looked at herself in the bathroom's dim light and then splashed more water on her face.

When she emerged Evan was back on the couch, and she noticed a few empty bottles of beer in front of him. The whole scene seemed very bacheloresque now that he'd been debachelored by having lost his apartment. He'd opened a fresh beer for himself and gotten her a glass of water. She took a sip and then kissed him. At first he hesitated but then he gave in to her. And though Anna was drunk, the long walk had sobered her somewhat, and she was not drunk enough to not take in the fact that she was with Evan in his house, on his couch, the shutters thrown open to the night. She couldn't help but imagine Simone and Aliki upstairs, that someone might appear at any moment. He briefly put his fingers in her mouth and they tasted of salt, and he made love to her slowly and his touch was gentle, his hands moving over her body deliberately but not urgently. The tenderness of it moved her, and she knew that this time it wasn't about love or lust or desire. It was simply about comfort, and this made her feel childish but also loved.

Afterward, she lay on his chest and inhaled, telling herself to remember what he smelled like, not the usual woodsy soap but the scent of beer and peanuts, cigarettes and sweat, and Evan talked quietly about this and that, unimportant, daily things. Anna felt herself falling asleep, wishing it could be like this all the time and wondering why it couldn't.

"Are you still awake, Anna?" he asked.

She murmured she was. She could feel his body tense up, and for a second Anna thought maybe she'd hear those words she had claimed she didn't care for but of course deep down wanted. She murmured something, telling him to go on.

He hesitated and shifted in his seat to reach his beer. "Simone is pregnant," he said.

She lifted her head off his chest and rubbed her eyes. She didn't say anything, and neither did he. She sat there for a moment, looking at him, and then she rested her head back on his chest. What was there to say?

All she wanted him to say was that he was sorry. For what, it didn't matter. To hear an apology would make up for the apartment, the pregnancy, the fact that not only was he still sleeping with his wife—what in the world had she thought?—but now she also had to have a constant reminder of that very fact. She didn't want what some girls wanted, gaudy baubles or expensive jewels or boxes of French chocolates; to her, these were only obvious markers of guilt. She didn't even want *I love you*s even though only a moment ago she had thought she did. What she wanted was to feel relevant, like her presence in his life had somehow altered it, that it couldn't be erased as easily as a rented apartment, a cleanly mopped floor, and boxed-up books. And then Anna had a very dark thought, one that somehow had never crossed her mind before. She had the power to make his life very miserable.

She fell asleep there, on his chest, and he slept too, and when those first hints of morning whispered through the open shutters, Anna stirred. The buses would start any minute. She quickly found her shoes and purse, used the bathroom, and slipped out the front door. Evan was stretched out on the couch, still asleep.

When she got off the bus in Halandri, the wild jealousy whirled inside her. Another baby? With Simone? Was it the baby that bothered her or just such an abrupt change in the status quo, first the apartment, now this? The square was slowly waking. A café owner swept the patio, and the air was filled with the smell of butter and sugar from the bakery, from which women in cotton housedresses already emerged holding white paper bags. She stopped and bought her favorite anise cookies and ate one right from the bag, the crumbs spilling onto her dress, instead of waiting for her coffee as she usually did. It was rare she saw Halandri at this hour and she was surprised to see her own old cat, Orpheas, stalking across the square, also returning home. Out of context, her pet looked like just another stray: hungry, and feral, and free.

When she finally got out of bed in the afternoon, she could hear her sister's voice drifting up from the veranda. Sophie had lived away from Athens six years, but now that she was back she didn't seem to know how to function away from the house. It had been so long that Sophie's presence still often surprised Anna. Anna wrapped herself in her robe and brushed her teeth. She washed her face, trying not to glimpse her reflection in the mirror. In the kitchen she poured herself a glass of juice, took an aspirin, and went on the porch to join her sister, who sat in her flowered sundress staring blankly ahead, her back straight, her legs spread apart, and her hands held over her belly as if she were in front of a pottery wheel, spinning something into being.

"Well," Sophie said. "Good morning. I was just going to wake you."

"What for?" Now her sister was going to act like her mother? At that moment, though, she didn't mind. She wanted to be taken care of.

Sophie shrugged. "You look like you had a good night."

Anna brought her hand to her hair, which was matted and tangled from Evan's couch. Her skin felt hot, and her eyes felt tender, from crying. "A long night, anyway," Anna said.

Sophie fidgeted in her chair a little. "I miss that," she said.

Anna shrugged. "It's good for things not to stay the same," she said, trying to convince herself. She did feel she had been pushed to some crucial point, as if she were teetering on the edge of something large and beyond her limited experience.

Sophie looked at Anna with a mixture of affection, pity, and envy. "Your hair looks like a dead animal left on the side of the road," she said. "Let me untangle it for you."

Anna returned with a brush and sat cross-legged on the floor, in front of her sister. Sophie tugged gently and carefully, methodically detangling each gnarled section.

"How's staying in Psychiko?" Anna asked.

"It's okay. We'll look for something else soon."

"An apartment?" Anna asked.

"Somewhere in Athens," Sophie said. "Near Loukas's work."

Anna was quiet a moment and closed her eyes. Having her hair brushed was so soothing, even though Sophie had to pull and tug to remove the tangles. "Evan has an apartment he's going to rent," Anna said. "I think it's available now."

Sophie didn't ask how she knew this; it didn't seem to cross her mind. "Really? That would be wonderful."

Her sister didn't miss a beat. She called Mihalis at Irini's—they finally had a phone—and then called Evan, as if it were the most natural thing in the world. Anna envied her sister then, the ease with which she could just call Evan, ask Simone if she could speak with him. The simplicity, in fact, was astounding.

August dragged, blank and hot. The thought of seeing Simone and Evan together was unbearable so Anna canceled her trip to Hydra and instead spent a week with her mother on Paros, swimming and sleeping and eating too much. When her mother tried to coax Anna to stay another week—Irini and Mihalis were on their way, and some family friends were renting a place nearby—Anna suddenly had the urge to go home. Being away was making her anxious.

Anna was not only completely alone in Halandri but completely alone in Athens. Panos had gone with some other boys to Mykonos, Stella was with her family on Hydra, and Sophie and Loukas had gone to Chios with some friends. Anna asked her sister if she would swim pregnant, and Sophie laughed as if Anna had asked if she would take a day trip to the moon. But what did Anna know of pregnancy? Besides, she couldn't imagine Sophie, her small body and large belly, in a bathing suit.

Given the situation, Anna couldn't take her eyes off pregnant women. It seemed, suddenly, they were everywhere, as if a ban had been lifted and all women of childbearing age were bearing. Perhaps it was the intense heat, the abandoning of jackets and sweaters and the exposure of skin, or maybe it was simply the result of staying indoors in those less pleasant months, but she couldn't remember the last time she had gone out and not seen a woman who was expecting. They were at the market, they were in the main square; they attempted to cover those bumps with shapeless dresses but their stances and flushed cheeks gave them away.

Anna did not want a baby of her own, but the combination of

Evan's wife's and Sophie's pregnancies made her feel left out, unimportant. Now any pregnancy was a reminder to Anna of her heartache. Yet until she had learned of Simone's pregnancy, Anna couldn't recall ever noticing or caring about pregnant women at all. The closest instance she could conjure was not even a pregnancy but a time a few years earlier when a woman had been arrested for breast-feeding her four-month-old in the park; the mother was taken away and kept for six months. Now it was as if all of Athens's women had kept their conceptions dormant for years, and slowly, like some sort of fish or shark, allowed them to continue gestation. As if all those impregnated during the junta were finally about to give birth, and they had taken to the street in droves, a feminine act of resistance.

What Anna knew was most maddening to the regime were just these things: that when they were in private, they spoke and argued and made love. In private, they could not be subjugated. They could resist, they could shout, they could do inappropriate, indiscreet things.

And maybe the possibility of such indiscretions was what brought her back to Athens when she, with no job, no school, no responsibilities, should have been relaxing by the sea in the day and going out until the sun rose again.

Her first night in Halandri alone felt liberating; Mihalis and Irini had stopped by on their way to the port to see if she was okay, and Mihalis had looked around the place, a little suspicious. "Just you here, all by yourself?" he'd asked. She told him she'd be fine. After they left, she fell asleep on the chaise longue on the terrace outside her bedroom and stumbled to her bed in the middle of the night. She stayed there until noon, and then she got up, got dressed, and took the bus to Syntagma. After she had had a coffee and some light lunch, she wandered through Evan's neighborhood in Kolonaki. When she passed his block, she looked for signs of life. His car was parked there, but there were no cars on Hydra, so they wouldn't have it with them anyway. She walked closer. The shutters were drawn in front, but something about the house didn't look completely abandoned. She surprised herself with such daring and also spooked herself out a little. She continued walking.

Later that afternoon, Stella called Anna and suggested she reconsider and come to Hydra. Her visiting aunts had left and now she was alone there with her parents and sister. There was room for Anna. "And your sister's gone now, isn't she?" Stella asked.

When Anna didn't respond immediately, Stella grew annoyed. "What—now you're going to worry that you'll see him each time we come? Or only come if he *is* here?"

"It's not that," she said.

"Then what is it? What could you be doing in Athens, in the thick heat? Entertaining tourists?"

Anna was quiet a moment. Yes, part of her wanted to return to Hydra, if for no other reason than to spot him, even if they never connected. But something about it made her feel she was chasing him now. It all felt so different. Maybe they had already had their good-bye. She didn't want to ask about him, but she did.

Stella sighed. "Fine. I did see him. Once, at the bakery in the morning," Stella told her. "With his daughter."

"Did he say hello?" Anna could picture the bakery in that famil-iar, crescent-shaped port. It was where they always went in the morn-ings for *tiropites*.

"He didn't see me. Listen, Anna *mou*. You know where to find me. You could probably find him here, too. I'll be here until school starts."

Anna thanked her and hung up. She couldn't articulate why she wanted to stay at home. It didn't make sense. Was it something as pathetic as being near the phone? Or was she avoiding him? She honestly couldn't figure it out. Being on Paros in particular had made her restless, wondering where he was, what he was doing. But going to Hydra would solve this. Perhaps she had replayed that first time there in her mind so many times that she wanted to preserve it.

She went out to the veranda and pulled a chair into the small bit of shade. Her mother's plants were wilting; she would remember to water them later.

She felt at turns besotted and angry, as if he had betrayed her. The whole notion was inane. Besides, how did she know what he was thinking? She spent inordinate amounts of time trying to figure out what was going on inside his head. But what did she know? He was certainly not a first-time adulterer. She had never even had a boy-friend before. If there were rules here, she had no access to them. She wouldn't even know where to look.

The next few days drifted into one another, and sometimes she couldn't remember what day it was, and what she had done, and if she had eaten. Anna was contemplating packing her bag and heading to Hydra or maybe even rejoining her mother, if for anything then for some human contact. Even her neighborhood felt oddly deserted; those who remained in town seemed particularly quiet, motionless in the intense heat. Only Vangelis remained active; she saw his cab idling around the quiet streets, off to the center of Athens to drive vacation-ers to the port, and she hoped he would take some time off soon.

Her fourth afternoon alone she lay on the couch with a glass of orange juice and a ferry schedule, checking to see when the next boats were leaving. Maybe she'd go somewhere else entirely different, find a boy her own age to have a fling with, maybe even a foreigner. Get her mind off things. The phone rang. Probably her mother, who had managed to check on her every day since she had come back, or maybe Stella, checking again to see if she was coming.

"Anna." It was Evan, and immediately his voice set her pulse fly-ing. "You're home."

"I am," she said. "Where are you?"

"Home, for now. Some friends just arrived from London, so I came back to meet them."

"Alone?" Anna asked, meaning, *Without Simone?*

"Then we're going back to Hydra together. Yes, just me." His voice trailed off. "I looked for you there," he said.

She didn't say anything, waiting for him to continue. All the things she had been thinking of saying seemed stuck in the back of her throat. All the things she had wanted to ask him.

"Can I see you?" he asked.

"*Can* you?" she asked. She didn't know if she was mocking him or teasing him. Maybe a bit of both.

"There's the girl," he said, "whom I've missed." The voice he used with her was lower, softer, more gentle than with others, and on these last few words particularly so.

She wanted to say, *I've missed you, too,* but the words wouldn't come out. Instead, she was imagining inviting him over when he interrupted her midthought. "Meet me someplace. Would you?" And against her better judgment, she said that she would.

He probably hadn't realized she was alone there, but he had a houseful of guests, and so he suggested the rooftop garden at the Grande Bretagne. Anna recognized the intent. The place would be teeming with tourists, and a place with such visibility also gave a surprising anonymity. Not that they hadn't met all the time, for coffee, for lunch, but meeting her on his few days back in the city seemed to be a little urgent. And the way he said, *Meet me someplace.* Such a brusque request, but beneath it something else.

She had become the kind of woman who slept with a married man, who rendezvoused in his second apartment, and who skulked to his house in the middle of the night and peeked through his windows. Now she was also the kind of woman who met him in fancy hotels? And what kind of woman was that? So quickly she had become what she never would have imagined herself to be that she could no longer even define it. She barely recognized herself. Or maybe he had simply unmasked it, there all along.

After Vangelis dropped her off in Syntagma Square, Anna walked in the opposite direction from the hotel. She didn't want him to see her walking into the Grande Bretagne; surely he'd wonder what she was doing in such an expensive place, particularly because he knew she preferred the same rinky-dink coffee shops he did. When she turned back, Vangelis was still idling, yet he wasn't watching her. Instead, he looked intently in the other direction, leaned back in his seat, almost mesmerized. Anna stopped to see what he might be looking at and noticed a slight young woman, a bit older than she was, standing in front of a café. She was pretty in a gamine sort of way, carried a sketch pad and a large purse, and wore a white embroidered blouse and low-slung bell-bottoms. Her glossy black hair was held back with a thick blue headband, but a lock had escaped and fell in her eyes. She pushed her sunglasses back and Anna watched Vangelis watch her as if she were the most interesting thing in the world. Then a curly-haired man came out of the café, put his arm on her shoulder, and the two of them sauntered away.

Vangelis still hadn't averted his gaze. He was obviously distracted, so Anna—in a yellow dress, brown platform sandals, her body smooth and tan—walked through the square, past the pigeons and the tourists and the children running in circles, and into the hotel as if she belonged there. Trying to appear inconspicuous, she slipped through the lobby and waited at the rooftop garden, as Evan had suggested. It was more crowded there than she had expected. She felt nervous being alone and wondered if she should have sat at the bar rather than at the linen-covered table. But no one seemed to bat an eye. She fidgeted with the napkin that she had absentmindedly draped onto her lap. Looking at the patrons around her, she was glad she had dressed up, had worn lipstick and pinned the front of her hair back and off her face, which she thought made her look appropriately older. She ordered an overpriced coffee, sweet, no milk, and looked out at Athens in the evening.

It was still light, and down in the square she could see all the tiny people having their coffees and *ouzos,* bowls of ice melting in front of them. The summer before her father had died he had taken her up to Lykavittos Hill, and she still recalled the marvel of seeing all those lights, of seeing the city, of her father pointing in the direction of Halandri and asking if she could see their house. She remembered wanting to please him, to see what she thought he wanted her to see, and she told him yes. He laughed. It was one of her favorite memories of her father and the only time she could remember being alone with him. Was that the last time she saw Athens like this? It seemed the most spectacular views of the city were the domain of tourists, views its citizens either took for granted or that didn't enter into their realm of thought at all. It was truly breathtaking.

Her entire body tingled with nerves and anticipation. She wasn't wearing her watch so she glanced over at the wrist of the man at the table beside her. Only ten minutes late. It wasn't like him to be late; in their meetings she was the one who was always running behind.

After half an hour, though, Anna acknowledged her worry. She ordered a glass of white wine. When the waiter set it down in front of her, she hoped she had enough money with her. And as she thought this, she knew, deep down, that maybe Evan wasn't coming.

She couldn't imagine why he'd suggest they meet and then purposely leave her there. She would have found a way to reach him
had the situation been reversed. He could have left a message, he
could have run in and said, *I've got friends in town, I'm running late,
I can't stay.* His house was not so far. And if he suddenly had grown
nervous about being caught, he could have called the hotel and left
a fake message: *Your uncle says he can't make it.* But he didn't do any
of these things.

As the sun went down, Anna watched the Acropolis change from a
pinky yellow to a dusky violet to looking as though it were gold-dipped
against a swath of velvet. The entire city twinkled, and looking out at
the glittery metropolis, Anna was able to momentarily calm her nerves.

But after an hour had passed her anger had reached a fervent
peak, bringing with it a wave of nausea, and she had to rush to the
bathroom for fear she might vomit. She sat in the stall awhile, listening to women come and go, speaking not only in Greek but in German, French, Italian. She thought, for some reason, of her first night
with Evan in Hydra, the way he had said it had been coming to this.
As if it were something that was in the way that simply needed to be
traversed so their relationship could deepen. Now she didn't see it that
way. This was *not* the only way it could have gone, and maybe they
had taken it to a dead end.

When the bathroom was empty, she emerged from the stall and
reapplied her lipstick. Digging through her purse, she was embarrassed to see the toothbrush and change of underwear she had brought
with her. What a sting of rejection. How she managed to convince
herself she was something more than just a fling, just another "other"
woman, was beyond her. What a fool she had been. What a happy,
delirious fool.

She remembered the way Panos had sneered that she was some
sweet thing placed on Evan's plate after dinner, and the way she had
thought to herself, *You don't understand.* But maybe she wasn't even as
substantial or significant as dessert. More like an after-dinner mint.
One you took absentmindedly on the way out of a café, shoved in
your coat pocket, and found, two days later, amid some thread and
lint. No. She was the thread and the lint.

Anna exited the bathroom and without paying her tab proceeded to the elevators. Back down in the lobby, she walked past the new arrivals waiting to check in, jet-lagged and weary, past the vibrant conversations in the gilded lobby, past the well-heeled guests waiting for cabs. She walked back out into the evening rush of the center of Athens; even in the quiet of August there were people double-parking, triple-parking as they stopped for cigarettes, a cheese pie, a newspaper. Anna crossed the street recklessly, sauntering across the middle of the avenue, the yellow cotton of her summer dress billowing behind her.

40

One day in October, a weighty, important-looking letter from Taki arrived. Taki had never written much, and since his daughter, Aspa, was born, ten months after the wedding that his family did not attend—though not by their choice, entirely—he had barely managed to write at all. Though when he did he always included some photos. The first letter was a birth announcement, in which the tiny Aspa looked more buglike than human; the second letter held a picture of Aspa plopped, belly down, on a blanket on Taki and Amalia's front lawn, in front of a bed of purple and yellow flowers. The baby wore a floppy red hat that covered most of her face. Taki had added short descriptions below the Polaroid shots, in blue felt-tip ink and his blocky, engineer-style letters: ASPA IN FLOWERS, AUGUST 1973.

Eleni walked to the den and picked up Christos's old letter opener, which was wooden and in the shape of a swordfish, endowed with painted-on eyes of dark blue and a red, green, and yellow smattering of something that Eleni had thought to be fins. It looked like a fish that would have been painted on some sort of prehistoric cave wall.

She wondered where Christos had ever found such a thing; it had been in his den as long as she could remember, and she never had given it a second thought. Now its strange little face and swordlike bill seemed a little ominous.

With the fish's long, pointed snout, she carefully coaxed the letter open. She remembered how Christos sat before his stack of mail and carefully opened each envelope at the side. Then, he'd proceed to read each piece, one by one. Sometimes, he'd save the envelopes until he wrote each return address in a leather-bound book he kept on his desk; other times, he'd toss them all in the wastebasket. Eleni found it to be tinged with melancholia, these neatly opened envelopes, sitting atop the pile of refuse.

A stack of Polaroids was enclosed with the letter. Aspa looked so much bigger now, less fetal, a real infant, dressed in pink pajamas. In the next picture she was naked and in the tub. Atop her head was a yellow washcloth, and she was shoving a toy rubber duck into her mouth. She looked just like Taki had at that age. Taki's hand held her up; she could see the blue stone of his university class ring, something he was proud enough to write her about and that was ever present in the photos he sent. His hand looked huge and hairy and out of place on Aspa's tiny back.

They say babies look like their fathers so the fathers won't abandon them. But what good was it, Eleni thought, when they abandoned them anyway? She always worried about a father's absence in his life, particularly in those important years between eight and eighteen, and she hoped he would know how to be a father. Then again, maybe without a clear memory of a father, he would become a better one, invent and imagine what a good father was on his own. Seeing her own son's child, and watching her pregnant daughter chatter about the baby's this and that, had left her questioning her capabilities as a parent. Had she been, ultimately, successful? Could she ever know? Was the distance between herself and her son normal, or had she done something to cause it?

Now that Taki was married, Eleni heard much more about his life, though not generally from him. Amalia was the one who made the phone calls, and Eleni was both flattered by this and suspicious of it. Those calls were expensive, and Eleni had found herself wondering what Amalia was trying to prove. That she was rich? Eleni soon realized that she was earnest in her intentions. Amalia perhaps felt guilty that Taki had fallen in love with her and settled in the States, though they both knew Taki never had any intention, wife or otherwise, of going back to Greece. And why should Eleni fault a woman who wanted to please her mother-in-law? She herself had only tolerated her mother-in-law, and when Christos passed away their relations grew first strained and then almost nonexistent. His mother never thought anyone was good enough for her son, and up until she had died, she blamed Eleni for his death, as if being married to her had somehow caused a vessel in his head to rupture and flood his brain with blood.

The next picture was of the three of them: Amalia, Taki, and Aspa standing in front of a large maple, vibrant yellow and orange. Some leaves fell from the tree, and they were captured that way in the picture: blurry and suspended balls of fire, tiny, bright explosions. Eleni looked at this picture for a long time. Here, Aspa wore a red wool coat that Eleni had sent, with dangling white pom-poms from the hood and yellow and white embroidery. Aspa's hands were up near her forehead and her tiny mouth was turned down into a pout. The next was the same setting but the hood was off, Amalia and Taki were grinning, and Aspa appeared to be shrieking with delight.

She had never met her granddaughter. Is this what it felt like, to be a grandmother? To simply be replaced by a new generation? It was not at all what she thought it would feel like. Looking at Aspa, Eleni wondered if she felt any differently about this baby than about others. But she didn't feel anything she didn't usually feel when in the presence of an infant, and she understood stories of mothers who adopted or of babies placed in someone else's care after a tragic event, how quickly they were able to bond. Because blood had nothing to do with it. It was something else entirely, that intense feeling of being needed, those little faces looking up at you with complete trust, that made you a mother. Love, she knew, was a bit proprietary.

Eleni didn't feel needed by this child at all. She had nothing to do with this baby's life, and this made her feel horribly lonely. She was the last to know of her conception and the details of her birth, and if she were lucky she'd see the baby every few years when Taki would come to parade her around, and they would all fuss in the proper, appropriate way. Aspa would know her grandmother to live in a far-off land. Taki would show her postcards of the Acropolis and Sounion, of the blue-domed churches of Santorini, of armless statues—things he'd buy in Detroit's Greektown in moments of nostalgia. Already, as she had imagined he would, he had settled in a suburb, where Greekness was probably as exotic as it got, and maybe Aspa would have the same one-sided, generic view of Greece that anyone, anywhere, could conjure.

When Taki had been a boy, Eleni had never imagined his leaving Athens, let alone Greece. He was the boy who hid beneath her leg at family gatherings, the boy who didn't want to go to school and screamed the whole way there, the boy who woke almost every morning with a stomachache and a hopeful look that he might be able to stay home. And certainly not someone who'd leave and not visit. His friend Spyro, who left at about the same time, had visited every summer, spending at least a month, sometimes more. Spyro's family had more money, but Eleni would have happily paid Taki's airfare. She had never offered, though, and he had never asked, and Eleni remembered that the distance between them was physical now but it had been there since his moody teenage years, when he grew into the opposite of the boy who attached himself to her leg.

Later, when Anna walked in, the pictures and letter were still on the table. She called to her mother, "Why didn't you tell me Taki was finally coming?"

Eleni hurried into the kitchen from the den. She had been preoccupied with the photos and had altogether forgotten to read what Taki had written. Anna held the letter in front of her now, her face shining like an August moon.

41

A few weeks later, Sophie and Loukas moved into Evan's apartment. Sophie would have rather stayed in the apartment in Victoria but didn't press the issue, considering the manner and condition in which she arrived. Her mother said there were still renters and she didn't want to ask them to leave so suddenly. Evan's place was smaller and the neighborhood was noisier but for now it would do. It was certainly bigger than her place in Paris.

One early afternoon, Loukas was at work, and Sophie was making lunch for herself and Anna. When Anna knocked, Sophie, hurrying to answer the door, bumped into the countertop with her belly. Anna looked beautiful, her hair shiny and her cheeks bright, a chic trench and gauzy scarf thrown over the rest of her stylishly antistylish clothing and her compact little body. Sophie felt a spot of jealousy. Or maybe a touch of wistfulness. It wasn't that she didn't like her life now—the pregnancy, living with Loukas back in Athens—she did, but she was filled with the sensation that she had missed something, a sort of undirected longing. Anna was only five years her junior, yet Sophie felt matronly and frowsy next to her, fat and clueless and insignificant.

Hadn't *she* been that same woman a few years before, full of determination and self-importance? She looked at the burgundy mohair sweater that Anna was wearing, the sleeves pulled down low over her hands. Hadn't it been hers?

She had the odd sensation of being thoroughly replaced. And sometimes she got the sense people expected no more from her, as a pregnant woman. Disassociated from the rest of society, utterly dispensable. Who were those women who said they felt nothing but sheer happiness when pregnant, who felt so peaceful and serene, Virgin Mothers incarnate? She was Virgin Mother discarnate. And, to boot, horny as hell, which she thought would go away soon enough but it kept persisting, even as her belly grew to gigantic proportions.

Loukas had developed a fixation these last weeks that he would somehow disturb the baby during sex, so she was left ravenous, for the most
part, with only her crazy, lusty dreams. A small part of her wondered
if he was disgusted by her pregnant self, if her body had changed too
much, if she smelled different, tasted different, just seemed like another woman altogether.

Anna hugged her sister, patted her belly, and absentmindedly
went through Sophie's mail. There was a letter from Taki, with pictures, from a month earlier. "It's just like Taki to visit in December,"
Anna said. "That way he can remember home as desolate and dirty."
She looked around the apartment wistfully.

"He might be here for the birth, too," Sophie said. "Though I'm
not sure he'll stay that long."

"Why would Taki come just because you were having a baby?
Then he would no longer be the star."

Taki approached fatherhood with the fervor of the converted,
and Sophie wondered whether, if she had been the one to give birth
first, he would have, in reaction, approached child-*less*-ness with an
equal enthusiasm. Then again, Taki had always thrown himself headfirst into things; there had been the time that Taki had acquired a
prayer rug, refused to eat pork, and convinced himself he was Mus-
lim. There had been Taki's Young Communist club, when he was six,
which he abandoned after one of their father's arrests, burning all the
club paraphernalia in a fire in an open field and declaring himself a
capitalist; there had been those plants, his veranda lined with all sorts
of potted greens, until one day, he seemed to forget they were there,
and they died.

Sophie knew, of course, this sort of fleeting interest would not
apply to his child but when Taki threw himself into something, he
acted as if he had discovered it. His letters were tinged with the tone
of authority, as if fatherhood had given him an omniscient wisdom
about the ways of the world, as if he were the first person to attempt
and accomplish such a feat. It annoyed her, a little bit, but she was not
nearly as bothered as Anna was.

"Oh, he'll still be the star," Sophie said. "I could have twelve
babies, but with Loukas's name, they're not as important." And she

agreed with Anna that a winter visit was strange, but her brother ("I've a family to support now") had taken a better-paying job that would begin after the New Year, and he would quit his old job before the American Thanksgiving. Sophie played along but felt uncomfortable with Anna's disdain. It was clear Anna felt a little abandoned by her siblings, who had not only left Athens but had now crossed over into the adult world of partnership and parenthood.

"Okay," Anna said. "Believe what you want."

"You don't have to be so spiteful." This was not the first time she'd found her little sister taking a harsh jab at their brother, though Anna seemed more agitated than the circumstances demanded.

"How are you liking this place?" Anna asked.

Sophie looked around the apartment: the tan couch, the green throw pillows. The kitchen was small but enough, and she loved the small porch off their bedroom. "It's nice," she said. "Thank you for mentioning it."

"Good," Anna said. "I'm glad it's working out." Then she tossed the picture from Taki back onto the table and excused herself to use the bathroom.

When Anna returned, her hair off her face and into a neat ponytail, Sophie asked, "Anna? Could it be that you're jealous? That we're all making a big deal about his arrival?"

Anna laughed almost maliciously. "And what if I am? Why is jealousy such a dismissed emotion?" Her tone sounded far more adult than Sophie would have expected. Anna stood up and poured herself a glass of water. Sophie dished out the *fasolakia*—green beans, tomatoes, and potatoes—and tossed the wild greens in lemon and oil.

"So tell me how *you* are," Sophie said.

"Fine," said Anna. "Busy with studying. Other things."

"Panos?"

"He's not my boyfriend," Anna said quickly. "Who has time for a boyfriend?"

"There's always time," Sophie said. "You just don't seem too interested. Hasn't this Panos been after you for years?"

"How do you know? You haven't even been here." Anna took a

long gulp of water. "What, I have to flash my breasts all day long to show I'm interested? In my physics class last year I was one of six women. The other seventy were men. Believe me. I have my pick."

"But you don't choose any of them," Sophie said. She didn't believe this.

"Why does a man always have to be involved? Aren't there other things in life, besides love?" Sophie saw that, despite the sharpness in her tone, Anna looked sad, suddenly. "A long story," Anna said finally, between bites. "But now I've got more important things to talk about." She leaned in across the table, and her eyes grew wide, like they were when she was a little girl. Her defensiveness lifted, and so did the bitter tone. "We're planning a big sit-in. A demonstration. Like the one at the law school." She stopped. Perhaps she thought she shouldn't be sharing her information with anyone. What did Anna think her sister was, a spy? And did she not remember that Sophie had left the country because she was afraid for her own and her family's safety? *I brought* bombs *back here,* Sophie wanted to say.

Anna stood up to clear their plates. "Don't mention anything I told you, okay?" She balanced the dishes against her chest, not caring about the sauce that dripped on her sweater. "I should be making *you* lunch," Anna said. "When the baby's born, I'll come over and cook."

Sophie wanted to hug her little sister then, she wanted to tell her she didn't mean to abandon her, and would she please forgive her, and she was here now. But those impressionable years could never be reclaimed; Anna had come of age as an only child.

Anna washed and dried the dishes, and she put them away without asking where anything went. Sophie's small kitchen looked not out onto a quaint street too narrow for cars, as it had in Paris, or a veranda that faced the garden, as it had in Halandri, but out to an alley wall that was always decorated with graffiti. Recently, someone had painted it all white again and written the slogan A GREECE OF CHRISTIAN GREEKS. Someone else, a few days later, had defaced it with the words of George Seferis:

Greece, Fire! of Christian, Fire! Greek, Fire!
Dead words! Why did you kill them?

Anna stared at the graffiti a moment. "Did you do that?"

"No," Sophie said, though suddenly she wished she had, and she could imagine Anna's judgment, *Of course you didn't*. "But it's Seferis."

"I know," Anna said, and rummaged through the cupboards. "Do you have anything sweet? What kind of pregnant woman doesn't keep anything sweet?"

Sophie told her there was chocolate in the drawer but wanted to say, *I'm more than a pregnant woman*. Was that how her little sister saw her? Is that how she acted? Anna found the bar, her favorite kind, and unwrapped it. She broke off a square and handed it to Sophie. "You're going to be a good mother, you know. And I wouldn't get married either. It's like voluntary confinement."

Despite her prior feelings of being judged, Sophie laughed. Maybe she was being too sensitive. She ate the chocolate. "Voluntary?" she joked.

Anna peered into the bedroom, and then she went and stood in the doorway. She opened the doors that led to the small terrace and Sophie followed her. "Can you still, you know . . . ," she asked.

"Can I *what*?" She smirked.

"Have sex?" Anna asked.

Sophie had never heard her sister even use the word, and she was startled by the straightforwardness of the question.

"What?" Anna asked. "I'm just curious."

Sophie nodded. "And sometimes, it's even better."

The younger Anna returned, embarrassed, timid, and Sophie's answer made her peevish. She was fidgety and her dark brows furrowed and for a moment Sophie felt as though she had won. Won what, though? "You asked!" Sophie said.

Anna averted her eyes and put her ear down on her sister's belly. "Boy or girl?" she asked, as if she'd be able to tell by listening.

"Do you have a preference?" Sophie asked.

"Boy. Definitely. It's easier to be a boy."

"Six or seven more weeks," Sophie said, "and we'll know." But though Sophie was acutely aware of her gestation clock, she could not comprehend that she had all that time to go before the baby came to term. She couldn't imagine keeping the baby inside her much longer.

She felt she had stayed her same size, with only her belly swelling and growing, to the point that she felt completely out of balance. From behind her on the street, men would hoot and whistle, and when she'd turn and expose her huge abdomen, they'd start in surprise and avert their eyes as if she were something disgusting and unnatural, or they'd scurry away with a look of shame, like they had hooted at the Virgin herself.

Now Sophie could feel a small hand (or was it a foot?) pushing on her side, and when she lay down at night, the baby wanted to do anything but sleep. She told this to Anna. "I think I have some sort of nocturnal creature inside me."

"Maybe you'll give birth to a kitten," Anna said, laughing.

This didn't make her laugh, though. Instead, she had to fight back tears, as if the possibility of something nonhuman were as real and attainable as the chance of its being a boy or a girl. She had never imagined how protective she would be of her unborn child, and the mere thought of schoolyard teasing or the common cold sent her into a fit of tears. *Dis*-balanced indeed, she thought. Discombobulated. Discomposed.

Anna didn't notice her sister's reaction. She stood up quickly, looking at the clock. "I have to meet someone," she said. "Thanks for the lunch." She hurried into the bathroom again and emerged wearing Sophie's lipstick, her hair down, freshly brushed.

When Anna left, Sophie watched her saunter down the road, her satchel at her side, the collar of her trench coat turned upward. Wasn't political engagement what Sophie had wanted, a sort of self-importance, some commitment? Her attempts had felt like one-shot deals, without momentum. It seemed, even from this one interaction, that her sister had assumed her role with more resolve and sophistication than Sophie could ever muster. And here was Sophie, eating lunch in her apartment and feeling as fat as a pig. Only less useful. A lumpen revolutionary, a *lumpy* nonrevolutionary.

How bold her little Anna had become. She now walked with such confidence, an almost bullish swagger that suggested, among other things, a lack of innocence. And the sexual charge that, boyfriend or not, seemed to go hand in hand with civil disobedience.

42

Evan had begun calling Anna at home again when he knew her mother was gone. Now that Anna was back in school, though, it was rare she brooded on the porch, waiting for the phone. Once, he had actually left a message with her mother, casually, as if he were simply a friend from school. They hadn't been together since Anna had traipsed to his house in the middle of the night, the night she found out Simone was pregnant. And they hadn't talked since he'd stood her up at the Grande Bretagne two months before. What did he want from her?

But when he caught her unawares in the university courtyard one sunny morning, she, trying to appear nonchalant, told him she had to meet her sister for lunch but she'd be out with friends later at a bar nearby. "If you want, you can find me there," she said. Evan insisted they meet somewhere more quiet, so Anna finally suggested a coffee shop a few blocks away, a place she liked but that Evan would find a bit too run-down.

When she walked in, he was already waiting. "You're mad at me," was the first thing he said. He smirked slightly. He wore a camel-colored cashmere sweater over a light-blue shirt, and his thick hair had glints of gold in it. She was always startled by how handsome he was, how perfectly his clothes seemed to fit him.

"I'm not," Anna said.

"You haven't returned my calls," Evan said.

"I never return your calls," Anna said. "I'm not allowed to. Besides, you stood me up."

"Of course you're allowed to," he said, revising things now. "And I had an excuse! You didn't let me explain. My friends arrived much earlier than expected. What was I supposed to do?"

I don't know, Professor, you figure it out, she thought. "It doesn't matter," she said.

"Will you please sit down?" he asked. She did, tracing her fingers along the chipped tabletop. She wanted him to take her hand.

Rejection was rejection, and it was odd and unfair how just a few small ones—the day at his house when she ended up babysitting, the time on the beach when he wouldn't even look at her, the stand-up—seemed to outweigh all those months and months of connection. She didn't want to be melodramatic, but she couldn't help it. It was how she felt.

"And now my sister is living in your apartment."

"You were the one who told her it was for rent."

"Wasn't it?" It suddenly occurred to her that perhaps it all had been an elaborate plan to break up with her.

"Of course it was. And Simone is thrilled to have Sophie and Loukas there. They're like family."

Anna prickled at this. Like family, he thought? The waiter interrupted them to take her order, but she brushed him off as she was brushing Evan off now.

Again he asked why she hadn't returned his calls, even though all this time she had never felt comfortable calling him at home. It had killed her not to dial that number, to not hear his voice, and instead she wrote him long, confusing letters that she never sent. Sometimes, when she'd reread them, she couldn't even follow her own train of thought.

"I'm sorry," Anna said eventually.

Evan looked right into her. "We never talked about any of this. After months and months of talking about everything."

"What's to talk about?" She tried to appear indifferent. "It is what it is. Was what it was." She fidgeted with the packets of sugar on the table.

"Was?" he asked. "Anna." He reached over the table and touched her chin.

She kept her head down and shifted in her chair. Oh, but when he said her name.

He continued, "You've been avoiding me."

"Have I? This semester has been busy. I can't believe it's almost November." She told him she had to go soon. That she had an exam.

"You said you were off to the bar," he said. "You don't want to talk to me."

"Of course I do. But I'm still a student. I've different priorities."

"You yourself said your professors were regime puppets. That your classes were pointless."

"*You* got your position back," she said, extending her hand to him. "They can't be all that bad."

He smiled, albeit wanly. "Touché."

Anna flagged the waiter down and asked for a glass of water and a small dessert. Evan added another coffee.

She continued. "A lot right now is pointless. But I still go through the motions." Maybe all this desire and longing was futile too, but she wondered if years from now she would still think of it that way, or if it would shine ever more brightly than other, more wholly requited desires.

"Are you purposely trying to hurt me?" Evan asked.

"I don't know. Am I? Hurting you?"

"I want to see you again," he said.

"Suddenly you want more of me? Well, you can't have that. And if you could, you wouldn't. You'd want others, all to yourself. There are always others." But the truth was she wanted him all to *her*self, and knew she could never have him that way.

The waiter set down their drinks and orders. They were quiet a while. Anna offered him a bite of her *galaktoboureko*. "It's good," she said. "Try some."

He declined but watched her eat.

"Come on," she said. But then she set the spoon on her plate and stretched back in her chair, flipping her hair out from where it had caught in her sweater. He watched her attentively. She liked the feeling.

Anna spooned up some custard and sticky *phyllo* and offered it out to him. "Just a little." He first tried to take the spoon from her, but she didn't let go. He leaned in, almost smiling, and took a bite. Anna looked down at the table and then drew her eyes upward slowly, meeting his.

He let out a sigh, almost a groan, and looked out distantly. "How long are we going to drive each other crazy like this?"

"What," she asked, "are you talking about?"

But Evan, exasperated, stood up abruptly and threw more money than necessary down on the table. "What would you have me do?" he asked. "Tell me."

She gave him an aloof shrug and lit a cigarette.

"I've got to go," he said. "I'll talk to you later."

"Ciao," she said, and looked at him with what he had called her haughty, bored face. He turned quickly, and soon his tense back disappeared into the crowded street.

When the waiter returned, she ordered another coffee and paid for it with Evan's money. She sat there, alone, a long time. When a few friends saw her in the window, they stopped for her. Otherwise, she would have sat there all afternoon and evening, staring out at the lit-up street.

It was true Anna was heartbroken. But she had also become angry.

She didn't know where it had started: a slow, steady upsurge. One too many condescending looks from the military police, her uncle's arrest, the way her mother always seemed on edge, looking over her shoulder. And also the personal—Evan, Evan, Evan. Maybe even it had started as early as her sister's abrupt departure, or that time in the stadium when she had first met Panos. But that semester, everything seemed to accelerate, and she felt the world was moving along far too quickly. Previously she had been sitting at the kitchen table, drinking tea and willing everyone to come back home, or stuck in bed, unable to move, or lying with an inappropriate man. Then, when another pardon had released many young people, some friends of Anna's among them, their experiences of beatings, of dirty cells, of humiliation both physical and mental, had finally rattled something in her. Coupled with wanting some self-protection from Evan and the way he consumed her, Anna was ready to stir things up.

Once she had been sitting with Mihalis in the morning on the veranda, and she had asked him why he was always writing. She was six or seven.

Mihalis had laughed. "What would you rather I did?"

Anna had shrugged, and Mihalis laughed again. "Play with you, I suppose?"

But when Mihalis realized she had been serious, he contemplated her question. "Because I have to," Mihalis said. "I can't *not* write."

This had confused her then—she couldn't imagine a compulsion or a drive to *write,* and she had taken it as some sort of homework he had. She nodded. Mihalis had tickled her, and she squealed. She was still small enough to be picked up, and he raised her into the air and beamed up at her, then lowered her and kissed her on the head. Anna remembered this clearly, being puzzled at his amusement. But those words stuck with her, *I can't not.*

She was not a natural leader, but leaders needed numbers, masses, protesters, those to march and pass out flyers and sit and take over buildings, and this mind-set freed her shyness and some power emerged from beneath it. Her fellow students were often amazed that she, a tiny young woman, was full of so much energy. And not a sweet energy, but intense and pointed, practical and compact. There was no longer anything diminutive about her, and she was able to command the attention of a room just by coming into it, a fact that would probably astound her family. It certainly astounded her and sometimes she was still uncomfortable with the attention. At home, her mother often didn't know if she was in the house or not.

So that morning in mid-November, she headed to the university, where dozens of others awaited. They had persuaded themselves that all of Greece was behind them, that it was up to them, those students who that morning had begun to barricade themselves in the Polytechnic. They would be responsible for bringing the dictators down. But they did not do so in the name of communism or Marxism or anarchy; they did so in the name of democracy. We are not radicals, many of them said. There is nothing radical about what we want. This is about basic human rights. This is about *life.*

They were protesting it all: the huge numbers of police files on students, sometimes for almost nothing; the spying and the infiltration of the campuses with agents provocateurs. They were sick of student groups being stifled, of not being able to walk home in the evening without worrying about being followed. For years they had tolerated this, and then, suddenly, it was no longer tolerable. It was that simple. A switch thrown.

Anna couldn't help but think of the American students who protested the conflict in Vietnam, those French students and the events of May five years before—she was among these young adults now, political and sexual and as much a part of what people were calling youth culture as anyone or anything. Evan could have his island homes and expensive cafés and his pretty wife with her babies. She would have something else.

Those past few weeks, on the phone or in cafés, they had their own patois, a jumble of code words, "the party" being the upcoming sit-in, "*feta*" for clubs, and "olives" for the provisions they would bring inside. "Lemons" were really lemons, as well as Vaseline, and would come in useful in the event of tear gas; it was better than water for washing out your eyes. "Wine" stood for medical supplies. *Feta* and olives and wine for the party. Who could object to that?

But as she joined her fellow students inside the university's main building, she thought there was only a large room of them, and then she noticed another, and soon Anna realized there were more students upstairs too and students filling the hallways and smoking in the stairwells, and it felt like that moment at a party where calm conversation swings to raucous roar in one giant exponential bound. She felt both self-righteous and baffled that beyond those university walls, the city passed its time no differently than the day before, and the day before that, and the day before that. The meeting had begun indoors, and they, almost three thousand of them, would together defy the powers that be. The discussions were serious and passionate, for the most part, though exhaustion sometimes gave way to silliness. Mimeographed faces of Patakos and Papadopoulos had been affixed to tongue depressors taken from the emergency medical kits, and the students paraded around wearing these masks, shouting out through the windows. Word had not yet gotten out. That soon would change.

By the time night fell, thousands of people filled the school's courtyards, and thousands more piled on the sidewalks in front, on the other side of the iron gates. Anna was stationed with Panos in a classroom, from where they were running a radio station. And to look outside at the masses in the streets, the angry demonstrators backing them up, it seemed to them that this would be the end. Outside, swarms of people held flyers and shouted and cheered, shouted things that in almost seven years had rarely been uttered at all. They pasted flyers onto cars; they sat and sang in the streets.

That first night, Anna barely slept amid the chaos. They had encouraged each other to nap, to take turns sleeping while they could. Anna wanted to avoid sleep altogether; with other like-minded students she made coffee and took various cocktails of pills. Finally, near evening of the second day, Anna and Panos rested on a small hallway bench. Anna was aware of the noise and energy around her but was unable to resist it. Her body was beginning to shut down. If she could only sleep for an hour or so, she'd feel better. In a voice that sounded hazy and dreamlike, she heard Panos say to her, "You don't really love him, do you?" but Anna couldn't answer, her body stuck again, unable to move.

There was her father, a memory, a dream, her father! Young and vibrant and happy, lifting her small self up to peer into the large record player, a piece of furniture in its own right. He let her lift the top to expose the turntable. New Year's Eve and a house full of guests, and Anna pointed to his favorite albums, a series from the Berlin Philharmonic. He said he'd play those later, that now it was time for something else, something for dancing. Anna handed him her lottery ticket, crumpled in her sweaty palms, too young to know what was going on but old enough to know the ticket held great potential. "Not yet," he said. "Soon."

Later, in the middle of the night, when a friend woke her to tell her to report to her post at the receiving window, where students gathered to accept food and medicine from those who felt brave enough to bring it, images of her father stayed with her. She looked for Panos, who had left his sweater as a pillow. She was cold so she wrapped it around her shoulders and went to the classroom where he and some others had the radio station up and running. She was proud of his raspy voice resounding from the school's public address system, "Testing: one, two, three. This is Radio Polytechnic." Over the radio they sang resistance songs and encouraged the rest of Greece to join them. Send observers, they told the embassies. Send journalists, they told the press.

43

Sophie waited for her mother, who had insisted on accompanying her to the doctor for her checkup.

After the initial shock of her pregnancy, her mother had shifted her energy from its conceptual to its physical state: how was she feeling, what was she eating, was everything going okay. Loukas had offered to come home from work and take her, but Sophie had protested. "I'm not an invalid," she had said. "I happen to have a baby growing inside me. Our *yia-yias* were probably working in the fields like this, washing clothes in the stream. They probably gave birth right out there amid the olive and lemon trees."

"I hate when you romanticize village life," he said.

He was trying to be cute, but Sophie was irritable. "I don't have some sort of debilitating condition," she said. "I'm just pregnant. It happens to a lot of people."

"It's not that I think you're fragile," Loukas said. "I just don't want you near the Polytechnic. It's getting completely out of control. Maybe you can reschedule your appointment."

"My mother is coming with me," Sophie said. This seemed to pacify him both because he didn't want her to be alone and because he had been worried about Sophie's relationship with her mother since they'd dropped back into Athens. They were happy with her mother's newfound interest.

Sophie was not dying to go out amid all this and *would* have rescheduled her appointment, but she hadn't felt the baby and its vigorous kicking for a few days, and she was worried. The doctor's office said yes, they were still seeing patients, and she should come in. "We should check on the baby," the nurse on the phone had said. *The baby.* Her pregnancy was so visible but the idea of a baby felt abstract. Until now, when it had grown strangely silent. But she kept this to herself.

Her mother arrived soon after, on edge. "Any word from Anna?" she asked.

Sophie told her once again there was none but that when she'd seen her days earlier, Anna had dropped hints. They knew she was among the thousands of students who had barricaded themselves inside the Polytechnic. "She just left that morning with her usual rucksack," Eleni said. "Nothing out of the ordinary."

"I can't imagine her telling you," Sophie said. Sophie, too, was worried about her sister, and she was both amazed and frightened by the angry throngs that had amassed outside the university. If she had not been pregnant, Sophie herself would have been there, holding signs and dropping off food and distributing flyers. But it was quickly becoming uncomfortable for her to do anything, and she could think of nothing more than the baby and the day she'd go into labor.

"It's getting crazy out there," her mother said. "The police have suddenly come out in droves, and they're using tear gas. Most of the roads are blocked off. Are you sure you want to keep this appointment?"

"We can walk," Sophie said. "I need the exercise, and we can go the back way, which should be clear." Even if the roads had not been blocked off, Sophie would have chosen to walk; sitting in the car gave her severe shooting pains down one leg. She was trying to stay as mobile and active as possible, even though her ever-increasing size seemed to ask otherwise of her.

Sophie's mother detected urgency in her voice and looked at her a moment. "Is everything okay?"

Sophie hesitated but then told her mother about the baby's stillness, and she frightened herself, uttering this aloud. Her mother's expression changed, though her tone didn't. "I'm sure it's fine." But she didn't fight with Sophie about rescheduling the appointment, and the two of them walked together, into the street.

Outside, Sophie could hear a collective roar, similar to what she'd hear from the stadium during a soccer match. Her doctor was only about eight blocks away, near Areos Park. She and her mother walked single-file down the narrow sidewalks, her mother in front, every so often turning back to make sure Sophie was still there. Finally, she stopped and said, "You walk ahead of me. I'll feel better if I can see you."

Sophie obliged.

The doctor's office was filled with frenzied energy; some had been injured in the protests, and Sophie felt strange, behind a closed door, discussing the progress of her pregnancy. The baby's heart rate was fine, and nothing looked out of the ordinary. "You shouldn't be worried," the doctor told her. "Just pay attention to its movements, its kicking. It's possible that you're just not noticing it anymore."

Sophie sighed. This was not very reassuring.

"Come back in a few days," her doctor said. "But you are on the right track."

The right track? Sophie thought. Putting it that way made it seem as though she was looking for something elusive. As though one false move, one wrong turn, and she'd suddenly become unpregnant, her belly vanished with no trace.

Though they had only been inside an hour, when they left the doctor's office, the atmosphere of the city had shifted as clearly as a lower-pressure system swinging in. Street activity had heightened. Cars sped around corners, and mothers with small children hurried them inside, closing the blinds on that sunny autumnal late afternoon. The sick, sweet smell of garbage burning made Sophie choke. They rounded a corner to find another group of students running past, carrying pipes and boards, makeshift weapons. A line of a poem flashed in her mind, *Our swords are taller than us.*

Sophie turned back to her mother. "What should we do?"

"Let's get home," she said, urging her ahead. "We're close."

But two blocks from the doctor's office, they were met by a large crowd, all running from the direction of the Polytechnic and from Sophie's place. One of the young women shouted. "Are you crazy? You can't be out here. Don't go that way, whatever you do."

One boy, no more than nineteen, noticed Sophie coughing and handed her a handkerchief soaked in water. "For the tear gas," he said. The boy and girl pounded on doors, frantically ringing buzzers. "Someone's got to let us in," one of them said.

"My God," the girl said, looking back at Sophie, just now noticing her. "We've got a pregnant woman with us."

Through the windows of one apartment, Sophie saw a group of adults sitting down for a perfectly calm late-afternoon meal. No one got up from the table to open the door, but after someone pounded on the window a man did close the shades. In other apartments, more of the same: the peering out of curtains, the dimming of the lights.

"We can't get to your apartment," her mother said. "Not now."

"Well, what are we supposed to do?" Sophie yelled, as much because of the noise as her anger and fear.

"We'll go to Lottery Place."

"What about the tenants?" Sophie asked.

"It's fine," her mother said. She took her hand and the two of them moved with the crowd, away from the university. Those narrow, pitted sidewalks, perpetually busted up for the endless sewer line repairs, seemed all the more treacherous. The students in the crowd warned them of snipers shooting from hotel balconies. Demonstrators had appropriated buses and threw fruits and stones and bricks at the police. Students started fires to break down the tear gas. In the distance Sophie could hear young voices over loudspeakers reading lists of things they needed: food, medicine, food, medicine. After a very close-sounding *pop pop pop* of machine guns and a few more loud screams, her mother grabbed her by the shoulders and asked if she was okay.

She was exhausted, and now her belly felt sloshed around and unstable, like it might detach. She could have been imagining it. "I'm okay," she said, gasping for air.

She and her mother quickened their pace. Her mother did not let go of her elbow. Some of the group split off; the fastest ones in front found shelter in one building. But just as Sophie was thinking she'd rather chance the tear gas and crazy militia than run another step, her mother squeezed her hand. "Just another block," she said.

"Oh, thank God," a girl behind them cried. It appeared that she and her mother were leading the way.

At the apartment building, her mother pulled out her keys and let them all in. The heavy steel door slammed behind them. She led Sophie and the students who were with them across a small foyer to the door of the apartment and didn't flinch at the scene inside. There, one woman was cleaning a cut on the leg of another. From climbing over a fence? Two students lay on the floor, exhausted, listening to the streams from Radio Polytechnic.

In the corner, a handsome man with wavy dark hair and large eyes stitched up a wound on a young woman's forehead. He and her mother exchanged glances. "It just started," he said. "When I arrived people were already waiting outside." Next to him was a box of medical supplies: bandages, ointments, antiseptics, and needles. Bottles of painkillers and sedatives.

Her mother, clearly in charge now, ordered Sophie to sit. A young woman in a recliner cleared it for her and then gave her a throat drop: the tear-gas-tinged air was irritating. Eleni brought Sophie a blanket and a glass of water, and Sophie sat quietly, her breath still heavy. "Stay here. Rest." Her mother then handed a clipboard to the girl who'd given up her seat. "As people come in, take down their names and their symptoms," she ordered. "Tear gas stings the eyes, but it can also cause suffocation."

Sophie listened to the shouts of the students on the radio, to the screech of cars and blare of sirens outside. Two others, who waited to be treated, told her of three consecutive explosions around the city. Nobody had been killed as far as they knew but there had been injuries, and Sophie felt sick thinking back to the materials she'd transported into the country. She just knew she was accountable for these explosions.

When she caught her breath, she phoned Loukas to tell him where she was and that she was okay. He insisted on meeting her.

"Okay," she said. She looked around the apartment, which was filling with people, scattered across the living room. "Just come to Victoria. But I'll explain when you get here." *I'm still piecing it together myself,* she thought.

And then she stood up and found her mother in the first bedroom, talking quietly to the handsome man whom she now introduced as Andreas, and he smiled at her warmly but remained focused on the girl's forehead he was suturing. He and her mother discussed whom to treat next. When he finished his last stitch, the girl winced. He tied the black thread off neatly. Another man waited patiently with a bruised lip and a broken wrist and a petite girl held her arm, crying in pain.

Sophie wanted to help but didn't know how, and just the sight of all those injured people made her feel faint. "I have to lie down," Sophie said. Her mother and an underground clinic, her sister probably a student radical. When had this all happened? Her mother quickly led her to the back bedroom, and Sophie reclined on a clean twin bed, and the way her mother put her hand on her forehead reminded her of being a child and sick with a fever.

Her mother was quiet and then, sensing Sophie's questions, said, "It's exactly what it looks like, Sophie *mou*." She took her hand and then said, "Call out if you need me." Sophie closed her eyes and tried to relax. Then she felt the baby, kicking, kicking, kicking. One small triumph, one small relief.

Very soon afterward, Loukas found her and embraced her, touched her belly, rubbed her legs with one hand and held her hand in the other. His eyes were red. "We're not going to go anywhere for a while. Just try to rest." In all their years together, she had never seen a tear leave his eye: not when he first had broken up with Estrella, not when he found out his father was sick, not even when he talked about his mother's death. He pulled Sophie to his chest. She let herself be held.

Despite all the activity, she was exhausted and soon fell asleep. Around midnight, she awoke to the sound of a newly arrived group of students, and she could tell that the apartment was far more crowded. "Tanks," they said, all of them out of breath. "Big, huge, barreling tanks."

44

Tanks slammed through the Polytechnic gates, crushing two students who had climbed on top. The police and military stormed through the hallways and released tear gas. They clubbed through the masses of students as though they were slashing wheat, and from inside the campus arose an echoing, bestial roar.

With Vaseline smeared around her eyes, Anna hid in the main building, near the room with the radio transmitter from which she had shouted slogans only moments before. In what she hoped would be an overlooked stairwell, she huddled into as small a shape as she could. This was where she and Panos had agreed to meet in case of an emergency, whatever that was. Falling, racing, scared footsteps pounded on the stairs above her, followed by the ugly, muffled trample of boots. The police ran their clubs against the railing—scare tactics—and Anna brought her hands to her ears.

Briefly, the sounds ebbed, and then a second wave of sheer noise blitzed through with a fresh incursion of soldiers into the building. She wanted to disappear into a crack in the wall, to become one with the sheer cement. She thought of the small spaces in her basement and the way she used to hide in them. Anna knew it was only a matter of luck she had not yet been discovered, that all it took was for one man to turn, to pause, to glance over his shoulder.

And then, a door above flew open, washing her in weak light. A policeman shouted, his gas mask moving like an angry snout. He shined his flashlight on her and his gruffness disappeared behind its blinding beam. He grabbed the neck of her sweater and pulled hard, nearly ripping it off her body. She thrashed and kicked and fought back, but the man got ahold of her throat and shoved her down the stairs. She tumbled to the bottom. Before she could get back on her feet, the man was on top of her again, kicking her in the stomach.

Something crushed inside her chest. She tried again to stand but a club to her spine crumpled her into a ball. She heard shouting in the distance. She closed her eyes and felt blackness overtake her.

They were shaking her, trying to wake her, but not too hard, she could tell. A cheek pressed against her face, a familiar smell. Panos. "She's barely breathing," she heard him say. "We've got to get her out of here." She felt herself be lifted up and carried. The throb of a heavy engine, the noxious smell of fumes, a clatter of soles on the sidewalk.

She finally opened her eyes and saw abandoned objects: book bags and sweaters, women's platforms, men's loafers, a few broken heels. Was she wearing her own shoes? She couldn't tell; she couldn't see her feet. She lifted her head slightly, felt a terrible pain in her chest, and moaned. She tried to focus on the back of someone's head before she slumped down again, staring at a frayed denim pocket. Panos was carrying her, running with her now. Her body jostled about. She wanted to talk but she couldn't move her mouth; her tongue felt swollen and huge.

And how her chest ached. Could it be that she had been knifed? Someone shouted: "Stop, please, stop!" She heard the screech of wheels, a blaring car horn. "Get in," a voice said in heavily accented English. "Hurry." She felt herself being slowly laid down. Only when the car sped away did she realize she was in a backseat, and this moments before the world retreated and again went black.

So she did not see the driver, a foreign journalist, a camera hung loose around his neck. She did not see the way he drove with one hand, a bloodied T-shirt pressed onto the other. She did not hear Panos tell the driver where to take them, nor did she hear that he wasn't sure, exactly, an address given to him by another student. Her head lay across Panos's lap, but she could not see his blood-crusted eyes, swollen like golf balls. She could not hear the tramp of tanks in the street, nor the sound of rifle shots, nor the bedlam of sirens that blared across the city. She didn't see the terrible lights playing across the dark skyline, the snipers from the hotel balconies. The students of Athens Polytechnic were still fighting, with their hands, their bodies, their stones. But Anna sensed nothing at all.

45

Outside the apartment, someone was furiously honking, and Eleni watched Andreas run outside. Through the window he called to Eleni, who was tending to students who had just arrived: a few held washcloths with ice to their heads; another sprawled on the couch, blood trickling from her ear; yet another lay slumped over a desk, remarkably asleep, his hand bandaged up and flopped in front of his head.

Eleni raced through the crowded living room and out of the building, where Andreas stood outside a running car talking to a boy with swollen eyes whom she immediately recognized as Panos. She knew then it was Anna, and she ran to the car where her daughter lay across the backseat, unconscious.

Andreas was taking her pulse. When he looked up at Eleni, his face had blanched. "She needs a hospital," Andreas said, and the flatness of his voice frightened her. "Now."

Eleni crawled into the backseat and let her daughter's head rest on her lap. Only then did she think to look up to see who was driving, a youngish man with a camera around his neck and long sandy brown hair. He was waiting for directions like some strange, polite cab driver.

"Athens General, Ippokrateio," she said. It was close by, and Dimitri was there for the night.

"On Vassilissis Sofias?" the journalist asked.

"Exactly," said Eleni. Panos got in the front seat next to him, setting aside the journalist's steno pad. They slammed the doors and raced up Alexandras Avenue, avoiding the scene at the Polytechnic. Roads were blocked off everywhere, but the journalist seemed to know his way around. He spoke to them in English but seemed to understand their Greek.

The streets were chaotic. People ran in all directions, and cars honked and fled through intersections. The journalist drove aggressively, every so often telling them something else he had seen, or some information about himself, in case they would suddenly decide not to trust him. He almost crashed into a motorcyclist and in trying to avoid him nearly ran into three students who limped across the street, their eyes shining in the headlights. "We're almost there," Panos said. "You're going to be okay." He looked in the rearview mirror a moment, meeting Eleni's eyes. If Anna could hear him, Eleni was glad she could not see that the calm tone of his voice did not match the terrified look on his face.

Eleni looked down at her unconscious girl. Was this the way her youngest daughter would leave the world, dumped into a backseat? She lightly touched her daughter's side and was startled to feel something—a rib?—jutting up from inside Anna's chest.

The journalist dropped them off right out front, and Eleni carefully got out. She ran inside and yelled for a stretcher. She felt as though her mouth had been shot with Novocain. She could barely form words. She hadn't even thanked her benevolent driver.

To the nurse at reception she asked for Dimitri, in surgery. He was used to calling the shots. She knew he would help them. "He's working," she said. "Call him."

They did, and Dimitri was downstairs immediately, commanding the nurses at the front desk like soldiers. While they raced out with a gurney to collect Anna, Eleni watched Dimitri corner an ER surgeon who seemed to just have finished an operation; he was coming to talk to the family, whom Eleni could identify because they all jumped up nervously and in unison. This surgeon, to whom Dimitri spoke quickly, glanced over at Anna as she was wheeled in. He pointed to the operating room, and Anna was whisked off behind those double doors before Eleni could say a word.

"I'm scrubbing in," Dimitri told her. "I'll be there the whole time. I promise." And then, he, too, was gone.

It was only then that Eleni noticed the injured were everywhere—in chairs, lying across the floor, crowding around the admissions desk. The staff was overwhelmed and overrun, and angry, urgent voices crammed the room. She walked to the front desk. She didn't recognize any of the nurses. "I'm a doctor in general medicine," she said. "Let me help." One nurse began to object, but another returned quickly with a coat and stethoscope. If nothing else, she could admit patients, fill out forms for those who couldn't. She could distinguish the desperately injured from the simply beat-up.

She started with Panos, his face ashen, slumped against the wall. He stared ahead at nothing in particular. Eleni noticed again his swollen eyes. His cheekbone was bruised, as if he had been struck.

After an hour, a young doctor came out to talk to Eleni. A rib had punctured Anna's spleen, which ruptured and flooded her abdomen with blood. Eleni kept her eyes on the doctor, waiting for more. "And?"

"They're removing the spleen. She'll need her leg in a cast. Some stitches around her left eye."

Eleni inhaled deeply and then let it all out. The hospital was at the height of triage. They wouldn't put her leg in a cast if she weren't going to live. They wouldn't have bothered to stitch up her eye.

"She's going to be okay," Eleni said to the people strewn out about the waiting room. And then she said it again, mostly to herself.

46

Those days after the Polytechnic insurrection, the injuries and deaths downplayed and the streets scrubbed of debris and blood, the powers that be arrogantly dismissed the events as no more significant than a mosquito buzzing around a bull's horn. Anna, of course, who was recovering in bed, knew differently. Behind the scenes, officials tracked down those they suspected to have been involved and *recommended* they sign something saying they weren't injured in the events.

A few days after, Anna, with her removed spleen and cracked ribs, her broken leg now plastered in a cast, had not yet been approached. Maybe because Dimitri had admitted her off the record;

maybe he had changed her name. She just knew that what had happened had been far more monumental than they had acknowledged, that the colonels were trying to deemphasize the event's influence—she had to believe this. It had gone on for three days, and their method of control, the tanks, the tear gas, the police with their clubs and their violence, in many ways suggested a complete lack of control.

Some days, Anna stayed on the couch all day and even slept there at night. Her mother had dragged a small table next to her and stretched the long, winding phone cord so Anna could answer it. She hated herself for hoping Evan would call. He had come to the hospital with flowers the day after her surgery, which her mother had given her when she'd woken up. The accompanying card simply read, *Perastika, sweet Anna mou. Many kisses, Evan.* A simple get-well wish. She knew her mother noticed the wave of brightness that must have swept over her face. Though when her mother had left the room, she cried, later blaming it on the effects of anesthesia. Her mother said she should call to thank him but she couldn't bring herself to do it. She hoped he would call her instead.

That night, the ringing set her heart pounding, some strange adrenaline buildup. She picked up the phone and cringed, feeling the pull of her incision.

"Anna?" the voice said. For a moment she thought it was Evan, and she sat up. But it wasn't. "It's Taki." His voice was groggy, as if he had just woken up.

The rare times Taki called she was either out or in bed, and she hadn't talked to him in a long time. Those nights he did call and she wasn't asleep, Anna knew she could just walk down the stairs and take the phone from her mother. But something always stopped her. The way her brother could interject himself into their lives with a phone call in the night, when it was a bright hour for him, bothered her. And she wasn't much of a conversationalist, always with so much to say but unable to say it.

So, for this reason, she couldn't give Taki the welcoming greeting he was looking for. She knew he expected a dramatic response when he telephoned. She wondered if someone had called him about her injury; undoubtedly, her mother had tried. Right now Anna felt Taki's departure was responsible for everything. She knew this was ridiculous but it didn't make her feel any better. "Hi," she said plainly.

"It's Taki," he said again.

"I know."

"How are you?"

She sighed, and Taki didn't speak either. It was certainly possible that no one had bothered to call him. As much as they sometimes missed him, Anna knew that it was partly resentment of him for leaving more than actually missing his presence. At least, that's what it felt like to her. She wished, though, she could be less cold. "Have you talked to anyone? Sophie?" she asked. She knew Taki and Sophie kept each other up to date even when the rest of the family wouldn't hear from them for weeks.

"She called last week. But she wasn't feeling well and had to get off the phone." He hesitated again, and Anna could detect some uncertainty in his tone. When her brother was nervous or cared about something he compensated by becoming almost apathetic.

"I broke my leg. And I had surgery; they removed my spleen, and I have a few cracked ribs."

"I'm sorry," he said.

"I have to stay in bed until God knows when. It hurts to cough. Or to laugh."

He asked her what had happened, exactly.

"Have you watched the news? The Polytechnic?" Though Anna had no sense of whether Greece would even make the news in the States, whether Americans paid attention to anything beyond their continental land. It wasn't a judgment call or a spiteful thought; she really simply had no idea how far their journalists would go to report the news, particularly with their country stuck in Vietnam. But, with all the other demonstrations happening internationally, she thought perhaps this might be something big. At least, she had hoped. But she had hoped for a lot of things. Now she just felt depressed. And she missed Evan more than she cared to admit, even to herself.

"Yes, of course," Taki said. "Athens is a madhouse, it looks like," he said.

Anna scoffed. Was this how he saw it, another unstable government of wild barbarians who couldn't keep things under control?

"But are *you* okay?" Taki asked.

Anna sighed. Where should she begin? How could she explain those last several months in one crackly long-distance phone call? "I'm fine," she said.

"I'll be there soon," he said.

Anna was excited to see her brother. But she couldn't help but think about all that she had done, in the name of democracy, in defense of the country, even for her family, and it was Taki who'd still fly in like some prince.

"I'm excited for you to come home," she managed to say. But when she said *home,* she felt immediately rejected. To Taki, Halandri was no longer anything of the sort.

47

The morning she and Loukas were to pick up Taki and his family at the airport and bring them to Halandri, Sophie woke with the feeling that this would be the day she gave birth. It was a little too early, she knew, but by the time she shuffled into the bathroom to wash her face and brush her teeth, the feeling had become muddled, and when she sat at the table with a cup of tea and some anise-flavored cookies, the sensation had disappeared entirely. Still, when she showered, when she dried her hair, when she shopped for presents for her niece, she was filled with a feeling of having forgotten something.

As many Athens winters as Sophie had lived through, she still imagined the city in spring: the flowers, the comfortable warmth, the verandas lined with all sorts of plants. Even though she knew this romanticization was unreal, it depressed her, her brother returning to this bleak weather. Sophie had never grown used to the cold of Paris, and she imagined Michigan was worse, but Taki had told her once that he welcomed the first snowfall; he liked to shovel his driveway and watch the neighborhood children build snowmen. But weather aside, Taki had moved from a city that slept and returned to a city that smoldered on the verge. How would he see his home now? How would he see her?

In the airport, Sophie was the first to spot them. There was Taki, a vaguely scared look on his face—he had always looked a bit scared, come to think of it, even if it was often hidden by impudence—and in his arms he held Aspa. She wore a dress of deep green velvet and already at eighteen months had a tumble of brown curls. She squirmed so much that Taki had to keep a tight grip around her tiny behind. His eyes searched the crowd. Behind him stood Amalia. If Amalia, his wife, held a grudge toward the family for not attending their wedding, she wasn't showing it. She just about floated across the airport floor, her arms outstretched, and embraced Sophie.

"Aspa," Taki said to his daughter. "This is your *theia* Sophie."

Aspa uttered something that Taki interpreted as a greeting. She clapped her hands and screeched at the top of her voice. "This is new," Amalia told Sophie as Sophie leaned in to give her niece a hug and a kiss. "Much to the chagrin of the other passengers on the plane." Aspa then focused her almond-shaped eyes, disproportionately huge, on Sophie's belly, and she stretched out her hand to touch it. *How is it*, Sophie thought, *that even the smallest child understands pregnancy, the essence of it, what it becomes?* She felt from her belly a strong, sharp kick, and she drew her hand there.

"Everyone is excited to see you," Sophie said.

On the way from the airport Sophie told Taki and Amalia about Anna: the Polytechnic, her spleen, the bruised-up body, the broken leg. Taki said he had heard it from Anna on the phone, but Anna, so reticent, hadn't divulged much. Sophie claimed Anna's "loss of appetite" was really a hunger strike. She only seemed to eat the ice cream her friend Panos would bring her. She was moody and alternated between smug and morose, Sophie said. But she looked okay.

"I'm sorry," Sophie said, interrupting herself. "Is this too much at once?"

Taki said it was not, but even looking out the window seemed to be too much for him. Loukas changed the subject to Aspa, and for the rest of the way home, Amalia and Loukas held up the conversation.

Back in Halandri, in the thin cold of early December, Sophie and Taki stood outside their childhood home. Sophie watched Taki fidget with Aspa's sweater, making sure its hood wasn't itching her face. To Sophie the child looked fine, and she knew her brother was stalling. Aspa, of course, was squirmy and anxious to get inside, as if she knew what awaited her: a grandmother, another aunt, presents. She was blissfully unaware of the power of familial guilt and grief.

Sophie was not sure what Taki was thinking. But because she herself had only recently returned, she knew exactly what he was sensing. While away she had forgotten the distinct scent of the house in Halandri, but when the door was flung open both Sophie and Taki were awash in it, the smell of the Ajax, of lemon, of their mother's rose perfume. She wondered if the street, too, had surprised Taki. When Sophie had returned from Paris she had still pictured it as unpaved, the old dirt road. But in reality it had been paved for years before she had left. She had a memory of standing on the porch with a toddler Anna balanced awkwardly in her arms and watching the milk truck blow dust in its wake. Now there was Aspa on the porch, making a sort of buzzing sound, leaning forward into the doorway. Amalia had already gone inside, met their mother, and smiled and called to Taki from behind the shield of the Polaroid.

When the picture snapped, Aspa squealed and clapped. Eleni took Aspa from Taki's arms as if it were something she had done hundreds of times before, kissing her on the head. In the doorway, Amalia took another picture, and then another. She set the photos down on the sideboard and followed the rest of the family to the kitchen. As she disappeared around the corner, Taki backed out of the house. "I'm going on the roof first," he said to no one in particular. And when Sophie returned to see what had happened to him, she found the door still open and Taki's small carry-on bag on the stoop.

48

Anna hadn't heard her brother come up the stairs, but instead heard a thump and scuttle as he scrambled down from the top of their house onto the balcony. She smiled, amused, as he opened the French doors into her room.

Anna sat up. "Hi, Taki," she said, as if her older brother always entered that way, up to the roof and then back down through the balcony.

"Wanted to see if I could still do it," he said. Then he exhaled. "It wasn't easy."

He came over to her and gave her a kiss and a hug. Fatherhood, or America, or simply his twenties, had made him soft; he looked pale and a bit paunchy, but still himself. He had long sideburns and a mustache. For some reason, she had expected him to look like an American soldier: short, buzzed hair, smooth-shaven face. But he looked just like any of the other Greek men his age, save for the bright sneakers he wore on his feet: brown and blue, new looking.

He hugged her and sat down at the edge of her bed, pointing at her cast. He let out a long, shaky sigh. "You okay?"

She shrugged. Anna wondered if this visit back was difficult for him. And just the thought of this made her a little angry that she was censoring herself to make her brother and his family feel comfortable. Things were not always comfortable. Why should they be for him? "The cast will come off, eventually," she said.

"No," he said. "I mean, are you able to get up?"

"With some help," she said. He surveyed the room, the pictures on the wall, the pile of clothes folded and stacked on the dresser. "Where's Aspa? Amalia?"

Taki grinned at the rickety sound of heeled shoes on the roof. Another set of feet was coming up the regular stairs. "Probably looking for me."

"Didn't you just get here?"

Taki shrugged. "I wanted to see the roof first."

He looked around her room, and Anna tried to see it through his eyes. Pictures of her friends, of rock formations and seashores, were tacked up in random patterns, haphazard. On the dresser was an assortment of various stones, collected from the beach. Then Taki reached into his pocket, as if just remembering something. He pulled out two small rocks.

"They're called Petoskey stones," he said. "I found them for you on the beach, in northern Michigan. It's fossilized coral," he added.

Anna felt the smooth, speckled stones in her palms. They were shiny, as if they were still wet. "I used Amalia's nail polish," he added.

"You have beaches there, in Michigan?" Anna asked.

Taki laughed. "Yeah," he said. There was a small knock and Sophie peered in. "Evan's here," she said, raising her eyebrows. And then she took Taki downstairs and left Anna alone.

It had been a month since Anna and Evan had spoken, and both could precisely recount their short, last conversation in the coffee shop, though neither would acknowledge as much. Evan appeared in her doorway carrying red carnations. It was now the second time he had brought her flowers, the second time anyone had ever brought her flowers. "Thank you," she said. She motioned to the nightstand, where he could set them down.

He hesitated. Anna invited him in but stared ahead. She was behaving like a sulking child, and she knew it, but she couldn't relax. She had no idea what to say.

"Your sister is very pregnant," he said.

Anna just looked at him. He sat carefully on the edge of the bed.

"I was worried," he said. She tried to imagine the situation if it were reversed. It was unfair his vague presence in her life was quietly recognized here—surely Mihalis had called him; how else had he known the day after—but hers in his would never be acknowledged. After all, he had a wife, and where would a twentysomething student, not even his own, fit in?

"I should have brought you some books," he said, glancing at the magazines spread on the nightstand.

"I haven't been reading much," Anna said. She knew, for some reason, that this comment would hurt him, as if books were a silly thing only he cared about, as if she had been humoring him all along.

Evan looked wounded, as she'd intended. And then she regretted it. But she wasn't ready to apologize. "I can't do much," she added. "My spleen was ruptured. By a large, angry man."

"What is the spleen for, then, if it can be removed?" he asked.

"What is anything for?" Anna snapped, though again she hadn't meant to.

The two of them were quiet for a moment, and Anna's mother appeared with a vase and arranged the flowers that sat forlorn on the dresser. She seemed unsure of how to handle this visit, so she treated him like she treated anyone else. "Evan, coffee is ready downstairs."

Anna couldn't tell if this was an offer or a command. Evan took it as the latter. "I'll be right down," he said. "Just thought I'd check on our little revolutionary."

Her mother adjusted the flowers one last time and then disappeared. If she hadn't figured it out before she surely had by now. Evan walked to the window. He stared at the neighbor on the roof, who was watering plants, a sort of last-ditch attempt before winter came full speed. He sighed. "You act like you're the only one who's hurting."

"Look at both of us. Who looks better off?"

"You know that's not what I mean," Evan said. He stared at her white coverlet. "What is it you would have wanted? That you want?"

"Nothing," she said.

"You knew that I—" His voice was gentle, and he couldn't seem to finish the sentence.

"That you're—" Anna paused, also unable to say the word *married*. "That you're unavailable. Yes. I understand that." She was offended that he even thought he had to bring it up. She remembered when Panos told her that nothing good would come of this. And yet she took a risk anyway, one that felt both irrational and completely instinctively *right*.

But what she *wanted*? What she wanted was for him to lean in and touch her face, her shoulder, to whisper in her ear as he'd done before. She added, "I don't know." She could not imagine herself in Evan's house, for instance, scurrying to bring him tea and the evening newspaper after his nap. The domestic principles that seemed to go hand in hand with coupledom did not appeal to her. Having a lover, to Anna, did not now and would never mean necessarily sharing space, or anything else, for that matter. Then why had she grown to feel so proprietary about this married man?

Evan was quiet. Anna watched him as he looked over her dresser, where she kept various mementos. Among them the wineglass she had stolen from his house, the first time she had been there. She had filled it with stones collected from the Hydra beach that first morning after. Anna hoped he didn't make the connection.

"I don't want things to end like this," he finally said, turning to her. "I don't want them to end at all."

Anna didn't say anything. She felt small and vulnerable there in her bed. The incision from her surgery throbbed. How could she explain to him that his existence alone broke her heart? It was best to keep things light. She knew she deserved more than this but she didn't want him to walk away from her. "Hey," she said. "Things are going to be fine."

Evan smiled, looked almost relieved. She could give him this much. "I hope so, dear girl," he said.

Anna studied Evan's face a moment, open and waiting. He leaned over and kissed her forehead, pulling her in close. *Stay here,* she wanted to say. *Sit here, on the edge of the bed.* But instead she pulled away. "Those are nice flowers, thank you."

"I'm sorry," Evan said. "I hope you know that."

She had survived a student insurrection. She had been kicked and beaten and left in a stairwell to bleed. Yet what devastated her the most was the man at her bed and those flowers at her bedside. She imagined he was only the first in a long string of heartbreaks; she imagined he would continue to come in and out of her life; she imagined her life as full and stretched out ahead of her, this experience only the start of many, experiences good and bad and difficult and splendid. Devastation and joy were so closely related.

Taki and his family were coming up the stairs. "I'm sorry, too," she said finally. But she still wasn't sure if they were apologizing for what had happened or for what had not.

49

On the drive to Halandri to see his nephew, his nephew's new wife, and their new baby, it occurred to Mihalis that he hadn't held an infant since Anna had been one herself. By the time she came along, babies had seemed less foreign to him, but Sophie, the first, had been another experience entirely.

When she had been born, he had been craggy and unused to city life, fresh from the northern mountains, and then from prison, and this new pink baby looked wondrous and fake, and he worried he'd somehow contaminate her just by his touch. "She's like a loaf of bread," he said, over and over.

How strange that, once again, this cycle repeated itself. He wasn't exactly fresh from prison, but it still felt that way; time seemed to go so quickly these days and sometimes he'd wake in Kifissia and for a moment expect to see Vangelis or Nefeli, would anticipate a draft and cold feet and loud morning announcements and would be stunned by the serenity and silence. In fact, it seemed he had just reentered Irini's house one more time, held a clean towel to his face, and wept. Now even the sight of the pregnant Sophie moved him.

Was this a sign of getting older? He had always been something of a loose cannon, but never one for sentiment and treacle.

In the backseat were copies of the American literary journal that had published his story, his first publication since the colonels had taken power. It had come with a sizable check in American dollars, and the editor, a man quite established and revered among the New York literati, had asked him for more work, a series of poems dealing with life under the dictators, details of the questioning on Bouboulinas Street, a memoir about island exile. He felt proud, and because the editor was such a self-identified iconoclast, the fact that he was being American-supported didn't bother him. Plus, the editor himself had written a lengthy introduction about the political situation in Greece, as well as excerpts from the Amnesty International report on the torture methods being used. He had included photos from the recent Polytechnic uprising, and Mihalis had found himself proudly telling the editor that his niece had been involved, that her voice had been heard over the radio, that she had stood at the small window grates on Patissia Boulevard and received food and medication for her comrades. That she had suffered harsh blows and persisted.

Then, as they neared his sister's house, driving down Kifissia Avenue, Mihalis and Irini passed two army officers loitering on the corner. They stood slumped and casual, more teenage hoodlums than commandants. They were no older than his nieces and nephew—most likely younger—and only pawns to the regime. Though Mihalis did not necessarily respect this, such obedience, he understood it.

One of the soldiers spotted Mihalis and tipped his hat, a wild grin on his face, as if he, too, were a subversive, some mole in the ranks disguised in official clothing. "The poet," he said, more to Mihalis than to his partner. He held up his cigarettes, as if offering one to Mihalis, but Mihalis flipped him the bird, American-style, and the boy looked shocked. Then Mihalis grinned wildly and shook his hands up by his ears, like some sort of lunatic. The boy's expression transitioned from one of affront to curiosity to wonder, as though he'd witnessed some inexplicable transformation. Then the light changed and they pulled through the intersection.

Irini, seemingly unaware, looked straight ahead at the road. But then she turned to Mihalis. "What is wrong with you?" she asked. Yet he could see her holding back a smile.

Mihalis settled back into his seat and watched his wife, her slim wrists draped over the steering wheel. Irini, with her soft voice, hummed something he couldn't recognize. And then she said, with a tone of great relief, "It's evident—even those boys know their time is soon to be up." She turned to him, raised her eyebrows, and continued humming.

Mihalis leaned his head out the open window, feeling the cool December air on his face. He wasn't sure he shared his wife's optimism, but he was happy she had it.

Something inside him rattled, unrestrained, a kind of happiness that had been shaken loose. "Resist!" he yelled out the window to no one in particular. "Resist!"

50

In all the commotion and bustle of their arrival, Eleni had barely said a word to Taki alone. He was in the basement now, probably going through his old things that she had stored there. So much of his teenage self still lingered in that house, and it seemed he had simply left it behind for a stable, respectable adult life. House, diplomas, wife, infant. Though Sophie, too, had come and gone, Eleni didn't think she felt that same dissociation from the city, the way an invisible line of demarcation existed between the time before his departure and the time after his return, with the middle filled in brightly, messily, like a child with a crayon drawing very deliberately, babbling.

Eleni was looking absentmindedly at the Polaroids Amalia had left on the small desk in the foyer when Taki came back in the front door. The house was quiet. Eleni handed him one of the photos and then looked at his face, in person. While he had lost some of his baby face, another vulnerable softness had emerged. Perhaps one of fatherhood. He looked at the photos a moment, and Eleni knew within them he recognized his bewildered, beleaguered self.

He set the photos down and turned to go upstairs. But instead he gave his mother a hug. He didn't have to say it, but this Eleni knew: somewhere, beneath the indifferent exterior, Taki was both happy and shattered to be back home.

He pulled away from her then, almost embarrassed, and Eleni pretended not to notice that he had been crying. "The jet lag is setting in," he said. "I'm going to lie down with the girls."

While everyone napped or walked or read, Eleni busied herself in the kitchen, looking already toward dinner. All her children back in the house again made her think about an earlier life. It wasn't that she didn't think of Christos often, but it came in waves, and sometimes she'd be so startled by his memory that she'd feel guilty for going so many days, weeks, without thinking of him. He was constantly in the back of her mind that day, when she washed her face in the morning, when she ran some last-minute errands, when she made up the beds. She thought of how she had gone through both her son's and daughter's respective arrivals and departures alone. She had now lived longer without him than with him, a painful and startling realization.

What did remain after someone you loved had died? Perhaps it was something other than love, a sensation similar to an amputee's phantom limb. Often Christos's memory was distant, the woman she had been with him almost like a friend she had known long ago but lost touch with. Other times, his memory was so sharp and clear that it seemed as though he were in the room with her, worry beads in his hands, talking away.

Her eldest daughter pregnant also reminded her of her own first pregnancy. As impatient a man as Christos could be, she marveled at the way he had sat with her when she felt sick, asked her how she was feeling, brought her lemons to suck on—this, strangely, was what she had craved. She thought that Christos would have liked to see Sophie pregnant, though probably not out of wedlock, and then

in the same breath she wondered if he would have found it unsettling, married or not; pregnancy, after all, implied sex, and he had
always been more horrified at the idea of their daughters growing
up than she had.

Fatherhood, for him, had been heartbreaking. She remembered so
clearly when Sophie first walked, his elation. But later that evening,
when Sophie was asleep, she had found him in the den, sitting in the
dark. Gently, she had asked what he was doing, not wanting to scare
him.

"Soon, she'll be at university, and then she'll get married, and that
will be that."

Eleni had sat down next to him, close, so their hips were touching, and took his hand. "Maybe we'll teach her how to use the toilet
first," she'd said.

Christos had been quiet, and he took off his glasses and cleaned
them with the sleeve of his sweater, the way he always did. Then he
laughed slightly.

"Or feed herself," Eleni said.

"Or bring me the afternoon paper," he added.

"Or cook us dinner."

And Christos truly laughed then, and so did she, but she knew
fatherhood would never be easy for him, not as the father of girls, and
however irrational he knew he was being, he couldn't help it. Just like
she knew, years later, she couldn't help but be angry at him after he
died, that he could abandon his family this way. As much as she knew,
rationally, that his early death was horrible—unpredictable, sudden,
shocking—she couldn't help but think, rather resentfully, that she
would die in her house alone, perhaps not having uttered a word in
days. It was her worst fear.

Evan had gone; Eleni had invited him to stay for dinner with the
family, though he politely declined. She had confessed to Mihalis,
after the hospital, that she worried Anna was involved with Evan,
and Mihalis answered that he was more worried Evan was involved
with Anna. He had a point. That distance in her eyes suggested
something untamable. Evan's face when he left had been wrought
with emotion. And over the past few months she had seen more

emotion cross her daughter's face than she had before, ever. What-ever was going on, it was safe to say Eleni should be worried about both of them.

Eleni peeked in on Anna. Still weary from the medicine, she was now fast asleep. Eleni knew her youngest daughter's life would not be easy. What would she rather have for her children, a life without event or drama but free of pain, or one both spectacular and difficult? And what would Anna want? She felt that these were the only two options, but if anyone had asked her where she thought she herself fell in this classification scheme, she'd have said her life was not yet over.

Amalia and Taki and Aspa, all jet-lagged and with sore throats, slept in Eleni's bed, which she had insisted they take. She couldn't help but look in on them, too. She had already purchased a crib to keep at her house for Sophie's upcoming arrival, and for Aspa, though probably by the next trip Aspa would have outgrown it. Who knew when the next trip would be.

Her children in the house, a new grandchild, another on the way. She felt a wash of nostalgia, deep, below her ribs.

The quiet denseness of a house of people sleeping soothed her; it reminded her of when her children took naps and the way the silence was so sweet and warm she could drink it. When the three children awoke, they'd run to the Xylino kiosk to grab their father a paper, and when he awoke, Eleni would have tea ready, and the three siblings would present him with his news.

Now, on the same couch where Christos had taken his afternoon naps, Sophie and Loukas slept. Awkwardly. They would have been more comfortable in Sophie's old bed, as small as it was, but instead the two of them lay next to each other, Sophie's head on Loukas's chest. Beneath the thin blanket, her daughter's giant belly rose and fell, rose and fell; it seemed that any moment, it would part open and a child would spring forth.

After Christos's death, after the burial, after the funeral, after the family and friends stopped hovering and appearing at their door with food, Eleni remembered how they all slept. They closed the shutters to not let any light in; she remembered the sight of her little children slumbering, exhausted from crying (or in Anna's case, from not crying but instead holding it all inside, six years old and tough as hell). She remembered the way the mornings became afternoons and then cicada-filled evenings, the way the smell of jasmine would sometimes capture her in her late-afternoon sleep, so strong and jarring. She remembered the way she'd wake with a terrible feeling that something awful had happened, and then see Christos's empty space and know that it had. She remembered hearing her children fix themselves snacks in the middle of the night, and the heartbreak of hearing them down there alone, and its intensification when she couldn't pull her body from the bed to keep them company. And once, during one of Sophie's late-night wakings, she had heard a man's voice through the grates in the floor and it had startled her. *Christos?* she thought, in the haze of a dream. In the morning, though, she found all three children and Mihalis, then also newly released from prison, asleep on the living room couch, in a heap, like puppies. On the kitchen table were the remnants of all sorts of snacks, some bones from leftover chicken, a bowl of soggy cornflakes, an orange peel (in one piece—Taki's), and a loaf of bread, a hunk torn off that had gone uneaten. What had made them all assemble in the kitchen together for a late-night feast?

And as they emerged from that post-funeral daze, they began to fall into a rhythm, though those days in early autumn when the children went back to school felt strange again, another new thing that was a first since he died. His first name day, the first New Year's, the first Easter. What she remembered most was wanting so badly to fast-forward their lives, to get to a point where it wouldn't feel quite so razor-sharp. Because the worst part of the grieving was not knowing that it would end, not knowing how much longer you would feel so bad, not knowing when, if ever, it would lift. Those days, endless days ahead of her, made her dizzy. If someone had just said, *There are twenty-two more days,* or *four hundred fifty,* or *two thousand,* she would have felt better about it. Just the day before, Sophie had confessed to her a similar sentiment, so similar that it had startled Eleni. Sophie wasn't scared of going into labor, per se, but she wished someone would tell her how long it would take beforehand, so she'd know. She wanted to know, she said, when her water broke, exactly how long it would be before she held her child. Down to the minute. Then, she said, it would be bearable. Even the way she articulated it, as if Sophie could read her thoughts.

When Christos popped into her mind now, like an unannounced but not unwelcome guest, his image was as clear as if he were right in front of her—his prominent nose, his deep-set eyes, his shock of dark hair that never seemed to lie quite right. Lately, Anna had taken to wearing his wool caps, somehow both boyish and strangely feminine on her thin body. She looked to Eleni like one of the models on the cover of a haute fashion magazine, dressed down just so, yet with an air of sensuality, coolness, beneath. Rock and roll. And once in a while, she'd look at Anna in one of those hats, and even though she had her mother's features, something about her expression, her gleaming eyes from beneath the brim, the upturn of her lips, the same sort of walk—part stroll, part march—and she'd think, *Christos.*

Genetics, she thought, was nothing short of magic.

Eleni felt tired but she wasn't sleepy; she made herself a cup of tea and went out onto the veranda off the living room, walking carefully so as not to wake Sophie and Loukas. She loved to be outside in early winter, when the rest of the country seemed to give up on the outdoors entirely. She huddled beneath a few blankets.

Later, the house began to wake. Eleni turned over and opened her eyes. The sky was lavender gray and the sun was about to set. She sat up and tightened her cardigan around her, pulled her shawl up over her face. She wondered if the neighbors had seen her, asleep outside in December. Certainly people slept outside all times of the year, albeit in tents, campers bundled in sleeping bags. It wasn't so strange; she had heard of stranger things. Cool air was good for your lungs, she had heard. But she wasn't sure where she had heard it, or if it was true. She let her sweater drop from over her mouth and took a deep breath. It felt good.

Upstairs, Aspa cried, awake again and hungry. She heard Taki walking around; how easy it was to recognize his steps. He went out to the terrace. Eleni could imagine him peering over the side, looking both ways, and then leaning his back against the wall, ready to smoke. She heard the clicks of his Zippo lighter, one, two, three. The smell of smoke drifted down to the veranda, and it was comforting. A pack of Dimitri's cigarettes was left on the small, white table next to her; she took one out, brought it to her nose, and held it. It's not that she wanted things to be perfect. In fact, she was becoming fond of imperfect. Imperfection was beautiful. If life wasn't so complicated, well, it wouldn't be so complicated.

Mihalis and Irini would arrive soon. The phone was ringing; maybe it was one of them, or some of Taki's old friends, waiting to see him. She heard Taki leave the terrace to answer it, like he always had, and she heard him speaking, like he rarely had. He called to her, and she assumed it was Dimitri, from work. But it was Andreas, Taki said.

Taki came out on the porch and told her he was calling to see how Anna was feeling. Eleni, on a whim, told her son to invite him for dinner. It might be messy. But she wanted her household to burst at the seams.

Then, from the slightly ajar doors that opened onto the porch, she heard Sophie mumbling something in the living room. She heard her slippered feet—her old slippers, she had somehow found them—padding to the bathroom.

"Oh," Sophie said quietly. And then, with more volume: "*Loukas.*" Hope and fear and excitement crowded his name.

Loukas mumbled back something, still asleep, but now Sophie was louder, not gentle at all, not the way you spoke to someone who was just waking up. Instead, her voice was convincing but composed, as if she were speaking in front of a crowd. "Hey. Loukas. *Loukas.*"

Before Loukas could answer, Sophie called for her mother.

Eleni stood up. This was it. *It won't be long,* she thought. *It won't be long at all.*

A Note on Sources

Though this is a work of fiction and therefore an act of the imagination, I have consulted numerous sources to try to capture the time and place as authentically as possible. I would like to specifically acknowledge Kevin Andrews's *Greece in the Dark* (Amsterdam: Adolf M. Hakkert, 1980) for its detailed accounts of life in Athens during this time and in particular for inspiring the scene in the Athens Stadium and for the details of the funeral of George Seferis. Amalia Fleming's *A Piece of Truth* (New York: Houghton Mifflin, 1973) inspired me with its beautiful evocation of the period and the mood those days after the coup. I'm also extremely indebted to the Pyrros Papers: The Greek Anti-Junta Struggle Collection, housed in the Special Collections Library at the University of Michigan.

The author is grateful for permission to reproduce the following material:

Kostas Karyotakis, "Sleep," trans. William W. Reader and Keith Taylor, in *Battered Guitars: Poems and Prose* (Birmingham, U.K.: University of Birmingham Centre for Byzantine, Ottoman and Modern Greek Studies, 2006).

Lefteris Poulios, "The Mirror," trans. Kimon Friar, in *A Century of Greek Poetry 1900–2000,* Bilingual Edition, eds. Peter Bien, Peter Constantine, Edmund Keeley, and Karen Van Dyck (River Vale, N.J.: Cosmos Publishing, 2004). Reprinted by permission of the Attica Tradition Foundation.

Yiannis Patilis, "The Song Never Stops," trans. Stathis Gourgouris, in *A Century of Greek Poetry 1900–2000,* Bilingual Edition, eds. Peter Bien, Peter Constantine, Edmund Keeley, and Karen Van Dyck (River Vale, N.J.: Cosmos Publishing, 2004).

Acknowledgments

When you're writing a novel, every conversation, every book, every act seems to weave itself into the process. I express deep gratitude to my earliest writing instructors at the University of Wisconsin—Madison, who encouraged my work even when I was a graduate student in physiology: Ron Kuka, Stephen Schottenfeld, and Judy Mitchell. I'm especially thankful to my wonderful professors at the University of Michigan, where I received my MFA in creative writing: Nicholas Delbanco, Eileen Pollack, Nancy Reisman, Laura Kasischke, and Peter Ho Davies. I'm also grateful to Andrea Beauchamp and the University of Michigan's Hopwood Program. Though I did not work with him directly, I also thank Charles Baxter, for his profundity, encouragement, and general mentorship.

My peers in the MFA program at Michigan read the earliest sketches of this book, encouraging me from the start, and I'm also thankful to Mike Hinken, Travis Holland, and Karen Outen for our discussions on the craft and project of the novel as a form. I'm particularly grateful to Elizabeth Ames Staudt, who has remained a thoughtful, careful reader, and whose talent, grace, and bigheartedness extend far beyond the page; to Sharon Pomerantz, for our long, rewarding discussions about novel writing; and to Elizabeth Kostova, for her unsurpassed energy, generosity, and strength. I thank Charlotte Boulay and Brian Girard for their warmth, humor, and late nights full of good ideas. I'm also grateful to Beth Chimera and Donovan Hohn, for their invaluable conversations, love, and friendship.

Two friends have been relentlessly supportive from the time I had my earliest, tiny triumphs: Steve Myck and the late Mark Gates, for the flowers and cards they sent every time.

For fellowships, support, and help with research I am grateful to the Special Collections Library at the University of Michigan; the Glen Arbor Arts Association in Glen Arbor, Michigan; the House of Literature in Lefkes, Paros, Greece; the Andreas Papandreou Foundation in Athens; the University of Missouri Writing Workshop in Serifos, Greece; and the Athens Centre. I am particularly indebted to the Camargo Foundation in Cassis, France, where I spent three months in the winter of 2011 doing final edits on this book; my inspiring colleagues there; and Connie Higginson and Leon Selig, who were the directors during my stay. A special thanks to co-fellow Stephanie Soileau for our evening terrace breaks and conversations about fiction and beyond. I'm also grateful to the Aegean Arts Circle in Andros, Greece, where I worked on an early draft of this novel, and particularly to its organizer, Amalia Melis, for her friendship and advice.

I extend warm gratitude to Motrya Tomycz, for the lastingness of her friendship and her creative spirit, and to friends in Ann Arbor, especially Giota Tachtara and Elizabeth Gramm, for our happy hours and lovely conversations. I'm grateful to Despina Margomenou and Panayiotis Pafilis for their help in my study of Modern Greek, to Keith Taylor, whose co-translation of Karyotakis gave the book its title, and to Christopher Bakken for those *tsipouro*-soaked evenings. I extend profound gratitude to Artemis Leontis and Vassilis Lambropoulos, for their careful reading, extraordinary generosity, and warm friendship, and also to the Modern Greek Department at the University of Michigan and the Foundation for Modern Greek Studies for their support.

I am thankful to the editors who responded so positively to my work: Ben George, Jodee Stanley, Cheston Knapp, John Freeman, Ted Hodgkinson, Laura Furman, Anders Dahlgren, Elaine Thomopoulos, and Linda Swanson-Davies and Susan Burmeister Brown. I extend sincere thanks to the editorial staff of *Fiction Writers Review*, particularly founding editor Anne Stameshkin.

I am indebted to Amy Williams, for her conviction, loyalty, and humor, as well as Bridget McCarthy and Susan Hobson. I'm also grateful to Anjali Singh, for her enthusiasm and discerning eye, and to

Michele Bové, Emer Flounders, Aja Pollock, Nina Pajak, and Wendy Sheanin, and the other professionals at Simon & Schuster for all their hard work.

I extend huge thanks—*xilia efharisto*—to my dear friends in Athens, particularly Adrianne Kalfopoulou for her close friendship, our ongoing exchange about life and literature, and for so much riotous laughter, and to Nick Papandreou for his warm solidarity, rewarding discussions, and his patience that was surely tried while reading several drafts of this manuscript. To my family in Athens, particularly Eleni Bakopoulou in loving memory, for her detailed letters describing the events of the period, and to Vassia Kappou, for her lively stories as well.

And I of course express deep gratitude to my family here: my brother, Dean Bakopoulos, and my sister-in-law, Amanda Okopski, for their love, joy, and artistic inspiration; and to the Chamberlin family, particularly my parents-in-law Mike and Libby. And without doubt I'm grateful to my parents: my father, George Bakopoulos, his wife, Pat Bakopoulos, and my mother, Luba Bakopoulos, for their continual, wholehearted, loving encouragement. Though my grandparents are no longer living, their influence has been profound.

And finally, to Jeremiah Chamberlin, for his brilliance, editing, and effusive support, and for joining me through life's beautiful messes and joys.

About the Author

Natalie Bakopoulos received her MFA from the University of Michigan, where she now teaches. Her work has appeared in *Tin House, Ninth Letter,* and Granta.com, and it has received a 2010 O. Henry Award, a Hopwood Award, and a Platsis Prize for Work in the Greek Legacy. She is a contributing editor for the online journal *Fiction Writers Review* (www.fictionwritersreview.com).